GUILT BY ASSOCIATION

MARCIA CLARK

GUILT BY ASSOCIATION

A NOVEL

Doubleday Large Print
Home Library Edition

MULHOLLAND BOOKS
LITTLE, BROWN AND COMPANY
NEW YORK BOSTON LONDON

This Large Print Edition, prepared especially
for Doubleday Large Print Home Library, contains
the complete, unabridged text of the original
Publisher's Edition.

Copyright © 2011 by Marcia Clark

All rights reserved. Except as permitted under the
U.S. Copyright Act of 1976, no part of this publication
may be reproduced, distributed, or transmitted in any
form or by any means, or stored in a database or
retrieval system, without the prior written
permission of the publisher.

Mulholland Books / Little, Brown and Company
Hachette Book Group
237 Park Avenue, New York, NY 10017

Mulholland Books is an imprint of Little, Brown and
Company, a division of Hachette Book Group, Inc.
The Mulholland Books name and logo are
trademarks of Hachette Book Group, Inc.

The publisher is not responsible for websites (or their
content) that are not owned by the publisher.

The characters and events in this book are fictitious.
Any similarity to real persons, living or dead, is
coincidental and not intended by the author.

ISBN 978-1-61129-605-1

Printed in the United States of America

**This Large Print Book carries the
Seal of Approval of N.A.V.H.**

To my sons

GUILT BY ASSOCIATION

PROLOGUE

He snapped his cell phone shut *and slid it into the pocket of his skintight jeans. The last piece was in place; it wouldn't be long now. But the waiting was agonizing. Unbidden, the memory of his only ride on a roller coaster flooded over him, like a thousand tiny needles piercing his face and body: eight years old, trapped in that rickety little car with no escape, the feeling of breathtaking terror that mounted as it click-click-clicked its slow, inexorable climb to the top of the sky.*

He shook his head to cleanse his mind of the memory, then abruptly

grabbed his long brown hair and pulled it tightly into a ponytail behind his head. He held it there and exhaled again more slowly, trying to quiet his pulse. He couldn't afford to lose it now. With the lift of his arms, his worn T-shirt rode up, and he absently admired in the little mirror above the dresser the reflection of the coiled snake tattooed on his slim, muscled belly.

He started pacing, the motel carpet crunching under his feet, and found that the action helped. Despite his anxiety, he moved with a loose-hipped grace. Back and forth he walked, considering his plan yet again, looking for flaws. No, he'd set it up just right. It would work. It had *to work. He stopped to look around at the dimly lit motel room. "Room" was using the term loosely — it was little more than a box with a bed. His eyes fell on a switch on the wall. Just to have something to do, he went over and flipped it on. Nothing happened. He looked up and saw only a filthy ceiling fan. The sour smell of old cigarettes told him that it hadn't worked in years. There were stains of undetermined origin on the walls that he thought were probably older than he was. The observation amused him. Neither the stains, nor the foul smell of decay, nor the hopeless dead-end feeling of the place fazed him at all. It wasn't that much worse than a lot of the places he'd lived during his seventeen years on the planet.*

In fact, far from depressing him, the ugly room made him feel triumphant. It represented the world he'd been born into, and the one he was finally leaving behind . . . forever. For the first time in a life that had nearly ended at the hands of a high-wired crackhead while his so-called mother was crashing in the next room, he was going to be in control. He paused to consider the memory of his early near demise—not a firsthand memory since he'd been only two months old when it happened, but rather a paragraph in the social worker's report he'd managed to read upside down during a follow-up visit at one of the many foster homes where he'd been "raised" for the past sixteen or so years. As it always did, the memory of that report made him wonder whether his mother was still alive. The thought felt different this time, though. Instead of the usual helpless, distant ache—and rage—he felt power, the power to choose. Now he could find her . . . if he wanted to. Find her and show her that the baby she'd been too stoned to give a shit about had made it. Had scored the big score.

In just a few more minutes, he'd say good-bye to that loser kid who lived on the fringes. He stopped, dropped his hands to his hips, and stared out the grimy window as he savored the thought of having "fuck you" money. He planned to extend a vigorous middle finger to the many foster parents for whom he was just a dollar sign, to all the ass-holes he'd had to put up with for a meal and a bed. And if he did decide to find his mother, he'd show up with some-thing awesome for her, a present, like a dress or jewelry. Something to make her sorry for all the years she'd let him be lost to her. He pictured himself giv-ing her whatever it was in a fancy, store-wrapped box. He tried to picture the expression on her face, but the image wouldn't resolve. The only photo he had of her—taken when he was less than a year old—was so faded, only the outline of her long brown hair was still visible. Still, the thought of being able to play the Mac Daddy puffed him up, and for a moment he let himself go there, enjoying the fantasy of his mother really loving him.

The knock on the door jolted him back to reality. He swallowed and struggled for a deep breath, then walked toward the door. He noticed his hands were shaking, and he quickly rubbed them on his thighs to make them stop. He slowly released his breath and willed his face to relax as he opened the door.

"Hey," he said, then held the door open and moved aside to let in his visitor. "What took you so long?"

"Lost track of the time, sorry." The visitor stepped inside quickly.

"You have it all?" the boy asked, wary.

The visitor nodded. The boy smiled and let the door close behind him.

1

"Guilty? Already? What'd they do, just walk around the table and hit the buzzer?" Jake said, shaking his head incredulously.

I laughed, nodding. "I know, it's crazy. Forty-five-minute verdict after a three-month trial," I said as I shook my head. "I thought the clerk was kidding when she called and told me to come back to court." I paused. "Now that I think about it, this might be my fastest win ever on a first-degree."

"Hell, sistah, that's the fastest win I done heard on *anythang,*" Toni said as she plopped down into the chair facing my desk. She talked ghetto only as a joke.

"Y'all gotta admit," I said, "homegirl brought game this time."

Toni gave me a disdainful look. "Uh-uh, snowflake. You can't pull it off, so don't try." She reached for the mug I kept cleaned and at the ready for her on the windowsill.

I raised an eyebrow. "You've got a choice: take that back and have a drink, or enjoy your little put-down and stay dry."

Toni eyed the bottle of Glenlivet on my desk, her lips firmly pressed together, as she weighed her options. It didn't take long. "It's amazing. For a minute there, I thought Sister Souljah was in the room," she said with no conviction whatsoever. She slammed her mug down on my desk. "Happy?"

I shrugged. "Not your best effort, but they can't all be gold." I broke the small ice tray out of my mini-fridge, dumped the cubes into her cup, and poured the equivalent of two generous shots of Glenlivet.

Toni shot me a "don't push your luck" look and signaled a toast.

I turned to Jake and gestured to the bottle. "Maybe a token?" I asked. He was a nondrinker by nature, but he'd occasionally join in to be sociable.

He nodded and gave me that little-boy smile that could light up a room—the same one that had warmed the hearts of juries across the county. His wire-rim glasses, wavy brown hair, and country-boy, self-effacing style—the dimples didn't hurt, though they were redundant—made a winning combination. Juries instinctively trusted him. He had a look that was almost angelic, making it hard for anyone to believe he'd even graduated from college, much less done all the backbreaking work required to finish law school and survive into his seventh year in the DA's office. I poured him a short dog of Glenlivet with a liberal dousing of water, careful not to give him more than he could handle. I was careful not to give myself more than I could handle either: a heavy-handed, undiluted triple shot.

Toni raised her mug. "To Rachel Knight: she put the 'speed' in 'speedy trial.'"

Jake lifted his cup. "To that," he said with a sly grin. "Until I beat her record."

I rolled my eyes. Jake had just thrown down the gauntlet. "Oh no, here we go," I said.

"Oh yeah," Toni replied. She narrowed her eyes at Jake. "It's on now, little man."

Jake gave her a flinty smile and nodded. They looked each other in the eye as they clinked cups. We all drank, Toni and I in long pulls, Jake in a more modest sip.

Toni turned back to the matter at hand. "Was this the dope-dealer shoot-out at MacArthur Park?" she asked.

I shook my head. Toni, Jake, and I were in Special Trials, the small, elite unit that handled the most complex and high-profile cases. Though Toni was as tough and competitive as anyone in the unit, she didn't live the job the way Jake and I did. It was one of the many ways Toni and I balanced each other.

Before I could answer, Jake said, "No, this was the one where the defendant poisoned his wife, then dumped the body off the cliff in Palos Verdes."

Toni thought for a moment. "Oh yeah. Body washed out to sea, right? And they never found a murder weapon."

I nodded.

Toni shook her head, smiling. "Evidence is for pussies," she said with a laugh. "You really are my hero." She raised her mug for another toast.

"I got lucky," I said with a shrug, raising mine to join her.

Toni made a face. "Oh please. Can you stop with the 'I'm so humble' stuff already? I've seen you pull these beasts together before. Nobody else drags their ass all over this county the way you do." She turned to Jake and added, "'Cept maybe you." She took another sip, then sat back. "Both of you are ridiculous, and you know it."

Jake and I exchanged a look. We couldn't argue. From the moment Jake had transferred into Special Trials two years ago, we'd found in each other a kindred workaholic spirit. Being a prosecutor was more than a career for us—it was a mission. Every victim's plight became our own. It was our duty to balance their suffering with some measure of justice. But by an unspoken yet entirely mutual agreement, our passion for the work never led us into personal territory—either physically or verbally. We rarely had lunch outside the building together, and during the long nights after court when we'd bat our cases around, we never even considered going out to dinner; instead we'd raid my desk supply of tiny pretzels, made more palatable by the little packets of mustard Jake snatched from the courthouse snack bar. Not once in all those long nights had we ever discussed our lives outside the office—either before or after becoming prosecutors. I knew that this odd boundary in our relationship went deeper than our shared devotion to the job. It takes one to know one, and I knew that I never asked personal questions because I didn't want to answer them. Jake played it close to the vest in the same way I did: don't ask, don't tell, and if someone does ask—deflect. The silent awareness of that shared sensibility let us relax with each other in a way we seldom could with anyone else.

"Well, she's not entirely wrong, Tone," Jake said with a smirk. "She did get lucky—she had Judge Tynan."

Toni chuckled. "Oh sweet Jesus, you did get lucky. How many times did you slip?"

"Not too bad this time," I admitted. "I only said 'asshole' once."

"Not bad for you," Toni remarked, amused. "When?"

"During rebuttal argument. And I was talking about one of my own witnesses."

My inability to rein in my colorful language once I got going had earned me fines on more than one occasion. You'd think this financial incentive would've made me clean up my act. It hadn't. All it had done was inspire me to keep a slush fund at the ready.

"There is an undeniable symmetry to your contempt citations," Toni observed. "What did Tynan do?"

"Just said, 'I'm warning you, Counsel.'" I sighed, took another sip of my drink, and stretched my legs out under the desk. "I wish I had all my cases in front of him."

"Hah!" Jake snorted. "You'd wear out your welcome by your second trial, and you'd be broke by your third."

"Thanks for the vote of confidence."

Jake shrugged. "Hey, I'm just sayin' . . ."

I laughed and threw a paper clip at him. He caught it easily in an overhand swipe, then looked out at the clock on the Times Building. "Shit, I've got to run. Later, guys." He put down his cup and left. The sound of his footsteps echoed down the hallway.

I turned to Toni. "Refresher?" I said as I held up the bottle of Glenlivet.

Toni shook her head. "Nah. I've had

enough of county ambience for one day. Why don't we get out of here and hit Church and State? We should celebrate the hell out of this one."

Church and State was a fun new restaurant in the old Meatpacking District, part of the ongoing effort to gentrify downtown L.A. Though how a restaurant that catered to a hip, moneyed crowd was going to make it with Skid Row just two blocks away was a looming question. I looked over at the stack of cases piled on the table where I kept my mini-fridge. I wanted to party, and with that gnarly no-body murder behind me, I could probably afford to. But the trial had taken me away from my other cases, and I always got a little—okay, a lot—panicky when I hadn't looked in on a case for more than a few days. If I went out with Toni tonight, I'd just be stressing and wishing I were working. I owed it to her to spare her that drag.

"Sorry, Tone, I—"

"Don't even bother—I know." Toni shook her head as she plunked her mug down on my desk and stood to go. "You can't even take time off for one little victory lap? It's sick, is what it is."

But it wasn't news, as evidenced by the lack of surprise in Toni's voice.

"How about tomorrow night? We'll do Church and State, whatever you want," I promised with more hope than conviction. I wasn't sure whether I'd be able to wade through the pile of cases and finish all the catch-up work by then. But I hated to disappoint Toni, so I privately vowed to push myself hard and make it happen.

Toni looked at me and sighed. "Sure, we'll talk tomorrow." She slung her laptop bag over one shoulder and her purse over the other. "I'm heading out. Try not to stay too late. If even your OCD partner-in-crime took a powder," she said, tilting her head toward Jake's office, "you can spare a night off too."

"I know." I looked toward his office. "What's up with that?" I laughed.

"Maybe his alien leaders told him to get a friggin' life," Toni said as she moved to the doorway. "And I've already got one, so I am now officially exiting the OCD Zone." She smiled and headed down the hall.

"Have fun!"

"You too," she called back. In a loud stage whisper, she muttered, "Ya freak."

"I heard that!" I yelled out.

"Don't care!"

I leaned back to rest my head against the cold leather of the majestic judge's chair. It was a tight fit at my little county-issue prosecutor's desk, but I didn't mind. The chair had mysteriously appeared late one night, abandoned in the hallway a few doors from my office. I'd looked up and down the hall to make sure the coast was clear, then whisked it into my office and pushed my own sorry little chair out to a hallway distant enough that it wouldn't be traced back. As I'd returned to my office, scanning the hallway for witnesses, I wondered whether someone had "liberated" the chair straight out of a judge's chambers. The possibility made my score even more triumphant.

I turned to the stack of case files and pulled the first one off the top, but within fifteen minutes I felt my eyelids drooping. I'd thought I'd had enough energy to plow through at least a few cases, but as usual I'd underestimated how tired I was. And the Glenlivet hadn't helped.

I listened to the last stragglers chatter their way out of the office. As the door snicked closed behind them, silence filled the air. I was tired, but I wasn't ready to go home. This was my favorite part of the day, when I had the whole DA's office to myself. No phones, no friends, no cops to distract me. I exhaled and looked out the window at the view that never got old. The streetlights had blinked on, and the jagged outline of the downtown L.A. office buildings glowed against the encroaching darkness. From my perch on the eighteenth floor of the Criminal Courts Building, I could see all the way from the main cop shop, the Police Administration Building, to the theaters at the Dorothy Chandler Pavilion and all the streets and sidewalks in between. The irony of being in the middle of those two extremes still made me smile. Just having an office with a window was a coup—let alone one with a spectacular view. But the fact that it had come with my transfer into Special Trials—the unit I'd worked my ass off to get into for seven years—made it a delicious victory.

Not that I'd minded working the routine felonies during my stints in the smaller Van Nuys and Compton branch courts. Seeing the same defendants come back to the fold with a new case every couple of years gave the job a kind of homey, family feeling. Sure, it was a weird, dysfunctional, and largely criminal family, but still. So it wasn't as though I was miserable when I worked the outlying courts. It just wasn't for me. From the moment I'd heard of the Special Trials Unit, based in the hub of the DA's office downtown, I'd known it was where I wanted to be. I'd been warned by the senior prosecutors in the branch courts about the long hours, the marathon-length trials, the public scrutiny, and the endless pressure I'd face in the unit. I didn't tell them that, for me, that was the allure. And being in the unit was even better than I'd imagined. On almost every case, I got to work with great cops and the best lawyers—for both the prosecution and the defense—I'd ever seen. Far from a detraction, the intensity of the job was exhilarating. Too often in life a long-desired goal, once achieved, turns out to be much less than expected—as they say, "Be careful what you wish for." Not this time. Getting into Special Trials was all I'd hoped for and then some, and I savored that fact at least once a day.

I tried to drag my mind back down to the

supplemental reports—updates on the investigation—that had been added to the case file during the last month, but the words were blurring on the page. I leaned back in my chair, hoping to catch a second wind, and watched the cars crawl down Main Street. The sky had darkened, and clouds were moving in.

I could tell my second wind wasn't going to arrive anytime soon. I decided to admit defeat and pack it in for the night. I got up, stretched, walked over to the table next to the window where I'd dropped my briefcase, and brought it over to my desk. I threw in five of the files—wishful thinking, I knew—picked up my purse, and grabbed my coat off the hook on the back of the door. I swung into my jacket and slung the strap of my briefcase over my shoulder, then reached into my coat pocket and flipped off the safety on my palm-size .22 Beretta. Then I kicked out the doorstop and headed down the hall toward the bank of elevators as my office door clicked shut behind me.

At this time of day I didn't have long to wait. Within seconds, the bell rang and I stepped into a blissfully empty car. The elevator hurtled down all eighteen floors and came to a shuddering stop on the first floor. It was a head-spinning ride that happened only at quiet times like this. I enjoyed the rush as long as I ignored what it meant about the quality of the machinery and my possible life expectancy.

As I walked through the darkened lobby toward the back doors, I stretched my eyes for better peripheral vision. I'd been walking to work ever since I'd moved into the nearby Biltmore Hotel a year ago. It seemed stupid to drive the six blocks to the courthouse, and I enjoyed the walk—it gave me a chance to think. Plus it saved me a bundle in gas and car maintenance. The only time I had second thoughts about it was after dark. Downtown L.A. empties out after 5:00 p.m., leaving a population that lives mainly outdoors. It wasn't the homeless who worried me as much as the bottom-feeders who preyed on them.

Being a prosecutor gave me an inside line on the danger in any area, but the truth was, I'd grown up with the knowledge that mortal peril lurked around every corner. So although I didn't have a permit to carry, I never left either home or office without a gun. The lack of a permit occasionally worried me, but as my father used to say, "I'd rather be judged by twelve than carried by six." I'd never applied for a permit because I didn't want to get turned down. There'd been a crackdown on gun permits ever since a certain sheriff's brother-in-law had fired "warning shots" at some neighborhood kids for blasting rap music from their car. And, to be honest, permit or no, I was going to carry anyway. Besides, I was no novice when it came to guns. Being my father's daughter, I'd started learning how to shoot the moment I could manage a shaky two-handed grip. If I had to shoot, I wouldn't miss. I stood at the wall of glass that faced out toward the Times Building and scanned the parking lot and sidewalk, as always, looking for signs of trouble. Seeing nothing, I pushed open the heavy glass door and stepped out into the night.

As I walked toward the stairs that led down to street level, I heard the sound of sirens, distant at first but rapidly getting louder. Suddenly the air was pierced with the whooping screams and bass horn blasts of fire engines. They were close, very close. Police cars, their sirens shrieking,

seemed to be approaching from all directions, and the night air jangled with wild
energy. I watched intently, waiting to see
where they were headed. The flashing
lights seemed to stop and coalesce about
four blocks south and east of the Biltmore,
in the middle of a block I knew was filled
with junk stores, iron-grilled pawnshops,
and low-rent motels. I'd never seen this
much action at a downtown crime scene.
My usual "neighbors"—druggies, pimps,
hookers, and the homeless—generally
didn't get this kind of "Protect and Serve"
response. My curiosity piqued, I decided to
find out what was going on. At least with all
those cops around, I wouldn't have to worry
about muggers.

2

Within minutes, I could see that the hub of the action was on the corner of 4th and South Broadway, just around the corner from Pershing Square—at one of those seedy pay-by-the-hour motels. I brilliantly deduced from the hose snaking in through the front door, and the fact that there was only smoke and no flames, that the firefighters had gotten on top of it already.

Sliding through the scraggly bunch of lookie-loos who'd gathered on the sidewalk, I got as close as the police line allowed and looked for a familiar face to ask what was going on. As another plume of smoke wafted out through the front door of the motel, the seen-better-days coroner's van pulled up. I peered through the haze and saw a head with a short crew cut pop out from the driver's side of the van. It was followed by a short, square body dressed in high-water pants, a blue Windbreaker, and Nike sneakers.

I was in luck. "Scott!" I yelled out. Scott Ferrier was a coroner's investigator. He'd become my buddy when I'd pulled my first homicide case, back in my baby DA days. He waved and trotted over.

"Does your mommy know you're out after dark?" I asked. Scott cut me a look. "This is a lot of firepower for a pimp fight, don't you think?"

Scott nodded. "Yeah, it's weird. If you want to hang around, I'll go see what I've got and fill you in."

"Okay if I wait here?" I gestured to his van.

"Yeah, just don't steal it," he said with a snort, knowing he'd have to pay someone to take the beat-up corpse jalopy off his hands.

Scott turned and wove through the throng of police and firemen and made his way into the motel. I slid into the driver's seat and tried not to think about the "passengers" that'd ridden around in the cargo space behind me.

A few more clouds of smoke drifted out as firefighters began to emerge from the building. One of them was rolling up the hose as he walked. They'd been here only a few minutes; if they were already wrapping up, this couldn't have been much of a fire.

I watched the hunky firefighters at work and was pondering the truth of the old saying—that God made all paramedics and firemen good-looking so you'd see something pretty before you died—when a deep, authoritative voice broke my concentration.

"Miss, are you with the coroner's office?"

I'd been sitting sidesaddle in the van, facing the motel. I turned to my left and saw that the owner of the voice was somewhere around six feet tall, on the lean side but tastefully muscled under his blue uniform, his dark-blond hair just long enough to comb. His eyes were a gold-flecked hazel, and he had wide, pronounced cheekbones, a strong nose, and a generous mouth. The bars on his uniform told me he

was brass, not rank and file. His name-
plate confirmed it: LIEUTENANT GRADEN HALES.
His skeptical look annoyed me, but his
presence made an already weird scene
even more so. What the hell was a lieutenant doing here? I mustered up my best "I
belong here" voice and replied, "I'm a DA,
but I'm waiting for Scott."

I expected that my status as a prosecutor would end the discussion. Wrong.

"I'm afraid you're going to have to leave,"
he said with a steely firmness. "Only crime
scene personnel are allowed right now."

High brass chasing me off a low-life
bust? Something was really off here, and
now I wasn't just curious—I had to find out
what was going on. "Well, I have to wait for
Scott. He's my ride." It was a lie, but I figured that would push Lieutenant Officious
out to greener pastures. Wrong again.

"I'll arrange for one of the patrol units to
take you home. Where do you live?"

Now I was pissed off. Since when does
a DA get tossed out of a crime scene?
Special case or no, this was bullshit.

I stepped down from the van. I was just
about to open my mouth and get myself
in trouble when the coroner's assistants

came out single file, rolling two gurneys carrying body bags. Suddenly Scott came running out of the motel and yelled to one of the assistants, "Get his glasses! Give me the glasses!"

The team rolling the first gurney came to an abrupt halt. They had been moving at a rapid pace, and when the assistant at the head of the line came to a sudden stop, the gurney kept moving and banged into his hip, causing him to yelp and curse. The other assistant, who'd been at the side of the gurney, quickly reached out and tugged down the zipper of the body bag.

Illuminated by the harsh streetlight, the face glowed a ghastly bluish white as the assistant lifted the wire-rim glasses from behind the ears and handed them to Scott. I'd been around more than my share of dead bodies, but the searing shock of what met my eyes made me reel and stumble backward into the side of the van. Then a firm hand gripped my arm, steadied me, and led me away from the scene. I looked up and saw that the hand belonged to Lieutenant Hales. I dimly realized that he was saying something, but I couldn't make the sounds turn into words. I shook my head slowly, as if trying to wake up from a nightmare. This couldn't be real, I thought, feeling as though I were watching a movie in slow motion with the sound turned too low. The coroner's assistants loaded the gurney into the cargo area, and I stopped, transfixed, still unable to believe what I'd seen. The lieutenant pulled me by the elbow with one hand and pushed me on the back with the other, leaving me no choice. I moved in stiff, jerky steps, like a windup toy whose key was on its last few turns. He steered me toward his unmarked car, and I numbly let him stuff me into the passenger seat and buckle the seat belt.

I must've told him where I lived, but I don't actually remember saying anything. I just remember staring blankly as the streets rolled by, telling myself it couldn't be, that I had to be wrong.

Jake Pahlmeyer, my office soul mate—dead. In a rat hole like this. I closed my eyes and told myself I'd been wrong. Irrationally, I refused to ask the lieutenant. If no one confirmed it, it wouldn't be true.

3

Lieutenant Hales pulled up to the Biltmore, guided me out of the car, and walked me to the front entrance. Through the fog of denial and disbelief, the shocked features of Angel, the doorman, floated before me.

"Rachel, what's wrong?" he asked as he opened the door and took the elbow Hales wasn't holding.

"She's had a tough night," Hales said tersely.

"I'll take it from here," Angel said proprietarily, with an accusatory glance at the lieutenant.

I didn't have the energy or the sentience to explain that it was nothing the lieutenant had done. I remained mute as Angel led me inside and steered me toward the elevator.

He managed to get me to my room, and I meant to thank him, though I'm not sure the words made it out of my mouth. All I know is that the moment the door closed behind him, I pulled out the bottle of Russian Standard Platinum vodka someone had given me a while ago and poured myself a triple shot.

I looked at the television. Was the story being aired yet? I decided I didn't want to know. And I couldn't bring myself to call Toni. Talking about it would make it real. Right now, all I wanted was oblivion. I tossed down my drink, then poured myself another and didn't stop pouring until I passed out cold.

It had seemed like a good idea at the time. Less so now, the morning after. I had a jittery, buzzy kind of hangover that told me this was going to be a really special day. I groaned as I got out of bed and crept into the shower. Somewhat revived, I called room service and ordered my usual pot of coffee and 2 percent milk, but this time I decided to treat myself to some real food—scrambled eggs and a bagel—instead of my usual egg whites and stewed tomatoes. Screw the diet; I needed some comfort food.

I ate as I stared at the blank television screen, daring myself to turn it on. Finally curiosity won out over denial, and I reached for the remote, dreading what I was about to see. But when I scrolled through the channels, I saw nothing. I tried again. Still nothing. I frowned—that was odd, very odd. I clicked off the television and enjoyed the quiet that settled over the room. In my current condition, the less noise, the better.

Not seeing the story mentioned on the news even fleetingly had left me feeling weirdly isolated, the whole experience of last night surreal. Now eager to talk to Toni, I quickly downed enough coffee to be semi-functioning and went out onto the balcony to check the weather. I pulled my fluffy robe around me and shivered at the cold bite in the air. The darkened skies told me that the clouds that'd rolled in last night were going to show us why. I threw on

gray wool gabardine slacks, a black turtleneck sweater, and black low-heeled boots.
I decided to pack my .357 Smith & Wesson revolver instead of the more compact
Beretta. After what I'd seen last night, I
was willing to trade a lighter load for more
firepower. I picked up my briefcase and
the black cashmere muffler that had been
a Valentine's Day present—for some reason it was the only souvenir I'd kept from
my last ill-fated relationship—wound it
around my neck, and walked out to the elevator. I punched the down button and
tried not to wince at the sound of the bell
when the doors slid open.

The brisk six-block walk to the courthouse marginally helped to calm some of
my jittery buzz, but as I approached the
metal detectors, I noticed that I was holding the .357 in my pocket in a death grip. I
flashed my badge, and the deputy waved
me through. Seeing an open elevator, I
ran for it and quickly jumped inside, then
endured what felt like a million stops on
the way to the eighteenth floor. I punched
in the security code on the main office
door and realized that I was going to be

right next to Jake's office. I wondered whether they'd put up crime scene tape to seal off his space and reflexively looked down the hall to see if it was there. Not yet. But the glimpse of his closed door undid me, and my eyes filled with tears. I blinked them back, then took deep breaths as I turned and walked up the hall, away from my office.

"Knock, knock," I whispered hoarsely, unable to bear the sound of my knuckles on the frame of Toni's open door.

Toni, who'd been working on her computer, turned to look at me. "My oh my, but you look like shit. So was it a very bad night or a very good one?"

I sank into the county-issue metal-framed chair that faced her desk. The sky had grown even darker in the few minutes it had taken me to ride up in the elevator. Right on cue, the first big, bloated drops of rain began to splat against the window. I took another deep breath, swallowed, and tried to make myself say the words I still didn't want to believe. "Tone," I began, then had to stop. A lump swelled in my throat as the enormity of it all hit me afresh.

Toni regarded me with alarm.

"Honey, what is it? You okay?" she asked.

"It's Jake. He's dead."

Toni reflexively looked in the direction of his office. "What?" She shook her head, her face closed in denial.

I nodded, struggling to stop a fresh wave of tears. Her face frozen in shock, Toni automatically handed me the box of Kleenex we all kept at our desks for victims and their families.

As I pulled a tissue out of the box, it occurred to me that this was the first time I could remember either one of us using it.

"How? He's, what, thirty-five?" Toni said as she focused on a point on the wall to the left of my head, trying to grasp the reality. "Was it a car accident?"

I shook my head and swallowed. "Somebody killed him, Tone."

"No," Toni said, shaking her head again. "That can't be," she said softly, almost to herself.

I told her what I'd seen the night before.

As I spoke, Toni folded her arms around her body and leaned forward.

"Our Jake—in that sleazebag motel. I

can't believe it. He was like my . . ." Toni broke off.

". . . little brother," I said, finishing the thought.

She nodded as her eyes welled up with tears. She bit her lip, then put a hand over her mouth, trying in vain to rein in her emotions. "It's so wrong for someone so . . . young and so sweet to be . . . dead," Toni said.

At her words, the last photo taken of my sister, Romy, with her sixth-grade gap-toothed smile, filled my mind, and my throat tightened with pain. I nodded, overcome, unable to speak. As always, I pushed the thought of Romy away. It did no good to revisit the memories that always ended in the same abyss of guilt and self-loathing.

I sat unmoving, trying not to think. Toni blinked rapidly and put a hand to her chest, as though to ease the ache in her heart. "Do you know if he has any family in L.A.? Or a girlfriend?" she asked.

In all the time we'd spent together, he'd never once mentioned his parents. But since we'd never really talked about anything personal, I'd never given it any thought until now. I scoured my memory for any personal snippet. "He never mentioned a girlfriend, but he did mention a sister."

"What in the hell was he doing in that hole anyway?" Toni asked, her features twisted in confusion. "And who on earth would want to kill him?"

I'd been asking myself the same things for the past several hours. I shook my head, and we sat in silence for a moment. I again tried to make sense of it. And again I failed.

"I guess the Feds will handle the case?" Toni asked.

"Yeah, it's a conflict of interest for us, so it'll go to the U.S. Attorney's Office."

Toni's intercom buzzed, and we both stared at it as though it were a UFO. It had to buzz a second time before she finally reached out and picked up the phone.

"Yes?" Toni answered. She listened for a moment, then said, "Yeah, she's here. Send him down."

I looked at her quizzically. Before she could reply, a cop appeared in the doorway. It took me a second to recognize him as the brass from the crime scene. He had a gritty, stubbly look that told me he hadn't been to bed yet, but his uniform still seemed remarkably crisp.

He nodded to Toni, then to me. "Lieutenant Hales, from last night," he said. "I drove you—"

"I remember, of course." My tone was frosty at best. Shooting the messenger.

"I was in the office for a meeting with your boss—"

"Eric?" I asked.

"No, Bill Vanderhorn."

I nodded to myself. Of course. With a case this politically sensitive, he wouldn't meet with the head of Special Trials—he'd go straight to the DA.

"The case going to the Feds?" I asked.

"Probably," he said noncommittally. His attitude made it clear he didn't want to discuss it, which annoyed me even more. If he didn't want to talk about the case, then what the hell did he want?

He seemed to sense my irritation. "I just wanted to make sure you were, you know, okay."

The warmth in his voice startled me. I looked up and saw that he was watching me intently, his expression one of concern. The personal interest flustered me and

made me uncomfortable, which only served
to increase my irritation. I knew that, as
Carla would say, I was just displacing my
grief with anger. Carla had been my childhood shrink in the aftermath of Romy's dis-
appearance. Twenty-six years later, with
five hundred miles separating us, she was
still a major force in my life. But I didn't
care what Carla would say. I'd burned right
through the denial stage of grief and was
eager to get to the fury. Anger was good. I
was comfortable with anger. And action. I
needed to do something about this. I wanted
to get the son of a bitch who'd killed Jake.

"How about telling us what you've got?
There's no point keeping a lid on it. The
news'll be all over the place within the next
hour, and we both know the DA's office
won't be handling the case."

Hales frowned and fell silent for a moment.

"She has a point, Lieutenant," Toni said,
using the velvety voice that usually made
men blubber and stammer.

Hales did neither. If anything, his expression seemed to get more strained. He
stared out the window, and I followed his

gaze. The rain was beating steadily now, and traffic had snarled to a stop on First Street. A cab that'd been barreling down Temple Street came to a brake-squealing halt inches behind the bumper of a brand-new Mercedes that was ambling slowly through the intersection. I saw the cabbie lean out and shake his fist and then lift a middle finger at the driver of the Benz, who continued to amble at his own pace, slowly and implacably. I shared a moment of empathy with the cabbie.

"Please, my name's Graden." He paused a moment. "How well did you know Jake?"

I could tell him a lot about Jake professionally—the good-luck "believe me" suit he always wore at closing argument, his favorite judges and least favorite defense attorneys, but I knew that wasn't what Graden was after. When it came to the personal things, I had nothing—I couldn't even have said whether Jake liked Chinese food. I frowned as I realized how bad that would look. But I knew Hales would find out for himself soon enough, and since he wasn't answering my questions, I didn't feel any obligation to answer his. I kept it short and sweet. "Pretty well. He's one of the best lawyers in the office and one of the hardest workers. Everyone in the unit liked him."

That actually said a lot, though I doubted Hales would know that. Special Trials was a small unit, just seven deputies, and the major-league egos assigned to the unit were always on the prowl for the big case, which occasionally led to some nasty politicking. Personally, I never got into that politicking—not because I didn't want the big case but because I was superstitious. I firmly believed that if you chased a case, it would come back to bite you.

But Jake never chased a case because he never cared about being a star—he just wanted to be in trial, so he'd take whatever came his way. This led to him getting more than his fair share of dogs, but it also meant that he was beloved by the piranhas in the unit. And the fact that he wound up being a star anyway said everything about how talented he really was. *Was.* My throat closed up again. I held my breath and willed the tears back as I looked out the window to give myself a moment.

Toni nodded her agreement. "I can't imagine a soul in the world who'd want to do him harm."

Graden looked uncomfortable, and I thought he was going to just clam up and leave. But after a beat, he took a deep breath and said, "Since you were close to Jake, you're going to be questioned pretty closely, so you'd probably figure it out on your own anyway. But I need you to keep this to yourselves. There's going to be a tight lid on this case for a while. Promise me you won't talk about this to anyone until there's an official release."

He paused, waiting for our nods of agreement.

"Jake wasn't alone in that motel room," he said quietly. "There was a young boy—school ID said he was seventeen years old. We found a nude picture of the boy in Jake's jacket. At this point, it looks like murder-suicide. Jake shot the boy, then himself."

4

I felt all the breath go out of my body as the words sank in. Disoriented, I peered through the pouring rain at the clock on the Times Building, then glanced at Toni. She was staring out into the hallway, looking like a punch-drunk fighter. I turned to face the lieutenant to tell him it couldn't be true, but my eyes wouldn't track. Momentarily dizzy, I couldn't find the words to put a sentence together. The ensuing silence felt leaden. Suddenly the buzz of Toni's intercom pierced the air.

For the second time that morning, we

both stared at the phone, then Toni slowly picked it up.

The lieutenant turned to me, his expression of concern now deepened. "I'm sorry," he said. Although I could see he felt awkward, I mentally gave him points for not saying the usual dumb things like "I know how you must feel" or "Time will heal the wound." No one knows how I feel, and time doesn't heal the wound. The wound just becomes a part of you.

I nodded, and the lieutenant glanced over at Toni, who was still on the phone and looking away from him, out the window. He quietly said good-bye and left.

A few seconds later, Toni hung up. "Eric called for a unit meeting in his office ASAP."

We exchanged a look. Neither of us was ready for a group appearance, but this wasn't an optional invitation. Grim-faced and dreading what was to come, we left Toni's office.

On our way up the hall, we passed by Jake's area and saw a cop approaching with crime scene tape. Toni and I exchanged another look. We didn't want to see that tape go up. We both veered off and turned into the hallway on the right to take the long way.

As we detoured around Jake's office, Toni gamely tried to distract us from the morbid reality. "He's interested."

"He who? And in what?"

"You. Couldn't you tell?"

I had no idea what she was talking about. "Who?" I repeated.

"Graden, the lieutenant. He's interested."

"Oh, for Christ's sake, Toni," I replied sourly. The moment the words left my mouth, I wanted to snatch them back. I was in one hell of a state if I was taking my upset out on her. "Sorry."

"Yeah, I know," Toni said, waving off the apology.

After five years of best friendship, we'd learned how to surf each other's rough spots. As we headed toward Eric's office, I deliberately kept my eyes turned away from the end of the hall so I wouldn't see the cop taping Jake's door. Even from where I stood, a strange stillness seemed to surround his office. The memory of all the nights I'd sat with him there, talking about our cases, laughing about something a witness had said, was so vivid I could hear his voice, see him toss a mini-pretzel into the air and catch it in his mouth. Never again. I couldn't bear the thought. I picked up the pace as we continued down the hall.

We marched into the anteroom of Eric Northrup's office. Knowing what was going to be said about Jake, I felt raw and defensive, ready for a fight. Melia Espinoza, the unit secretary who was also known as Gossip Central, was on the phone, her hand covering the mouthpiece to muffle her words.

"We're here to see Eric," I said.

"Hang on a sec," she said as she covered the phone, then looked up at us and replied, "He's on the phone, and the rest of the unit isn't here yet, so . . ."

The look on my face told her not to tell me to wait, so she stopped the sentence just short of a trip to the hospital.

"I'll have to call you back," she said into the phone quickly, then hung up.

"You know the meeting's about Jake, right?" she asked.

"No, but obviously you do." My tone was no more inviting than my look.

"You know, I always thought he was

nice—kind of nerdy, but you know . . . now this, *ay, Dios mío*. I don't get what he was doing in a place like *that*." She said it with a mix of accusation and distaste that made me want to slap her. Hard.

"We don't know the story yet, Melia," I said, angry at the way she was so quick to believe the worst. I hoped the lieutenant was right about keeping a lid on the sordid details. The location of Jake's death alone would raise enough nasty speculation, and I knew there'd be plenty of it. I needed to start getting used to it now or I'd wind up going postal.

Melia raised her eyebrows, then looked at me sympathetically and said, "I'm sorry, *mija,* I know he was your friend, but you didn't hang with him, right?"

Hang with him, meaning outside the office. "No, but—"

"Sometimes people have dark sides you don't know about."

I stared at her for a moment, waiting for the inanity of what she'd just said to sink in. Fortunately I managed to bite back several remarks that would've ensured all of my messages would be lost for at least the next year. Further opportunities for dis-

aster were averted, as the rest of the deputies appeared in the anteroom. Eric opened
his door and, cradling his phone, motioned
for all of us to come in, and Toni and I
filed inside with the others.

As Head Deputy, Eric had a "corner
pocket" office with a conference table, lots
of space, and a panoramic view. The furniture was still the usual government-
utilitarian ugly, but Eric had warmed it up
with photographs of his wife and toddler
twin boys. The boys' artwork hung on the
wall next to his desk. I'm a fan of kid art.
The largest piece depicted a Santa Claus
and a fire engine. I supposed an argument
could be made for a thematic link between
the two subjects, but I strongly suspected
the connection more likely lay in the art-
ist's access to the color red. Years of training afforded me these astonishing insights.

Eric, who'd been on a call when we all
filed in, hung up as we got seated. Looking as though he'd just lost his own son,
Eric ran his hand through his permanently
mussed hair, rolled his shirtsleeves up to
his elbows, and got right to it. "I know everyone's heard about Jake by now. I'm going
to ask all of you to withhold any judgment

until the investigation is complete," he said, looking at each of us one by one. He did not appear optimistic, and I couldn't blame him. But I liked him for making the effort.

Eric continued, his voice gruff with emotion. "For now, I want to say that I'll really miss him. He was a great lawyer and a great person, and an asset to this unit."

As I glanced around the room, I was pleasantly surprised to see the look of devastation on the faces of my fellow deputies. It was one of those rare occasions when my low expectations of others went unfulfilled. Then again, they didn't know that Jake had been found with that kid's picture in his pocket.

Eric paused to collect himself. "I have the unfortunate duty of having to deal with the business end of things," he said, clearing his throat with obvious discomfort. "As you all know, Jake carried a heavy caseload. He has ten open cases that I've got to assign. The good news is that only four of them really need to be worked up."

He began to hand out the case files, one or two to a deputy. He got to me last. "Rachel, I'm giving you the one that probably needs the most work-up." He handed me the file. "You've got the Densmore case."

Densmore—the name was familiar, but I couldn't place it.

Eric filled me in. "Victim is a minor, her father is a big-time doctor, pediatrician. Very influential. We've got no suspect in custody, and Daddy's pushing us to make an arrest and wrap up the case."

Then it hit me. "Jake just got this last week, right?"

Eric nodded. "Vanderhorn specifically asked for you or Jake. You were in that no-body murder trial, so . . ."

Jake had told me about it. When the DA himself assigns a case, it's serious. It was only a single-count rape case, not the high-profile murder cases we usually handled in Special Trials. In fact, when Jake gave me the rundown, I found that I couldn't even remember when I'd last had a live victim. I'd asked him what made the case Special Trials material. Now the conversation came back to me:

"Guess."
"No," I said.

"Come on, just one guess," Jake teased.

I sighed, feigning annoyance, but the truth was, we both loved playing the riddle game. "Okay, fine. Densmore is Vanderhorn's baby-daddy."

Jake gave me a disgusted look. "Biological impossibility—an unworthy effort, Ms. Knight."

I crossed my arms and waited. Seeing that I wasn't going to keep playing, Jake finally relented.

"Densmore's a real piece of work. I said, 'Hello, I'm—,' and didn't even get my name out before he started telling me what a big Vanderhorn supporter he was. Then I did the math, all by myself in my little head, and guess what I realized?"

"It's a reelection year," I groaned.

"Clichés are clichés because they're true, right?" Jake laughed, shaking his head. "So, big shock, Vanderhorn wants daily updates on our progress—"

"Jeez," I said disgustedly. "I feel your pain, Jakie, I do. But I cannot lie—I've probably never been happier to be unavailable for duty."

"Yeah, I wouldn't have minded letting you take the fall on this one either," Jake admitted with that impish grin of his. "Guess it's my turn in the barrel, but feel free to try and buy your way out of any guilt trips you may be having."

"Not a problem," I joked. "I'll stock up on pretzels and mustard."

"Actually, I was thinking you'd want to offer to take the next dog that comes along," he replied.

"It's a guilt trip, Jake, not psychosis."

We both laughed.

The memory made my heart ache, and I felt hot tears spring to my eyes. Alarmed—though Eric would've understood, I've never liked to get emotional in public—I swallowed rapidly to recover and flipped open the file. The first thing I saw was that the investigating officer—the detective in charge of the case—was Hughes Lambkin. Not so fondly nicknamed "Useless." He was a notoriously dumb load. Nothing could have sobered me up faster.

"Can I pull my own IO?" I asked.

Eric looked at me silently for a beat. "I'll back you, but don't get your hopes up," he said, his tone broadcasting what I already knew: getting the captain to approve a change in investigating officers was a fantasy. But I'd never get the case off the ground with Useless, so I had to try.

Eric adjourned the meeting, and we all trooped out with our newly assigned case files. I'd noticed that Toni had flipped through hers and read the summary Jake had prepared while Eric was doling out the rest of the cases, so as we walked down the hall, I asked, "What'd you get?"

"A double. You'll love this: three-defendant case, all illegal Russian immigrants. They wasted the guys who brought them over to do a credit card fraud scam, then they dug the bullets out of the bodies so the ammo couldn't be traced to their guns—"

"Smarter than the average bear so far," I remarked.

"Right, so you'd think they'd know better

than to leave behind the knife they used to dig out the bullets."

I smiled in spite of myself. "And the cops made their prints on the knife."

Toni nodded and grinned. "Sounds like you got something special too."

"A one-count rape, no defendant in custody, a worthless sack for an IO, a father who's in bed with Vanderhorn," I said.

"So it's a lot like mine, except without the evidence and with lots of pressure," Toni remarked dryly.

"Exactly." I seemed to be on a roll for getting cases with no evidence. "Maybe I should start a new unit: Crimes withOut Witnesses—COW. It'll be a small unit, consisting of just me, but I'd get to be the boss. What do you think?" I paused. "And no milk jokes allowed."

"I think you must still be hungover."

That was a fair guess. Back in my office, I sat down at my desk with a *whump* and picked up the phone. I'd tried to make light of it, but this case was going to be serious trouble. I'd have to solve it and win it . . . with the victim's daddy and the DA breathing down my neck.

"This is Rachel Knight. Can I have Bailey Keller, please?"

Bailey Keller was one of the best detectives on the force. From day one in the academy, she'd shown a rare combination of athleticism and brilliance that had foreshadowed a meteoric rise to the rank of detective and an assignment to the Major Crimes Division of the LAPD. The fact that on her third day of training she'd walked into a mom-and-pop liquor store to buy a Red Bull and wound up single-handedly busting a trio of gangbangers who'd been in the process of robbing the owners hadn't hurt her prospects either. On top of all that, she was the kind of natural pretty that didn't need makeup, and she had the obnoxious ability to be able to eat whatever she wanted without gaining an ounce. Toni and I regularly plotted to kill her for that particular gift. During our first case together, involving a serial killer who specialized in older women, Bailey and I had become fast friends. But it was her professional help that I needed now.

Bailey let herself be found.

"A little early for drinks, isn't it, Knight?" she asked. "Not that it's a problem."

"It's not, but we'll do the drinks later." I filled her in on the Densmore case. "I need you on this one. I can't get stuck with Lambkin."

"'Useless,' huh?" Bailey thought for a moment. "I have an idea. I'll call you back in about an hour."

We hung up, and I began to read through the file. Having a case like this, with a rummy like Lambkin for an IO, was a nightmare I wouldn't wake up from until either the case or my career was over. I must have looked at the phone ten times when, one hour and five minutes later, Bailey called.

"You owe me," she said in her rich contralto that was now tinged with a note of smugness. "Big-time."

I wanted to kiss her, hug her, offer to bear her many children.

"How'd you manage?"

"If I told you . . ."

"You'd have to kill me, yeah, I know." I didn't tell her, but from what I'd seen of this case, that might be a favor. "Can you set up a meeting with the victim and her parents?"

"Meet me downstairs at three thirty," she said, then hung up.

That was Bailey. A real blabbermouth.

5

We'd gotten lucky—traffic was moving on the 101 Freeway, and it took us only an hour to make the half-hour trip to Sunset Boulevard, heading west. The rain had stopped abruptly, and blue spaces peeked between gaps in the clouds, allowing random rays of sunshine to beam down on cars that flew alongside us. We were set to meet the Densmores at 5:00 p.m., and it was only a quarter till, so Bailey took the climb up through Pacific Palisades slowly, giving us a chance to get the lay of the land.

Usually the outskirts of a community are devoted to low-rent living options, small

tract homes, drab apartment buildings—
they always remind me of the Baltic and
Mediterranean Avenue squares on a Mo-
nopoly board. But this being "the Palisades," one of the toniest neighborhoods
in L.A., no such reminders of real life were
allowed. Here, the homes at the edge of
the community were at least four thousand
square feet, and none sold for less than
seven figures.

Water fell over fake rocks and shot up in
spouts in the man-made pools that her-
alded the entry to the gates that encircled
the Cliffs. Carefully manicured lawns and
colorful flowers covered the grounds in
front of, and the hills behind, the large
wrought iron gates. Huge, well-tended
weeping willows hung over the drive that
led up to the guarded entry. The "shack"
that housed the security personnel was
styled like a country cottage, with mullioned
windows and wooden doors with decora-
tive iron hinges. A uniformed guard was
standing outside the door, and when Bailey
held out her badge, he took it and inspected
it, then waved us through. "Yes, Dr. Densmore is expecting you."

La-di-da, I thought. As we headed up

the hill toward Susan Densmore's home, the lawns grew progressively bigger and greener, and the houses more palatial. Some were the one-story ranch style, albeit many thousand square feet thereof—not the kind of split-level, vinyl-sided ranches I grew up around, naturally—but there were also Tudor styles with dormers and brick fronts, and Mediterranean Modern styles painted in pale yellows with white columns and tiled roofs. Though architecturally eclectic, the neighborhood uniformly screamed money—big money. Predictably, the only people on the immaculate tree-lined streets were gardeners and nannies, tending dutifully to their employers' impeccable pets, pools, plants, and children.

We pulled into the semicircular driveway of a two-story Tudor-style home that had wings extending to the right and left, and headed up the brick paved walk between banks of perfectly tended white rosebushes. A Porsche Cayenne with a bike rack was parked in front of the four-car garage.

"Ten thousand square feet, would you say?" I asked.

"Not counting the guesthouse we'll definitely find out back."

As usual, Bailey was dressed perfectly—a camel-colored trench coat and off-white turtleneck sweater that complemented her fair skin and short blond hair. And at a slender five feet nine, Bailey pulled off the tight cigarette-leg slacks better than I, at five feet six, ever could. I comforted myself once again with the knowledge that I could get away with wearing higher heels. It wasn't much, but it was all I had. We reached the massive oak double doors. Bailey ignored the heavy brass knocker and punched the doorbell. Even the chimes sounded rich. A matronly Hispanic woman answered so quickly I thought she had to have been waiting by the door.

"You are the detectives?" she asked.

Her English was careful, her expression skeptical. Why do people still think detectives have to look like Joe Friday?

"Right," Bailey said, keeping it short. We'd explain exactly who was what to someone who cared.

The housekeeper nodded and motioned us inside.

Ordinarily you'd call it a foyer, but this? This was a lobby. The ceiling was easily thirty feet high, and the floor was a wide, circular expanse of cream-colored marble dotted with terra-cotta-colored diamonds. A gleaming teak elephant stood to the right of the door, its mouth open and waiting for umbrellas. A circular staircase on my left led to the second floor, where an open hallway branched off to the north and south, no doubt leading to the separate wings I'd noticed outside. On my right was a thickly carpeted and heavily draped drawing room. Just beyond that was an open, formal living room with French doors and windows that offered a view of the park the Densmores called the backyard. As the housekeeper led us toward the living room, I could see an outdoor kitchen; plush, brick-colored patio furniture; a huge swimming pool with a waterfall; and rolling grounds punctuated by jacaranda trees, bronze statuary, and hundreds of bushes that were obediently flowering in multicolored hues, although it was the dead of winter.

A perfectly groomed, rigorously fit-looking man stood up and extended his hand. A little taller than six feet, he had sharp features, precisely combed hair, and a piercing dark gaze.

"Dr. Frank Densmore," he said.

There was a slight challenge to the way he said it. I was in just the mood to meet that challenge.

"Deputy District Attorney Rachel Knight," I replied, giving his hand an extra-firm shake. "I'm the DA who's been assigned to the case." He gave my hand one and a half pumps, then dropped it. Done with me.

I gestured to Bailey. "This is Detective Bailey Keller. She's going to be the investigating officer on the case."

Bailey got the same requisite one and a half pumps.

He turned back to me. "I heard about Jake Pahlmeyer. I'm sorry."

He didn't sound all that sorry. "Yes, it's a tragedy," I said, trying to keep my tone neutral. I wondered what he knew of Jake's death. Judging by his tone of voice, I guessed it wasn't much. This told me that Densmore wasn't a longtime member of Vanderhorn's inner circle. Though, come to think of it, I'd bet Vanderhorn wasn't talking to anyone about what the police suspected. Still, I made a mental note to find out exactly when Densmore had jumped on the Reelect Vanderhorn bandwagon—before or after his daughter's rape. It wouldn't matter to the case; I just wanted to know who I was dealing with.

Densmore turned abruptly to Bailey. "What happened to Detective Lambkin?" Jake's death meant nothing more to him than a change in personnel, and his tone implied that someone should have run that change by him first. Not that I expected him to rip his clothes and douse himself with ashes over Jake's passing, but I'd seen chimpanzees with more empathy.

Bailey didn't miss a beat. "He's been called out to handle a cold case that's going to require some travel," she said. "Your case needs full-time attention, so they put me on it."

Damn, she was good. I could already tell that Daddy Densmore was the type who always thought he deserved more than what anyone else got, and I was right. I could see by his satisfied expression that Bailey's words had had the desired effect—there'd be no more questions about why she'd taken over for Useless. And now the mystery of how Bailey had gotten rid of Lambkin was solved: she'd drummed up a no-pressure case that would give him "travel bennies." How she'd managed to do *that* was something I didn't want to know.

"Good. Hopefully you'll be able to move this along now," Densmore replied, looking across the room.

I followed his gaze to the woman and young girl seated on the giant gold-and-beige-striped couch. A family portrait that hung in the traditional spot over the mantel showed them sitting in an almost identical position: Father Frank standing behind them with a proprietary air—his girls. Susan Densmore had Alice in Wonderland long, golden hair and delicate features that came from the maternal end of the gene pool. Her mother wore her hair in a low ponytail, while Susan's hung pale and straight, down to the middle of her back. Both were slender and sat primly, ankles crossed, hands folded in their laps like Lladró figurines. I bet it was some kind of fun to live in this house.

"Janet, my wife, and, of course, Susan," said Frank Densmore, motioning toward them.

As though she'd been waiting for her cue, Janet unfolded, and I reached out to take her hand as she stood.

"It's a pleasure to meet you, Mrs. Densmore," I said, and noticed her grip was surprisingly strong—quite a contrast to the demure pose.

"Please call me Janet," she said as she glanced over at her daughter.

Susan took her cue and stood gracefully but was unable to meet my eyes as she reluctantly reached for my hand. "Nice to meet you," she said politely, her voice barely above a whisper.

"I'm glad to meet you too, Susan," I said. An air of sadness and shock floated around her like the broken tendrils of a spiderweb. The sight pulled at my heart. I knew that emotionally broken feeling very well—the world-shattering discovery that the safety net of security she'd always taken for granted was just a fairy tale. Whatever had happened here, Susan would never be the same. It'd been a while since I'd handled a case with a live rape victim, but my past experience had taught me that rape victims often don't know who they hate more—the cops and prosecutors who make them relive the nightmare over and over, or the animals who put them in the position of having to do it. It would take some winning over to let Susan know I understood that.

"I hope you realize we already know who did this," Frank Densmore said impatiently as he lifted his pant legs slightly and sat down in the leather wingback chair, careful to keep the crease straight.

I noticed that Susan suddenly stiffened, and Janet glanced warily between father and daughter.

I always loved it when witnesses let me know they had it all figured out. But this time I was prepared, because Jake had put a note in the file to that effect. The tension in the room after Densmore made his remark told me there was dissension among the ranks. I wanted to see how this played out. So I raised an eyebrow but said nothing.

The father steepled his hands and peered over them at me. "Susan's been tutoring a boy from Sylmar—part of an ill-advised program at her school to bring young people from diverse backgrounds together. As soon as I saw him, I knew he was a gangbanger. I told Janet to get Susan out of the program, that he was bad news, but she wouldn't listen." He flashed a look of irritation first at Janet, then at Susan, who'd obviously colluded to defy him.

"Assuming he is a gang member, what makes you think he did it?" I asked, deliberately keeping my tone neutral.

"Isn't it obvious? He saw all this," Frank said, gesturing at the vaulted ceiling and everything it sheltered, "and got jealous and angry."

That explanation seemed to fit a burglary a lot better than a rape, but I had no desire to get into a debate with him. Opinions didn't matter; evidence did. "We'll be looking into all possibilities, Dr. Densmore," I said calmly, knowing my refusal to jump on his bandwagon would piss him off.

"Do your job," he said dismissively, then continued, "but please don't waste a lot of time looking around. It's very clear who did it, and I don't like having it dragged out."

"I'd imagine it's pretty hard on Susan too," I said dryly. My sarcasm was lost on good old Frank, so I turned to the daughter. "Would you mind showing me where it happened?"

"They've already processed the area for evidence," Densmore said, his expression broadcasting how much he'd loved having crime scene techs roaming around his house. "Of course I won't object if you want to make sure nothing was missed, but I would think there isn't much left to do."

I didn't think this was the time to share the joke about "Useless" Hughes Lambkin, so I just nodded. Densmore stood up, intending to lead the way.

I stopped him. "No need to join us. Susan can show me around for now. I just want to get a sense of how it happened—it helps if I can visualize the scene." Taking a page out of Bailey's book, I added, "I don't want to take up any more of your time than necessary."

Kiss-ass behavior generally goes against my grain, but I could suck it up and brown-nose with the best of them when I wanted something. Right now, I wanted to talk to Susan alone, without Dr. Blowhard in the way.

Densmore frowned, and I saw him glance protectively at Susan. That, I understood and appreciated.

"We won't be long, Dr. Densmore," I said, attempting to reassure him with my look and tone of voice that we weren't going to put his daughter through a grilling session.

He looked at me for a moment, then nodded reluctantly. "Fine. Let me know if you need anything. I'll be here," he said, a hint of warning in his voice.

"Will do," I said.

Susan led Bailey and me up the wide spiral staircase with slow, leaden steps, gripping the polished mahogany railing like an arthritic ninety-year-old. We turned left at the top of the stairs and followed her to the door at the end of the hallway, which sported a framed poster of Albert Einstein. Not what I'd expected to see on this girl's bedroom door. I noticed that the glass covering of the poster was sparkling clean—it had likely been dusted for fingerprints and in need of a thorough scrubbing after the crime scene techs had finished with it. The fact that it had been returned told me nothing useful had been found.

Susan took a deep breath and opened the door, then stepped in and stopped to the right of it, unwilling to go any farther than she had to. Bailey and I filed past her into a bedroom that was larger than most houses.

It had a sitting room lined with closets and a huge bathroom with a steam sauna shower. The south wall was almost fully occupied by a set of glass French doors that led onto a balcony overlooking the back grounds. Her king-size bed—covered with a custom duvet colored in soft rose and blue flowers—was to the left of the window, just five feet away.

"So, Susan, what grade are you in now?" I asked conversationally, although I already knew she was fifteen years old.

"I'm a sophomore," she replied in a small voice that sounded like she was closer to twelve.

The rape-kit exam indicated she'd probably been a virgin too, and judging by her shy demeanor and buttoned-up style, I'd bet that was true. Of course, I couldn't be sure until I asked her; looks could be deceiving. Not that it mattered from a legal standpoint—rape was rape regardless—but knowing Susan's specific situation would let me find the right tack in handling our interviews and preparing her for court. To do that, I had to establish some rapport so she'd open up and talk to me—no easy task after what she'd been through. I gazed out the window and wished for the thousandth time that rape were punishable by penis removal . . . with a rusty knife.

"You go to Pali High?" I asked. Ordinarily I'd have assumed that a girl living in a mansion and neighborhood like this went to a private school. But Palisades Charter High School was no ordinary public school. Due in no small part to the generous donations that were solicited throughout the year, it had all the perks of a private school and then some.

Susan nodded but said nothing more. I continued with nonthreatening get-to-know-you questions. "How is it being a sophomore? A little better than your freshman year?"

"I guess, maybe." Her gaze slid off to the doorway, where I figured she'd like to be headed. Out of the corner of my eye, I saw that while I was trying to loosen Susan up, Bailey was looking around the room, gathering some firsthand impressions.

I tried again, hoping to help her let go of what had happened in this room. "What's your favorite subject this year?"

Susan shrugged, still not looking at me. "I don't know. English, I guess."

Aha. A hook. "Really? That was mine too. What are you reading?"

"*Animal Farm* by George Orwell," she replied with as much animation as I'd seen since we shook hands.

"I read that too," I said, smiling. "What'd you think of it?"

"Um, I liked it, actually," Susan said, tucking a strand of hair behind her ear. "At first, you just think it's funny, but then it's, like, about so much more. You know?"

"Yep. That book was so good, even school couldn't ruin it," I remarked with a little smile.

I was rewarded with Susan's conspiratorial grin and brief nod. I hated to spoil the moment, but I knew we'd have to start talking about the case sometime. I intended to ease in and let her tell as much as she wanted to for now, then fill in the parts she couldn't handle at a later date. I looked around the room for a moment, then back at Susan. This time, she returned my gaze. She was ready.

6

"Were you awake when he came into your room?" I asked.

"No, but I know he came in through there," she said as she pointed to the French doors that led to the balcony. She looked at the bed as her next words poured out in a torrent. "I was asleep. Then he jumped on my bed. He pushed a pillow over my face, and I couldn't breathe. I thought I was going to die." She paused after she said this and took a breath.

I would bet there were times she'd wished she had.

"Susan, we don't have to get into the details right now."

"It's okay . . . I'd rather just tell you and get it over with, you know?"

I really did. If the questions that force you to relive the nightmare are unavoidable, it's better to answer them right away and get at least that part of the suffering over with. Postponing the inevitable only added days of dreaded anticipation to the pain. I nodded and squeezed her arm for support, then gestured for us to sit on the upholstered chest at the foot of the bed. As we moved into the room, I scanned the view through the French doors and made a mental note.

Susan took another deep breath. Staring at the floor, she began to speak. "I never saw him. All I know is I woke up with him on top of me. I tried to scream, but I had the pillow in my face, so nothing came out. Then he pulled up my nightgown and . . ."

She stopped, and I waited for her to recover. I hated putting any rape victim through this, but it was especially awful with Susan. She seemed so young, so vulnerable. Just like Romy. As it had countless times before, my mind replayed my last moments with her: my seven-year-old self saying, *"Come on, Romy, you're not even trying! Hide better!"* Romy, shaking her head good-naturedly, walking away. The memory tightened my chest with pain and guilt, and I had to force myself to breathe past the moment.

I was about to prompt Susan to continue but thought better of it. There was no need. I knew her rape kit had not yielded any semen, but that wasn't surprising—her vaginal swab had revealed lubricant of the type generally found on condoms. So he was a careful rapist, but he hadn't been careful enough. They'd found DNA on the nightgown that didn't match Susan or anyone else in the house. That was the good news. The bad news was that it didn't match anyone in the state database either. Whoever had done it didn't have a criminal record, or had one in another state, or hadn't been asked to submit bodily fluids. I'd already made a note to myself to check and see if the so-called gangbanger Susan had been tutoring was in the DNA database. Ordinarily I'd have been fairly certain that the first detective would have taken care of something this routine, but with Useless Hughes Lambkin, you had no such assurance.

Based on the photographs and doctors' reports I'd seen, there was a thinning to the hymen, which indicated there'd been sexual penetration, and there was some degree of vaginal tearing. It was better than nothing in terms of ruling out consensual sex, but it wasn't a slam dunk. The fact that a condom had been used didn't help much either. Still, from what I'd seen so far, Susan would make a compelling witness. Providing I could find someone to arrest.

"Did you see any part of him—his face, maybe in profile? Or his back? Do you remember any particular smell?" I asked.

Susan shook her head thoughtfully. "I've tried to remember, but I was afraid to pull off the pillow until he was gone. In case he might come back and . . ." She stopped and frowned to herself.

"I don't blame you. I would've been afraid too, Susan," I reassured her.

She nodded, took another breath, and

continued. "I think he left through the balcony, because the French doors were still open, and I would've heard if he'd left through my bedroom door."

I nodded. The French doors opened onto a semicircular balcony. Those doors now sported a not-so-decorative bolt-style lock. I scanned the room. Probably the crime scene tech had gotten all there was to get, but again, with Lambkin in charge, I had reason to doubt. Bailey noticed my look and nodded.

"Susan, would you mind if we had another crime scene technician take a look around?" Bailey asked. "We'll be neat."

"I don't care. I don't sleep here anymore," Susan admitted. "I took the maid's old room. I don't even get dressed here."

I couldn't blame her. I got up to go, but Susan reached out and touched my arm, stopping me.

I turned to her.

She darted a furtive look at the doorway, then whispered with urgency, "Don't listen to my dad. It wasn't Luis. I know it wasn't!"

Luis, the gangbanger, I knew from the file.

Struck by the vehemence in her tone, I asked, "What makes you say that?"

Susan shook her head sadly. "I know you must think I'm some little sheltered rich girl, and I am. But I'm not stupid. And I know Luis. He worked hard. He was looking to get out of his . . . situation. He might be a lot of things; he probably is. But he's not a rapist. And he'd never hurt me."

"Are you . . . ?" I began.

She shook her head rapidly. "He's just a friend."

"Any idea where we might be able to find him?"

Susan dipped her head and looked at the floor. "No. I never knew where he lived. And I haven't seen him since . . ."

We knew he'd been in the wind ever since the rape, which did not help his cause any—Susan knew it too. It wasn't proof beyond a reasonable doubt, but I couldn't blame Frank Densmore for thinking otherwise. I always kept an open mind to all possibilities in the beginning of a case, but I had to admit that finding Luis was at the top of our to-do list.

I looked at Susan. Rich and sheltered, she certainly was, but she was a tough little thing for all that. And her willingness to stand up to her father for this Luis guy was impressive, even though it might be ill-advised. I had a feeling Daddy was always right, even when he wasn't. Densmore didn't seem like an easy person to stand up to.

We headed downstairs, and all of us were relieved to find that Daddy Dearest was gone.

"He had to go back to the office," Janet explained. "He's running six pediatric health centers," she said apologetically. "All the kids in the neighborhood go to him. And then he's got his charity work," she said, a tinge of pride creeping into the apology. She sighed. "He's spread awfully thin."

He didn't seem the saintly type, but there was no benefit in arguing the point with Mrs. Densmore. I figured nearly all of his clinics were in high-dollar neighborhoods. More businessman than doctor nowadays, Densmore rarely saw patients. "Not a problem," I said.

"By the way, I noticed the bike rack," Bailey said, nodding toward the Cayenne in the driveway. "Who's the cyclist in the family?"

"Both of us," Janet replied. "But Frank's

the real enthusiast. He does those marathon rides for charity. I tried it once, but . . ." She shook her head and gave Bailey a measuring look. "I bet you can do them."

Bailey nodded. "On a good day."

That, I knew, was bullshit. Bailey was a monster on two wheels.

Janet looked at me questioningly, but I shook my head. "Not me. Those crazy rides are a bridge too far." This pulled a little smile out of Janet. I got her permission for a "do over" for the crime scene techs in Susan's bedroom, and we said our good-byes for the time being.

As I got into Bailey's car, I noticed a twenty-four-hour neighborhood patrol vehicle roll by. It said PALISADES SECURITY—24-HOUR PATROL on the driver's-side door.

"We should check out the security patrol for this joint. They might have some ideas about who had access to the house," I said.

Bailey nodded. "They might be on that list themselves."

"Might be," I agreed. It wouldn't be the first time the security was actually the culprit, though I expected the background checks for a company that worked in

neighborhoods like this were pretty thorough—if only to avoid the inevitable lawsuit if a baddie slipped through the cracks.
"Did Useless door-knock the neighborhood?"

"Report says he did, but he doesn't list
any leads. My bet is he kissed off whatever the uniforms got as a dead end so he
wouldn't have to do the follow-ups. I'm
starting over with my own team," Bailey
said, her voice grim and shaded with disgust. "We'll run rap sheets on everyone,
check ties to the Densmores, alibis—the
whole shootin' match. Start with neighbors
tomorrow."

"Make sure someone's working on
finding our gangbanger Luis Revelo while
you're at it—"

"Got it," Bailey interjected.

She hated when I stuck in my two
cents—especially on the obvious stuff. This
never stopped me.

"Lot of workers in a place like this too," I
continued. "Pool men, gardeners, personal
trainers—"

"Contractors, architects, carpenters,
decorators—yeah." Bailey's tone told me I
was pushing it now.

"Decorators?"

She shrugged. "Can't get stuck on stereotypes."

The decorators I'd met wouldn't even walk *around* a ladder, let alone climb one to break into a young girl's bedroom, but Bailey was right about stereotypes. "Have at 'em."

We headed east on Sunset, now at a crawl through the thick commuter traffic.

"What do you think?" Bailey asked.

I watched as the neighborhood gave way to meaner streets and tiny storefronts bearing signs in foreign languages — moving backward on the game board, going from St. Charles to Oriental to Baltic and Mediterranean, heading toward "Go."

"This guy Luis dropping out of sight like that? Seems awfully obvious, don't you think?" I asked rhetorically.

"Does."

I nodded. "I hate that." But I also knew better than to fight it. Just because it was obvious didn't mean Luis wasn't our rapist. I'd long since learned that criminals generally aren't the brightest bulbs in the chandelier — if they were, we'd never catch them. And, as my old mentor used to say,

"When you hear hoofbeats, think horses, not zebras."

"Did Useless run the guy?" I asked.

"Not likely. I'll take care of it," Bailey replied, making a note in her new cell phone.

"What happened to your BlackBerry?" I asked. Bailey was a gadget freak—the first to get the best in techie hot stuff.

She offered her iPhone to me. "Old news. This thing makes the BlackBerry look like a typewriter."

I shook my head and refused to take the phone. "You should know better by now. I'll break it before I can even pick a ringtone."

"True," Bailey said, and abruptly pulled her gadget back and dropped it into her pocket.

I watched a young girl in skintight jeans and Converse sneakers bobbing along to a tune on her iPod as she walked a ratlike dog. The dog, stopping suddenly to pee on a bus bench, pulled her backward and caused her earpieces to fall out. She looked completely befuddled for a moment, as though this were her first experience being out in the world without piped-in music. Maybe it was.

The sight of the young girl brought me back to Susan's father. "Old Frank's a piece of work, though, isn't he?"

"A real dick," Bailey agreed. "He's the type who yells his own name when he comes."

I shot her a look. "Must you? Now I've got that picture in my head." I squeezed my eyes shut to block out the image of Frank Densmore in the throes. *Yech.*

Bailey shrugged.

She had an inborn gift for the gross-out, but growing up with three older brothers — not to mention working with cops — had raised her game to Olympic levels.

I deliberately turned off the image of Densmore and considered what bugged me about him. It wasn't just that he was a control-freak know-it-all; it was that no matter what was going on, it was all about him — even his daughter's rape. But, to be fair, I had seen some genuine concern for her. And if he'd bought his way into Vanderhorn's inner circle just to get special attention for his daughter's case, that was some evidence of real devotion — albeit in a sickening, influence-peddling sort of way. And, as it turned out, the sort of way that worked.

"You ever notice how rich people's clinics are called 'health centers'?" I asked.

"Yeah," Bailey replied with a smirk.

After a moment, her expression darkened. "Tell you what, Knight. If Luis isn't our guy, we'd better find something to work with in Susan's bedroom, because otherwise this case is looking like a dead body in a locked room." Bailey's tone was sullen as she continued. "By the way, have I thanked you yet for getting me into this?"

"No, you haven't. But you've always been the ungrateful type," I replied.

Bailey gave me a sideways look.

"Still, we do know one thing," I said. "The rapist definitely knew the Densmores. There's no way anyone who hadn't been in that castle would know how to dodge the security patrol and find her bedroom."

"And do it in the middle of the night," Bailey added.

7

It was nearly 8:00 when Bailey pulled up to the Biltmore. I was tired, hungry, and ready for a drink to smooth out the last frayed edges of my hangover.

"Feel like a short dog?" I asked.

"Maybe several," she said as she parked in a loading-only zone.

We got out, and I deliberately avoided Rafi's eyes as we approached the door. The valet was already not a big fan of mine, since I almost never drove my car. This wasn't going to make my stock rise any higher with him. Angel, the doorman, saw me skulking past the valet stand and smirked knowingly as he let us in.

As always the sheer beauty of the hotel lobby struck me afresh: the stained glass set into the soaring dome ceiling, the ornately cut Lalique chandelier, the plushness of the huge Oriental rugs spread over dark henna-colored marble floors. In the far corner next to the bar, the soft rain of a waterfall fountain spilling over an Italian-tiled wall lent a soothing grace note to the opulent ambience. Walking into the lobby always felt like I'd been enfolded in the embrace of a Rubenesque duchess.

To my right stood a group of very blond middle-aged couples beside a mound of luggage bearing Lufthansa stickers. Adorned in clunky sandals, black socks, and Bermuda shorts—deliberately snubbing both L.A. winter and fashion—they waited as their leader tried to claim their room reservations in a thick accent that the clerk was struggling mightily to decipher. I nodded to Tommy, the night manager, who gave me a brief smile and a wave. As he moved toward the clerk, I heard the group leader's voice grow louder. Though it never works, everyone tries to scale the language barrier with volume.

I pulled open the heavy, darkly tinted glass door of the bar and felt the familiar hush created by thick carpets, soft lights, and rich upholstery. The door closed slowly behind us as we stepped into the cool, quiet darkness. Frank Sinatra sang "Witchcraft" over the muted tinkle of glasses, and I took in the scene as we moved toward the bar.

A group of four older men in conservative dark suits huddled in one of the forest-green leather booths to the right of the fireplace. In the middle of the room sat two young bare-legged women in tight, expensive suits, sipping cosmopolitans on one of the overstuffed sofas—either lawyers or hookers trying to look like lawyers.

My buddy and favorite bartender, Drew Rayford, was drying a manhattan glass as Bailey and I climbed onto the leather stools at the end of the long, brass-trimmed mahogany bar. We sat beneath a photograph of a famous jockey, the horse's bridle in one hand and a winner's cup in the other.

"Rachel, Bailey," Drew said, nodding to each of us. I could feel Bailey heat up next to me as she nodded back at Drew. He looked particularly elegant tonight, in dark slacks and a white shirt and black vest that emphasized a disgustingly narrow waist. The white collar provided a sharp yet stunning contrast with his black skin, and the single diamond stud he wore in his left ear glittered as he moved through the soft light emanating from behind the bar. Tall, gorgeous, and smooth as silk, Drew had too many options when it came to women. Unfortunately for them, his priority was opening his own upscale bar one day, and he intended for that day to come sooner than later. Socializing was last on his list. As a result, I had a feeling no woman saw him half as much as I did.

"Ladies?" he asked.

"Glenlivet rocks, water back," Bailey replied.

"I'll have a Bloody Mary," I said.

"I see," Drew said with a small smile.

A Bloody Mary at night meant only one thing—hangover time—and no one knew it better than Drew. It's the downside of living here. Everyone knows me . . . and my habits. I rolled my eyes. "And we're having dinner," I added.

"Well, good for us. I'm guessing you'll be wanting this too," he said as he scooped up a glass of ice, filled it with water, and put it on the bar in front of me. I waited until he'd moved off to get the menus and our drinks. I slugged down most of the water in one long gulp and pushed the glass over in front of Bailey, not wanting Drew to know that he'd accurately assessed my condition—seriously, couldn't I have some privacy?

"I feel used," Bailey said, giving me a sidelong glance.

I reached for the silver tray of snack bowls that Drew filled with something different every week. Tonight's offerings were kalamata olives, endive, and spicy almonds. "You heard anything about Jake Pahlmeyer's case?" I asked Bailey as I treated myself to an olive.

Before she could answer, Drew brought our drinks, then gave us the menus and spread large white napkins out on the bar in front of us.

Bailey looked at him for a beat. "Thanks," she said with a slow smile.

Drew looked back at her for what seemed to me an obnoxiously long time.

"You're very welcome," he said with a little smile of his own before he moved down the bar.

I almost groaned out loud. "You've got to be kidding, right?" I whispered. "He'll boink you once and then bounce you out. You do remember that I live here, and you'll have to keep meeting me here after it's over?"

"What makes you so sure he hasn't 'boinked' me more than once already?" Bailey took a sip of her whiskey. "Besides," she said matter-of-factly, "nobody bounces me out."

If I took this any further, I'd wind up with either too much or too little information. Neither option appealed to me, and besides, I had bigger fish to fry at the moment.

"Whatever," I said dryly. "So tell me what's up with Jake's case."

"The FBI has officially moved in," Bailey replied.

I took a drink of my Bloody Mary. The first sip went down like oil in a rusty engine. I inhaled deeply and finally began to relax.

"So now that the Feds are in, are you guys out?" I asked.

"Not yet. We're 'cooperating' with them."

"Who's the liaison?" I asked. Usually, when agencies worked together, each one had a point man to make coordinating the work more efficient.

"Hales. You know him?"

"We've met," I said noncommittally, taking another pull of my drink.

Bailey caught my evasive tone. "Tell me you're not one of them."

"One of what?"

"Don't give me that 'one of what' crap. One of his babes." She took a long sip of her drink. "He's got a friggin' fan club of panting pussies," she said, her mouth twisted in disgust.

"That's lovely, Emily Dickinson."

"Call 'em like I see 'em," she replied. She popped an almond into her mouth.

Bailey's "grossitude" notwithstanding, this meant that if Toni was right, Hale's interest in me was no cause to pop out the Dom—it was just another day that ended in "y." Never one for crowds, I decided I could take a pass on joining Hales's Hotties.

"Please," I said as I reached for another olive. "Have I ever been anyone's 'babe'?"

I looked at Bailey, who conceded the point. "Not that I've ever seen."

"Right."

I told her how I'd met Lieutenant Graden Hales. Bailey nodded, serious for a moment. When I'd finished, I drained what was left of my water and attacked the Bloody Mary again.

Bailey looked at me speculatively. "He may be a little too popular for my taste, but I have to tell you, Hales does seem like a good guy," she said as she lifted her glass. "It wouldn't be a bad idea for you to try and move past Daniel."

I opened my mouth to argue that I *had* moved past Daniel, that it'd been a year since I'd broken up with him. But I knew what Bailey meant, and although I hated to admit it, I knew she was right. It hadn't been a clean break. Daniel Rose, a world-class criminal defense attorney, had become one of the most sought-after Strickland experts—lawyers who give expert testimony on the competence, or lack thereof, of other lawyers—in the country. I'd met him when a rapist-murderer, whom I'd gotten life without parole, had tried to get his conviction overturned by claiming his lawyer was incompetent for failing to present an insanity defense. I'd put Daniel on the stand to refute his claim, and from our very first meeting, I could feel the electricity in the air between us. I'd had no idea that he'd felt it too until the day we won.

Daniel's testimony had torn the defense ploy to shreds. Within minutes after Daniel left the stand, the judge denied the motion to overturn the verdict. Daniel had called me at the office that evening to find out how the judge had ruled, and when I told him, he proposed a celebratory drink. The drink had turned into dinner, hours of talking until the wee hours, and then lunch the next day. By the end of the week, we had plans for the weekend.

What we had in those first few months was idyllic. Experiencing that kind of happiness was completely foreign to me. Daniel was my lover, my best friend, my cheerleader—and someone who could give me a game. Challenge, thrills, and comfort, all in one package. For the first time in my life, I let myself get wrapped up in a relationship with a man instead of holding him off at arm's length. I was afraid but filled with wonder—a pale cave creature basking in its first exposure to sunshine.

If I'd given it a moment of rational

thought, I could've predicted what the death knell of our relationship would be—but I didn't want to know. And so the corrosive forces seeped quietly and imperceptibly into my subconscious, then bled out, inch by inch, into the space between us.

Daniel, being a nationally recognized expert, had speaking engagements and court appearances all over the country. But when we met, the season for lectures had just ended, so I didn't realize how much time he usually spent on the road. When the season picked up again six months later, he was traveling, doing lectures and court appearances that kept him on the road for at least two weeks out of every month.

Without even realizing it, I began to back away. Suddenly I couldn't find the time to take Daniel's calls, then I forgot to call him back, and on the days he was in town, I always seemed to have to work later than usual—which, given my habitually late hours, meant that on some nights I didn't leave the office till nearly midnight. At first Daniel accepted my excuses—a gnarly case, a recalcitrant witness—but eventually he began to ask if there was something wrong. A very faint voice from deep inside whispered that there was, but I didn't want to hear it. Daniel, on the other hand, didn't have my powers of denial, so finally, over what was supposed to be a romantic candlelit dinner at his house, he asked me point-blank if I was seeing someone else. Horrified, I'd sat speechless. When I made my voice work, I managed to ask him how he could think that. He told me: all the nights I'd been too busy to see him, all his calls that I hadn't taken—and never returned. I told him that there was no one else, and that was the truth. But I also told him that the only reason I'd been so scarce was that I'd been overwhelmed with a double homicide I'd been preparing for trial. Although I'd wanted to believe that was the truth, it wasn't.

The truth was, my old scars—the ones that had always screwed up my relationships, the ones I thought I'd finally vanquished with Daniel—were reemerging. Carla, my shrink, called it a problem with object constancy. Having suffered the early traumatic loss of Romy, I never learned emotionally that when people leave they also come back. And so every time Daniel left town, a part of me, on a deep subconscious level, sealed up against the pain of the complete loss my child-self knew was bound to happen. Of course, I didn't know that at the time. It wasn't until after we'd broken up that Carla pointed it out and I realized what had happened.

The saddest part is that even if I had known earlier, I couldn't have brought myself to tell Daniel. It made me feel weak, which I hated, and beyond that, I didn't want to tell him about Romy. Because worse than having to admit weakness was having to admit guilt.

Daniel and I patched it up, but problems left unresolved never go away; they just hide in dark corners, where they fester and simmer—and eventually boil over. Over the next six months, Daniel would periodically point out that I was withdrawing again. I'd make excuses; he'd forgive me. We limped along that way for the rest of that year. But finally, just before Christmas, I accepted the fact that my demons had defeated me again, and I told Daniel goodbye. The sadness and tears in his eyes pierced my heart with a physical pain. The year that followed our breakup had rounded the sharp edges of that pain but hadn't washed it out. Time and again, I'd notice that I hadn't thought about Daniel for a few days and I'd congratulate myself on being over him . . . until I caught a glimpse of him in the courthouse. Then all the old feelings, mixed with the despondency of loss, would flood through me, leaving me with an ache so strong it stopped my breath. Bailey and Toni never argue when I say I've gotten past it, but they both know better. I'm hoping that if I keep on saying it, someday it'll be true.

"So Graden's riding point on Jake's case," I said, bringing us back around to the more immediate issue.

Bailey nodded. "The working theory right now is that the kid they found with Jake was blackmailing him. Kid's nude picture was in Jake's shirt pocket. Jake couldn't pay—he cracked and decided to check out and take the kid with him."

"Is that so?" I said, suddenly incensed by the cavalier judgment. "Did anyone ever stop to consider that nothing about this fits the person Jake actually was? Not a fucking thing!"

Bailey raised an eyebrow. "The person Jake actually was? Something you want to tell me about you and—"

"Of course not," I said heatedly. "It's just not right. He was a good guy, and he deserves better than to have everyone believe . . . this crap."

Bailey nodded as Drew reappeared. While she ordered dinner (in the most sultry voice I'd heard outside of a James Bond movie), I forced myself to power down. It wasn't Bailey's fault that everyone was taking this crime at face value. When Drew turned to me, I was tempted to again throw dietary caution to the wind and get the shrimp scampi Bailey had ordered, but I took pity on my waistband and got the salad niçoise instead. Drew made a face that said "Again?" but I ignored him. He probably hadn't gained a pound he didn't want since he was born.

As Drew left to turn in our orders, I said, "Sorry, Bailey. I'm just wondering why no one's digging below the first inch. I knew Jake pretty well, and I—"

She put up a hand to stop me. "You're preaching to the choir. But I want you to prepare yourself. How well did you really know Jake? Did you go to his crib? Did he come here? Did you meet his family? His girlfriend? You ever do anything together except work in an office?"

I just shook my head. And as far as I knew there was no girlfriend. An unbidden tendril of doubt snaked its way into my thoughts. At Jake's age, and with his looks and charm, there should have been a woman, a man—*someone* in his life, past or present, who should have come up in conversation at least once. Closemouthed as I was, I'd certainly mentioned Daniel's name a time or two. I didn't like the way this was making me feel. "Look, I'm not saying you don't have a point, okay? I just want to make sure they don't close the case before they've explored all the options."

"Why don't you talk to Hales?"

"I have. He basically said the same thing you did. And he's being really closemouthed about it for some reason," I groused.

"He's probably under pressure not to leak."

I took another sip of my drink and pondered what I could do on my own. Being a prosecutor, I was not, as they say, without resources.

Bailey looked at me appraisingly. "What're you going to do?"

"Not sure yet."

Drew brought my salad and Bailey's scampi. My stomach growled as I inhaled the rich aromas floating up from her plate.

Bailey smiled. "Want a bite?"

"Thought you'd never ask," I said, picking up my fork.

"And . . . Rache?"

"Yep?" I said as I concentrated on getting my fork under a good, healthy chunk of Bailey's shrimp. It melted in my mouth, and I savored the mix of flavors for a moment, then realized that Bailey was waiting to get my attention. I looked up at her.

"I'll help."

I stopped midchew. Going out on a limb for a friend is one thing; stepping off a cliff is another. If she got caught reaching into this cookie jar, she'd get in big trouble for digging into a case that wasn't hers. I didn't know what to say. The better part of me wanted to stop her, but the part of me that wanted to solve this case told me to shut up and accept her offer. I left the better part of me muzzled and hog-tied in the corner. The only thing I could say for myself was that I'd try to minimize Bailey's exposure and ask for her help as little as possible. I couldn't find words big enough to stretch around the gratitude I felt, so I just nodded and let my look of thanks and the beat of silence say it for me.

Bailey took another sip of her drink. The taste of her scampi had left my mouth watering for more. Unable to resist, I lifted my fork and took aim at another piece of shrimp. Proving there were limits even to a friendship as close as ours, Bailey pulled her plate away protectively.

I reluctantly withdrew my fork and turned my attention to my salad. Eyeballed a slice of hard-boiled egg. Pretended it looked delicious.

8

I opened my eyes the next morning, saw it was only 8:30, and burrowed deeper into the thousand-thread-count Frette sheets. Bailey had arranged to have the crime scene people meet us at Susan's house at 10:30 a.m., so I'd told Melia that I'd be "out in the field" on the Densmore case. Going to crime scenes was a great way to get out of the office and, in this case, a rare chance to sleep in.

It was a clear but brisk morning, so I dressed warmly in a long stretchy wool skirt and knee-high boots. I felt a lot better now that I'd run out of hangover, and I

swore I'd never do that to myself again. I
called Rafi, the valet, and asked him to
pull my car out for me, to make up for the
tip he didn't get when Bailey parked at the
curb last night. I hardly ever drove, so I
didn't worry about setting a financial pre-
cedent I couldn't keep up with. I winced as
he pulled my little Accord out to the curb.
It was looking pretty dusty, and I didn't
have time to hit the car wash. Hell of a way
to show up in Richie Rich–land. Oh well. I
plugged in my iPod and hit my jazz-mix
playlist. I floated along to Stanley Turren-
tine and Maceo Parker and barely noticed
the traffic.

By the time I got to the Densmores'
manse, Bailey had arrived and was standing in front of an open car trunk, talking to
the crime scene tech. I was glad to see
that it was Dorian. Short, square, and no-
nonsense, Dorian, one of the few veteran
female criminalists, had processed more
crime scenes in her twenty-two years on
the job than most of us had ever heard of.
Trust Bailey to make sure we got the best.

"Hey, Dorian, you're back," I said. She'd
been in the Firearms Identification Unit for
the past year.

"Yeah, I liked it for a while, but I missed the field," she said. That response, for Dorian, was a long, windy story. She hoisted her crime scene analysis kit out of her trunk. "Shall we do this?"

"I doubt you'll find any prints," I said as we began to walk toward the house. "This guy was pretty careful, so I'm thinking hair or fiber is more likely."

Dorian nodded. The same housekeeper from before answered the door. She motioned for us to enter. This time, Dorian got the skeptical eye. Gratified it wasn't just me, I looked for Dorian's reaction; if she noticed, she didn't show it. We tromped up to Susan's room, and Dorian set down her kit; pulled on latex gloves, paper bootees, and a hairnet; and went to work.

"I'm guessing you two have already been in here," Dorian said as she entered the room. We nodded. She gestured for us to stay at the doorway, shaking her head in mild disgust.

She was right. We should've stayed out until she'd processed the scene, though by now everyone and his duck had clomped through the room; still, extra care at any point couldn't hurt. I reflected that the

world would be a better-run place if Dorian
were in charge.

"I'll need your hair samples and whatever you were wearing—for elimination.
Hers too," she said, nodding in the direction of the housekeeper. "And the parents,
and anyone else who had access. I'm
guessing there's quite a list."

Bailey and I nodded obediently, and I
again glanced at the French doors of Susan's bedroom, trying to imagine how the
rapist had gotten in through a second-story
window. Even with the balcony access, it
had to be a pretty steep climb. It was no
mystery how he'd gotten away—in a house
this big, he was probably already on the
freeway by the time anyone heard Susan
screaming. I decided to go get the lay of
the land outside Susan's window.

"I'm going to walk around," I told Bailey.

"Feel free to join her," Dorian said point-
edly, looking at Bailey before returning to
her inspection of the window.

I tried to hide my chuckle under a throat-
clearing maneuver—and failed. Bailey
raised her chin, snorted, and stomped
down the hall. I sauntered behind her, taking in the scenery I hadn't had time to

notice before. Original artwork lined the walls—a little too modern and abstract for my taste, but I recognized the artists and knew that the paintings cost a small fortune. No expense was spared: everything, down to the smallest detail—an antique miniature crystal bell that rested on an imported Italian credenza of inlaid wood, a thick silken rope of subtle golden hues that held back the drape in the drawing room—was unique and of the highest quality. This was more money than I'd ever been close to. I kept my peasant hands to myself and moved quickly toward the back of the house, through the predictably enormous kitchen—two dishwashers, two Sub-Zero built-in refrigerators—and out the servants' entrance to the backyard.

Bailey, who'd briskly preceded me, was standing on the patio behind the house, under Susan's balcony. I joined her and looked up, judging the height to be about twenty feet, then scanned the area for means of access. It didn't take long. Leaning up against a tall peppertree was a painter's ladder that looked as if it could've extended out to forty feet.

"You see any signs of painting going

on?" Bailey asked as she looked around the property.

I shook my head. We walked across the rear patio. Sure enough, painters were working on the balustrades of the balcony that led into what I guessed was the master bedroom.

"If you had any doubt about our perp being someone who knew the family . . ." Bailey shielded her eyes with her hand and gazed up at the house.

"I didn't, but this clinches it. Whoever it was knew where to find Susan and knew that there was a ladder available."

Which made this a creepier rape than most. While it's true that a vast majority of rapes are committed by someone known to the victim, it's usually a date-rape situation. This MO had the feel of a serial rapist—but serial rapists didn't pick victims they knew. Nothing about this fit.

We headed around to the front of the house. "Think Mrs. Doctor is around?" Bailey asked.

As we passed by the living room window, I thought I saw a flash of movement. I motioned for Bailey to join me as I moved up the front walk and rang the doorbell.

The housekeeper answered again, this time looking even less excited to see us. I asked, "Is Mrs. Densmore in?"

She eyed us skeptically, as though we might just be playing around and really didn't need to see the lady of the house. I put on my serious Humphrey Bogart face to show her we meant business, and she sighed and motioned us into the foyer, then left us there. Two minutes later, Janet Densmore emerged, looking as if she'd stepped out of an ad for the St. John clothing line.

"Sorry to bother you," Bailey said in a voice that clearly conveyed the opposite.

"Please—I'm happy to help however I can," Janet said gracefully and with apparent sincerity.

"I wanted to ask you," I said, "does Susan go to your husband's clinics?"

Janet shook her head. "His first clinic was in a bad area of town, so we didn't want her . . . exposed. By the time he started to open clinics in safer areas, Susan was already seven years old and she'd gotten used to her own doctor. So we didn't see any real need to switch her."

"Where does Susan go, then?" I asked.

"Why are you asking?" Janet queried.

"I'm just looking for places where some-one might have information on Susan that she's not aware of. Because whoever did this knew where she slept and how to get to her," I replied.

Janet looked stricken. "But a clinic? I wouldn't have thought . . ." She sighed to herself and stared off for a moment, suf-fering with the thought that Susan might have been stalked.

"We just have to consider everything at this point, Mrs. Densmore—," I said.

"Janet, please," she said. "But doesn't it make sense that it was the boy she was tutoring?"

"It absolutely does," I replied. "But, like I said, we can't afford to ignore any possi-bilities just yet."

That seemed to comfort her somewhat. "I'll be glad to give you the address of the health center," she said. She paused and smiled to herself. "But I doubt you'll need to talk to her doctor. He's about seventy-five years old. I don't see him climbing through any windows at this point."

We shared a brief smile before I contin-ued. "I've got the list you gave to Jake of all the places Susan visits regularly and all the people that come to the house. Is there anyone you want to add?" It was a surprisingly short list. The only thing missing had been Susan's clinic. Even Useless had been able to run down—and exclude—just about everybody on it already.

Janet thought for a moment, then shook her head.

"Just two more quick things," I said. "We're going to need hair and fiber samples from you and your husband, the housekeeper, and anyone else who had access to Susan's room. Unless that's already been done?" I said, and paused to let her confirm what I already knew: that Lambkin hadn't done squat.

She shook her head. "Will someone come here, or do you need us to go in to the station?"

"We'll have Dorian do it here. And can you tell us when the painters started work on that balcony? The one off the master bedroom?"

Janet nodded. "He came in through the window. Of course." She looked down at the floor for a moment. "I believe it was about a week before the . . . it happened.

But I can go back through our paperwork and pin down the exact date, if you like."

"I would, thank you. That's all for now. We're going to check on Dorian's progress, if you don't mind."

"Not at all. Shall I have Esperanza show you the way?"

"I think we can manage." We turned to go. "We'll be out of here as soon as possible."

"Take your time, and please don't hesitate to ask for anything. I'm happy to do whatever it takes. I want that monster in jail."

She didn't seem the emoting type, so I knew that if she was showing us this much, she was seething inside. I couldn't for the life of me figure out what a class act like her was doing with a putz like Frank Densmore. Dupe that I am, I never want to believe it's just about the money.

"Thank you, Janet," I said. "So do we."

She nodded and headed toward the back of the house to continue whatever she'd been doing. We'd gotten halfway up the staircase when I heard a key turn in the lock at the front door and saw Susan slink in. She closed the door behind her softly and didn't notice us at first. I checked my watch: 12:30. It seemed early for her to be out of school.

I had a feeling this had been happening a lot more than anyone knew, and I had no doubt about why. Teenagers are drama queens by nature. No matter how sympathetic her peers were, the tragedy that Susan had been through would be a hot Twitter topic for weeks to come. After what had happened to Romy, I knew firsthand the living hell of being the object of that kind of attention.

"Hey, Susan, how're you doing?" I asked quietly. I hoped my tone conveyed that I wanted to help keep her secret, and I deliberately made no reference to the fact that she was home several hours too early.

Startled, Susan looked up with a guilty expression. I gave her a reassuring smile. "We're going to see if the crime scene tech found anything. You want to come with us?"

I don't agree with the notion that victims should be kept in the dark about investigations. I don't think it spares their feelings; I think it just makes them feel more powerless. I prefer to let them tell me if they don't want to know — at least then it's their choice.

"Uh, sure," Susan replied with some surprise.

We moved quickly and quietly up to Susan's room and stood in the doorway. I could see that Dorian had thoroughly dusted the windows and frames of the French doors, and all points in between them and the bed. Several little paper baggies were lined up in orderly rows on the floor, and she was checking her notations on a clipboard. Hair and fiber evidence is best preserved in a paper bag so it can breathe and stay dry. I noticed that all but one of the baggies had been folded over at the top.

Dorian looked up. "They took the bedding, right?"

"Yeah, even Useless knew enough to do that," Bailey remarked.

"Anybody look at it yet?" Dorian asked. Her tone telegraphed the answer she expected.

"No hit on the database with the nightgown, so no rush. It's sitting in the clean room," Bailey replied.

The crime lab was so swamped, it

wouldn't move on any more of our evidence until we hooked someone up. Someone, for example, like Frank Densmore's number one suspect, Luis.

"Find anything?" I asked Dorian.

"Maybe, don't know." She picked up the unsealed paper baggie and came over to us. "Found these caught in the headboard," she said, holding the baggie a couple of feet in front of us. We leaned forward for a better view, which prompted her to abruptly pull the bag away. "Stay back, and use your damn eyes."

I squeezed Susan's arm to let her know Dorian might bark but she wouldn't bite, and we pulled back. Dorian tilted the baggie toward us, and we looked in. There were a few tiny pieces of light-colored hair. I looked over at the headboard. It was wood of some kind, painted white, with ornate scrollwork. I could see how hair might get snagged on it if someone bumped into it. Only Dorian would've noticed a few tiny, light-colored hairs on a swirling white surface. But since Susan was blond, I didn't see what the big deal was. I looked at Dorian quizzically.

"They're synthetic," she remarked.

"Like from a wig?" I asked.

She nodded. "Or a doll. She ever took a doll to bed with her, the hair could've transferred." She turned to Susan. "You keep any dolls in here?"

Susan went over to a large white armoire with gold accents and opened the doors. Three shelves were lined with dolls of all kinds—Barbie, Skipper, and a bunch I didn't recognize. It would be a nightmare of a job to do all the comparisons and find out whether the hairs from the headboard had come from any of them. But if the dolls could be eliminated as a source, the hairs might be a clue.

Dorian scanned all the dolls, and I could feel her mentally assessing the hours it would take to examine and compare them all. She turned to Susan and said, "I'm going to have to take them."

Susan nodded mutely.

"Don't worry, we'll bring them back," I said.

Susan nodded again but said nothing. And as I watched Dorian package each doll in a separate baggie, I couldn't help but feel that we were carting out the last few vestiges of Susan's childhood.

9

I was glad I'd brought my own car. I wasn't in the mood to be sociable during the long ride back downtown. Truth be told, Bailey didn't look all that jolly herself. We got into our separate cars, and I drove back to the Biltmore, my iPod silenced. After giving my car to Rafi—whose quick grin told me I was worming my way back into his good graces—I walked to the office. Some days the walk helped my mood. This wasn't one of them.

But it did make me realize I was hungry. I'd had my usual egg-white omelet for breakfast, and by now I'd long since burned through it. My stomach growled audibly as I ran for the courthouse elevator. I managed to squeeze in just as the doors were closing. Since it was the end of the lunch hour, the elevator was packed to capacity, and I turned to face the doors as I held my breath. Toni had once told me that the air in those elevators was a breeding ground for disease — too many germ-infested people jammed into a too-small space. I've tried not to breathe in crowded elevators ever since.

I sprang out at the thirteenth floor and headed for the snack bar, weaving my way through the crowds waiting for the afternoon court session. I spotted Toni peering through the glass door of the refrigerator, searching for something edible. It was always a challenge.

"See anything good?"

Toni looked at me and rolled her eyes. "Good? I'm just hoping for nontoxic."

We settled for a turkey and swiss on whole wheat and a diet soda, and walked out into the corridor just as the last of the waiting crowds filed into the courtrooms.

As we moved toward the elevators, I saw Lieutenant Graden Hales speed into Department 125 carrying a sheaf of papers—probably police reports. Toni followed my gaze. "Want to go and see him in action?"

I didn't really have time to play hooky. I was sure the stack of phone messages, motions, and general casework had grown impressively high. But I was feeling blue after the day's events with Susan, so I decided a brief distraction might be a good thing.

"What the heck," I said.

I saw Toni glance down the hallway toward Department 130—Judge J. D. Morgan's courtroom. Her expression told me their on-again, off-again romance was in its "off" phase. Whether by her choice or his this time was anyone's guess. They took turns pulling the cut-and-run trigger.

She turned back, saw me watching her, and shrugged. I patted her on the shoulder sympathetically, and we walked into the court's anteroom. One of the retiree court-watchers followed us in and looked at us curiously, then opened the door and shuffled into the courtroom. I looked in as the door closed behind him and saw that the jury was in the box and Graden was on the witness stand. The defense attorney was just standing up to cross-examine. We filed into the back row next to the retiree and his court-watcher cronies and sat down.

As I listened to the cross-examination, the simple case unfolded. The defendant had gotten into a fight with his girlfriend at a party. Someone had intervened, and the defendant had then left the party and lay in wait for the girlfriend behind a Dumpster that was near her car. When she walked to her vehicle, he jumped out and fatally stabbed her.

The defense attorney was trying to get Graden to concede that there were a lot of other people at the party who could have done it. But Graden was one tough witness—calm, collected, and immovable. After about twenty minutes, I could tell the defense attorney had hit the wall and was fishing around for a face-saving way to wrap up the cross-examination. He should've quit while he was behind.

"In fact, Lieutenant Hales," the lawyer boomed, "isn't it true that Sonia Fontina was the last one to see the victim alive?"

Graden paused, then calmly replied, "No, Counsel. Your client was the last one to see the victim alive."

The defense attorney tried to object to the answer, but the objection was over-ruled and the attorney moved shakily to his seat. The prosecutor wisely chose not to mess up a strong finish and declined redirect.

Since we were tucked into the back of the room among the court-watchers, Graden didn't notice us as he stepped down from the witness stand and strode out.

Toni watched him leave, then turned to me. "Good witness, though he's kind of a smart-ass."

Personally, I liked my witnesses with a touch of smart-ass. "Yeah, but you've got to admit, it was a pretty sweet jab."

"'Twas," Toni said with a small grin, then sighed. "Guess it's back to the salt mines."

We quietly slipped out and headed up-stairs.

Back in my office, I slogged through my case files until the sun dipped behind the Times Building and the sidewalks were nearly emptied. That lovely end-of-day quiet had descended over the DA's office. I exhaled, stretched my arms over my head, and leaned from side to side to work out the kinks in my neck and back as I looked out at the darkening sky. At this time of year, nightfall came early and quickly. Now that I'd caught up on my backlog and pushed forward on the Densmore matter, I could afford to ponder how to move on Jake's case. Wanting to lean on Bailey as little as possible, I took out my cell phone and scrolled through my list of contacts. I stopped when I got to the letter "F" and looked up at the clock on the Times Building. It said 5:20. I dialed my buddy Scott Ferrier, the coroner's investigator. I got lucky—Scott hadn't left yet.

"Guess the reports are done on Jake by now," I said as I thought how strange and awful it was to be talking about a coroner's report on a friend.

"Don't ask, Rachel."

"Too late, I just did. Besides, you know the file's safe with me."

"It's too risky. If someone finds it on you, it's my ass."

"Who's going to find it on me? The

cleaning crew? All I have to do is put the file in the middle of my floor—believe me, they'll never see it."

"I don't know . . ."

Sensing weakness, I pounced. "Lunch at Engine Company Number Twenty-eight, on me." The old converted firehouse was one of Scott's favorite restaurants.

He sighed, defeated by the lure of gastronomic ecstasy. "When?"

"Tomorrow," I said, trying to keep the triumph out of my voice.

Scott agreed and I hung up, satisfied. With that coup, I felt as if I'd put in a good day's work. Time to quit while I was ahead. I packed up, thinking I should hit the gym for a workout, but I just couldn't get up for it. Then I remembered it was Wednesday: Chinese takeout night. I consoled myself that the hike to Chinatown would at least qualify as cardio and headed out. The Oolong Café had been Toni's find. She'd had to talk me past the garish pink-and-green neon sign, but I was glad she did. The food was surprisingly good—and the service was fast. Within minutes, I had a big grocery bag filled with fried rice, orange chicken, and beef chow mein, and a separate smaller bag that held a carton of steamed vegetables.

I moved briskly up the west side of Broadway in search of a particular spot. When I hit the corner of Broadway and 1st, I found it: a pile of dirty blankets, on top of which sat a well-worn Lakers hat.

"Hey, missy, how ya doin'? How ya doin'?" said a gravelly voice so deep it seemed to come from the center of the earth rather than from under the blanket heap.

"I'm well, Cletus," I said. "And you?"

"Can't complain," said the voice in the blankets.

"I had a taste for orange chicken tonight," I said as I put the bigger bag down next to him.

A hand snaked out and pulled the bag closer. "Smells like you got chow mein in there too. Good choice, good choice."

"Thanks," I replied. "Take care of yourself."

"No, *you* take care," he called out.

"Bon appétit," I replied as I waved.

Me and my sad little carton of steamed veggies headed for home.

10

The next morning dawned windy and cold but clear. I decided to treat Scott by taking the Accord. Once again, it occurred to me that I ought to get it washed. On the other hand, someone who drove around in a car with dead people probably wouldn't notice a few empty coffee cups.

I picked Scott up just before noon so we could beat the lunch rush. After twenty years, Engine Co. No. 28 was still a popular spot. It always reminded me of the old grill restaurants up in San Francisco. The firehouse that had been on this spot in 1912 was now restored, with mahogany booths and a great bar, and the original fireman's pole still stood at the far end of the restaurant.

I ordered a Cobb salad, and Scott had the short ribs. My friend, paranoid, kept looking around after we'd been seated, so I steered clear of any conversation about Jake's case. I forced myself to make small talk and twisted my napkin under the table as the minutes slowly dragged by. Finally the waiter brought the check. I paid in cash to avoid any further delay, and when we got into the car, Scott opened my glove box and pulled the report out of his jacket.

"Lock it up," he said, sliding it inside. "And don't let anyone see you with this."

I nodded and tried not to set a land speed record getting Scott back to his office.

After I dropped him off, I drove to Elysian Park, a pocket of green near the downtown police academy. I parked under a tree at the end of the lot, where no one could get close. Scott might be paranoid, but it was better to be too cautious than risk screwing him over.

I quickly flipped through the physical descriptions of Jake and the boy found with him—Kit Chalmers—and cut to the chase. No indication of smoke inhalation for either of them. So they were both dead by the time the fire got going. That might mean someone else had caused it. Jake didn't smoke, but it was likely that Kit did. So maybe Kit had lit a cigarette and left it to burn. Or the fire might've been caused by faulty electrical wiring. Damn. Too many options. I turned to Scott's section. The coroner's investigator lays out the crime scene, though not usually in as much detail as the police report. But Scott's descriptions were always meticulous, and this one was no exception. He'd noted all kinds of disgusting debris, such as used condoms in the bathroom, old cigarette butts, even a rubber "tie"—what junkies use so they can fix. Lovely. I supposed it was possible that one of those cigarette butts could've caused the fire—if the filter had kept it from being consumed. Seemed unlikely, but it was a possibility since the fire had been extinguished fairly quickly.

The FBI should be comparing any DNA on those butts to Jake and Kit, I thought. Though even if it turned out that none of them matched either person, it wouldn't exactly be a big clue. A place like that probably got vacuumed twice a year.

I turned to the toxicology report. Traces of THC—marijuana—in Kit's blood, but Jake was completely clean. No surprise there. Tarring in Kit's lungs confirmed he was a smoker. The possibility that the fire had been started by his cigarette had just gotten stronger. And if it was Kit's cigarette, my theory that someone else might have started the fire in order to destroy the evidence would go out the window.

I jumped ahead to the cause of death. As predicted, for both it was a gunshot wound to the head. An unregistered .38 Smith & Wesson was found near Jake. Gunshot-residue tests showed a couple of particles on his right hand. Not much for a suicide, but GSR was so inexact anyway. Though it wasn't Scott's job to interview witnesses, I flipped ahead to see if any were mentioned. Nothing. Even in a flophouse, people would've heard two gunshots, wouldn't they? And if they did, wouldn't they at least try to look out and see what was going on? If I could get my hands on the police reports, I'd be able to find out. If no one heard anything, that might indicate that a silencer was used. Since, according to Scott's report, no silencer was found at the scene, that could mean a third party *had* been involved.

It was a slim reed, but we all know what they say about beggars. I drove back to the office, marginally cheered. I pulled into the county employee lot, and Julio, the security guard, let me park close to the building. I again promised myself a workout when I got home and looked at my watch as I hiked up the stairs. It was a quarter to three already—time flies when you're reading stolen coroner's reports. I quickly trotted inside and ran to catch the elevator.

I was hurrying down the hall to my office when Melia called out to me. "*Mija,* come back."

I put it in reverse and leaned into Eric's anteroom. "Yes?"

Melia nodded toward the boss's office. "The jefe wants to see you."

Eric was on the phone when I poked my head through his doorway, and he made a circling motion with his finger, indicating that whoever was on the line was going on and on, then motioned for me to sit down. I mouthed, "No problem," and he smiled.

I sat and took advantage of the moment to enjoy the 180-degree view. From this perch eighteen floors up, I had a clear bird's-eye view of the people moving on the streets and sidewalks below. To my left, a young black man in jeans and a hoodie walked down Spring Street in graceful time to the music coming through his head-phones.

Eric cut in on his caller, his tone exas-perated. "Again, I need to get a little more information before I can give you any an-swers. Why don't I call you back later?" He rolled his eyes at me and shook his head.

I nodded sympathetically, then looked out the window again and saw that the young black man was closer. Now I could see that the jack on the end of his head-phones was swinging freely in the wind, attached to nothing.

Eric ended his call. "Sorry about that," he said.

"No worries. What's up?"

Eric sighed, never a good sign, and

made a face that told me he didn't want to have to say what he was about to say. I braced myself.

"Frank Densmore called."

"Ahh, yes," I said, not surprised. "And he's pissed off because . . . ?"

"He wants this case wrapped up. He knows who did it, he told Jake who did it, then he told you who did it, and he's tired of waiting for the police and the DA's office to catch up with him."

I raised my eyebrows. "Catch up with him—very nice."

"We're going to have to try and keep him happy. He's got Vanderhorn's ear—"

"Really?" I interjected. "I was thinking of another part of the DA's anatomy."

To Eric's credit, he looked just as irked as I felt. "He wanted to talk to you this afternoon, and when he couldn't find you, he found me."

Uh-oh. I suddenly saw where this was going, and it wasn't good.

"Rachel, I know you're not happy with the assumptions being made about Jake and what happened. But it's not our case, and you're looking at some serious charges of insubordination if you keep poking around. I'm prepared to be sympathetic . . . this time. Understood?"

I nodded, forced out an insincere apology, and excused myself before he had a chance to read my insubordinate mind.

I headed back to my office, plopped down in my chair, and mulled over my options. I supposed I could put in a mollifying call to Daddy Densmore, but I'm a lousy ass-kisser, and odds were good I'd just make things worse. Besides, I'm a big believer in behavior modification—if I called him now it would just reward him for bringing Vanderhorn into the picture and ensure that he'd do it again whenever he wanted to yank my chain. Better to give Densmore no response and show him who's boss.

Vanderhorn was another matter. Him, I couldn't ignore. I sighed to myself. I guessed I could manage a little bit of ass-kissing for the sake of keeping my job. Unfortunately there was only one way to back Vanderhorn off. Explanations would mean nothing. He'd want proof of progress. Otherwise known as new evidence. A suspect in custody would be nice, for instance. I picked up the phone.

"Hey, it's Rachel Knight. Is Dorian there?"

I waited while the tech who'd answered the phone yelled around the office.

"Not here. Probably on her cell, though," said a young male whose voice I didn't recognize. These days crime scene techs moved in and out of the Scientific Investigation Division (SID) as though it were a Motel 6. Old warhorses like Dorian were an increasingly rare commodity.

"I've got the number, thanks," I replied, though he hadn't offered to give it to me.

I hung up and dialed again. After four rings, she answered. "Yep?"

"It's Rachel. Any news on the hair and fiber?"

Dorian snorted. "Sure, I've only got about five thousand dolls here. Just give me a sec while I finish the last four thousand."

I hadn't really expected any results yet—we'd seized more than thirty dolls from Susan's bedroom, so even a rush job would take quite some time. But perfectionist Dorian didn't do rush jobs, so I knew this was going to be a while. I'd put in the call so I'd have something to bring to Vanderhorn as a peace offering. Dorian read the brief pause in the air like a large-print book.

"Tell your boss he can have it fast or he can have it right, but he can't have both," she barked.

"From what I've heard, fast is his thing . . . if you know what I mean," I replied acidly, annoyed not only at having to appease Vanderhorn but at Dorian's busting me for it.

"Creatures in space know what you mean, Knight. Tell him you'll have results soon enough, and if he doesn't like it he can kiss my ass," Dorian growled, then hung up.

Next I called Vanderhorn.

He wasn't in; probably checking the part in his hair or bleaching his teeth—smoothing his path to reelection. Glad to avoid talking to him, I cheerfully left word that hair and fiber results were on the way. Then I sat back to consider what else I could do on the Densmore case. We'd reprocessed the crime scene, and Bailey was already having Luis Revelo's rap sheet run. Uniforms were checking out everyone else we could think of with access, such as the house painters, the security-patrol guys, and all the neighbors and their worker bees. In just a few days, we'd covered a lot of ground.

There was nothing more to be done at this point but wait for some leads to pop up so we could follow them. At a dead end on my most pressing official case, at least for the time being, I turned my thoughts to my unofficial one and considered my next move.

The way I saw it, I had to pursue the case on two fronts: the off-duty part of Jake's life, and the background and associates of the kid they found with him, Kit Chalmers. I could do at least the initial legwork on Jake's life myself. I called a buddy in the Planning and Training Division, where all new DAs started and where the background information on us was stored, and steered the conversation around to Jake and his next of kin. It wasn't hard—the whole office was obsessed with the subject. After getting what I could, I hung up, then dialed again.

11

Five minutes later I was weaving my way through the crowd in the downstairs lobby on my way to the Police Administration Building, affectionately known as PAB. The sidewalks were crowded, which surprised me, so I checked my watch. It was 4:30 already. Ass-covering is very time-consuming. The late-afternoon hour explained the mass of bodies and cars in front of the building: the exodus out of downtown had begun. This was a lucky break for me, because it would decrease the chance I'd get caught at what I was about to do. If I wanted to keep my job, and I did, I'd have to get smarter about when and where I made my moves and be sure to have cover stories in place. Going to see Bailey was safe enough, since we were working the Densmore case together, but I didn't want to use Bailey any more than I had to.

I tried to imagine what they'd do to me if I got caught digging into Jake's case again. Transfer me out to East Jesus to try sprinkler-use violations for the rest of my career? Very likely. Suspension . . . and then a transfer to the aforementioned outpost? Also likely. Termination for insubordination? This was an uncomfortably distinct possibility. The thought set my stomach roiling. And if they did fire me, what would I do? Go into private practice and defend the scumbags? I shook my head—been there, done that, straight out of law school. I couldn't go back. So what did that leave—exotic dancing? Not enough chest, too much smart-mouth. In fact, my smart mouth was going to be a problem in all employment endeavors this side of Fox News. Bus driver, cocktail waitress—you name it.

Ruminations on all the ways my pursuit of Jake's case could lead to my demise kept me occupied right up until I got off the elevator at the third floor in PAB. At that precise moment, I remembered that Hales was Bailey's lieutenant, which meant that he worked there too. The fact that he was standing at the elevator also helped jog my memory.

"Hey," I said.

"Hey," he replied. "How're you doing?" His voice conveyed something unexpected. I think it's called kindness.

I felt a little electric jolt in my gut. I resolutely ignored it. "Okay, I guess," I said with a nonchalant shrug. *Look at me, playing it too cool for school.*

The elevator doors began to close, but he stuck his hand inside and held them open. Macho, but not too. Or maybe just polite. My judgment's not great.

He looked at me for a long beat. "We're still on your friend's case, Rachel. I want you to know that I won't let the Feds shut it down until we've got it right."

I nodded to show my appreciation. I decided he didn't need to know that I was here to make sure of exactly that.

The elevator began buzzing in protest,

and Graden stepped inside. I waved and turned to go, but he pulled out the stop button to silence it, then called out to me.

"You ever eat lunch?" he asked with one of those lazy, lopsided smiles that probably worked well for him. The fact that I was aware of this meant it was working for him now too.

"Sometimes," I said.

His smile got bigger as he released the stop button and replied, "I'll call you."

I turned to go, then stopped. "I'm not going to be in the office much," I said, wanting to let him know that I'd be hard to find. But the door closed before my protestation could register.

I tried to put that signature smile out of my mind as I headed for Bailey's desk.

She was hunched miserably in front of her computer. She loved gadgets but hated computers. Probably because the latter were associated with paperwork. I have yet to meet a cop who loves paperwork. So not only was I jeopardizing her career, but I was torturing her in the process. The very definition of an all-purpose friend.

I rolled a chair up next to her. "What'd you get?"

Bailey snuck a look around her desk to make sure no one was watching, then replied, "The boy, Kit Chalmers, has a record."

Since Kit was a young kid whose life had ended in a downtown motel that charged by the hour, this was about as surprising as finding an ex-con in a car wash.

"What's he got?" I asked.

"All misdemeanor crap. Starting at about age nine, he's got petty theft, possession of marijuana, giving false information to a cop. But the most recent one is the kicker." Bailey paused for a beat. "Prostitution."

Exactly what I didn't want to hear.

"How long ago was it?" I asked.

"Two years ago."

"So Kit was . . ."

"Fifteen," Bailey replied.

"Anything after that prostitution bust?"

"Nada."

Bailey and I exchanged a look, thinking the same thing. By the time he'd been busted for prostitution, Kit had likely been criming for more than six years—just because he'd been caught at age nine didn't mean it was his first venture. So it was very hard to believe that he'd suddenly gone clean at the age of fifteen; he'd been busted far too often for too long. Everything about this was weird. And not in a good way.

"Did we file a petition on that last case?" I asked. Since juvenile cases weren't considered criminal and were supposed to be "for the benefit of the minor"—yeah, right—they had their own terminology. So instead of filing charges in a complaint, you filed allegations in a petition. Instead of being convicted of charges, a juvenile had his petition "sustained."

Bailey tapped a few keys on her computer to bring up what she'd found. "In Eastlake."

Eastlake Juvenile Court was just south of downtown, and its proximity to gangland territories meant that it was heavily trafficked by the most heinous offenders. I'd heard they filed more murder cases there than we did in the Criminal Courts Building, which explained why the parking lot for court personnel was surrounded by a cement wall that was topped with barbed wire.

"Does it show the disposition?" I asked, meaning what kind of sentence he got.

I had a hunch about this, and I hoped it was wrong.

Bailey frowned at the screen.

"Move over. I know where to look," I said as I nudged her out of her seat and planted myself in front of her computer.

I'd just started to scroll down when a deep voice that sounded way too close said, "I'm sure it's just an alarming coincidence that you're looking into Kit Chalmers's last case."

I barely managed to keep from jumping out of the chair. As soon as I could breathe, I half turned around to see who it was. Standing side by side were two clean-cut, solid-looking men dressed in blazers and slacks. Typical FBI-issue.

"Yeah, funny, isn't it?" I said, forcing a light, offhand tone. I knew very well that if they reported me for sticking my nose into the case after the warning I'd already gotten, I'd be toast. But men in authority are like horses—show fear, and they'll knock you around; act blasé, and they'll leave you alone. I wasn't about to let them know that I could barely hear them over my thudding heartbeat.

The blonder of the two replied, "I'd hate to get a DA fired for insubordination because she didn't have the smarts to know that 'recused' means 'hands-off.'" His tone told me he wouldn't hate it all that much.

"Well, this DA does know what 'recused' means," I said brightly. "Now it's your turn: do you know what 'mind your own fucking business' means?" I leaned back and smiled winningly.

They didn't look "won." Ted and Fred each gave me what was supposed to be a meaningful look—their version of the last word—and walked off.

Bailey folded her arms and tracked the goons' progress through the squad room with a steely glare. I knew she'd wanted to get into it with them, but that would only have made it a bigger deal. I turned back to the screen and drew long, deep breaths through my nose to slow down my pulse as I scrolled through the court docket. At first the letters wouldn't settle into recognizable patterns, but after a few seconds the effort to concentrate calmed me down and I was able to make sense of the entries.

By the time of his last arrest, Kit Chalmers had racked up five "sustained petitions." For a sixth bust as relatively serious as prostitution, I figured he should've gotten a camp commitment. Camp is the middle ground between short-term detention hall and the prison facility euphemistically called CYA—California Youth Authority.

But he didn't get a camp commitment. In fact, he didn't even get detention-hall time. He got HOP: Home on Probation. A bullshit sentence that was no sentence at all. It basically meant he went home and just had to stay out of trouble—he didn't even have to report to a probation officer. By all accounts, this was one sweetheart of a deal. Bailey echoed the sentiment when I pointed to the screen to show her what it said under "Disposition."

She spoke in an incredulous whisper. "And nothing since then?"

I shook my head. I didn't like what I was seeing, but I continued to scroll down through the page, hoping for some explanation that would take the bad taste out of my mouth.

"Well, I guess that's it," Bailey said as I got to the bottom of the page without finding any more information.

"Not quite," I said softly as I moved the cursor back up the page, looking for one last entry.

And there it was, the answer I'd dreaded: Jake's last assignment before joining the Special Trials Unit two years ago had been deputy in charge of Eastlake Juvenile. The sweetheart deal on Kit's prostitution bust was given by none other than Jake Pahlmeyer.

12

There was more bad news in this than just the dumping of a prostitution case; a kid like Kit was unlikely to have kept his nose clean for the past two years. Of course, there were innocent explanations, and I'd fight for every one of them. But a low hum of suspicion had begun to thrum in the back of my brain at the fact that there was nothing at all in Kit's juvenile file since that prostitution bust. And although I may have been the first to connect those dots, I definitely wouldn't be the last.

Bailey and I sat staring at the screen as we silently absorbed the impact of all this.

Then, aware that Feebies Ted and Fred, or God knew who else, could look over our shoulders again at any moment, I pushed back from the desk and let Bailey shut down the program and erase our trail. She worked quickly as I packed up my brief-case. We left the building without saying a word.

It was 5:30 now and the streets were almost empty. When we got to the corner of First and Main, I glanced around to make sure Ted and Fred weren't hiding behind a lamppost.

Bailey pressed her lips together. "Looks bad, Knight."

"I still don't believe it," I said. But even as the words left my mouth, I knew that rivulets of doubt had begun to seep into my image of Jake.

I stared down the street and watched a battered taxi rattle by, headed for the free-way entrance on Broadway. Above, the black velvet fingers of night were reaching out across the sky, engulfing the last rays of sun, deepening the chill in the air. I shivered under my wool-lined coat and picked up the pace in an effort to get warm, then looked back at Bailey.

"I'm not giving up," I said, "but I'll understand completely if you—"

She raised her hand abruptly, cutting me off. "I'm in it as long as you are."

"I'm serious, Bailey. This could get really ugly."

She stopped walking and looked at me squarely. "I'm guessing it *is* going to get really ugly, and fast. But you're right: it's not all the way there yet, and we both know anything can happen from here. I'm in."

Her show of support was a much-needed balm on a wounded memory. I couldn't express what I was feeling in words, so I did the next best thing. "Feel like El Chavo?"

The cozy little dive served up some of the best Mexican food and margaritas this side of Baja.

"Perfect."

As we headed for Bailey's car, "The Crystal Ship" by the Doors—one of my favorites among the rock classics—began playing on my cell phone.

"That's Toni," I said as I pulled out the phone.

"Tell her to join us," Bailey said. "I haven't seen her in a while."

Twenty minutes later, we pulled into the

tiny parking lot and wove around to the old adobe building adorned with strings of multicolored Christmas lights that stayed up year-round. We walked into the claustrophobic vestibule, where we were greeted by Blanca, the owner's wife, who looked more like the owner's daughter.

"Your friend is already here," she said with a smile as she gathered up two plastic-coated menus and gestured for us to follow her down the narrow stairs. Our eyes adjusted to the dim light and we found Toni already seated at one of the long picnic-style tables. Looking around the room, I marveled again at how something as simple as tiny multicolored lights could give a place such a warm, rosy glow. It felt like an endless party.

We ordered a pitcher of margaritas and filled Toni in on what we'd learned. She remained steadfast. "It's gonna take more than this to make me believe Jake was a homicidal-suicidal pedophile."

The simple, defiant statement stiffened my spine, and I could feel Bailey's spirits lift too. In unison, we raised our glasses in a silent toast and took a long, delicious sip.

"So now what?" Toni asked.

"I've got a few ideas," I began, then paused to look around the room, catching Bailey's expression as I finished my scan. Her look confirmed what I was feeling. "Later," I said as I looked steadily at Toni, sending a message. She nodded.

We weren't the only ones in the business who liked to hang out at El Chavo, and I'd already been busted twice for butting into Jake's case. I didn't need to go for strike three.

I considered telling them about Graden Hales's elevator invitation but decided against it. Nothing had happened yet, and maybe nothing would ever come of it. And there was also the possibility that since I'd been officially warned off the case, and Bailey was risking her neck to help me, she'd be less than pleased to find out that the cop who was heading the operation—her boss—was getting flirty with me. Now that I thought about it, she might be right. It *was* a little too close for comfort. *Speaking of which . . . ,* I thought as I turned to Bailey.

"What's up with you and Drew?" I asked her.

"Details—now," Toni demanded.

Bailey laughed, and we all leaned in as she regaled us with the tale of her amazing date with Drew at the Rooftop Bar at the Standard. Two margarita pitchers later, Bailey called in and got a patrol car to give us a ride home. The officer turned out to be a hottie. A proud example of the LAPD's finest. Toni rode up front with him. I think she might've kissed him good night. He bore up with selfless dedication: "To Protect and Serve." The motto was still alive and well in L.A.

13

I woke early the next morning, only slightly the worse for wear after last night's dining experience. I had a meeting set up with Jake's sister, Jennifer, whose number I'd cadged from my buddy in the Planning and Training Division. I didn't know what she could offer, but anything was more than I had now. As I got dressed, it struck me as tragic that a person could work with someone so closely for so long and yet know so little about him. We are, in essence, a lonely species. I hiked up to the parking lot behind the courthouse, where

I'd left my car. Its dusty exterior was wet with morning dew — muddy dew. Lovely.

Jennifer lived in a duplex apartment on a quiet tree-lined street in Glendale, a bedroom community just ten minutes north and west of downtown L.A. There were old-fashioned planters lining the front windows, and blue hydrangeas were in full, luscious bloom. Everything grew like crazy here. Back in the '40s or '50s, the whole town had been slated for orchards, so they'd trucked in the best-quality soil. The orchards had given way when the real estate became too valuable to waste on fruit, but the soil kept on giving. If you spit out a pumpkin seed, by next week you'd have a pumpkin patch. I pressed the buzzer at the side of the screen door and stepped back so as not to crowd the entry. Through the door, I could hear the television playing a morning news show. I had time to hear that it wasn't the usual lame jousting between airheaded anchors, so it couldn't have been a network program. Probably CNN. A serious person, this Jennifer.

She answered the door breathlessly; I'd obviously caught her in the middle of getting ready to go to work. Although I knew

from Jake's bio in Planning and Training
that she was twenty-nine, just five and a
half years younger than Jake, she could've
passed for a high school junior. Petite, no
makeup, soft wavy brown hair that fell past
her shoulders—Jennifer was the female
version of Jake. The resemblance made
me feel close to her, even as it caused a
lump in my throat. But whereas Jake visi-
bly burned with an intense energy that
powered his rapid speech and passion for
work, Jennifer gave off a soft blue, lower-
wattage reserve. The sun and the moon.
And I could tell from the way she barely
held my fingers when we shook hands that
this was not a people person.

"Hi, Jennifer, I'm Rachel Knight. Thank
you for seeing me. I know this is a hard time
for you."

She opened the screen door and stepped
back to let me in. "No, actually, I was glad
when you called," she said as she pushed
a strand of hair behind her ear. "I never met
any of Jake's friends. . . . In fact, you're the
only one he ever mentioned by name," she
said in a soft, sad voice.

Did this mean I was his only friend? Or
was I the only person he could tell her

about? I immediately choked off the un-wanted thought, but I could feel the threads of a memory being woven together in my subconscious.

"Did someone from the office call you?" I asked.

"Oh yes. Yes, they did. But, um . . . it's just . . . not the same, you know . . . ?" She trailed off, and her eyes darted away. She directed me to the living room, and as I took a seat on the sofa, I tried not to dwell on how horrible it must have been to lose a sibling under such circumstances, and on top of that not to have anyone close to him to share memories with. I'd suffered many agonies with the loss of Romy, but none had involved ugly speculation about who she'd really been. I couldn't imagine how much worse that would be. Assuming, of course, that the speculation about Jake was untrue. I looked around the room as she settled on the couch. A house can tell you a lot about a person.

Jennifer had cleverly chosen to furnish the small space sparsely—just a sofa, a coffee table, and a mini entertainment center against the opposite wall. It was a room uniquely devoid of personality—just one framed photo of her and Jake on the fireplace mantel, and judging by the clothes they wore in the picture, I could tell it was at least five years old. No plants, no pets, no artwork. This place could have belonged to anyone.

"Oh, can I get you coffee or . . . anything?" she offered as she started to get up.

"No, thanks," I said, gesturing for her to sit back down. "I want you to know that I wasn't Jake's only friend. Everyone in the office loved him."

Jennifer bit the inside of her lip and nodded silently. I could see she was holding back tears. She didn't want to cry on a stranger's shoulder—or maybe anyone else's either. The decor told me that Jennifer wasn't the sharing type.

"Are you a lawyer?" I asked.

She shook her head. "No, I'm a psychologist."

That would not have been my first guess. I deliberately kept my expression neutral. "Do you have your own practice?"

"I'm not that kind of psychologist. I do testing for research. Right now I'm working on the data for the next edition of the *DSM.*"

This, I could totally see—as a researcher,

Jennifer didn't treat patients; she compiled the data that would be used to figure out how to treat patients. The *Diagnostic and Statistical Manual of Mental Disorders* is a sort of bible for the mental-health profession. Shrinks who testify for the defense at trial often refer to it when they're trying to tell the jury why the defendant wasn't responsible for the rape, murder, and burning of a dozen women in their eighties. I love this kind of testimony the way Keith Olbermann loves Bill O'Reilly.

"I got the impression you and Jake were close," I said.

My impression didn't come from what he'd said, because Jake never offered any personal details. It was more in the way he'd spoken of his sister, the warmth and real affection in his voice when he said her name.

"We were," Jennifer said as she looked up at the photo on the mantel. "When we were growing up in New York, we did a lot together. Even shared an apartment in the East Village for a while—before it got all hipped up and expensive."

Her gaze drifted off as she smiled at the fond memory.

"Did you move out here with your folks?"

Jennifer blinked quickly, and I saw that my question had brought her down to earth with a thud.

"No. Jake and I . . . we got tired of the cold, and we both liked the idea of California. So we saved up and moved out here together."

She looked down at the floor and swallowed. I'd known this meeting would be painful, but the tightness in my throat told me it had outstripped my expectations. I gave Jennifer a moment to recover, then asked, "How long ago was that?"

"Ten years ago. He put himself through law school; I got a scholarship and majored in psychology. We still had dinners when we could, but we both got busier and busier, so we saw less of each other . . ." She trailed off as she paused again to collect herself, then continued. "By the time he joined the DA's office and I got this job, we'd see each other maybe once a month for dinner or something."

I watched her remember and nodded, encouraging her to continue.

"But, you know, he was still there for me. No matter how busy or tired, he was always there when I needed him." Suddenly Jennifer, her features twisted with pain, burst out, "And he wasn't some sick child molester! I don't care what anybody says, it's a disgusting lie!"

She covered her face, bending over and sobbing. I moved toward her and put my arms around her. She leaned into me and cried as though it were the first time anyone had offered her any sort of comfort. Maybe it was.

I smoothed her hair and gently rubbed her back.

"I know," I said. "Jake wasn't that guy."

I hoped. More than ever, I wanted to squash all the doubts—mine and everyone else's. Meeting Jennifer had made me doubly determined to prove Jake's innocence. I explained that I intended to dig into the case to find out what had really happened. "So do you know anything about his personal life? What he did in his spare time?"

"Spare time?" Jennifer gave a short, mirthless laugh. "We didn't believe in it. Like I said, we had dinner once a month. We'd go out or I'd make dinner here."

She noticed me looking toward the

small, immaculate, and fairly untouched kitchen and added, "Mostly we ate out."

I nodded with a little smile. "I live in a hotel, and the part I like the most is room service."

"That would be wonderful—no dishes, ever," she said, and smiled. It was a nice smile. I wanted to help her keep it.

"You didn't know of any friends or people outside the office he hung around with?"

She shook her head. "I didn't think he had any. I don't," she said quietly.

I was struck by the naked honesty of the statement. These two were classic loners who'd barely been able to stay connected—even to each other. For both, the only real bond they'd had was to their jobs. And now Jennifer didn't just feel alone; she really was alone. Her isolation was complete. I felt what she was going through as though it were me—probably because, in so many ways, it *was* me.

I tried to get some additional information, but after a few more minutes of fruitless inquiry, I admitted defeat. Jennifer had given me all she had, and right now she was engulfed in a grief that went beyond the pain of Jake's death.

I told her that I'd be in touch and that she should call me any time she felt like it. She said she would. I didn't believe her. That was okay; I'd keep checking in on her until she saw that I meant it—or told me to stop. I said good-bye and squeezed my eyes shut as I hugged her at the door.

I walked to my car, planning the lunches I would set up for her with the deputies in the unit. They were sharks at work, but they'd show up for Jennifer. I turned left onto the freeway and headed back downtown in traffic that wasn't horrible. It wasn't until I neared the Broadway exit that it occurred to me she hadn't once mentioned their parents.

14

I sat at a stoplight at the intersection of Temple and Broadway and watched the mix of workers and witnesses make their way through the crosswalk to the courthouse. The last stragglers were a pregnant mother and her toddler boy, the latter stopping to pick up a gum wrapper that was glinting in the sun. *"No, papi, es sucio,"* she chided as she grabbed his hand and pulled him, toes dragging along the street, toward the sidewalk.

The light changed, and I pulled through the intersection. As I turned right onto Spring Street, heading for the employee parking lot, the memory that had begun to tweak me during my meeting with Jennifer finally emerged from the shadows. I pulled into a spot and let it play out.

I'd just come back from court after a long session wrangling over discovery with four of the biggest chowderheaded defense attorneys I'd ever had the misfortune of meeting. I'd stopped in Jake's office to do some venting and found him hunched over his desk, head down, talking intently into the phone.

"Don't worry," Jake said, his tone softly reassuring. "I'll take care of it, okay?"

He listened a moment, then looked up and saw me standing in the doorway. He mouthed, "I'll meet you," as he gestured toward my office.

I nodded and moved on. A few minutes later, Jake came in, shaking his head.

"Sorry. I was just talking to my IO on that stalking murder," he explained. "He's kinda new, needs some hand-holding."

"Sure," I replied.

But I'd known it was a lie. I'd recognized the number on the display screen of his phone. It was for Central Juvenile Hall.

I hadn't understood why he'd lied, but I'd let it go. There were plenty of innocent reasons for Jake to talk to someone in juvenile hall, some of which might well have required secrecy. Like, for example, a juvenile witness who was cooperating with the prosecution and in danger of gang reprisal. I'd still found it weird that Jake didn't trust me with that information, but I'd figured he thought it was better to be safe than sorry.

Now, of course, there was another, far more sinister possibility to consider. The memory, and what it might mean, was deeply disturbing. How could I have been that wrong about Jake? How could I have missed seeing a side of him that was so despicably perverted? I wanted badly to prove that it wasn't true, that the call hadn't meant anything. But that would require some digging, and I didn't know of a safe way to do that.

Angry and frustrated, I turned my thoughts to Kit Chalmers. I thought there might be a little more wiggle room for us to look around in his life without getting caught, but not much. And it wasn't as though I had nothing else to do. I was under a lot of pressure to move forward on the Densmore case, and then there was the rest of my caseload. The press of having too much to do closed in on me, and I had to force myself to relax, slow down, and think.

I looked around for cops, then, holding my cell phone in my lap, I flipped it open and dialed Bailey's number.

"Meet me in my office," I said. She hung up without bothering to reply.

I stopped in the snack bar for coffee, and by the time I got back to my office, Bailey was already there, her feet up on the side table under the window, staring down at the street below.

"What took you so long?" I said as I dropped my purse on the floor next to my desk and flopped into my chair.

Bailey turned her head to face me without changing her position. "You meet with the sister?"

I nodded and filled her in. She grunted. "So all possibilities are still open—and she ruled out nothing. Fantastic."

Then I told her about Jake's phone call with someone at juvenile hall.

Bailey raised her eyebrows and fell silent. "We can't check phone records without getting noticed," she said finally.

"Yeah."

"Could be completely innocent," she added.

"Could be."

We both sat quietly for a moment as we shared the same thought: we couldn't rule out the ugly possibility that the phone call might have been evidence that Jake had a suspicious interest in fringe children.

There was nowhere to go with this train of thought at the moment, so I changed the subject to something I hoped would prove more productive. "Did you run the gang-banger kid, Luis, on the Densmore case?"

"I did. Had to kick some rookie ass to get the job done, but, of course," Bailey said as she brandished a sheaf of papers, "that's not a problem for me."

Not only was it not a problem, but I knew that Bailey actively relished the chance to call out the slackers.

She began to read: "Busted for possession of marijuana when he was twelve, arrested for burglary when he was fourteen." Bailey paused for effect. "No convictions."

"Really?" I said, incredulous. Bailey nodded, equally disbelieving. It was so easy to get convicted in juvenile court that the only surprise was when someone didn't.

"Busted last year for possession of cocaine, claimed the stuff was left in his car by someone else—"

I raised my eyebrows at the common "some other dude did it" defense. Bailey nodded her acknowledgment and continued. "Pled guilty anyway for two days' detention, basically time served."

"And no one ever took a buccal swab for his DNA?" I asked.

Bailey shrugged. "It was all chicken-shit stuff."

"Still," I said, annoyed. Every rapist had to start somewhere. Who said it couldn't be with a bust for cocaine possession? "He still on probation?" I asked.

Bailey continued to read, then replied, "Yep. Hang on." She shuffled through the papers. I signaled to her that I was going to the restroom, and she waved me away.

When I got back, she was dropping her cell phone into her jacket pocket. "We've got a meeting with the probation officer in"—she consulted her watch—"half an hour."

I nodded. If we went right away, we could just make it. The only problem was that when I'd left Glendale after my interview with Jennifer, I hadn't had an appetite, but now my stomach was feeling hollow. "I'll need to grab something from the snack bar on the way down."

I called Melia. "Would you let Eric know that I'm going out to Pasadena with Bailey on the Densmore case?" I asked. I especially wanted it noted that I wasn't working on Jake's case, for extra brownie points.

"Uh, yeah," Melia said absently.

I'd probably interrupted her in the middle of swooning over the bios of the cast members in Hollywood Men, a popular beefcake strip show. "Gustavo likes walks on the beach at sunset . . ." Ordinarily I wouldn't have cared, but this time it was important that she have the information ready in case there were any more visits from Vanderhorn.

"Melia, it's important. Focus, okay?"

When she finally sounded as if she was half there, I repeated the message, then asked her to read it back. After I spelled the name "Densmore" for the third time, I thought she got ahold of it. I hoped for the best, picked up my briefcase and coat, patted the pocket to make sure my .22 was still there, and gestured to Bailey that I was ready.

We made it to Pasadena so fast I barely had time to finish my chicken Caesar wrap. I wiped my mouth with the pathetic excuse for a napkin provided by the snack bar and checked my face in the mirror for crumbs. By the time I was done, Bailey had parked.

The nondescript building could have been any standard government-issue structure, with cinder blocks and ugly green institutional paint. Bailey flashed her badge, and the bored-looking receptionist waved us on and buzzed us through the security door.

Luis Revelo's probation officer was a heavyset black man with an open, friendly face, casually dressed in a powder-blue polo shirt and khakis. According to the sign on his desk, we were speaking to someone named Tyrone Jackson.

He signaled for us to have a seat while he finished scanning his file on Revelo. After a few minutes, apparently satisfied he'd plumbed its depths, he closed the file, rocked back precariously far in his chair, and said, "Luis didn't give me any trouble. No new busts, no dirty tests." He looked from me to Bailey. "So what else can I do for you?"

"When did you last see him, Mr. Jackson?" I asked.

"Tyrone," he corrected as he flipped to the end of the file. "We had a meeting scheduled for January twenty-fourth, but according to my notes, he never showed up. Said he was sick, so I gave him a pass on that one."

I looked at Bailey. January 24 was the day after the rape.

"Did he ever reschedule?" Bailey asked.

"Nope, but since he wasn't in any trouble, I figured it was no emergency." Tyrone gestured to a three-foot-high stack of files behind him. "Got enough emergencies to keep me busy without worrying about the kids who manage to keep their noses clean."

I wouldn't have had a problem with his logic if it weren't for the fact that Luis Revelo was standing tall as suspect numero uno in a rape case. In my book, that qualified him as one of those emergencies. But

I had the feeling that if Useless had contacted Tyrone, he hadn't given him the 411 on the Densmore case. With Bailey's next question, I learned I was right.

"Has anyone told you that Revelo is a person of interest in the rape of a young girl in the Palisades?"

Tyrone frowned. "Definitely not." He paused, then said, "Didn't make him for that kind of offender, but it wouldn't be the first bad surprise I ever got."

"Can you call him in, tell him it's just a routine check-in?" Bailey asked.

For an answer, Tyrone picked up the phone. After the space of about three rings, he asked for Luis in heavily-English-accented Spanish. When he hung up, he said, "His mom says he's asleep, worked all night." He turned to Bailey. "You got a warrant?"

She shook her head. "Not enough for that yet."

"Which is why you need me," Tyrone said.

Bailey and I nodded.

"Okay, let's do this," he said as he stood up and clipped his badge and gun to his belt.

15

Luis Revelo lived on the wrong side of the tracks in a working-class neighborhood in Sylmar, a city in the North San Fernando Valley. Heavily Hispanic, the town had been a relatively quiet, respectable little burg until the gangbangers had moved in and turned it into a war zone. There were still pockets that were populated by the sort of decent, hardworking poor of all races that used to be typical of Sylmar, but they were under siege.

We pulled up in front of a "yard" where the only things growing were spare tires, neglected toys, and empty beer bottles.

The paint on the front door had peeled to the point where I could no longer tell what color it had been, and the trim on the left side of the frame was gone. We walked up the front path, kicking empties out of our way as we went.

A small woman with a long, unkempt braid answered the door.

"Ms. Revelo?" Tyrone said.

She looked old enough to be Luis's grandmother, but she was probably his mother. Aging happened a lot faster when life was this hard.

"Sí. Estás buscando a Luis?"

The fact that she'd immediately known who we were looking for showed she had few illusions about her son.

"Sí, yo estoy el oficial de—"

"Sí, sí, entiendo," the woman said, cutting him off as she gestured toward a door inside the house. She pointed to a room and said, *"El está durmiendo."*

Tyrone motioned for us to wait at the doorway. We didn't have a warrant and had no legal authority to arrest him in his house. Tyrone strode directly to the door and knocked loudly. "Luis, this is your probation officer. Open up."

No answer. He knocked and called out again, this time louder. No response. "Luis! I'm coming in!"

Now we heard the sound of glass breaking and a loud thump. Tyrone put his shoulder to the door as Bailey pulled out her .44 to back him up. I put my hand into my coat pocket, flipped off the safety on my .22, and ran around the outside of the house.

Just as I rounded the corner, I saw a young barefoot male in a wifebeater and jeans running toward the backyard fence. I fired a shot into the air and called out, "Police!"

But of course he already knew that— that's why he was running. I hesitated for just a fraction of a second, unsure that I could justify the shoot. We didn't have him for the rape yet, and he wasn't wanted for anything else, so he wasn't necessarily a fleeing felon. That moment of hesitation was all he needed. Luis, or whoever it was, threw himself over the fence and out of sight. One second later, Bailey and Tyrone flew out the back door and ran for the fence, but it was no use. I turned to see if anyone else had been flushed out of the house, but I saw only the thin fabric of a cheap curtain floating through an open bedroom window.

"Damn!" Tyrone said, his chest heaving as he tried to catch his breath. Bailey, who was barely breathing hard, had some more colorful observations.

I pocketed my .22-caliber Beretta a little too violently. "It's my fault," I said. "I had a clear shot. I should've taken it."

"No cause for lethal force," Bailey said matter-of-factly.

Not to mention the fact that I had no gun license.

Tyrone had been leaning forward, his hands on his knees, trying to get his breathing under control. He straightened up. "I'll file the notice of probation violation so you can get a warrant into the system," he said. He turned to me. "We'll pick him up sooner or later, don't you worry."

I wasn't worried about whether we'd pick Revelo up; it was just the "or later" part that didn't thrill me. "We need to make this sound like a win," I said, "or Frank Densmore'll be on the phone to Vanderhorn whining that we let his prime suspect slip through our fingers."

"She's got a point there," Tyrone remarked . . . and got a steely glare from Bailey for his trouble. He put his hands up. "I'm just saying." We wended our way back to the car as he pulled out his cell phone to get the probation-violation ball rolling.

By the time Bailey and I got back to my office, we'd agreed on the spin. I called Eric and gave him the spiel so he could feed it to Vanderhorn.

"We were just about to haul him in, but someone tipped him off. He's in the wind, but we've put a no-bail warrant out for him. Given the way he rocketed out of there, I'd say he's looking pretty good for the rape. We don't know of anything else hanging over his head. So, bottom line, you can tell Vanderhorn the case'll be wrapped and ready for trial as soon as we get him."

"But we don't know how soon 'soon' is." Eric sighed. "Okay, I'll pass it along. You going to tell Densmore?"

"I was thinking you should let Vanderhorn do it. It's his buddy. Besides, it'll let him feel useful for a change," I replied.

I could hear the smile in Eric's voice as he said, "Never thought I'd see the day when you put 'useful' and 'Vanderhorn' together." He paused, then continued on a

more sober note. "I have no doubt Vanderhorn will jump at the chance to give this
news to a potential campaign supporter
like Densmore, so you should expect that
call to be made by the end of today. Once
Densmore hears this, he's going to expect
an arrest in about five minutes. Stand by
for major flack if it doesn't happen."

I'd just closed my cell when it went off
in my hand. The default ringtone, "FM" by
Steely Dan, played as I stared at the unfamiliar number. I flipped the phone open,
thinking it was probably a misdial. It was
Graden Hales. It figured. I was tired and
frustrated, and in a bad mood because
I'd lost Revelo, and Bailey was watching.
When else would he call?

"You must be hungry by now," Graden
said playfully.

I noted that he'd called me on my cell
phone though I'd never given him the number. I shouldn't have been surprised—after
all, he was a cop. "You could've called me
at the office. I'm here."

"The point was to impress you with how
resourceful I am."

It wasn't a big intrusion, I had to admit. I
gave my cell number to defense attorneys

all the time. Still, it bugged me a little. "You've definitely made an impression," I said dryly.

The pause on his end told me he was smart enough to sense that this particular superpower wasn't my favorite.

Bailey lifted an eyebrow to show me she'd noticed this wasn't a work call. I couldn't tell her it was Graden, since I hadn't told her about his lunch invitation and it wasn't the kind of news that could just be dropped in her lap. I'd been meaning to say something about it, and now I wished that I had. I nodded, confirming that this was personal, and mouthed, "I'll tell you." Bailey nodded back, motioned for me to call her later, and left.

Graden's tone was conciliatory. "I'll make you a deal. Have lunch with me tomorrow, and I'll get you a blocked number. No one will have it. Including me."

That was pretty quick on the uptake. I remembered Bailey's warning about him being a babe magnet, but lunch wasn't a huge commitment. Besides, what did I have to lose? I took a look at my calendar. It was packed with pretrial hearings on all my other cases. I'd stacked them up to get it all over with at once.

"Tomorrow's a nightmare. What about next week?"

We settled on Tuesday.

"How does noon sound?" he asked. "I'll meet you in front of the building."

I said that sounded fine, but no sooner had I closed the phone than my apprehension began to mount. I wasn't that good at making new friends, unless they were sitting in a jury box; first dates always made me nervous and grumpy. Then it occurred to me that I could use the opportunity to pump him for information about Jake's case. The thought immediately relaxed me.

I spent the rest of the afternoon preparing for my upcoming hearings: which cases I'd make offers on and which ones would have to "plead to the sheet"—plead to all charges with no offers and no deals. By 5:00 p.m. I was good and ready for a playdate. I walked down to Toni's office.

"How about Charlie O's?" I asked. A cozy, no-frills jazz bar, Charlie O's was one of our favorite hangs.

"I'm gonna convert to whatever deity sent you with this message of mercy," Toni said. She'd been hunched, bleary-eyed, over her computer, and now she leaned back and blew out a long breath. "I'm not really in the mood to drive, though. You mind letting me crash on your couch tonight?"

Toni's house, a small but charming two-story, two-bedroom, was perched at the top of one of the narrow, winding streets in Laurel Canyon. It was a tough road to navigate even in daylight, so she'd frequently bunk in with me after a night out rather than hazard the drive in darkness. And since Toni and I basically wore the same size, she didn't have to worry about packing for the occasion. Of course, Toni, being Toni, occasionally groused that my wardrobe choices were boring—she had a more feminine, frilly fashion sense (and she was a little better endowed than me)—but I handled that by reminding her that if she didn't like the offerings, she could just wear the same clothes she'd worn the day before. This was akin to telling her to don a hair shirt and leg chains.

"Not a problem," I said.

"Bailey coming?" Toni asked. "I haven't seen that girl in . . . forever."

"It's been a day," I replied, amused. "I'll call her now."

Bailey agreed to meet us at the hotel at

7:30. Back in my room, I changed into jeans and tucked them into knee-high motorcycle-type boots. I added a Harley-Davidson vest that laced up the sides. Toni found one of my few pairs of strappy sandals and picked out jeans to go with the rose-pink cashmere pullover she'd left in my room after a previous outing. At 7:25, our finishing touches completed, we ran downstairs just in time to see Bailey pull into the driveway.

Charlie O's wasn't swanky. It was small, with cottage-cheese-style ceilings that'd been darkened by the smoke of a million cigarettes back in the day when that was still allowed. The walls were lined with portraits of jazz greats: Miles Davis, Sonny Rollins, McCoy Tyner. A lively painting of the exterior of Charlie O's that'd been done by a veteran cocktail waitress hung at the end of the wall near the back door, where the regulars entered.

It was a great night. Tenor-sax player Pete Christlieb was leading a tight quartet, and the martini was almost certainly the best one I'd ever had.

"Here's to surviving the week," I said, lifting my glass carefully.

"I heard that," Toni said with feeling.

We clinked and drank, then soaked in the music and exhaled. When the band took their first break, Toni and I ordered another round of drinks. Bailey, as the designated driver, switched to club soda and lime.

"I'm going to door-knock the Densmore hood again myself on Monday. See if I can dredge up any witnesses," Bailey said after the waitress left.

"You don't think Luis is our guy?" I asked.

"I want to make sure all other options are ruled out by the time we find him so we can move on it."

I looked at Bailey as closely as the dim light would allow. If she was willing to do the scut work of door-knocking the neighbors herself, something was up.

"Densmore called your captain?" I asked.

"He did," Bailey admitted.

I sighed and we all picked up our glasses, and that was the end of shoptalk for the night.

16

I'd planned to start my morning at the usual 7:30 and set my alarm accordingly. As usual, life did not cooperate. The phone blasted me from a deep sleep to a jerked-upright, heart-pounding, and confused state of alertness at the barbaric hour of 4:30 a.m. I yanked the phone up, punched the talk button, and croaked, "'Lo?"

"Rachel, it's Elan."

My blurry brain got as far as asking, *Elan? Who?* when he continued, "From hotel security. Someone's hit your car—"

"Huh?" I said, still fuzzy. "But it's in the garage—"

"Yes, your car is in the garage. And you need to come down here, because I'm about to call the cops," he said with exaggerated patience.

"I'm on my way," I said, and slammed the phone back down. A rush of adrenaline propelled me to a standing run for the closet. My brain tried to sort out what had happened, but it kept hitting dead ends. I washed up, ran my hand through my hair, and threw on jeans and a hoodie sweatshirt-jacket. Toni was sleeping peacefully on the foldout couch, so I tiptoed out of the room and ran for the elevator.

As I rode down to the garage, I tried to remember where Rafi usually parked my car, but when the doors opened, that problem at least was easily solved. All I had to do was follow the blaring horns and whistles of the alarm. I ran toward the noise, remote control in hand. The moment my little Honda came into view at the far end of the garage, I frantically began to press the button. The blasting stopped, and the contrasting predawn silence made the air feel like a solid mass. The echo of my footsteps seemed to be coming from a distance, adding a surreal, out-of-body quality to an already bizarre moment.

I'd been expecting to see that my car had been the victim of a hit-and-run, and I dreaded the damage. When I got within twenty feet of the car, I wished it *had* been a hit-and-run. Bright, splashy spray paint covered the hood, the trunk, the doors, and even the roof in writing that was amazingly clear. "Lil' Loco" of the "Sylmar Sevens" had been here; my little econobox had been tagged within an inch of its life. And just in case I'd thought a quick paint job would handle the problem, the word *"puta"* — whore — had been gouged into the driver's door so deeply it went right down to the tinfoil.

The Sylmar Sevens had to be Revelo's gang. This was their way of warning me off their homie. Just beneath the disorientation and anger, I felt a thrill of victory. This meant we'd found our rapist. Densmore was right. Damn. I turned to Elan, who was taking pictures with a fancy-looking digital camera.

"Thanks for giving me the call first," I said.

"Sure," he said absently as he continued to click off photos of my car.

"You don't have to do that for me. The cops'll take care of it," I said as I hit Bailey's cell number.

Elan was viewing the series of photos he'd just taken, and it was a moment before he'd processed what I'd said. He looked up for a moment and replied, "These aren't for you."

I looked at him, hand on hip, waiting for the explanation I knew I wasn't going to like. I wasn't disappointed.

"It's for a pictorial book I'm doing . . . L.A. scenes. My brother-in-law's an agent. He thinks he can find me a publisher." He began to circle my car again. It made me squeamish somehow, as if some pervert were taking creepy photos of a toddler.

At least he didn't want to be a director. Bailey showed up a little later with a crime scene tech so bleary-eyed, I wondered whether we'd wind up with pictures of the ceiling. I turned my back to the tech and said to Bailey under my breath, "Put the squeeze on Elan for his photos. He's got about a hundred."

Bailey sauntered over to him as she pushed open her leather bomber jacket to reveal the gun on her hip. I figured Elan's photos would arrive on her desktop in about five minutes. Along with some BS confidentiality agreement for her to sign promising not to publish the photos without his permission.

When the tech left, I assessed the damage to my now multicolored car. "I suppose it'll still drive okay."

"'Cept for the four slashed tires," Bailey pointed out matter-of-factly. "'Course, the way you drive, it'll handle about the same."

In all the excitement I'd somehow missed the fact that my car was sitting a lot lower than it should've been. Now I looked and saw that the tires were indeed history. The paint was one thing—I could get the worst of it covered over fairly cheaply. But tires?

"How'm I supposed to afford four new tires?"

"You're not. At least not for now. Until Luis Revelo's locked up and we have a bead on his gang, you'll be carpooling with me."

I opened my mouth to protest, then

abruptly closed it as Bailey's words sank in. The reality was that the trashing of my car was meant as a warning and possibly a death threat. My earlier adrenaline rush was replaced by a cold pit of fear in my gut. *They know where I live,* I thought. *They know what I drive.* I shoved my hands into the pockets of my jacket to hide the fact that they'd begun to shake, and my right hand instinctively searched for the comfort of my .22 Beretta, but then I remembered that I'd left it in the room. A sense of weakness and vulnerability suddenly washed over me—something I particularly detested. Ordinarily I would've balked at the loss of autonomy Bailey had suggested, but now I was ashamed to admit it felt like a damn good idea. Still, I didn't want Bailey to report this—at least not yet.

"Do me a favor and don't call this in right now."

"Why?" Bailey asked, puzzled.

"Because if the office finds out, they'll put a tail on me."

Bailey nodded and finished the thought: "And that'll be the end of any work on Jake's case." She paused for a moment, then nodded again. "It won't be long before we hook up Revelo. Once we've got him and it's a public thing, they'll leave you alone."

"Exactly," I replied. Gangbangers could be dumb, but they weren't stupid. The Densmore case was going to get some ink, and once Revelo got hooked up for it, there'd be no point in taking the risk of getting caught going after the prosecutor. If they scared off one deputy DA, the office would just assign another. Besides, the Sylmar Sevens had drug dealing and car thefts to attend to; they couldn't be wasting precious time on a no-money proposition like chasing off a DA.

I saw that Bailey was yawning. Now that the excitement had died down, I was starting to feel it too. Yawns being the contagion they are, I covered my mouth as I felt a jaw-splitter coming on.

"Want to crash upstairs?" I asked. "Toni's on the foldout, but we can push her over."

Bailey nodded. We rode the elevator up to my floor, and when I opened the door, we found Toni still asleep, snoring and oblivious. Bailey and I shared a smile. I whispered, "'Night," moved into my bedroom, and quietly closed the French doors.

I placed breakfast orders. "And add an extra order of bacon," I said into the phone. After all that action I figured I could afford it.

17

"How on earth did I sleep through all that?" Toni asked as she offered up the second pot of coffee.

Bailey declined; I accepted with gusto.

"You could sleep through the Apocalypse. Remember that trip to Vegas?" I asked.

Toni shot me a hard look. "I was tired, and we'd been at the crap table all night."

I laughed, remembering. "Couple in the room next to ours really got into it," I said to Bailey. "From what I could hear, someone had lost more than they were supposed to.

The screaming went on for an hour, then they started throwing things. Then they started throwing each other. That seemed the propitious moment—"

"Propitious?" Bailey said, an eyebrow cocked. "Isn't it a little early for that kind of talk?"

"She's getting her 'lawyer' on," Toni remarked dryly.

"The propitious moment to call the manager. Turned out everyone in that wing had heard it, that's how loud it was." I paused and tipped my head toward Toni. "Ms. Thang over here slept through it all."

Bailey chuckled as Toni threw a piece of bagel at me. I ducked just in time and heard it hit the wall behind me. I snaked my fork over to Bailey's avocado, turkey, and swiss omelet and speared a bite. It was delicious.

"Speaking of getting my lawyer on, Bailey," I said. "Now that we've probably got our prime suspect for the rape, we should finish ruling out the others."

Bailey nodded. Even if we lucked out with a good DNA match, we couldn't stop the investigation now or the defense would make it look like we went for the most obvious, convenient suspect and let the "real" culprit get away.

"I don't have a solid alibi for that weird security guy yet," Bailey said. She saw me raise my fork a second time and pulled back her plate defensively. "Tell you what: you let me eat my own damn food, and I promise I'll do some more checking into him."

" 'Weird' and 'security guy'—isn't that redundant?" Toni remarked.

"Kind of," I said, now turning my attention to Toni's French toast. I surreptitiously picked up a piece with my stealth fork.

"Are you ever goin' to live with what you order, girl?" Toni asked with mock exasperation.

I ignored the rhetorical question. "What about that gardener with the prior for statutory rape?" I asked Bailey.

"Still checking on his alibi," she replied. "But I did find out that the case got busted down to a misdemeanor. She was sixteen going on seventeen, he was barely eighteen, blah, blah, blah—you know the story."

I did. Sometimes things are less than they seem.

"But I'll run it down, just to be on the safe side," Bailey assured me.

"So where're you at with Jake's case?" Toni asked as she put her napkin next to her plate and pulled out her compact mirror and eyelash curler. Even though it was Saturday and Toni was likely headed for nothing more exciting than her laundry, she always looked fantastically perfect. My makeup "routine" tended to consist of whatever I had patience for at the moment, so the results on any given day could be unpredictable.

"I'm at a dead end for now with Jake's background, so I'm going to go after Kit. Starting with his school records," I replied. Bailey gave me a questioning, skeptical look. "What? I know people—I can't make some calls?"

"Just let me know what you find out," Bailey said, then tossed her napkin onto the table and headed for the bathroom, where I kept her extra toothbrush and comb.

I put the silver cover over my plate of half-eaten egg whites and moved to the mirror in the living room. I shoved my hair into a ponytail, threw a black muffler around my neck, and pulled on my wool-lined black trench coat. Black on black, I was Rachel Knight, Sexy Spy. With just a dab of syrup on her cheek, I noticed.

"Rache, you got a coat I can borrow?" Toni asked. "I'm gonna freeze my hind-quarters out there."

Clouds had gathered, and it was looking overcast and brisk outside. I gave her my peacoat. Bailey came back, looking disgustingly fresh, and held the door as I pushed the room-service table into the hallway, then we all headed out.

"Want me to run you back to the office?" Bailey asked.

"That'd be lovely," Toni said. She'd left her car at work when we'd gone to Charlie O's last night, and she wasn't the type to enjoy the hike the way I did. I suspected the strappy sandals she was still wearing had something to do with it. Toni had packed yesterday's work clothes into a laundry bag and had put on my new V-necked red sweater.

"That looks so good on you I might not want it back," I told her.

Toni tossed her head as if she were in a hair commercial. "Don't hate me because

I'm beautiful." She laughed. "You'd rock this sweater too, girl. It's a good red."

I took a step back and looked at her. It *was* a good red. I loved that Toni knew things like that.

We all got into the elevator. Bailey turned to me. "Where're you headed?"

"Not far," I said. "Just the Hall of Records."

"Hall of Records. On a Saturday?" Toni asked.

The elevator opened onto the lobby, and we all moved toward the front door. "I'm meeting Kevin," I said. "I'll explain later." I didn't want to discuss my mission in public.

I wanted to walk. It would help to clear my head and calm my nerves. But even with my fully loaded .357 in my purse, I was still unsettled by last night's events. Bailey dropped me at the corner of Temple and Broadway, and I got out and waved good-bye. As I entered the Hall of Records, I admitted to myself that the probable death threat the Sylmar Sevens had issued weighed heavily on me. Clearly I was not going to get any party invitations from them. I consoled myself with the knowledge that it wasn't personal. After all, they didn't know me. With a little bit of luck, they soon would. Then they'd really hate me. That thought cheered me as I rode the elevator up to Kevin's office.

Kevin Jerreau, a buddy from our baby DA days, now a deputy in charge in Juvenile, had agreed to meet me at his office. He was surprisingly surfer-boy handsome for a prosecutor, and all the girls in my newbie training group had had a crush on him. It had cracked me up to watch them angle to sit next to him during classes or at lunch, because I could see what they apparently couldn't: Kevin was gay. And we took to each other on sight. Given the lousy track record I'd had with men, even back then, I found his company relaxing. Kevin, on the other hand, had been glad not to have to deal with yet another panting female he'd have to disappoint. He'd turned me on to hip-hop music, prompting me to call him the straightest gay man I'd ever met. In exchange, I'd turned him on to jazz—which prompted him to take up with a tenor-sax player.

He waved me over and took the sheet of paper I handed to him. "This the kid they found with Jake?" he asked as he swiveled away from me to type on his computer.

"Yeah, and I've already been flicked for nosing around the case, so if you—"

Kevin waved me off. "When you asked me to come in on a Saturday, I knew what it meant," he said, squinting at the screen, then sighed and put on his reading glasses. "Marsden High," he said.

Kevin looked at me sideways. "You know Marsden High?"

I shook my head.

"Very tough school, high dropout rate." He turned back to the computer. "Your kid was a junior. Never made above a D on anything." Kevin continued scrolling. "Oh, now shut me up for the liar I am, he got a C in Auto Shop. Go, Kit."

"Any disciplinary actions? Suspensions? I need a thread to pull here."

Kevin leaned forward. "Five million tardies," he said as he continued to scroll. "And . . . one bust for truancy."

Bingo. I sat up. "When?"

"Two months ago."

"Yes." Now for the money shot. "Was he with anyone?"

Kevin turned back to the screen. "Two

other kids, both from the same school." Anticipating my next request, he wrote down their names on a legal pad next to the keyboard, then tore off the page and handed it to me.

"You're the best, Kev," I said as I looked at the page, then folded it up and shoved it into my coat pocket.

"Damn right I am, though this is definitely not the reason why." Kevin sat back in his chair and folded his hands across his middle as he looked at me thoughtfully. "How come you haven't asked?"

"Asked what?"

"Whether or not I knew Jake was gay."

"Because if he was involved with Kit, he's not gay. He's a pedophile," I replied flatly.

Kevin nodded with a sad smile. "Thank you."

We exchanged a long look, and I was struck by how hard it still was to be different in this world. Somehow Kevin had always made it look easy.

18

On Monday morning, I put in a call to the principal of Marsden High, then I phoned Bailey and asked her if she'd like to join me.

"I was just thinking how much I missed high school," Bailey replied.

She agreed to meet me out in front of the building in ten minutes. Knowing it could take me that long just to get an elevator, I quickly grabbed a legal pad and the page with the names of Kit's partners-in-truancy and headed out.

As I pushed open the large glass door to exit the building, I could see the early promise of a sunny, clear day ahead. There was a slight nip in the air, but the sky was a brilliant blue and the sunlight was starting to get thicker, in preparation for spring. Typical L.A.—we'd only had a couple of chilly months, but the city was already giving up the pretense of winter. I was glad I'd left my muffler at home.

The high school was on Sycamore, just west of downtown, in a bleak, low-rent stretch of concrete office buildings and family-run grocery and liquor stores. The school looked as if it belonged on the East Coast: one monolithic two-story brick building with a wide front walkway that led to two sets of tall glass doors. One of those doors was boarded over with plywood. They needed to either switch to metal or make the glass bulletproof. All in all, it was an imposing edifice. Making it even more so was the surrounding ten-foot fence and metal front gates. Bailey circled the school, looking for a parking space, but the streets were packed with cars. We wound up parking four blocks away, next to a vacant lot. The air was still chilly enough to let us see our breath as we hoofed it to the school.

At this time of day, the gates were open: as we passed through, I felt as if I were entering a prison. I had no doubt that most of the student body felt the same way every single morning. A teenage boy with spiked, superblack hair, eyeliner, and multiple piercings burst out of the school, banging open the front door, and I saw that there were metal detectors just inside. I pulled out my badge so I could keep my gun, and out of the corner of my eye I saw Bailey do the same. It was comforting to know that we'd be able to shoot our way out if we needed to.

We turned left down a cavernous hallway. "Nice place," Bailey said sarcastically.

I replied with a grim smile. It was many things, but nice wasn't one of them. The floor was brown linoleum, the walls last saw paint when the Beatles were still touring, and the air smelled of rubber, sweat, and disinfectant. They say that about 40 percent of the California state budget goes to education, but you couldn't prove it by the looks of Marsden High.

Juanita Esquivel, secretary to the principal, Colin Reilly, looked at us over the tortoiseshell frames of her bifocals. "Can I help you?" she asked in a voice that managed to sound both stern and bored.

I wondered briefly how one was supposed to address a principal. By his title? Mister? I opted for the kiss-ass approach. "We're here to see Principal Reilly. Deputy District Attorney Rachel Knight and Detective Bailey Keller."

"Oh," she said with an expression like she'd just smelled spoiled yogurt in the mini-fridge. "Whyn't you have a seat. I'll tell him you're here." She pointed a long red nail at uncomfortable-looking wooden chairs set against the wall next to the door.

I remained standing—partly to annoy her and partly because I didn't want to consider who or what else had last occupied those chairs. Bailey stood, arms folded, with her back against the wall on the other side of the door. Her look said that Juanita would be wise to make sure the principal met with us very soon. The secretary eyed Bailey nervously, showing a well-honed instinct for self-preservation.

Five minutes later, we were seated in the spare, run-down, uninspiring box of an office that Principal Reilly called home. A couple of dying miniature cacti in clay pots behind his desk were his only concession to interior design. The one thing I could say for his office was that it fit in perfectly with the rest of the school.

"Call me Colin," he said, shaking our hands and inviting us to sit. He reminded me of a beefy Irish patrol cop. Thick of limb, heavy featured in an attractive way, he carried himself like he had a sap in one pocket and a throw-down gun in the other. Working here, he probably did. "So what can I do for you?"

"We're looking into some background information on Kit Chalmers." I paused to see if the name rang a bell.

It took a moment to register. "The one that just got killed. Yes, sad business." Reilly's voice showed this wasn't the first time he'd lost a student to a violent death.

I wanted to ask whether he'd been visited by the FBI, but if he hadn't, I didn't want to give him reason to question what we were doing here. The fact that he didn't ask led me to conclude that the FBI probably hadn't contacted him yet. This made me feel superior and insubordinate all at once. It was shaping up to be a very good day.

"I'm looking into a truancy bust about two months before he died, and I'd like to talk to the kids he was busted with," I said.

"They're Marsden students?" he asked. I nodded, and he turned to his computer.

I gave him the names.

"I show them as still enrolled. Morning attendance reports aren't in yet, so I can't say whether they're here today. According to our records, when they got the truancy bust, they were loitering at the mini-mart a couple of blocks away, smoking and pan-handling," he said matter-of-factly.

"So you wouldn't remember any details, I take it?"

He shook his head with a small smile. "That's not exactly a standout event around here."

"You have a yearbook we could look at?" Bailey asked.

He reached behind him to the metal bookcase against the wall and pulled out a large hardcover book emblazoned with MARSDEN HIGH SCHOOL and the picture of a marlin. Marsden Marlins—I had to admit, it had a ring to it. He handed the book to Bailey. She took out her digital camera, then opened the book and began turning pages.

"Mind if we borrow that copy?" I asked.

"Nope, just bring it back. It'd look bad if the principal didn't have a copy of the year-book." Reilly glanced at his watch. "Anything else?"

"Do you have any property Kit may have left here, by any chance?" I knew it was a long shot, but I had to ask.

"I know we cleaned out his locker. Nothing there but textbooks and some old weed that was mostly seeds," he said. "I can check with his counselor, though."

"That'd be great," I replied.

I joined Bailey in scanning the yearbook while Reilly called the counselor. When he hung up, he said, "She confiscated his cell phone the last time he was in school."

A cell phone. The way kids lived on them, this should be the Fort Knox of information. "She still have it?"

"We'll find out. She's on her way over."

Ms. Wilder, the counselor, whose curly brown hair made her look so young I thought she was a student, showed up less than a minute later. Her hands were empty. *Damn.*

We introduced ourselves, and she said, "I want to help any way I can. I'm a little uncertain, though," she said hesitantly. Then she reached into the pocket of her thick knit cardigan and pulled out the Holy Grail: Kit's cell phone. I held on to the arms of my chair to keep myself from knocking her down and taking it from her.

"You mean about letting us see his phone?" I asked as I began to mentally list all the reasons she should. I watched her eyes dart around the room, considering the issue. "Is it a privacy thing?"

She looked at me gratefully. "Yeah, I sort of feel like . . . like I owe him this sort of respect, you know?"

I nodded and gave her my most sincere "I'm on your side" look. "I do. And I'd feel the same way," I said, my nose growing. "But I think Kit would want us to get into his cell phone if it meant finding out who killed him, don't you agree?"

"Well, we already know who killed him, don't we?" she asked tentatively. She was a tentative sort of person—I could tell. The kind who was uncomfortable with declarative sentences.

"Not necessarily," I said, giving her my most heartfelt "I wish I could tell you the whole story" look. "There are still a lot of questions," I replied.

"Oh."

I could feel Bailey next to me inwardly gagging, and I knew she was losing patience with this dance. I didn't blame her, but I sensed that the heavy-handed approach would backfire with this young woman.

"Would you feel better if we just borrowed it for a little while and only used it to find friends who might know something?" I asked.

She wrinkled her forehead, then replied, "I think . . . that might be okay. Like I said, I want to help, I just . . ."

"Well, then, that's what we'll do," I said, and held out my hand.

She reluctantly dropped the phone into it. I was careful not to look triumphant.

Relieved of the burden of the cell, she pulled out a tissue and dabbed her eyes. "If I'd known it was going to be the last time I ever saw him, I'd have told him how special I thought he was."

"How special was he?" I asked.

She looked at me suspiciously, unsure whether I was making fun of her, but when my expression remained neutral, she relaxed. "He was smart, and he was a dreamer. If he'd had any kind of family support, he'd have been headed for college and maybe an acting career. He was really very handsome."

Ms. Wilder sighed, then looked at her watch and said she had to get back to her office. Eager to examine the cell phone that was burning a hole in my jacket pocket, I said my good-byes and thanks to Principal Reilly. It was almost noon, and when we stepped out into the hallway, the rising disharmony of a throng of teenage voices rose up and swelled over us. I looked in the direction it seemed to be coming from, then looked at Bailey.

"Shall we?" I asked.

19

The sound led us to a cafeteria the size of a football field, populated with hundreds of adolescents in the act of grazing through the offerings in the glass-shielded food carts that lined the perimeter of the room. Acned faces, multihued hair, piercings, and tattoos, with a small smattering of those who in my day would've been labeled preppies.

I scanned the crowd for the faces of Kit's fellow truants, but it was like playing *Where's Waldo?* with moving figures. I thought about how to make use of this moment. Then I pulled out the cell phone and powered it up, hoping the battery still had some charge. There wasn't much, but it was enough for what I had planned. I searched through the dialed numbers. When I'd found the three that recurred the most, I hit the send button for the first one. It was hard to hear over the din, so I watched the room and tried to pick out the movement I was looking for. I didn't see anything. Bailey shook her head—she hadn't either. I dialed number two and watched again. This time I saw a ponytailed Asian kid among a group of young males reach for his cell phone. On a hunch, I dialed the third number.

And got lucky. A black kid with a retro 'fro standing next to the Asian kid pulled out his cell phone. "Yo," he answered.

"You missing Kit?" I said.

I thought I saw his face go slack, though from where I was standing across the room, I couldn't be sure. I kept the phone to my ear, waiting for an answer as I pointed him out to Bailey. We circled around so we'd come up behind him. As we got closer, I could see he was still holding the phone to his ear, but no words were coming out.

Finally he asked, "Who is this?"

By the time I was about ten feet away, I told him, "Turn around."

He turned and took one look at Bailey and me, then tugged on the Asian kid's shirt. They both started to back away. Before they could bolt, I called out, "Don't do it." They kept backing slowly, so I added, "I've got your names. We can find you whenever we want."

The kids close enough to hear us fell silent and watched intently. These students weren't the kind to be easily intimidated by authority. If the two boys put up a fight, they'd likely get some support, and this was not the place for us to pull out guns. "We're not here to bust anyone. We're here to investigate. Nothing more."

The two stopped moving and watched us, and especially Bailey, warily, but they stayed put and let us approach. The other students slowly turned back to their groups, though they continued to dart surreptitious looks at us.

"You're Eddie," I said to the Asian kid, "and you're Dante," I said to the black kid. My "gaydar" told me Eddie was on the team, but Dante had the vibe of a straight kid. It wasn't an obvious thing—they dressed like all the other teenagers milling around us. It was more a matter of the way they stood and moved.

They wouldn't commit to their names and looked back at us, impassive. *Prove it.* Were kids in general that much tougher now? Or just these kids?

"You ever hear about Kit having something going on with a DA?" I asked.

That got a reaction. They immediately shook their heads, and Dante asked, "You're talking about that guy that killed him, right?"

"Right," I said, biting back the urge to go on the defensive for Jake. This wasn't the time. "You ever hear Kit talk about someone named Jake?"

They again both shook their heads without hesitation.

"No," Eddie said.

"Never," Dante echoed.

There was nothing equivocal about the way they'd responded. They really didn't know—about a prosecutor, or about Jake.

"You know whether Kit had any 'regulars'?" The likelihood that they'd share that kind of information with me was slim—assuming they even knew—but what did I have to lose? I watched their reactions carefully. Dante stared off toward the window that faced the street and said nothing, but Eddie slowly shook his head.

"If he did, he never told me about it," Eddie replied. Then, in an arch bitchy-queen style, he added, "Probably didn't want the competition."

"That'd be my guess," I replied.

Eddie gave me a little smile. I turned to his friend. "Dante?"

Dante exhaled and shook his head, a small frown wrinkling his brow. "I don't remember him ever talking about a regular."

The answer seemed sincere, so I moved on. "When was the last time you saw Kit?"

They both shrugged.

"You don't remember? Seriously? A friend gets murdered, and you don't remember the last time you saw him?"

Dante looked around the cafeteria and Eddie looked out the window, but neither one of them answered my question. I could almost hear them planning their exit. For some reason, they'd both decided they'd done enough cooperating. I could feel Bailey getting ready to step in and be a little more persuasive, but we didn't have anything to threaten them with—at least not yet. Right now, the smart move was to back off and leave looking like good guys.

"Whatever you thought of Kit, you know what happened wasn't right. If you help us, nobody'll know. I promise we'll keep it quiet." Which was true. I *had* to keep it quiet if I wanted to keep my job. I didn't feel the need to share that with the boys. I handed them my card and told them to call me, then turned and walked out. Bailey gave them one more hard look and followed.

I could feel about one hundred pairs of eyes follow us as we left the cafeteria. We walked down the front steps of the school, and I exhaled loudly as we hit the street and headed for Bailey's car. The sidewalks were still relatively quiet, except for the mom-and-pop grocery and liquor stores, each of which was showing its own particular signs of life. We briskly covered the four blocks to Bailey's car in silence, lost in our own thoughts. Mine were largely devoted to my decidedly unfond memories of high school. Apparently Bailey's were too.

"High school sucks," she remarked with disgust.

"My sentiments ex—"

At that instant—we were just steps from Bailey's car—the air cracked with the sound of a shot fired at close range.

"Holy shit!" Bailey said.

We both hit the ground; I saw a bullet ricochet off the sidewalk ahead of us, spitting up a spray of concrete inches from my face. Another shot nearly split my eardrums, this time even closer. I heard the bullet ping loudly off the fire hydrant just ahead of me.

Everything seemed to move in slow motion as we each whipped out our guns and simultaneously rolled to shelter behind a parked car. I held my gun out in front of me, though I had no idea where to aim. Ears still ringing from the shots, I quickly scanned the area across the street but saw nothing—unless I counted the freaked-out shoppers who'd jumped out of their skins. A grapefruit and two avocados rolled out of the grocery bag one of them had dropped before running for cover.

We both rose into a crouch and looked through the car windows, our guns at the ready, but there was nothing to see. Bailey jerked her head in the direction of her car and signaled to me to stay low. *No shit,* I wanted to say. I bit back the impulse to tell her I thought we should skip. We duckwalked, staying in a crouch to make ourselves smaller targets, and ran for Bailey's car.

We crawled in from the passenger side to give us cover. As soon as we were in, Bailey hunched down, gunned the engine, and peeled out. I slid down in my seat and tried to look over the dash to see where the shots might have come from, but as we flew out of there, I realized they could've come from too many places—the alley between the gas station and the Korean acupuncturist, a window on the floor above the Armenian grocery store, or behind a myriad assortment of parked vehicles. I gave up and stayed low in my seat as Bailey jerked the car through the streets at a speed that left my stomach several blocks behind us.

When the adrenaline rush ebbed somewhat, I started to think about who'd done this. It had to be personal. There'd been no gang "hit up"—the usual "Where you from?"

that precedes a random gang shooting, and they didn't usually target women our age anyway. But there was a gang-style brazenness to it, which made it likely that the Sylmar Sevens were behind it. When Bailey had cleared us out of the immediate area and slowed down enough to make conversation a little less life-threatening, I said, "I want to say this was the Sevens."

Bailey, who was continually darting looks into the rearview mirror, gave a short nod. "A long way out of their territory."

"So's my hotel. The only way they could've known about either place was by following us from the Criminal Courts Building."

"True," Bailey agreed.

"Though from what I've learned, the Sylmar Sevens aren't exactly a big-time operation. Don't get me wrong. They've done their share. But I'm having a hard time believing Revelo's important enough to be worth all this work . . . and risk," I said.

Bailey turned right, toward the bridge that would take us over the freeway and into downtown.

"Not much risk so far. We haven't caught anybody, right?" she said dryly.

She had a point. "I suppose it's possible.

Maybe if they merged with a bigger gang, and Revelo's the new shot-caller . . ."

I completed the thought mentally: then the BGs—baby gangsters—of the new and improved Sylmar Sevens would want to impress the new boss and shot-caller by taking out the prosecutor that was causing him trouble. And from their perspective it was a win-win situation: if they didn't get caught, they'd look like heroes, and if they did get caught, they'd look like even bigger heroes.

These were not comforting thoughts.

"If we're going to call this in, we'd better get back there and do it now," Bailey said as she continued to drive down Broadway toward the Criminal Courts Building.

The sound of sirens, distant at first but fast approaching, told me we didn't have much time to decide.

20

It hadn't been an easy decision. At first I thought that maybe we did have to report the shooting. But upon reflection it occurred to me that in a neighborhood like that, with gangs on all sides, a random shooting to claim new turf was a far more logical explanation than the possibility that we were being targeted by the Sylmar Sevens—a small-time gang with limited resources. And the downside of reporting the shooting was that—if I got lucky, at the very least—I'd get a full-time tail, which would effectively end my work on Jake's case. If I didn't get so lucky, I'd get busted for sticking my nose into a case I'd specifically been warned off of—a firing offense.

I told Bailey, "I admit, our chances of solving Jake's case are probably going to get somewhat slimmer if we're dead, but if I'm right and this was random, then we'll have shut ourselves down for no reason."

Bailey didn't like it, but I eventually wheedled her down . . . on one condition: "You don't leave the office without me. Ever. You never leave for work before eight a.m.—"

Fine by me. I'm not exactly nature's freshest flower before noon anyway . . .

"—and when you do walk to the courthouse, you wear a vest."

That momentarily cooled my jets. I hate those things with a blinding passion. Stiff, hot, uncomfortable—but worst of all they make you look like Frankenstein. I opened my mouth to protest, but Bailey held up her hand. "Nonnegotiable, Knight."

I capitulated.

But this morning, as I opened my closet doors, I reflected that it was a hell of a day to take my first crack at working a bulletproof. Today I was having lunch with Lieutenant Graden Hales, which meant I had enough wardrobe issues on my hands without worrying about body-armor couture. I don't have a lot of patience for dress-up, so deciding what to wear usually takes less than three minutes. But now I uncharacteristically found myself noodling over my choice of wardrobe. I didn't want to look like Dita Von Teese, but I didn't want to look like Gertrude the Security Guard either. The goal was to seem slick but not slutty. This is not as easy as it seems. My cobalt-blue sweater was flattering but clingy—too slutty. My starchy white blouse with metal cuff links was court worthy but mannish—too blah. Finally I settled on a charcoal-gray cashmere turtleneck thin enough to tuck into a pair of high-waisted wool trousers and finished it off with low-heeled boots—people downtown usually walk to lunch, and I didn't want to suffer through a multiblock hike on spiky heels. The only thing left to decide was outerwear.

I considered which jackets would fit over the bulky body armor, then walked out onto the balcony to get a feel for the weather. It was brisk, but the sky was a cerulean blue that said clouds were unlikely, and the sun was a brilliant diamond that promised it wouldn't stay this cool for long. The air was scrubbed clean, not a shred of smog in sight. As I had many times before, I thought that days like this were probably the norm for L.A. back in the '30s. I decided on a roomy cream-colored blazer but had to settle for carrying my .22 Beretta, because the pockets weren't big enough for the .357. I wouldn't ordinarily have made that compromise, but since I'd be wearing the vest, I still felt loaded for bear. Especially since, after I got to work, I'd be with one cop or another all day—and they got to carry .44s.

On my walk to the office, I told myself that I was moving fast so I could squeeze in some aerobic benefit to make up for all the gym days I'd missed recently. True or not, my effort was significantly encumbered by the stiff, heavy bulletproof vest that made me feel like I was climbing up the side of a building. After just two blocks, I was already out of breath. Terrific. If someone wanted to shoot me now, the vest was my only hope, because I sure as hell couldn't outrun them. As I slogged my way up the hill, I reconsidered the possibility that the shooting yesterday might have been a random event. The more I thought about it, the more I convinced myself that it had to be. I sincerely doubted that ours was the first unreported shooting in that area, which meant it would probably be impossible to figure out what kind of bullets had been fired at us. The more I thought about it, the happier I was that we hadn't reported it. Though, given the sirens I'd heard, it was likely someone—maybe a teacher at the school—must have.

I picked up my pace and furtively looked around for baggy clothing or tattoos. I keyed in on the guy selling churros from a push-cart. I thought his pants looked pretty loose. He caught my gaze. When our eyes met, he started to give me what probably used to be his sexy smile. He looked like he was about ninety, and his sexy smile needed work. It'd probably been a very long time since he'd seen someone checking out the junk in his trunk. Unless someone was looking at his car.

I blew out a sigh of relief as I briskly pushed through the doors of the Criminal Courts Building and ran for the elevator, but a familiar sight brought me to a stomach-lurching halt. There was no mistaking that thick shock of salt-and-pepper hair. Or the sound of that rich baritone voice. Daniel Rose, my ex. My heart beat slow and hard as I watched him chatting easily with a couple of prosecutors at the bank of elevators. My vision blurred, and suddenly I couldn't breathe. I quickly turned away and moved into the crowd near the metal detector. Of all days to run into Daniel, I thought, it had to be today. Since our breakup, dating was a rare occasion for me. My last date—a mini-break for coffee in the outdoor café of the Ahmanson Theater—had been four months ago. What kind of sick twist was it that I had to see him today? Feeling defeated by fate, I waited for his elevator to arrive and finally allowed myself to breathe when I heard the ding and saw the doors close. I moved out to the nearest elevator on leaden feet and punched the up button.

On the eighteenth floor, I ran into Toni as I was getting off the elevator.

"Hey, you!" she said. Then she stopped and looked at me more closely. "What's up? Are you okay?"

I nodded wordlessly, not wanting to tear up in front of the whole world. Toni pulled me into the ladies' restroom across the hall. Luckily we had the space to ourselves.

"I just saw Daniel downstairs," I said quietly. I swallowed and tried to push the lump out of my throat.

"Oh my God, I'm so sorry, honey." Toni put her arms around me and patted my back.

I held on to her and breathed for a moment, grateful for the comfort. After a minute, I pulled away. "Thanks, Toni," I said. "I just feel like I'm never going to get over him, and I'm sick of feeling this way."

"And you'll keep feeling that way until you *are* over him. You know what I mean?"

"No, I really don't."

"You'll be hurting until you won't be anymore. It just takes time," she said gently. "And you'll probably always feel at least a *little* something when you think of Daniel, because he's a good guy. That's how it is with the good guys."

I nodded.

"And you also haven't really tried to see anyone else. That's keeping it fresh too." Toni looked at me with a steady gaze.

I returned her stare for a moment, then looked away. Toni and Bailey had been trying to get me back out in the mix for at least six months. So far I hadn't been able to make it past a single cup of coffee, let alone into a relationship. But I didn't tell her about my lunch date with Graden because I was seriously thinking about canceling, and I knew Toni would try to talk me out of it. And I admitted to myself that I probably hadn't told her before this because, deep down inside, I'd had a feeling I'd want to get out of it anyway.

I hugged her again.

Toni leaned back, held my shoulders, and looked me in the eye. "You going to be okay now?"

I nodded. "Work beckons," I said with a rueful smile.

"Your great escape," she agreed. "I'm around if you need me. Okay?"

"Yeah." I sighed. I knew I wouldn't want to talk about it, though. I never did.

Toni gave me a knowing smile. She knew that too.

We walked out into the hallway. The ding of the elevator sounded, and Toni trotted out to catch it. She stepped inside and blew me a kiss, and I smiled and blew one back. I punched in the security code and made my way toward my office, lifting my hand to wave to Melia as I passed by Eric's anteroom. Her head was bowed, and she was staring down into her lap, reading one of her tabloid mags under the desk. That meant Eric had probably just left for a meeting, because she knew better than to let him catch her at it.

I tried not to look at the police seal on Jake's door as I headed for my office. The bright-yellow tape was like an open wound. Part of me wished they'd take it down; another part of me was glad, because it meant the case was still open.

With those happy thoughts, I opened my office door to find my intercom buzzing.

I quickly slipped out of my jacket and began unfastening my vest as I answered. It was Melia.

"Mark Baransky on the . . . uh . . ." Melia stuttered to a stop, having forgotten the name of the case he was calling about, although he'd probably just given it to her seconds ago. *Poor thing,* I thought, *it must be hard to remember dumb old case names when you're concentrating on important stuff like which celebrity is banging someone else's wife's daughter.*

"The Duncan case. I've got it, Melia," I said, then switched over to the line with the blinking light and kicked my vest under the desk. I couldn't let anyone know I had it, or there'd be questions.

"Hey, Mark, your guy ready to plead?" His client Ramon Duncan had murdered a husband and wife during a home-invasion robbery. The office had decided to go for the death penalty, but I'd told the lawyer I could probably talk the brass into a sentence of life without parole if his client would plead to the sheet.

"Yeah, and he's asking for death. Says he knows how busy you are and doesn't want you to have to bother with a trial."

Lawyers are fun. "I'm glad someone finally understands. Tell your client that I'll put a letter in his file about how grateful we are for all his tips on the Aryan Brotherhood." A note like that about the notorious prison gang would get his client killed within minutes.

"Knight, you're a riot." He laughed a little uncertainly.

I didn't join in the mirth. Let him squirm. "What's up?"

"I'm going to run a few motions, try to

get some evidence thrown out, but I've got a trip to Greece planned, so I won't be able to do it at the next setting. I'll need a continuance," Mark said.

"Let me make sure I've got this right: you want me to agree to put the case over so you can have time to take a vacation before you come back and try to gut my case."

"That's about it. But, look, fair's fair. If you've got any trips planned, I promise to go along with a continuance for you. Deal?"

This only rubbed salt in the wound, because not only did I not have time to go anywhere, but I couldn't really afford any trips—especially not to Greece.

"Yeah, I'll take you up on that offer real soon," I said sarcastically. Defense attorneys have to deal with the miseries of representing criminals, but the money they get is a nice consolation prize. "You are such a putz, Mark. What date do you want?" I said, looking at my calendar.

The morning flew by after that point. There was a lot to catch up on. By the time I finished making and returning calls, it was noon. After the way my day had started, I'd lost my appetite for a lunch date. I'd just begun to hope that I was being stood up when Lieutenant Graden Hales called.

"Want to meet me outside the building?" he asked.

My "sure" came out a little frostier than I'd intended. Without much enthusiasm, I made a token effort at a touch-up of lip gloss and eye shadow, tried and failed to fluff up my hair, and threw on my blazer. I decided I could dispense with the vest for now—after all, I was going to be with a cop. I grabbed my purse and headed out to the elevator as I devised ways to cut this lunch as short as possible.

21

He wasn't standing on the sidewalk in front of the building when I got there, so I glanced at my watch to see if I'd made un-usually good time in the elevator. I hadn't. It was almost a quarter past noon. Maybe he'd given up? Feeling more relieved than disappointed, I was about to head back into the building when someone in a new black 750Li BMW honked the horn insis-tently. I looked up and down the street to see who wasn't getting the message. A car in front of the BMW pulled away from the curb, and the BMW pulled forward. When the passenger window slid down, the driver leaned over.

"Sorry, I forgot to tell you I'd be driving," Graden said apologetically.

Or maybe *what* he'd be driving. What was a cop doing with a hundred-thousand-dollar car? Maybe he was one of those people who lived in lean-tos so they could drive some fancy wheels. Somehow I hadn't made him for that kind of guy.

"Not a problem, Lieutenant." I got in and buckled up, wondering what I'd gotten myself into.

He looked at me and gave a small smile. "Does 'Graden' sit okay with you? Or at least Hales?"

"I think I can manage Graden." I didn't tell him he could call me Rachel.

He pulled out into traffic, and I glanced at him sideways. I noticed that he had a slight tan—in winter. What was that all about? And he was wearing an expensive-looking gray sports jacket and white dress shirt, open at the neck. A tasteful patch of chest hair peeked out just at the top of the V. And no gold chains. Thank God. I settled back into the cushy leather seat as he navigated. The streets were packed with aggressive drivers and pedestrians who'd been crowded off the sidewalks and were weaving their way through the gridlock. When he'd managed to squeeze out the other side of the snarl and headed toward Beaudry, I asked, "Where are we going?"

"PDC. I'm in the mood for a Bloody Mary. Sound good?"

It sounded more than good. The Pacific Dining Car was an actual old railroad dining car that had been converted into an intimate, Frank Sinatra / Dean Martin–style restaurant with great lobster, steak, and one of the best bars in town. It was a favorite of mine, and it was known for making great Bloody Marys too. But it was pricey, so the PDC was strictly a special-occasion place for me. Graden pulled into the driveway and handed the keys to the valet.

The host, Fred Astaire in slacks and a navy-blue blazer, greeted Graden by name and led us to a quiet booth in the bar area. Behind the bar was a full wall of liquors from just about everywhere in the world. The pin-dot lighting made the bottles glow like jewels in the cool darkness, and the bartender, in his shirtsleeves and apron, was backlit, making him look like a painting from the '50s come to life. As we slid into the booth, the host flipped open the linen napkin that had been folded on the table and set it expertly in my lap, then did the same for Graden. He handed each of us a menu, and the lieutenant ordered a Bloody Mary, as threatened. Although I didn't usually drink at lunch, I decided, since I didn't have any court appearances and my heavy work was done, to splurge and ordered one too.

I was lousy at making small talk and didn't want to pretend otherwise. But that left me with shoptalk—I'd be good with it, but experience had taught me that not everyone shared my appetite for all work, all the time. I'd planned to use this lunch to find out what was happening on Jake's case, but given Graden's past tight-lipped attitude, it seemed smarter to hold off and wait for the right moment.

He solved the problem for me. "I hear you and Bailey have a pretty hot lead on the Densmore rape case."

The knot that I hadn't even known was in my stomach began to unravel. I brought him up to speed, ending with our efforts to chase down our prime suspect, Luis Revelo.

"Have they run the rape kit through to see if it matches anyone in the database?" he asked.

"Yep. No hit. But that doesn't mean Revelo's not our guy. For some reason, he managed to dodge the DNA-testing bullet."

"Low-level rap sheet?"

I nodded. "Chicken-shit stuff, mostly a year or two ago. Seems to have cleaned up his act, or—"

"Gotten much better at it," he said. "Some of these shot-callers are smart. They keep their hands clean and let the little guys do the dirty work."

"They're getting more like politicians every day," I agreed.

Graden chuckled, and the white-coated waiter brought our Bloody Marys and took our orders. We both stirred and then sipped appreciatively.

"Perfect," I said. Just enough Tabasco and spice to give it a kick, not so much that you couldn't taste anything else.

We chatted on about our other cases, and the conversation flowed effortlessly over common ground. There was an easiness between us that went beyond our careers, though I couldn't really pinpoint why. All I knew was that this was one of the most fun, stress-free, unawkward first dates I'd ever had. My quest to squeeze information out of Graden about Jake's case lurked in the back of my mind, but I didn't want to force the issue and possibly spoil not only our lunch but my chances of ever getting him to talk to me about it. I decided to wait and see if our conversation took us there naturally. I can be patient when it matters. After the waiter brought our orders—Graden opted for steak; I chose the grilled trout—I mentioned the lawyer who'd called to get a continuance so he could go to Greece.

"Great time of year to go," Graden mused with a faraway look. "I spent ten days in Crete last year. Love that place." He went back to his drink, so he didn't see my look of disbelief. First the late-model BMW, then the PDC for lunch, now Crete. *What the hell?*

Finally he glanced up and saw my expression. "I sell dope on the side," he said with a grin.

"Oh good. I was worried you might be doing something sleazy. Like movie-set security."

He chuckled and I waited for the explanation. He gave it.

"I loved video games as a kid. Actually, 'addicted' is more the word for it. I got into making up my own games after a while. It was just a hobby. I never considered doing it full-time," he said.

"I'm guessing you didn't play Grand Theft Auto," I remarked. The cops were always getting shafted by the crooks in that game.

"No, that was a little after my time," he said. "Probably a good thing. I would've lived a life of crime and wound up getting prosecuted by you." He smiled.

"I might've cut you a deal, you never know," I replied.

Graden smiled even wider, then continued. "My brother, Devon, is a computer whiz, works at Hewlett-Packard. Growing up, he was one of those kids who always knew what they wanted to do. It took me a little longer. While I knocked around doing odd jobs, trying to figure out who I wanted to be, I'd dream up video games. After I got into the police academy, I came up with Code Three."

I nodded.

"You've heard of it."

"I have," I replied. Code Three—cop lingo for "in pursuit"—was a megahit.

Graden smiled very briefly in acknowledgment. "Frankly, it wasn't my favorite. But Devon was dead sure it would sell, so on his days off he worked on the program. In the meantime, I graduated, got on the force, and lost interest in video games. I told Devon to let it go, but he kept plugging away. Five years later, he'd finished the program and found a buyer—"

"And the rest is history."

Graden shrugged noncommittally. "Pretty much."

I took another sip of my Bloody Mary and tucked into my trout.

"Can I get you another one?" Graden asked, gesturing at my nearly empty drink.

I considered it for a moment, tempted, but declined. "Thanks, I might need my brain for a little longer."

Graden followed suit.

I was struck by his dismissive attitude toward his success. "I'd imagine that game made you rich enough to quit work."

Graden half nodded. "Probably."

"So why don't you?"

He put down his fork and took a sip of

water before answering. "It was kind of a fluke, you know? I don't trust it. At some point, maybe even tomorrow, the kids will decide it's not cool anymore. You'd be surprised how fast money runs out when you're just spending and not earning." Graden picked up his knife and fork and cut another piece of steak. "I don't take risks when it comes to paying the rent."

"And yet you're a cop," I remarked. "Hardly a risk-free proposition."

"But it's a steady paycheck," he pointed out.

I nodded even as I thought his logic made no sense. I knew something about video-gaming money—it was huge, especially for a success like Code Three. Yet that wasn't enough security for him, so he stayed in a job that was frequently life-threatening. It was an unusual paradox—one I'd bet had stemmed from an unstable childhood. These kinds of complications made people so interesting.

Graden chewed his steak for a moment, then grinned. "Besides, you've seen me in my uniform. *I'd* do me in that uniform."

I laughed almost as hard as he did.

"I have a confession," he said.

"Listening," I said, intrigued and only mildly alarmed.

"You live at the Biltmore Hotel."

He knew where I lived? First my cell phone number, now this.

Graden picked up on my reaction. He looked at me, his expression mildly puzzled. "I took you home, remember?"

Right. On the night of Jake's murder. "Of course." I smiled, embarrassed. "Sorry."

And now that I thought about it, why was I all het up about Graden finding out where I lived when gangbangers had already done the same?

"My confession is that I can't figure out how an underpaid civil servant can afford a luxury hotel."

"I could let you dwell in the mystery."

"But that would be cruel and, I'm guessing, very unlike you."

"How would you know?" I said.

Graden gave me a measured look. "Fair enough," he said mildly. "And?"

For a moment, I toyed with the idea of thwarting him, but since I really didn't mind telling the story, I relented. "You remember the Biltmore CEO's wife who got killed last year?" I began.

Graden squinted, searching his memory. "Sheriff's case, right?"

I nodded. "There was some big muckety-muck meeting, and the CEO decided to bring his family to the hotel, combine business with pleasure. He got stuck in a late dinner meeting, so his wife went to the concert at the Disney Hall alone—"

"And she got robbed and murdered in the underground parking lot by a meth freak," Graden interjected. "I didn't know that was your case."

"Yeah, I'd been staying at the hotel for about a week when I caught the case. Just a weird coincidence." I sensed that the question about why I was staying there in the first place was on the tip of his tongue. The truth was, when my mother was diagnosed with melanoma two years ago, I'd moved into her house to take care of her. When she passed away six months later, I couldn't bear to move out at first. It'd been a comfort to see my mother's furniture, the pictures on the mantel, her dishes—it felt as though she were still there. But after my breakup with Daniel, everything changed. Suddenly the house became a symbol of loss, and what had been my cocoon was now a dark place from which I'd had to escape. Not wanting to talk about any of this, I moved on quickly. "Anyway the CEO let me stay at the hotel for free while the trial was going on so I wouldn't be distracted with having to move. When I got the asshole defendant sent up for life without parole, the CEO gave me such a good deal on the suite, I couldn't afford to leave."

"For how long?" Graden asked.

"I keep offering to leave, but he always tells me not to look a gift horse in the mouth, so I'm following orders," I said.

"Which for you is certainly a first," he remarked.

It didn't take a detective to know that much about me. The thought brought me back to the Densmore case. "You happen to know anything about the Sylmar Sevens?" I thought he might remember something from his patrol days.

He frowned, thinking, then said, "Valley gang—specializes in burglary and dope."

I nodded.

"You a meat eater?" Graden asked.

"Is that some kind of guy code for something else?"

"Yeah, it's code for 'Do you eat meat?'"

"Oh, sure."

"You've got to taste this." He speared a piece of his steak on his fork and held it out to me.

I hesitated for just a fraction of a second at the intimacy of the gesture, but I took the fork from him. The steak was so tender it practically melted in my mouth, the rich, full flavor of it unfettered by unnecessary sauces or marinades.

"Fantastic, thank you. Is that the rib eye?" I asked, handing the fork back to him.

He nodded. "It's always good here, but this time it's spectacular. What about the Sylmar Sevens?"

"I was wondering whether they'd merged with another gang, gotten bigger lately."

"Why?"

I'd been giving the whole situation a lot of thought. Something about it didn't hit me right. "It just seems like a big, dumb move to do a rape in the Palisades, where they know the cops will go nuts—especially since our suspect was being tutored by the victim."

"Someone else in the gang did it to show off?"

"Maybe. Or maybe someone did it

knowing we'd suspect Revelo, and they wanted to get him out of the way so they could take over as the new shot-caller." I didn't share the additional thought that maybe Revelo's loyals were fighting back by warning me off.

"And if the new gang is big enough, it'd be worth a risky move like that to take over as leader," Graden said, thinking aloud. "I can check it out for you."

"Revelo's still in the wind, so it'd be nice to have all the background before he's in pocket."

Graden's phone rang, and as he checked the number, I looked at my own cell. Two thirty. I couldn't believe it. Where had the time gone?

When he looked up, I said, "I've got to get back. I—"

He waved off my apology. "No problem. Me too."

When the waiter came with the check, I reached into my purse, but Graden stopped me.

"I've got this," he said.

I'm not sure why, but I didn't want him to pick up the tab. "At least let's split it," I countered.

Graden paused and took in my determined expression, then replied, "How about you pay next time?"

He really knew how to end an argument.

22

"Thanks for lunch," I said as Graden pulled up in front of the building.

"I'll call you," he said.

I nodded and opened the passenger door.

"Soon," he added with that lazy smile.

I gave him what I hoped was a nonchalant smile of my own and trotted into the building. It was fun to feel pursued again—it'd been a while. But I wished I'd found a good opening to ask him about Jake. I promised myself I'd make it happen the next time, no matter what.

On my way up to the eighteenth floor,

while holding my breath among the masses, I tried to figure out what I was feeling. I'd had a much better time with Graden than I'd expected. But for some reason I was also a little unsettled. I might've given the question more thought, but when I reached my office I found Toni sitting in my chair, her feet up on my desk.

"Where'd you go? I was looking to go out for some sushi," Toni said.

"And you thought you'd find some in my desk?"

She looked sheepish. "I got comfortable. This chair's amazing. And then I found your pretzels." Toni looked around my office. "Man, you've got a lot of cases."

"You ate all my pretzels?" I said, hand-on-hip indignant.

"Please, like I'd eat that junk," Toni said with disdain. "But, seriously, where've you been?"

"I had lunch with Graden."

Toni sat up and let her feet fall to the ground with a thunk. "Graden," she said. "Lieutenant Graden Hales? No kidding?"

"Nope."

Toni had a surprised smile on her face. "How'd it go? Does Bailey know?"

"Not yet, but I'll tell her as soon as I can, so don't worry about having to keep a secret," I reassured her.

"And Graden?" Toni prompted.

I thought about it for a moment, sorting through my feelings. "I guess it went pretty well."

"Pretty well?" Toni remarked with a wry smile. "Compared to all the others, that's a home run." She looked pleased. "Well, I'll be damned," she said as she stood.

"It was just a lunch, Tone."

Toni waved her hand as she walked to the door. "I know, I know. But it's progress, isn't it? One meal at a time."

I wasn't sure, so I didn't answer.

"Oh, will you stop," Toni said, giving me an exasperated look. "Fine. It's better than nothing. How's that?"

I nodded, grinning. "About right."

"I hate it when you get all gushy like this," Toni said. She started out of my office, then stopped. "Oh, and I owe you a bag of pretzels." She took two more steps, then stopped again and said over her shoulder, "And a roll of mints." Then she turned and wiggled her fingers behind her head as she left. "Later," she sang out.

I checked my messages. The usual defense whining for deals and continuances. I shuffled through them quickly until I got to one from Olive Horner, Kit Chalmers's last foster mother. I was surprised to hear from her. I'd been leaving her messages for the past couple of days, ever since Kevin had given me her name, but I'd given up hope when my calls went unreturned. I picked up the phone and punched in the numbers. On the fourth ring, a tired-sounding woman answered. I heard kids screaming over a daytime soap opera in the background and cringed at the mental image conjured by the sounds.

"Ms. Horner, this is Rachel Knight . . . from the DA's office."

"You gonna help me get my county payments? They owe me for three months on the baby."

Mystery solved. She'd returned my call for the promise of cash. "Sorry, ma'am, I don't work in that department. I'm a prosecutor. I only handle criminal cases. I called to talk to you about Kit."

"Oh." She paused a moment to absorb the unexpected shift, then said, "Well, Feds already talked to me."

The FBI had managed to find someone after all. I had to tread lightly, or Olive would start wondering what was up.

"We just have a few more questions. Some areas they probably didn't cover. We'll be happy to come whenever it's easy for you, and we won't take more than a few minutes of your time," I replied, trying to sound official and undesperate.

Olive paused long enough for me to hear a male voice in the background promise that a fascinating career as a dental hygienist could be mine. I pictured a job leaning over open mouths all day. I decided to stick with prosecuting.

"Well, okay. But I don't know what I can tell you. I mean . . ."

She trailed off. I could imagine what she was thinking. It wasn't just that she'd spoken to the FBI; it was that he was dead, and there was nothing more to do about him. It wasn't cold so much as it was pragmatic. In a life overfilled with obligations and not enough means to meet them, grief was a luxury she couldn't afford.

"I won't take much of your time. Really."

Olive fell silent, and I listened to the drone of the television and the shrill screams of children. After a moment, she sighed. "Come on over. But make it before six o'clock. I've got dinner to get to. You know where I live?"

I confirmed the address and directions and then punched Bailey's number. We were on the road by 4:00, which is rush hour wherever you are in this city. Olive and her brood lived just outside Silver Lake, about ten minutes from downtown as the car was supposed to fly but double that in this traffic. We crawled along Temple, taking the surface streets to avoid the impossible gridlock of homebound freeway travel on the northbound 101.

The night sky was already encroaching in purples and grays, but the final rays of sun slanting low across the hoods of the cars flashed a blinding light that made the visibility near zero. It was almost as bad as the whiteout of driving in a thick fog. I always marveled at how L.A. drivers managed to avoid major road carnage at times like this.

The house was on Madera, just a few blocks outside the gentrification efforts that had promised to turn Silver Lake into a hot spot. Now, some ten years since that promise, the effort showed only in a small pocket of the neighborhood. The areas outside that enclave might as well have been in any lower-income ghetto. The quaint shops, chic restaurants, and sophisticated home renovations stopped abruptly at an invisible boundary. Across it, there was nothing but run-down, tiny adobe-style homes with postage-stamp yards largely gone to seed, and apartment buildings that hadn't been maintained since they went up in the '60s. Crowded between the homes and apartments were down-at-the-heels grocery shops, windowless bars, strip joints with garishly painted walls and faded signs, and liquor stores that sold no booze that cost more than ten dollars a bottle.

I slumped down in the passenger seat and imagined what it would be like to live here. I ruminated on the unfairness of a world where the Frank Densmores lived like royalty, and the Olive Horners lived like paupers. By the time we pulled up in front of the faded-yellow ranch-style house and its dying front lawn, littered with broken trikes and discarded dolls, I was in one heavy funk of a mood.

As I followed Bailey through the little

front gate, I saw that she was feeling it too. I let her do the door-knock and told myself we'd get out of there as fast as we could.

I heard the faint din of a television and the plastic voice of a talking action figure. A woman's voice called out, "Just a minute." Eventually a bored teenage girl appeared with a baby casually slung on her hip. With the opening of the door, the faint din turned to a roar, and the smell of cheap food cooked in lots of grease was thick in the air. The baby played with the girl's long, mousy brown hair. The girl didn't seem to notice.

"Hi, I'm Rachel Knight from the DA's office, here to see Olive Horner. This is Detective Bailey Keller."

The girl's hands were wound around the baby, so I couldn't do the usual introductory handshake. She invited us in, then yelled over her shoulder, "Mom!" She gestured with her head that we should go into the tiny living room that housed the blaring television. I felt something—a Frito—crunch under my shoe as I walked inside and was transported back in time. I hadn't thought about Fritos since I was twelve. The living room was predictably crowded with toys, kids' blankets and pillows. Baby bottles and half-empty juice cups competed on nearly every surface with half-eaten Pop-Tarts, open cheese-and-cracker-combo packages, and other assorted prefab-food delights.

I looked around for an open space to sit and found none. I'd resigned myself to standing when Olive came in.

All her colors were faded, as though she'd been run through the wash too many times, and the sag of her features spoke of little sleep and too much worry for too many years. She looked me up and down, then threw a Power Ranger and a stuffed tiger off the couch and waved us over.

"Sorry about the mess," she said wearily. "Hard to keep up."

"You've got a lot on your plate, Ms. Horner. I'm just grateful you could make the time for us," I said.

"Call me Olive—I already feel like the Old Woman Who Lived in a Shoe, don't need to feel any older." She brushed back her hair, exposing gray roots at the sides.

"How many kids do you have?" Bailey asked, her tone understanding.

"Right now, I've got five—four are foster care, but the teenager's mine. They tell me the baby's probably going to wind up adopted. He's a cute little thing. Tell you the truth, I'll miss him." Olive sighed. "But since the state's behind on his payments, I'll be glad to see him get into a decent home where they can give him what he needs."

The struggle of her life was a palpable presence in the room. I felt tired just looking at her. The only thing I could think to say was "I'm sorry," but that was useless, and Olive wasn't looking for my pity or anyone else's. The only thing I could do for her was get out of her hair as soon as possible.

"How long did you have Kit Chalmers?" I asked.

Olive threw a stuffed Clifford the Big Red Dog onto the cluttered coffee table and sat down on the chenille-covered rocker across from us. The baby on the teenage girl's hip had either grown bored with the girl's hair or gotten hungry, and he started to cry.

"Janzy, give me the baby," Olive said. The girl looked glad to be rid of her burden as she unloaded him into Olive's outstretched arms, then sauntered out of the room.

When Olive had gotten the baby settled in with a bottle, she continued. "He was already fifteen years old and busted for prostitution by the time I got him. CSSD called him a challenge. Still, I couldn't blame him, coming from where he did." Olive shook her head sadly at the memory.

The Child Support Services Department used euphemisms like "challenge" to avoid stigmatizing a kid. I thought that was like closing the barn door after the animals took off. "You know something about his mom?" I asked. If Kit's mother was still in the picture, she might lead us somewhere.

"All's I know from the agency is that she was the usual meth-head loser and that Kit'd been passed around between foster homes since he was a baby." Olive patted the infant's bottom comfortingly and looked down at him affectionately as he held his bottle in a death grip. The sight made my heart ache for all the babies who'd never see a mother look at them that way. "Little ones," she said fondly. "You got to focus, or they get into some serious trouble." Olive's expression suddenly hardened as she said, "Only damn thing those meth freaks can focus on is a pipe."

"You know whether Kit still had any contact with his mom?" I asked.

"Not as far as I could tell. And not with his last foster parents either," Olive said with a grunt of disgust. "What a bunch of useless losers. Let him run the streets and just collected the checks. Like to see them get nailed for it." She peered at me skeptically. "Don't suppose you could do anything about that either, right?"

I thought for a minute. "We might. We'll definitely look into it."

"As far as you know, was Kit still hooking when he died?" Bailey asked.

"He said he was working at Target, in the stockroom."

"But you didn't believe him."

"I was born in the morning but not yesterday morning. I tried to tell him why it was bad to be throwing himself around like that. But it was too late," she said, shaking her head sadly. "Sometimes, when I get 'em at that age, they can still listen. But Kit—that kid was one tough case. He'd feed me a load of crap about what he was up to 'cuz he didn't want me to toss him out like the others did. I told him I'd never do that—but he didn't believe me. Maybe if I'd had more time . . ."

She frowned, and the lines on her forehead and around her eyes deepened into crevices, a preview of the apple-doll face she was going to have way too soon.

"Which Target did he supposedly work in?" I asked.

"Down on Santa Monica Boulevard, by La Brea."

The location was on the outskirts of West Hollywood, affectionately known as Boys-Town because it was largely a gay enclave.

"He hang with anyone you know of?" I asked.

Olive thought for a moment. "I seem to remember a couple of young guys, but they only came round a few times. And there was a girl—had a weird name, Teecheetah, or . . . Janzy! Hey, girl! You remember that girl Kit used to hang with? What was her name?"

Janzy sauntered in, eating Jell-O out of a plastic cup. "You don't gotta yell, Mom, I can hear you." She turned to us and said lazily, "I think she was, like, his girlfriend."

The baby had finished his bottle, and Olive placed him on her shoulder to burp him.

Janzy reached out for the baby. "I can do that, Mom." Olive handed him over, and Janzy settled the baby on her shoulder and began to gently thump his back. "Her first name was T'Chia—I can't remember her last name, but you can find her easy. She works at that Target on Santa Monica, and she's real short, orange hair in spikes, pierced nose, spider tatt on her neck."

Anywhere else, that description would be enough to pick her out in a crowd. Not in L.A. But at least someone really worked at Target.

"Did Kit ever say anything to you about the DA they found him with, Jake Pahlmeyer?" I asked.

"No." Olive shook her head slowly. "Not that it means anything. That kid never told me much, and what he did tell me was mostly lies. But I'd sure like to know what really happened. I know this'll sound bad, but I can't say I'm real surprised. Kit was hell-bent on disaster—I could see that from a mile away."

Janzy chimed in. "He wasn't, like, evil or

anything. He was just trying to make it, find a place in the world, but it never worked out. Like, he wanted to be normal, but he just didn't know how. He'd bring home stuff for the kids when he could, play with them sometimes. But then he'd be gone—we wouldn't see him for days." She paused, remembering. When she spoke again, her voice was angry. "Anyways, he didn't deserve what happened to him, you know?" She paused the burping to roughly brush away a tear, then tossed her hair back with a flick of her head and walked out of the room, toward the rear of the house.

"I gotta agree with her there," Olive said. "Whatever he was, an' I know it wasn't great, dyin' in that motel room wasn't what was comin' to him."

I thought Olive was probably right on all counts.

23

I usually leave my card with witnesses so they can call if they think of anything they forgot to mention. But since neither Bailey nor I was supposed to be there, I just told Olive we'd be in touch, mentally prayed she wouldn't mention seeing us if the FBI talked to her, and headed for the car.

We pulled away from the curb. "Target?" Bailey asked, looking straight ahead.

"Yep." We didn't know when T'Chia was working, but since we were sort of close by, I figured we might as well give it a shot.

I don't know whether I'd rather be lucky or good, but it was definitely nice to get lucky. T'Chia Arendt was there, and when we told her why we'd come, she agreed to spend her break talking to us in the fast-food court at the front of the store. Bailey and I commandeered one of the small, molded plastic tables and waited for her. The pizza smelled like it'd been there for hours, but it made me hungry anyway. The trout I'd had for lunch had been tasty but not filling. And pizza always makes my mouth water—even the stale, cardboardy specimens in the glass case.

"What're we going to say if someone from the task force sees us here?" Bailey asked.

I was watching what the shoppers in the checkout line were buying to see if there was anything I just had to have. I've found some amazingly good deals there in the past. A pair of comfy-looking white capris had snagged my attention, so it took me a moment to refocus.

"We tell 'em we heard about a great sale on bras?"

"Sure," Bailey said dryly.

T'Chia hurried over and pulled out a chair. Janzy's description had been right on the money. Just over five feet, T'Chia wasn't so much plump as roundish. Her hair was black at the roots, and it shot out from her head in orange spikes. The spiderweb tattoo, replete with resident spider, spread across her neck, from which she'd hung a skull necklace. So far, so good—or at least consistent. But she'd taken a different tack from the neck down, with a pink bolero sweater, a short plaid skirt, and half-laced black Doc Martens. I'm completely on board with fashion as an expression of individuality, but T'Chia seemed to be expressing several individuals.

I tried to make my smile friendly and suppressed the chuckle that wanted to bubble up. "Thank you for making time for us. We really appreciate it."

T'Chia gave us a polite nod and got right down to business. "I don't know if anyone told you this, but Kit and I, we were totally in love. People talk all kinds of shit—" She stopped abruptly, her eyes round with alarm at having used a swearword in front of us.

There was something sweet about that.

"Please don't worry about that . . . shit," I said with a smile. I am so cool.

She nodded, relieved. Probably didn't

know how to get through more than a few sentences without hitting a four-letter-word bump. I could relate.

T'Chia leaned in, her expression intense, earnest. "They say he was, like, sketchy, and I know he was into some nasty shit, but he was good inside, you know? No one knew him like I did."

The lines were delivered with maximum heartrending angst. Teens can wring drama out of the way paint dries, but having been in love with a boy who'd been killed under strange and mysterious circumstances was the jackpot of teen tragedy. Unless he then turned into a vampire. *That* was the mega-jackpot.

"How long had you been together?" I asked. T'Chia had made it sound like they'd been sweethearts since their sandbox days.

"Three months."

Three months?

T'Chia continued, unaware of how this answer might have undermined her profession of eternal love. "But we kind of hung around for a couple of months before that, since the semester started," she added.

Oh. Five months, not three. Now it all made sense.

Abruptly, she stood. "I'm going to get a drink. You want anything? I can get it for you. I get a discount."

It was a gracious offer, but we declined. It was bad enough we were talking to Kit's girlfriend; we didn't have to compound it by accepting freebies from her.

She returned in a jiffy, big plastic cup in hand, and sat back down.

"You guys ever hang out after school?" I asked.

"Yeah, but he'd mainly visit me here. I didn't have a lot of free time, between school and work."

This relationship was sounding less and less like Romeo and Juliet and more and more like Fagin and Oliver Twist—Kit cadged free drinks and food, and T'Chia got to pretend she had a boyfriend.

"You know who his friends were?" I asked.

She shrugged. "He didn't really hang with anyone all that much. Maybe Eddie and Dante. He brought them here a couple of times."

The kids we'd spoken to in the school cafeteria. We'd have to push harder on them. From what I'd seen so far, they seemed to be the only real connection Kit had.

"What about the DA guy they found him with? You ever hear Kit talk about him?" I asked. It stung to call Jake "the DA guy," but I didn't want to let on that this was a personal thing for me.

"Nuh-uh." She shook her head, thinking. "But he once told me he knew someone important who always had his back. Maybe that was him?"

An interesting wrinkle, and maybe a glimmer of light. If it was Jake, then maybe it was an innocent thing and Jake was just being kind to a kid with a rough life. Then again, it might also mean Jake was being much too "kind." I steeled myself for the answer to my next question.

"You think he might've been, uh, involved with that person?"

T'Chia's face suddenly reddened and her eyes teared up. "Kit was not gay! Those asshole FBI guys tried to say the same thing, but it's not true. I knew Kit was into some weird stuff—I'm not stupid! But deep down he was good and sweet, and I'm friggin' tired of people saying that shit about him!"

"I'd be pissed off too, T'Chia," I said. I meant it, but I had the ulterior motive of needing to calm her down. If she had any more information, I needed to get it fast and get out of there. I was becoming increasingly nervous about sitting out in the open with her.

"Did Kit talk to you about coming into money soon? Any big score?"

"Not that I remember," she said. "I mean, he talked about making it big all the time, but that was just, like, win-the-lottery talk and stuff."

But I'd seen her eyes flicker away as she answered. I knew I'd hit on something. I knew if I pushed her to answer right now, I ran the risk that she'd lie to get rid of me, and I didn't have enough information yet to call her on it.

I needed to dig around so I could come back with enough ammunition to keep her honest. For now, I'd let her think she'd pushed me off. But I'd be back to get the answer. No matter what it was.

24

I woke up the next morning feeling refreshed. I'd ended the day before with a decent workout and a dinner of grilled veggies, then fallen into bed early. The clean and healthy respite had done me good, and I was in an energetic mood. I made my usual vow to make a habit of this . . . and pretended that this time I meant it. I slipped a Herbie Hancock CD into the player to accompany my morning preparations for the day and hummed along to "Driftin'" as I finished my coffee standing in front of my closet, trying to decide what to wear.

I had no expectations of seeing anyone I cared to impress—I resolutely refused to admit to myself that "anyone" meant Graden—and since I didn't have to be in court, I opted for comfort. It was another sunny day so far, but I could see clouds to the west that might roll in quickly. Toni had returned my new red V-necked sweater, so I pulled it on, along with a pair of black wool gabardine slacks and medium-heeled short boots. And, of course, the hated vest. Maybe I'd eventually get attached to that thing and want to wear it everywhere. I pulled my lined black leather jacket over it awkwardly. Maybe not. Then I had a change of heart. Since I had to wear it anyway, why not make the best of it? I took off my jacket, walked over to the mirror, and turned from side to side. I squinted and tilted my head to the left. Viewed from that angle, the vest almost made me look hot. If you liked flat, boxy women. It was all a matter of perspective.

At this point Herbie was wrapping up "Watermelon Man." I pulled my jacket back on, slipped the .357 into my purse, and headed for work.

Fifteen minutes later, I was taking the

long way around the hallways to avoid Jake's office. I knew I'd have to get over this at some point, but it didn't seem to have happened yet. I looked down the hall and noticed that Toni's door was open. It was an unusual but welcome treat for her to be in this early. I walked over and leaned in the doorway. Toni was engrossed in a file, so I knocked to let her know I was there.

She glanced up, and I noticed that she was looking particularly stunning—perfectly coiffed and made up in a jade-green blouse and tight beige skirt.

"What's going on?" I asked.

"I'm in trial on that double homicide I picked up from Jake."

"Oh, you're picking a jury, then? Let me know if you want me to come and look at anyone, give a second opinion."

"No jury today, just motions," Toni said simply.

The too-casual tone was the final tip-off.

"You're in J. D. Morgan's court," I said, amused.

Toni struggled to keep her expression neutral. "I wanted to run this Miranda motion by you," she said, sidestepping my cross-examination. "It might be a problem."

I raised an eyebrow. "Be glad to. In fact, why don't we talk about it over dinner? We can hit Pace. My treat."

Pace, Toni's favorite restaurant, was an intimate dinner house in Laurel Canyon, tucked into a pocket behind the Country Store, where Jim Morrison used to do his grocery shopping. Unflashy but tastefully boheme, with great food and wine, it was a popular insider hang for the Hollywood crowd.

Toni gave me a hard look. "And if I don't have any dish on J.D. and me, you still buying?" she challenged.

"Who are you kidding?" I said, amused. "There'd be a story to tell if all you did was pass each other in the hallway."

Toni acknowledged the point with a rueful smile.

Her on-again, off-again commitment-phobic but never dull relationship with Judge J. D. Morgan was a great source of entertaining material for me. Not that I blamed her for the attraction.

J.D. typified the description "rakishly

handsome," with steel-gray hair, blue eyes that really did twinkle, and a killer body that came from his years on the force and love of amateur boxing. Decades ago, the transition from cop to superior court judge was fairly common. But when the LAPD started to take hits for being unruly cowboys, governors became leery of appointing them to the bench. Nowadays the LAPD has largely outgrown that rap, but it's almost as hard to find an L.A. judge who's a former cop as it is to find a monogamous politician.

Even so, Judge Morgan was the kind of guy who'd have been appointed by any governor at any time. He wasn't the intellectual type, but he was whip-smart with life experience, and a born raconteur with an infectious laugh. Those qualities provided him with an endless collection of invitations to parties thrown by an eclectic bunch of hosts, from hard-core gang detectives to the L.A. Philharmonic crowd.

I'd met him when my arson case got sent to his court for trial. I was braced for a nasty slugfest. The defense attorney, whom we called Snarol, a brand of snail poison—picture the face of a pissed-off snail; that's what he looked like—was known for his short temper and vicious personal attacks. On our first day of pre-trial motions, Judge Morgan had asked what issues we needed to resolve before we started picking a jury. Sure enough, Snarol had jumped to his feet, steam whistling out of his ears.

"The prosecution has been hiding critical evidence! She just handed me these transcripts of my client's statement this morning!" he practically yelled, brandishing a sheaf of papers. "This is outrageous misconduct, and I fully intend to take this to the State Bar!"

"Your Honor, I've given counsel those transcripts three times. Today is actually the fourth. There is no—"

J.D. held up his hand to stop me. "Ms. Knight, I've seen the proof of discovery. I know exactly when you turned them over." Then he looked at the defense attorney, his deep baritone relaxed, even congenial, but firm. "Counsel, I need you to hear me loud and clear: we don't try lawsuits that way in my court. I'm going to give you a piece of advice, and for your sake, I hope you take it: When you go after the prosecutor like that, all I hear is you've got nothing—not the law and not the facts. You want to win a motion in front of me, you'll remember what I just said." It was like magic. For the first time ever, Snarol acted civilized. J.D. often admitted that he was no great legal scholar, yet he had a Zenlike sense of balance. As a result, lawyers on both sides liked him because, in the end, everyone got a fair trial.

The story of Toni and J.D. began by accident. I was about to go into closing argument on my arson case when I realized I'd forgotten a file I needed. With only ten minutes before the jury was due back in, I didn't have time to go up to the office and get it, so I'd asked Toni to bring it to me. The moment she walked into the courtroom and said, "Excuse me, Your Honor," I'd seen the light jump into his eyes. After that, they were hot and heavy for a few months, and they'd seemed to be perfect together. As it turned out, a little too perfect.

Once word got out about the romance, everyone in the building started asking when they were going to set the date. Within a week, they'd both started to backpedal away from each other faster than Russian circus bears. Because one of the main things they had in common was an aversion to commitment. Yet they couldn't completely stay away from each other—that's how good their chemistry was. So every time their paths crossed, they'd pick up where they'd left off and have one hell of a great time—until one or the other got phobic again. Though they couldn't date while the trial was going on, Toni being in J.D.'s court meant they'd certainly get back together once it ended.

A shrink would have a field day with them . . . if either one would go.

"Give J.D. my best," I said. As I turned to go, I added, "And I can see you're already giving him yours."

Toni's pen hit the wall behind me as I walked out into the hall.

I unlocked my door, kicked up the doorstop, and sat down in front of my computer. I had a raft of e-mails from defense attorneys and one from Master Control Freak, aka Daddy Dearest: FrankDensmore@ DensmoreClinics.com. I was surprised his address wasn't MasteroftheUniverse.com. I'd been giving him periodic updates via e-mail to avoid talking to him in person.

Even then, it took a lot of restraint not to tell him what to do with his increasingly irritable, condescending, and amazingly long-winded communications about our failure to bring the obvious culprit to justice.

I was reading the most recent example when my cell phone rang.

"You in your office?" Bailey asked.

"Yep."

"Stay there," she said, then hung up.

I tried to focus on the task at hand while I waited for Bailey to arrive—and failed miserably. What was so urgent and so secret that she couldn't say it on the phone? Fortunately for my impatient self, I didn't have long to wait.

"You won't believe this," she began, striding briskly into my office. "We got a call about a burglary in progress in the Palisades last night."

I looked at her, my eyebrows raised. The Palisades again. I'm not a fan of coincidences, but on the other hand, a burglary in a rich neighborhood is a fairly commonplace event.

"Close to Susan's house?" I asked.

"Close enough. We caught the suspect hiding in another neighbor's backyard." Bailey paused to look at me meaningfully, making sure she had my full attention. She did.

"Our perp is a baby gangster. And his crew?" she said, pausing for effect.

"The Sylmar Sevens," I concluded.

So much for coincidence.

25

I sat back in my chair with a thump. "The Sevens hitting the Palisades makes no sense at all." A well-policed hood like that isn't usually a gang's first choice, especially while there's still heat on the shot-caller for a crime committed in that same area. The more I thought about it, the more it seemed suicidal for them to hit the neighborhood so soon after Susan's rape. It was like hanging a GUILTY sign around Luis Revelo's neck.

Bailey had been watching my reaction. "My thoughts exactly," she said.

"Anyone talk to the guy yet?" I asked.

"They tried. He clammed up, wants his lawyer."

"He got one?"

"Not yet."

Until his lawyer showed up and said otherwise, there'd be no talking. So unless the suspect asked to talk to the cops first—unlikely, given his behavior so far—there was nothing we could do.

For the moment, the conundrum of what the Sylmar Sevens were doing in the Palisades would go unsolved. I turned my attention to Jake's case. "What are you hearing about the double?" I asked. "Any word on physical evidence, stray hairs? Fibers?"

"They're not calling it a 'double.'"

"Screw them. It's not a murder-suicide until I say it is."

"I'll let the FBI know," Bailey said, deadpan. "Anyway, I have no news. They've been keeping everything under lock and key." Bailey paused. A sly look crossed her face. "But I know someone you could ask . . ."

It dawned on me suddenly that I'd forgotten to tell her about my lunch with Graden. Much as I hated to play into her hands after that innuendo, I couldn't put it off and risk her hearing about it from someone else. That would hurt her feelings. Besides, her innuendo actually was my game plan: I *did* intend to squeeze Graden for information.

"I forgot to tell you," I began. I filled her in. When I finished, she looked at me in disbelief.

"You forgot?" she asked.

I shrugged. "And we got busy."

Bailey shook her head, but she was smiling. "It's you. I buy it." She looked out the window for a moment before she said, "It's hard not to shit where you eat, isn't it?"

"Thank you, Elizabeth Barrett Browning," I said dryly. "I assume you mean it's not so smart to date the guy who's heading up the murder investigation on Jake's case."

"No, I mean the opposite. The case won't last forever. And we all work these crazy hours, so where else would we meet someone? I mean, you almost have to shit where you eat."

"You know, I was kind of hungry until you started talking." This was Bailey's way of endorsing the date with Graden, but it was making me queasy.

"Come on, it's just a figure of speech. 'You don't—'"

"Stop," I said, holding up a hand. "Seriously. I'd like to find an appetite again by next week."

Now it was Bailey's turn to shrug. She stood to go but hit a more serious note. "You're wearing your vest, right?"

"Yes, Mother."

Unfazed, she replied, "Call me when you're ready to roll."

I hadn't needed the reminder. Just this morning, the hotel manager had called to ask me, as delicately as possible, when I intended to do something about my car. I had to admit, my little Accord hadn't looked all that great next to the Benzes and Rolls in that garage to begin with, but now that it'd been turned into a mobile tribute to the artistic renderings of Lil' Loco, it stuck out like a Cracker Jack ring in a Tiffany display. I'd been putting it off, but I'd have to get it fixed up soon. The bodywork was going to cost me a chunk of change.

But that wasn't the only reason I hadn't done anything about my little car. For all my solid logic as to why the shooting had been random, the possibility that there might be someone out there gunning for me—literally—was unnerving. And so was that train of thought. I prefer not to fix-ate on life-threatening problems I can't fix, so my mind groped for an alternative. It settled back on Jake's case.

Maybe it was time to stop fighting the pedophile angle and go straight at it. I turned the problem over in my mind as I stared out the window and watched the sidewalks fill with the 4:00 homebound crowd. Desiree, my favorite tranny, in thigh-high boots with a leather miniskirt and her perennial long, wavy blond wig, was making her way up Spring Street in strong, confident strides, looking straight ahead, daring all who passed to ignore her. She always made me smile.

By the time the office had cleared out, I had a plan. Turning to my computer, I tapped out an e-mail to PedoAlert, a vigi-lante group headed by Clive Zorn that was dedicated to the capture of pedophiles and child pornographers. I met him during a child-murder case I'd handled a few years back. The case had been presented to me as a battered-child case, and they'd arrested the nanny. The injuries didn't present a clear-cut case for murder, and there was a strong possibility the jury might buy the nanny's story that the child's neck broke after a fall down the stairs—a scenario that could've led to a complete acquittal.

Clive had called to alert me to the possibility that there might be sexual abuse involved. There were no overt signs of this on the victim, and I'd been warned that Clive and his group were trying to make a name for themselves by claiming there was sexual abuse on high-profile cases so they'd have an excuse to horn in. I'd been leery of him at first when Melia had given me the message saying he'd called. But curiosity, combined with paranoia—at the thought that something might've been missed—made me return his call anyway. When Clive told me that he didn't want any publicity and that he just wanted to give me some tips on what to look for, I'd been surprised. I was still suspicious, but I'd listened.

An hour and a half later, my hair was standing on end—I'd heard more than I ever thought there was to know about all the possible signs of child molestation. I went back to the detectives and made specific requests for follow-up investigations. Among other things, they found a hidden cache of kiddie porn that featured our victim. Since the age of two. Taken by her nanny. And, in several, the nanny had shaken and abused the child in ways that left no bruises. A dicey case turned into a first-degree-murder conviction that sent the nanny to prison for twenty-five years to life.

Since then, I'd recommended Zorn to every deputy I knew and talked him up to reporters every chance I got. Clive had been effusive in his gratitude for my support, so I knew he'd be willing to help. Sure enough, within minutes of my hitting send, my phone rang. I snatched it up after the first ring.

"DA's office, Rachel Knight."

"I'd say it was nice to hear from you, but I'm assuming it's about another pedophile." Clive's surprisingly soft voice had fooled more than one target during the group's sting operations.

I told him what I knew about Jake's case.

"And you want to know what we can find out about your victim, right?"

"Right."

"I'm going to need a copy of Kit's photo-graph—the one that was in Jake's pocket."

I exhaled sharply. I'd been afraid of this. "Can you do any kind of search based on a description?" I asked. Getting a copy of the picture might be impossible, but I thought I could find a way to sneak a look at the pho-tograph.

"I can try, of course. But your definition of a short nose could differ from mine. What you call dark-brown hair might be medium brown to me. So even if your vic-tim's picture is on the Internet, I might not recognize it." I could tell Clive was just be-ginning to wind up for one of his lengthy, precise, and detailed explanations. This was the downside of Clive Zorn. It made him an amazing engineering professor, but it could also make me want to jump out of the window.

He continued in his maddening, nothing-will-rush-me pace. "So you see, Rachel, even if I were to assist you in performing the search after you had described the picture to me, even *you* might not remem-ber the details well enough to recognize his photograph on the Internet, especially if there's distortion of any kind. And, of course, *my* chances of finding a match based only on your description are slimmer still."

He was right. "Yeah, I get it. I'll work on it."

He wished me luck, we said our good-byes, and I hung up. I knew what I had to do, and as much as I hated it, I did it.

He answered on the first ring.

"Graden Hales."

"I know," I said, deadpan. "I dialed the number."

"Just one question," he replied, not missing a beat. "How many times did you get kicked out of class?"

"None. All of my teachers loved me." I managed to say it with a straight face.

"And if they tell me something different?"

"Of course, they'll be lying." Fibbing wasn't my strong suit, so I got to the point. "How about a quick bite at The Cover?" It was a speakeasy-style bistro hidden behind an unmarked door at the back of a historic diner that had been built in the 1930s. Dark, quiet, and fairly new, it hadn't yet been discovered by the Criminal Courts crowd. The Cover would give us plenty of privacy.

"Sounds great," he said. "When?"

When I didn't respond right away, he managed not to sputter.

"You mean right now?"

"I know it's short notice. But, honestly, I need a favor. You may not like it, but even if the answer's no, we've still got to eat, right?"

Graden paused just long enough to make me wonder if he'd hung up on me. "Okay, I'm in. I'm intrigued—and hungry. Meet me downstairs in ten. I'll swing by and pick you up."

26

The soft light emanating from the small glass lamps that hung from the ceiling created a chic but intimate feeling. And it was comforting to see that there wasn't one recognizable face in the crowd. We both ordered salads, but Graden followed his up with beef bourguignonne, while I boringly stuck to roast chicken. Not that it wasn't good, but Graden's dinner looked better. I strained to keep my eyes off his plate.

I didn't really want to ask him for Kit's photo, so I let openings slip by as the internal ethics battle waged inside me. Finally, when the waiter came to clear our dishes, I knew it was do-or-die time. I was just about to take the plunge when Graden put his napkin on the table and leaned forward.

"Okay, Knight. You've been fighting with yourself for the past half hour. Out with it."

I didn't know whether I was impressed or annoyed that he'd read me so easily. "I need that photo they found on Jake. The one of Kit Chalmers."

Graden lifted an eyebrow and looked somewhat taken aback. I'd known it was a lot to ask. Now I realized it was probably too much, and I felt embarrassed and awkward.

Finally Graden spoke. "What for?" he asked.

I explained about my contact in the vigilante group. "If he can find this photograph on the Internet, or others that look similar, I might be able to figure out who took the picture and dig into other possibilities."

"Such as?"

"Everyone's been assuming that Kit was blackmailing Jake. I've been thinking — half of that isn't such a bad hypothesis. But maybe the person Kit was blackmailing wasn't Jake." I knew the theory had holes, and Graden immediately went for the biggest one.

"Then why was Jake the person in the room with him? And why was the photo hidden on Jake's body? And why would Kit bring the photograph if what he wanted was Jake's protection?"

"Obviously I don't have all the answers yet," I said glumly.

"Or any," he said.

I nodded.

Graden continued. "And I hate to keep shooting you down, but the motel clerk remembered that Jake asked for Kit's room number just before the shooting." He looked at me meaningfully.

I gazed down at the table. It wasn't big news, but it didn't help matters either. I wanted to argue that if Jake was up to no good, he wouldn't have spoken so openly to the clerk. But obviously if he'd planned to be dead, that wouldn't have mattered to him.

"There's more."

Graden's tone of voice told me that this time "more" wasn't going to be better.

"We checked Jake's cell phone records. He got a call from Kit earlier that day." Graden paused. "And that wasn't the only one. We found calls between Jake and Kit going back for the past two years."

"How many?"

"Not a lot, not a little. Seemed like every couple of months one or the other would call."

I inhaled slowly, absorbing the news. It wasn't exactly a signed confession, but it didn't help any. I sat gloomily as the weight of it all settled over me.

"Sorry, Rachel," Graden said.

"No, no." I shook my head. "I have to know. If it's true about Jake, then I'm going to have to deal with it." I considered everything again. "But I'm not there yet."

Graden nodded grimly. "I agree. I just want you to be prepared."

I appreciated the thought, if not the implied prediction, and we sat in silence for a moment.

He looked around the room, then turned back to me. "If I do this, you'll have to be extremely careful. That photograph is going to have to stay way under wraps."

The tightness in my chest relaxed, and my shoulders, previously hunched around my ears, dropped down as a sudden wave of relief washed over me.

"And you can trust this vigilante guy not to flash it around or talk about how he got it?" Graden asked.

"Oh yeah," I said with certainty. I'd have to make Clive understand the photograph had to be kept under lock and key without letting him know that his possession of it was illegal. It was a fine line to walk with a big drop on the wrong side of it.

Graden watched me closely. "For both our sakes, I hope you're right," he said finally.

I nodded with as much confidence as I could muster and signaled to the waiter, who'd been standing near the bar with nothing to do. He came quickly, carrying dessert menus. The early diners had left, and the restaurant was quiet. I knew it was just a momentary lull in the action before the real dinner crowd showed up, but for now Graden and I were at one of only three occupied tables.

I turned to him. "Dessert? I hear the crème brûlée is to die for."

"Let's share," he said. "I'm pretty full."

I handed the menu back to the waiter. "One crème brûlée, two spoons, coming up," he said, and left.

"I'm going to ask a favor from you too," Graden said.

"Yes?"

"Next time, don't suffer. I get the feeling you don't like to ask for much. But I don't get bent about being asked for help, especially when it's for a worthy cause. So from now on, you want something, just tell me. I'll do what I can."

The waiter brought the crème brûlée and set out two spoons.

We clinked silverware, broke into the perfectly browned, crispy top layer, and savored the first mouthful. The firm yet creamy pudding was just sweet enough without tipping over into sugary. We didn't talk again until we were both scraping the bowl.

"You'll have to give me some time to get my hands on it when no one's looking. It'll probably be a few days. Where's a safe place to get it to you?" Graden asked as I paid the bill.

"My place. We can meet in the bar. No one we have to worry about ever goes there."

"A girl who's got a bar in her home," Graden remarked with a smile. "You know, there's only one thing that could top that."

"Let me guess. Room service?"

He grinned, getting up from the table. "Are we all that easy to read?"

"Just the ones who're breathing."

27

The next day, I came into the office determined to bury myself in work and stay distracted. I didn't want to think about the increasing likelihood that things were exactly as they seemed with Jake and Kit. Lunch was a turkey wrap at my desk as I worked nonstop, making my way through one case after another. After a few hours, I took a short breather to stretch and look out the window. I noticed that the guard in the parking lot behind the building was asleep in his kiosk. It made me glad I wasn't driving my car to work. Break time over, I turned back to my desk and pushed through the stack of defense motions, sorting out the ones I'd need to answer in writing. I'd had my head down, nose to the grindstone for an unknown amount of time, when I heard Toni's heels come clicking down the hallway. I thought it was early for her to be out of court already, but when I looked up at the clock tower, I saw that it was already a quarter to five. Time flies when you're in avoidance mode.

I called out, "Hey, Toni. How'd it go?"

Standing in my doorway, she looked all amped up. *Here we go again,* I thought, *the Toni and J.D. Show.* It'd be nice if they could manage to hang in there.

"You win every motion, or did he throw the defense a bone or two?" I joked. There was no way Judge Morgan would ever let his relationship with Toni affect his rulings, but I saw no reason why that should stop me from teasing her about it.

Toni rolled her eyes in answer. "He won't let me get in the ADW priors, but I don't really need them. Otherwise my case is looking pretty good . . . knock on wood," she said, rapping on the door frame.

"That's metal, and I agree, you don't

need any assault priors to nail these guys. Your case is solid," I said.

But we both knew that trials were unpredictable things—with just a few of the wrong words from the wrong witness at the right time, a sure winner could turn into a dog—so trial lawyers were notoriously superstitious. That's how I knew that tomorrow Toni would wear her lucky navy "believe me" suit when she started jury selection.

"How you doing?" she asked.

"Had dinner with Graden."

Toni stepped in, closed the door, dropped her briefcase, and sat down. "Talk about burying your lead, girl." She let her shoes drop to the floor and put her feet up on the other chair. "Okay, let's hear it."

I filled her in.

She looked at me shrewdly. "So now he knows you're a pit bull, and now you know he's got a heart."

I nodded. "I just hope this favor doesn't ruin us both."

"Dangerous business, messing around with evidence on an FBI case," Toni agreed. She paused and checked her watch.

"Damn. I've got to run," she said as she hurriedly slipped on her shoes and stood up.

"Where to?" I asked. Toni couldn't date the judge during trial, and I knew she wasn't seeing anyone else.

"I started a water-aerobics class at my gym last week. I've got five minutes to get there," she said, picking up her briefcase and opening the door. "Call me later," she said. "Unless you're in handcuffs." Her laugh echoed down the hall as she walked away.

I assessed the pile of motions on my desk. I'd whittled it down to one motion to suppress a defendant's confession. I could prove the case without it, and generally speaking I wasn't big on using confessions anyway. They were almost always a Trojan horse, a mixture of admission and avoidance, filled with "yes . . . but"s. If a defendant wants to bullshit the jury, let him do it on the witness stand, where I have something to say about it. I wouldn't cry if the judge threw out the confession, so I decided to file a canned response and use the extra time for a workout.

Outside, the late-afternoon sun had waned, but it was still light out. The days were already lengthening, stretching out to reach for spring. I pulled on the hated vest, threw my jacket over it, and felt the reassuring weight of the .357 as I slung my purse over my shoulder. I paused at the door as I remembered I was supposed to call Bailey to come and get me. But it was early, and there were plenty of people in the streets. I decided I could let her have the night off. As I trotted down the hallway, I made a mental note to ask Toni what she thought of her water-aerobics class. It'd be a nice change from my no-frills metal-and-mirrors gym routine.

The last stragglers hurried down the sidewalks toward bus stops and parking lots, their figures casting long shadows on the concrete—a parallel universe of narrow giants that marched smoothly through lampposts and sparsely planted trees. I kept my pace brisk, realizing that night was falling more rapidly than I'd expected.

I'd just cut through Pershing Square when, out of the corner of my eye, I noticed an old Lincoln stop in the middle of the street just ahead of me. I'd barely had a second to register how strange that was when two dark figures leaped out of the backseat, reached me in a couple of long, fast strides, and took me by the arms. I reflexively pulled back and away and started to lift my foot to stomp on an instep when one of them threw a blanket over my head.

They quickly grabbed me by the head and feet, hoisted me up, and ran for the car. I kicked and bucked and tried to scream, but the blanket muffled the sound. I felt myself tossed onto the floor of the backseat, and the hump in the middle hit me in the stomach, winding me. I tried to catch my breath, but between the blanket and the sudden blow to my solar plexus, I couldn't seem to get any air. I began to panic, and my breath came in short, raspy spurts. I felt the two men jump into the backseat, one at each end of me. I heard the car doors slam and then the engine gunning. The car peeled out, slamming my face into the front seat. I gasped in pain and struggled for air that would not come. I felt my head swim and tried to fight what I sensed was coming, but it was too late. My last thought was that no one would find me until I was beyond caring. Then everything went black.

28

I woke to the rumble of the engine and the sensation that I was hurtling through space. Unable to see, I panicked, thinking I was blind, then remembered they'd thrown a blanket over my head. I blinked a few times to reassure myself that my eyes were working. I had no idea how long I'd been unconscious, or in what direction we were headed.

There were at least three people in the car with me, the two in the backseat who'd snatched me and the driver, but no one spoke a word. From what little I'd had the chance to see, the assholes who'd grabbed me seemed dark-complected. My mind flashed immediately to Hispanic, then to gangbanger, then to the Sylmar Sevens. I wanted to be wrong about this, because if I was right, then I was dead.

I needed a plan. *Did I still have my gun?* Slowly, trying to keep them from seeing any movement, I wiggled my hands. They weren't bound. So far, so good. I carefully flexed my left foot. My feet were free too. Even better. But my purse was gone, which meant my gun was gone. That was bad, really bad. I had my vest on, but that wasn't much comfort. A vest wouldn't do squat for a head shot. I fought off the sinking feeling that rode a new wave of panic. *Focus,* I told myself. They'd have to get me out of the car to shoot me. No one wants the mess of someone bleeding out in his car if he can avoid it. That meant at least a few exposed moments that would give me a chance to fight. I tried to remember the street-fighting moves I'd learned from a former date who'd taught Krav Maga. I'd just replayed the kneecap crusher when I noticed that traffic sounds were receding and the streets were getting quieter. As the city noises fell away, I smelled the damp greenness of trees and grass.

Bad had suddenly turned to much, much worse. I thought about all the popular local body dumps where my carcass likely wouldn't be found for months. Griffith Park was the closest, which would explain the fresh smell of growing plants and nature. I tried not to give in to the fear, tried to stay focused on a decent plan of action. But just then the car pulled onto gravel and slowed to a stop. No more time for plans. I willed my breathing to slow down and focused on what my first move would be when they pulled me off the floor of the car.

The jerk who was sitting near my head wrapped his arms around my torso in a bear hug that pinned my arms to my sides, then pulled me up to a sitting position in the middle of the seat. With the blanket still draped over my head and body, he stuck what felt like a .44 semiautomatic into my neck while the other jerk gripped my elbow at an angle I knew would cause a nasty break if I made any sudden moves. I braced myself for the shot that would tear through my throat as my mind, numbed with terror but hyperalert, took in every smell and sensation. Then a voice from the driver's seat said quietly, "Okay, now."

I inhaled sharply, thinking this breath might be my last, and steeled myself against the searing heat of a bullet. Instead, someone pulled off the blanket.

As my eyes adjusted to the dim light, I realized we were in MacArthur Park—just minutes from downtown—and I was staring into the face of suspect number one: Luis Revelo.

29

"I apologize for the uncivilized intro," Luis Revelo said in a soft voice. "You probably won't believe it, but it's not my style." He pronounced "probably" *prally* and gave "style" two really long syllables.

Having just a second earlier believed I was about to shuffle off this mortal coil, I was in a somewhat insane, reckless frame of mind. "Unlike rape," I barked, my voice raspy, "which apparently *is* your style."

"No, ma'am. It ain't—isn't," he corrected himself, trying hard to impress. "See, I knew you was—were thinkin' like that, so I had to find a way to tell you. Susan was my

friend and my ticket out. She was helpin'
me go for my GED so I could get into community college, then a four-year for my
MBA. No way was I goin' to fu—uh, screw
that up."

"So you kidnapped a DA," I said, "in order
to explain that?"

His brow wrinkled in consternation.
"What was I gonna do? Walk into the cop
shop, tell 'em I didn't rape that girl? What
you think they gonna say? 'Oh, sorry, man,
have a nice day'? You and I both know it
don't work like that."

I looked at him, my eyes narrowed. He
twisted around to face me full on and continued.

"They throw me in the slammer first, ax
questions later. Then I sit there and rot
while they drag their feet checkin' out my
story. Meantime, someone else moves in
on my turf. Or I get shanked by some Peck-
erwood or Crip in the joint." He paused,
giving me time to absorb the intricacies of
his dilemma.

I said nothing, but I privately figured he
was "prally" right.

"'Sides, I had to try and get to you and
'splain somehow, 'cuz, see, I got nuthin' to

lose," he said, loosening himself from the binds of grammar in his desire to explain. "Long as you guys keep thinkin' I did it, I'm on the run. Can't do nuthin' 'cept hide. Tha's no life. I figure I take this one shot with you. It don't work, I fly south. Least in Baja, life's cheaper."

I could understand the logic. What I didn't understand was why I should believe he didn't rape Susan Densmore.

"And I'm supposed to just take your word that you didn't do it, because—?"

"No." He frowned, thinking. "What you want me to do?"

The gun that was still firmly planted in my neck did not exactly inspire a spirit of cooperation. "For starters, you could tell your buddies here to stand down."

"Sorry," he said. "Manny, back off the piece."

Manny, for whom no deodorant was any match, obediently removed the gun. It felt good enough to put me in a bargaining mood. Trying to ignore the smell of overactive sweat glands from my seatmates, I considered my options. They'd banged me up some and scared the shit out of me, but I couldn't argue with Luis's take on things. And if he really hadn't raped Susan, then I wanted to move on and find out who did. The more I thought about it, the more I realized I had a lot to gain from this bizarre collaboration. Strange times call for strange measures. I was ready to drive this deal home.

"You'll take a DNA test and a poly," I said. "Those come up clean, we'll forget about . . . this." I looked at the creeps flanking me. "If not, your ass is mine."

"It'll be a clean test, no funny stuff, right?"

"You see me laughing?"

He looked at me closely, then slowly nodded. "Okay." After a pause, he added, "But when I pass and whatever, I walk out of there, right?"

"I'll walk you out myself," I promised.

"Deal," he said as he reached out between the front seats to shake my hand.

"Not yet." I shook my head. "You messed up my car, cost me for four new tires, and shot at me. I want the assholes who did all that or it's no deal."

Luis looked at me quizzically, then stared at my escorts. They shrugged at him and looked at each other, then back at Luis. "Nobody fired no—'scuse me—*any* shots at you," he said. Then, focusing on what was obviously the most important event to him, he asked, "No shit, they effed up your ride?"

"One of your *pendejos* tagged and dragged my car so bad it looks like a raggedy soup can. Then some of them followed me and my detective to Marsden High and took shots at us," I said, my tone getting crankier by the second.

This time, I had to admit, the looks of shock on all their faces were fairly convincing.

"Marsden High? What'd we be doin' there?" Luis asked, looking honestly puzzled. He shook his head emphatically, then leaned toward me. "Come on, Ms. Knight, you know how it works. No one makes a big move like messin' with a DA or a cop 'less I call the shot. And I din't—I *didn't* — give a green light on that shit," Luis said heatedly, ending on a note of disgust. He shook his head. "That kinda craziness screws it up for all of us. Some dumbass messes with a cop or a DA, next thing you know, they're up our asses twenty-four/seven and we can't do no bizness."

"And banging's all about business?" I said, skeptical but mildly amused.

Luis nodded seriously. "Some *cabrones* out there're just plain loco, crimin' alla time, just gettin' in trouble for no reason. Don' accomplish nuthin'. That stupid shit gets you nowhere. Tha's not me. It's 'bout makin' the money," he said matter-of-factly. "And *familia.*"

I paused, thinking. I wasn't quite as confident as Luis that none of his minions had gone rogue, but if I asked him to check in with his homies, I knew that would only make him lose face. And besides, if he came up clean for the rape, there'd have been no reason for the Sevens to stick their necks out to get to me or Bailey.

"One more thing," I said. I had a single last piece of business to do with him right now. It was a big one. And now, when I had his full attention and real leverage, was the time to spring it.

"Yeah?" he said warily.

"We've got one of your baby gangsters in custody right now—"

Luis looked at his homies again; they looked back at him blankly. I got the feeling they looked that way a lot.

"You haven't heard?"

Luis shook his head, his expression dark. "Who you talkin' about?"

"Hector Amaya."

Luis turned to the other two. *"Sabes algo?"* (You know anything?)

The other two shook their heads, their expressions shocked. "Nada."

"What's he busted for?" Luis asked.

"Burglary," I replied.

He nodded. His reaction, or lack thereof, told me that this was an approved activity. So as far as he was concerned, it was no harm, no foul. Time to see what he did with the rest of the information.

I continued, "About three blocks from Susan's house."

Luis frowned, and his demeanor suddenly went white-hot. "What the—?" His nostrils flared as he turned an accusatory look on the two bangers next to me.

This time, one of them found the power of speech. "I din' hear nuthin' 'bout this, I swear."

"Me neither," said Manny.

"This doesn't help your case any," I pointed out.

Luis nodded, his fury palpable. "Looks

like shit," he agreed. "I din't have nuthin' to do with it." He took in my skeptical expression. "You don' believe me, I get it. But how'm I s'posed to prove it?"

I leaned back and looked at Luis for a moment. "I'll tell you how. Hector dummied up and asked for a lawyer. You get him to talk to me. We'll see where it goes from there."

Luis turned sideways and stared out the passenger window as he cracked his knuckles. For the first time, I noticed he was probably over six feet and fairly buffed. The loud cracks coming from his hands told me he'd used them for more than just picking locks. Still staring out the window, his expression grim, he said, "You're going to have to get me in to see him. He's not gonna talk 'less he hears from me in person, an' he can't talk on the phone."

I nodded. Jail calls were routinely taped and monitored . . . and used in trial, as more than one defendant had learned the hard way.

Luis nodded solemnly. "He'll talk to you. Count on it."

I felt an unexpected wave of sympathy for

the baby gangster. And now I understood why he'd asked for a lawyer. If Luis was telling the truth and he'd pulled this job on his own in an unapproved territory, he was in big trouble. The best thing he could do was suck it up, do the time, and hope the powers that be—i.e., Luis Revelo—would cool off in the interim. But if he talked to the cops, he'd be branded a snitch, adding insult to injury. He'd lose gang backing for all time. That would mean he'd not only have to worry about getting shanked by rival gangs in prison, but he'd be at risk from his own people as well. Talk about a death warrant.

"You won't be alone with him, so don't think you're going to take care of some of your own business on my watch," I warned. Though Luis didn't seem the type who was dumb enough to shank Hector during a visit, I didn't want to take any chances.

Luis looked at me and sighed. "Lady, please. I got enough troubles without that shit. You don't think I know it?" He shook his head. "But how you gonna do it without getting my ass busted? I'm on probation. I'm not allowed to visit nobody in jail."

I thought for a moment. "You got a decent suit?"

He looked insulted—as though I'd asked him if he knew how to fence a diamond bracelet. Luis tilted his head, looked down his nose, and said, "What you think we wear to funerals, lady?"

30

Manny's sweat glands had gone nuclear after Luis found out about the baby gang- ster's burglary, and the smell was gagging me, so I called shotgun for the ride back to the Biltmore. Luis was amused by a DA who called shotgun, so it was a win-win move. Just ten minutes later, he stopped across the street from the hotel and turned to Manny. "Give the lady back her piece."

Manny passed me my purse, then handed over the gun in a smooth, practiced move that kept it below window level. "Nice gun," he said as he eyed it covetously.

I slid Manny a warning look, snatched

the gun out of his hand, and protectively slipped it back into my purse. Luis and I settled on our next time and place. I got out and patted the roof of the car, and Luis zoomed off.

I headed for the hotel, feeling like the ground was tilting under my feet. Angel, the doorman, smiled, then looked at me closely. "You okay, Rachel?"

"I'm good. Just a little tired," I said, on autopilot. My body moved toward the bar before my brain could register where it was going. Muscle memory.

The moment I realized where I was headed, I began to imagine Drew's warm, welcoming smile and the cool bite of a Ketel One martini flowing over my tongue and down my throat. Feeling as though I were walking through space, I crossed the last few feet to the bar and savored the solidity of the polished wooden door under my hand as I pushed through. The sounds of the lobby behind me shut off as though I'd stepped through an air lock. I enjoyed the hush for a moment, then turned and looked for Drew.

I saw with relief that he was there, talking intently to someone seated at the bar.

The movement of the door caught his eye, and when he looked up, I was surprised to see the expression of shock, and then anger, cross his face. The object of his attention turned around. Bailey. Her drawn, tight-lipped face stopped me in my tracks.

In all the . . . "confusion," as Clint Eastwood would put it, I'd forgotten that the whole debacle had happened because I'd broken my promise not to leave the office without her. I wasn't sure how long I'd been off the radar, but I could see from her expression that it'd been long enough to put her through hell.

I wished I could've delayed this confrontation until I had my sense of gravity back, but unless I turned and ran, I had no choice but to get this over with now. I sat on the bar stool and held up my hand. "I'm sorry, I know I screwed up. Something weird happened. But let me have a martini before we get into it. Please."

Either my appearance or my tone of voice let them know that it was serious, because Drew went to fix my drink while Bailey exhaled without saying anything and studied my profile. I sat facing forward, saying nothing. I'd just realized my hands were shaking and I didn't trust my voice not to crack, so I sat silently. Drew brought me the martini, and it took all my attention to make my shaky hand lift the glass. I felt some of the drink slide over my fingers before I could get it to my mouth and take a long sip. Once I got it there, the cool drink worked its magic, and as it slid down my throat, I felt the warm, familiar buzz spread through my chest and crawl up the back of my head.

My ragged nerves now somewhat under control, I took a deep breath and told the whole story. When I finished, Bailey picked up her untouched Patrón Silver on the rocks and drained it in one gulp. Drew poured himself a shot of Glenlivet and did the same.

He reached out and took my hand in both of his. "Promise me you won't be that big an idiot again," he said, looking deeply into my eyes.

I nodded wordlessly, feeling myself starting to choke up.

"Jesus," Bailey said as she looked at me, swallowed, looked away, and shook her head. Then she grabbed me by the shoulder in a grip so strong I winced. "I want to hear you say it," she said as she stared into my eyes.

"I promise."

She continued to hold my gaze for another moment, then released my shoulder and looked away, maybe picturing my near miss with an untimely demise. Or maybe thinking, after what I'd put her through, it wouldn't have been so untimely.

Uncomfortable at being the focus of concern and desperate to put the experience behind me, I shifted gears. "The upside is that we can probably rule out the Sevens as our personal problem. And I think Luis can actually be useful to us."

"Being useful to anyone would be a refreshing change for them," Bailey replied dryly. She gave me a look that said she knew why I'd changed the subject and that she was also going to let me get away with it.

Grateful, I asked Drew to pour us another round.

He patted my hand and moved off to get our drinks.

I turned back to Bailey and laid out my plan for getting Luis into the jail to squeeze some information out of the baby gangster.

Bailey thought it over, then replied, "It's worth a shot."

"Of course, the downside of finding out that our problem isn't the Sevens is that we have no idea who's been coming after us," I said.

I reached for the silver condiment tower and grabbed a handful of raw almonds. Suddenly my stomach had realized I wasn't dead after all, and it woke up with a vengeance, grumbling thunderously.

"Not 'us,' Knight. You. And, actually, we might," Bailey said as she grabbed some of the kalamata olives from the bowl on the lower tier of the tower. "We should order. I'm starving."

"Wait. We might?" I asked.

But Bailey was signaling to the waiter. She ordered a filet mignon and steamed broccoli. I got a filet of my own and a spinach salad.

Drew put our drinks down in front of us. Then, a smile tugging at his mouth, he asked, "She really got you wearing a bulletproof?"

I turned to Bailey. "You had to tell him?"

She shrugged, and Drew chuckled softly

as he moved off to the other end of the bar, where a waiter stood impatiently.

"You were about to say something about another suspect?"

Bailey nodded. "We were going to check out the security patrol in Susan's hood, right? Well, I just got the records. One of the guys on duty that night missed three of his checkpoints."

We'd noticed that the security patrol was the high-tech kind that required the guards to punch their codes into boxes at various points along the route throughout the neighborhood. The box recorded the date and time they checked in. The fact that a guard had missed three check-ins on that particular night was plenty suspicious.

"Did he go off the radar for the rest of the night?"

"Don't know yet. But all three misses happened right around when Susan was raped," Bailey replied.

"Hmph," I said insightfully. "Sounds interesting. Is he still in pocket?"

"Far as I know."

"We'll be finding out for sure . . . ?" I asked.

"Tomorrow. We're going to drop in and pay him a casual visit."

"Casual," meaning unannounced.

The waiter approached with our food, and I watched with ravenous eyes as the steam rose tantalizingly from the plates in his hands.

"Rachel," Bailey said with a serious expression.

I tore my gaze off the food with an effort and looked back at her.

"No more flying solo."

"You don't have to tell me again, Bailey," I said with sincerity. "And I really am sorry."

Bailey nodded. I meant it, and she knew it.

The mouthwatering smell of filet mignon dragged us both out of the heavy moment, and we tucked into our steaks without further comment. When I came up for air, I took another sip of my martini and was finally feeling relaxed enough to think about how differently I'd thought this night was going to end just an hour ago. This steak wouldn't have tasted nearly as good if I'd been lying dead at the bottom of a ravine. I lifted my martini and drank to that.

31

The next morning, my aching ribs reminded me to plot a suitable revenge against Manny and his ham-handed buddy. I rolled out of bed gingerly and put on a robe. Then I called the office and told Melia I'd be out in the field on the Densmore case. I poured myself a cup of coffee and took it out onto the balcony to feel the day. The sky was gray and hazy, but the promise of sun and warmth was in the air. I inhaled and enjoyed the experience the way I never had before. There's nothing like a brush with death to make you appreciate the simple act of breathing.

I pulled myself off that morbid thought and went back to the matter at hand: wardrobe. I was going to be in the county jail and out in a security-guard "shack" with Bailey, so I ruled out skirts and dresses and went with a tan light-wool pantsuit and cream-colored silk blouse. Being with Bailey meant I didn't have to wear my vest, and just the thought of that made me feel lighter. I kicked the vest into the closet, packed my briefcase carefully with the rest of my outfit, and went downstairs.

Bailey was already idling in front of the hotel by the time I got there. I loaded myself into the passenger seat and we headed east toward the county jail on Bauchet Street. I attended to the final piece of my outfit as she drove.

"What do you think?" I asked her when I finished.

She glanced at me, then turned back to the road. "I think you're a weird-looking blonde," she said, then smirked. "Which means you look like a typical defense attorney."

My plan for meeting with the baby gangster and Luis Revelo required me to be disguised. Thus my artful blond wig and glasses. I didn't have much business with the county jail, so I didn't think people would see past the costume. But if anyone checked the records to find out who'd visited the little gangster—something I routinely did with all defendants—my name could not appear. Hector Amaya had "lawyered up." No one in law enforcement could legally ask him anything at this point, so my being here was completely out of bounds. I couldn't just hang back and send in Luis Revelo either. For one thing, he'd be acting as my proxy—just as bad as me going in myself; and for another, I didn't know if I could trust Luis yet. Plus, trustworthy or not—and even if he could muscle Hector better than I—Luis wouldn't know how to get what I needed out of the baby gangster. So Luis and I had to do this together. This significantly increased my legal jeopardy, because on top of the fact that I wasn't allowed to question Hector, it wasn't exactly kosher to bring in the shot-caller of the gang to strong-arm a junior banger. In fact, getting caught might well land me in the cell next to Hector's. All in all, this was one hell of a perilous mission. So Bailey, who was more likely to be recognized, was going to wait safely outside during these proceedings.

The Los Angeles County Men's Central Jail on Bauchet Street was less than five miles south of the office buildings of downtown Los Angeles, but the imposing monstrosity of a building—the largest jail in the world—enveloped everything within a one-mile radius in a profound desolation that blocked out all normal civilization. We bumped over long-abandoned railroad tracks in the middle of the street and went under a bridged highway. As we climbed out onto Vignes, the concrete behemoth came into full view. Surrounded by walls and razor wire, the jail epitomized all of the ugly dehumanization of incarceration, and a sense of hopelessness hung over it like a permanent cloud. Across the street, seedy but brightly painted and lit signs for bail bondsmen crowded next to one another, shouting out colorful names: THE ACE OF BAIL, BAD BOY BAIL, DISCREET BAIL BONDS.

We drove past the jail, and I found Luis Revelo sitting in his car, parked on the side street I'd specified, the engine idling loudly. He'd dressed up as I'd instructed, but he looked miserable. Considering how he'd set up our last meeting, this didn't bother me.

I got out, briefcase in hand, and knocked on the passenger window. He looked startled at first, until I said, "It's me, Luis. Let me in."

A slow smile spread across his face as he hit the unlock button. I got into the passenger seat, closed the door, and started to unpack his props. Luis tilted his head back to look at me out of the corner of his eye and said, "You look good like that. Kinda hot."

I stared at him, then handed over his legal pad, file, and glasses. "Your name is Enrique Vasquez, and you've been my paralegal for three years."

"I'm just a paralegal? Whyn't you make me a lawyer?"

I stared at him again, and he shrugged. "I'm jus' sayin'. You already go to all the trouble, may as well."

"Just pull off the paralegal thing, and don't get fancy, okay?"

He shrugged again. I opened the car

door, and we both got out and headed for the jail.

Luis looked back at his car, his expression worried.

"Something happens to my ride, you gonna take care of it? I don' trust this hood," he said, looking around suspiciously.

"Focus, Luis. Eye on the ball here," I said as I marched ahead of him. Luis reluctantly picked up his pace, and we advanced toward the gates of Mordor. I turned back just before we got to the entrance and saw that he was slouching along, hands in pockets in typical banger fashion.

"Take your hands out of your pockets, stand up straight, and try to act like you actually work for a living."

Looking offended, Luis slowly complied, retorting, "I do work. I work all kinds of jobs."

"Any of them semilegal?"

He gave me a wounded look, then shrugged again. "Pretty soon, all of 'em be legal. Why you think I was studying with Susan? Not gonna be doin'—doing," he corrected himself, "this banger shit forever. 'S no kind of life, you know?"

I thought this was a pretty ironic conversation to be having on the steps of the county jail just before we lied our way into the attorney's visiting room—so we could muscle a defendant who'd invoked his Fifth Amendment rights.

As I led the way to the lawyers' window, the sounds of metal clanging and voices echoing off the hard floors and ceilings mingled with the smell of sweat, disinfectant, and stale air. I always tried to brace myself for the sensory overload of jail visits, but it was futile. Like a morgue, everything about the place assaulted eyes, ears, and nose . . . and stayed there for hours afterward. I reflexively drew shorter breaths to keep the tendrils of foul mists out of my system.

I stopped at the counter that held visiting forms and filled one out, then went over to the cage, where a heavyset, bored-looking female sheriff's deputy sat behind bulletproof glass. I pushed down the trickle of nerves that fluttered up my back and covered with an elaborate show of arrogant impatience.

I spoke into the round metal grate: "Beatrice Danziger to see Hector Amaya. This is my paralegal, Enrique Vasquez. I'll need an attorney room." I'd been tight with the real Bea in law school. But she'd gone into family law and I joined the DA's office, so we didn't have much chance to see each other anymore. Still, we'd remained good friends. When I told her last night that I needed to borrow her ID for the day, she'd been amused and willing to help. Since she'd never practiced criminal law, there was no chance anyone here would recognize her ID, and with the blond wig, I could pass for her well enough. Lucky for Luis, his cousin Enrique was dually blessed with an uncanny resemblance to Luis and a remarkably clean record. Heart pounding with awareness of just how illegal this all was, I tried to cover by tossing Bea's State Bar card and driver's license into the metal chute with a cavalier flip of the wrist. Like I was annoyed at having to go through the empty formality.

The guard pulled the tray toward her, picked up the cards, and frowned as she looked down at my ID. I looked around as though I were bored to death while my imagination danced with pictures of myself being pushed against the wall and handcuffed. It's not easy looking bored with thoughts like these, and I could feel heat rising off my scalp from the effort. She looked up at me, then down at the driver's license, and I thought she could actually hear my heart beating.

"His ID?" she said as she slid mine back out in the chute and nodded at Luis.

I took a moment to let the blood find its way back to my brain, then nodded and gestured for Luis to put his license into the chute. Luis complied, and for some reason she didn't frown this time. She briefly looked at the license, dropped it into the chute, and shoved it back out to him. Feeling a little miffed at how much less scrutiny he got, I missed the fact that she had said something to me.

"I'm sorry?"

"You'll have to wait. Attorney rooms are all busy right now."

I nodded and sent my briefcase and Luis's legal pad and file through the metal detector, then stepped to the door. When the deputies on the other side had finished having their way with my briefcase and gave the "okay" sign, she buzzed us through. The jail was huge but poorly equipped for private visits. I'd anticipated the wait because I knew there were only five attorney rooms.

We stood against the wall and watched the row of visitors talk through the glass that separated them from the row of inmates. It was largely mundane stuff—whether they'd sent food/clothes/books/pictures, how the mom/girlfriend/wife/kids were doing, and the usual litany of complaints about their lawyers, who never saw them and just wanted them to cop a plea.

I tuned them out and thought about all the effort Bailey and I'd gone to for this meeting. The jeopardy wasn't just mine either. If it got out that Hector had a visit from a DA, he'd be dead within twenty-four hours. When it came to snitches, bangers had a policy of shanking first and asking questions later. I was going to be good and pissed if, after all this, the kid had nothing of interest to say. I vowed to beat it out of him with my bare hands if I had to.

A deep male voice boomed out and broke into my Dirty Harry reverie. "Attorney for Hector Amaya?"

I gestured for Luis to join me, and we moved toward the beefy sheriff's deputy who was standing next to the row of attorney rooms.

"He'll be in room five," the deputy said

as he motioned us to the last room in the row and held open the door on our side.

"Thanks," I said as I entered and pulled out a chair.

"Take one more look at that briefcase, ma'am."

It was interesting to see how the other half lived. He'd never have done that if I'd come here as a DA. I turned over my brief-case and he rifled through it for a while, then gave it back to me.

"How long you going to be?"

"About ten minutes, but it could be longer."

"You've got an hour," he said, then left and closed the door behind him.

I looked around at the glass walls that enclosed our little Cone of Silence. They were smudged and dirty with grime that had probably accumulated for the past ten years, and the air was even staler in this little enclosed cubicle. I wasn't claustropho-bic, but spending enough time in this filthy bubble could convince me otherwise. I spread out my file and legal pad on the badly banged-up metal table that was bolted to the floor and patted the chair next to me. "Take a load off, Luis." Luis was standing, looking out at the waiting visitors, his expression fierce.

"Luis. Get a grip. You're a paralegal, here to help with an interview. You're not here to trip down memory lane."

Luis slowly lowered his gaze and sat down, muttering to himself.

"What? What's your issue now?" I asked, annoyed.

"Jus' wonderin' what's it like for Droopy. This place is intense, and he's jus' a lil' guy, you know?"

Of all the bangers in the world, I had to get Mr. Sensitive. Droopy, I assumed, was Hector Amaya's gang moniker. I wondered why they were always so unflattering. Me, I would've at least picked something like Foxy or Jet. Which, I supposed, explained in part why I wasn't gang material.

I saw a pale and skinny young sheriff's deputy escorting an inmate down the corridor toward us. He was so small, his county-jail jumpsuit swam around him like a parachute. He looked to be about twelve years old. His hands were shackled to his waist, and his feet were chained at the ankles, so the two made slow progress. When they got closer, I understood the

Droopy moniker: his eyes sagged down at the corners, giving him a perpetually sad look. Hector, aka Droopy, was indeed a little guy—short and thin, with the long wiry arms that made him a perfect cat burglar. But the colorful tattoos that lined them meant short sleeves would be a dangerous fashion choice.

The deputy unlocked the door on his side, and I watched as Hector entered the room and realized suddenly who was with me. His eyes bulged and his face turned ashen, but I had to hand it to him—he otherwise kept it cool and uttered not one sound as the deputy put him into the chair. I waited until the door had closed securely behind the deputy and he'd taken his seat outside before addressing Hector.

"As far as anyone will ever know, I'm your defense attorney, and this is my assistant," I said, gesturing to Luis.

I continued, "I'm actually the prosecutor on the rape case involving someone Luis knows pretty well. And she just happens to live very close to where you got caught the other night. Which just happened to make everyone think that the Sylmar Sevens were working that hood. And this gave us the unfortunate impression that Luis was the rapist."

"Pissed me off good, *ese*," Luis said, his voice menacing.

Hector shrunk in his chair and looked down at the table, unable to meet Luis's eyes, which were trained angrily on his face.

Luis leaned in and said in a low but raw-voiced whisper, "What the fuck you thinkin', pullin' a job like that without askin'? You forget who's the shot-caller?" He spoke with a quiet intensity and menace that showed me what kept him on top of the heap known as the Sylmar Sevens.

Hector drooped so low in his chair that he'd probably have slid onto the floor if he hadn't been shackled into it.

"I guess I'm goin' to have to find a way to remind you," Luis said. "Look at me when I'm talkin' to you, *pendejo*." Hector obediently looked up as much as his still-bowed head allowed. "I got a lot of people in here. They can take care of you . . . or not. You understan'?"

I had to walk a fine line, letting Luis flex his muscle to make this kid talk without being a party to a felony. Misdemeanors were my limit.

"I can't be hearing threats, Luis," I said quietly, with as little challenge as possible, then gave Luis the power to keep Hector's respect by letting him work the interrogation. "He needs to tell us now why he picked that hood and that house."

Luis looked at Hector like he was a turd hanging off Luis's shoe. "Tell the lady," he said.

Hector took a deep breath, then blew it out and shrugged. "I don' know. Was stupid, but I never meant for it to come down on you, Luis, you gotta believe me," he said.

I would've felt sorry for the kid, but I didn't really care whether he meant to frame Luis or not. "What made you choose that neighborhood and that house? And don't tell me your grandma lives in the area," I said.

Hector swallowed hard for a minute, and I watched his Adam's apple bob up and down before he managed to squeak out, "Really, it was jus' bad luck. No reason. I jus' was ridin' around with my homies and we drove by this place and it looked real good, so I decided to hit it." He paused to breathe and looked between Luis and me, trying to gauge our reactions.

This was total bullshit. Hector looked good and scared, but for some reason he wasn't coming clean.

"Pinche cabrón mentiroso," Luis spit at him. "You bring all this trouble down on my head. I'm givin' you the chance to start makin' it right, and you disrespectin' me with this fuckin' shit?"

Hector's chains were his "tell." He was shaking so hard they rattled loudly under the table, sounding like Ebenezer Scrooge's ghost of Jacob Marley. Luis continued to stare at Hector, his brows knitted, his expression thunderous.

"Luis, I know I got no right to ask, but if I give it up, you gotta get me protection in here or I'm dead, man. I'm dead." Hector had tears in his eyes, and his already high-pitched young-boy voice got even higher. This was starting to really worry me. What had this goofy kid gotten himself into?

Luis paused and stared at him for several beats. The rattling of Hector's chains punctuated the tension in the air. Then, in full *Godfather* mode, Luis slowly nodded. "You have my word," he said softly, sitting back in his chair.

Hector's chest heaved, and he began to sob. Luis looked away to give him a measure of privacy, and I did the same. When the sobs had reduced to sniffles, I looked back. Finally Hector began to speak.

"Was this dude tol' me he knew a house, real rich people, they were gonna be gone for the night. The back door would be open. There'd be cash an' jewelry an' he'd let me keep the cash—"

Hector stopped abruptly and looked at Luis. The shot-caller's nostrils flared as he rasped, "Why don' you think? Think! Some *vato* you don' even know gives you all this, you don' say to yourself, 'Hector, this shit's too good to be true'? *Qué tonto estás!* You see? This is why you have to ask permission." He stabbed his finger at Hector's head. "Because you don' got nothin' up here."

Hector again bowed his head and nodded. "I shoulda known. But I thought if I pulled this off, you'd let me move up."

Move up the corporate ladder of the Sylmar Sevens. I supposed it was always good to have goals.

"Was it true, was the back door open?" I asked. This was a key point.

"Yeah, it was, but—"

"But the people were home," I finished for him. Either the "dude" had left the door open himself because he had access to the place, or he knew the family's habits well enough to know that they left their door open all the time. Either way, it was an inside job.

Hector nodded.

"This dude got a name?" I asked.

"I never knew his name."

Of course not. That would be too easy. "Describe him," I said.

"White guy, kinda big. Long black hair, wears it kinda slicked back, in a ponytail."

"Beard, mustache, soul patch?"

"Nah."

"Any tatts?" I asked.

Hector nodded and tapped the left side of his neck to indicate where the tatt was, and I heard the chains rattle again as he began to bounce his knee nervously. His reaction to my question told me why he'd been so scared.

"AB?" I asked.

Hector nodded again, and Luis grunted as he sat back in his chair. The AB, or Aryan Brotherhood, was one of the oldest, most powerful, and violent prison gangs. Hector would definitely sleep with the fishes if they found out he'd ratted on one of their own. But nowadays they weren't as big as the Sureños, a Hispanic prison gang that went back to the original Mexican Mafia. Ultimately the bigger, badder gang would make sure nothing happened to Hector if Luis had enough pull. The baby gangster and I were both hoping he did. But what weird quirk of fate caused a young Hispanic gangbanger to cross paths with an AB guy?

"Where'd you run into him?" I asked. Hispanic gangbangers and white-supremacist groups didn't mix as a general rule.

Hector licked his lips and looked from me to Luis. "You gonna go arrest him?"

"Eventually, if we find him. But we'll have you safe by then," I said with more confidence than I probably should have. With prison gangs, there was never really such a thing as "safe." Lucky, maybe, but not safe.

Hector didn't look entirely convinced, but it's not like he had any choice.

"I seen him at the Oki-Dog," he replied.

If it was the place I was thinking of, it was a dive with mostly outdoor eating. Located on Fairfax, it was literally a place where, in the words of Jim Morrison, all the "creatures meet." Punkers, bangers, all-night druggies, wannabe actors, high schoolers trying to be cool—they all congregated at the Oki-Dog.

"You see him there a lot, or just this time?"

Hector shrugged. "I seen him there a few times before."

I pulled out as much more of a description of the guy as I could, and when I'd run out of questions, I turned to Luis. "You got anything?"

Luis shook his head, and we stood up to signal the sheriff's deputy that we were done. The shot-caller started to pick up his file, then stopped and looked down at Hector. "You my homie, so I'm takin' care of you for now. But that can end, you mess up again, *m'entiende?*"

Hector nodded quietly. I wondered whether Luis really had the power to protect him from the Aryan Brotherhood. I'd find out soon enough, when we picked up Oki-Dog man. And then the answer would come swiftly.

32

Luis and I emerged from the jail, blinking into the forgotten sunlight, and made our way to Bailey's car. I ripped off my wig and glasses the moment we pulled away from the curb. Bailey drove us to a nearby clinic, where she had connections that would get Luis's inner cheek swabbed and blood drawn, no questions asked. I filled her in on what I'd learned from Hector as she drove, and she absorbed the news without comment. Uneasy with our alliance with Luis, Bailey wouldn't say any more than she had to in front of him. I should've been even less enthused with his company, but for some reason I believed he did aspire to something more than being the gang shot-caller.

As we walked out of the clinic, I found a nearby waste container and dumped the long blond wig. I didn't want to keep any evidence around. Luis seemed disappointed. "Looked kinda hot, you ax me, but whatever." He finished rolling down his shirtsleeve and said, "We gonna get my poly done now or what?"

We all got into the car. Bailey and I looked at each other. Getting Luis into the station to do a polygraph exam without anyone realizing who he was would be very tough. If he was spotted, they'd lock him up no matter what we said, and that would mean I'd get nothing more out of Hector if I needed it. Besides, a deal's a deal. I'd promised to keep him out of custody if he delivered, and he had. And I wasn't a big fan of polygraphs anyway. Bailey turned a quick left, taking us back to Bauchet Street.

Luis was tugging on his cuffs and straightening his shirt collar when he looked out the window and saw where we were heading.

"Uh, excuse me, what we going back to the jail for?"

Bailey continued to drive, and I said nothing.

Luis cleared his throat and tried again. "I don' want you ladies to take this the wrong way, but you mind if we get this thing going? I got things to do, you know?"

For some reason, maybe a bit of payback, I decided to let him twist a little. Besides, I was intrigued. "What things?"

"Got to help out with the kids today. My ma's not feeling good."

I twisted around to look at him, trying to figure out whether he was yanking my chain. But he returned my gaze, in dead earnest.

"We'll skip the poly. We don't need it. We've got your DNA, that's good enough."

Luis's face reddened and his brows knitted. "What? No! Tha's not right, man," he said, shaking his head vigorously to demonstrate just how wrong this was. "You promised me a poly—what if they make a mistake with the DNA or somethin'? They can screw that stuff up real easy. I don' trust it. Why you doin' me like this?" Luis said heatedly. He looked at me suspiciously. "You tryin' to set me up?" He looked down and shook his head as though there were nothing left to trust in the world. "After the way I hooked you up in there . . ." He jerked his head toward the jail, then looked at me, wounded.

It was one for the books: a felon begging for his polygraph. If I'd had any doubts about his innocence, they were definitely gone now. No one is so confident in his ability to fake a poly that he'd beg to take one.

"No, Luis. I'm not 'doing you like this.' I think the DNA's going to show you didn't do it, and we don't need to waste any more time . . . yours or mine. And, by the way, you can tell everybody that they definitely don't screw up DNA *all* the time. But we're going to need you to stick around. We may need your help with Hector again, so don't be making any vacation plans, got it?"

Luis looked at me. "Vacation plans. Tha's very funny. I bet your homies think you're a riot."

I saw Bailey suppress a smile as she pulled into an empty spot at the curb across the street from Luis's car. He looked it over through the window, his eyes narrowed, searching for any signs of defilement. His expression told me it had survived the ordeal of being parked next to the Hellmouth.

Luis started to leave our car and then stopped with one foot on the ground. "Listen, just make sure your DNA person knows what he's doin', okay?"

I nodded.

He looked at me, then sighed and got out and sprinted to his car.

Bailey and I watched as he folded himself into the driver's seat and fixed his hair in the rearview, then gunned the engine and pulled away.

"Think he's really going to help out his mother?" Bailey asked.

"For the next couple of hours, maybe. After that . . ."

"Yeah."

Bailey drove us onto the freeway heading west, for the ultimate experience in contrast: from the bowels of hell to the luxe of Pacific Palisades to check out the errant security guard who worked in Susan's neighborhood. I rolled down the window and leaned my head out into the wind. I could feel my hair becoming a tangled mess, but I didn't care. Ever since we'd left the building, each inhaled breath had recycled the noxious smell of the jail back through my sinuses, and I had to get it out. I tilted my face up and took deep, cleansing breaths of carbon monoxide.

When Bailey got off the freeway, I made a halfhearted effort to pat my hair and fix my face. By the time she turned west on Sunset, I felt as if I'd gotten the worst of Bauchet Street out of my system.

When we drove up to the guardhouse, the top half of the door was opened, giving us a view of a state-of-the-art surveillance system, with monitors on the walls that showed continuous views of the streets and registered the time and date of each vehicle's entry. Even Useless had known to grab the videotapes, so we already knew they hadn't picked up any activity near Susan's house. But since the rapist had gone in through the backyard and the residents hadn't been ready to let Big Brother plant cameras on their actual properties yet, that was no surprise.

"Hello? LAPD," Bailey said, holding up her badge.

A round, rosy-cheeked guard in shirtsleeves who'd been rocking back in his ergonomic chair sat up from the bank of monitors with a bang and an eager-to-please smile and came to the door.

"What can I do for you, Detective?" he asked. His enthusiasm told me that he had a very boring job. His name tag said he was DIRECTOR OF SECURITY NORMAN CHER-NOW.

Bailey graced Norman with one of her professional "just the facts, ma'am" smiles and replied, "We're looking for Deputy Pickelman. Deputy Duane Pickelman."

He began to bob his head up and down rapidly, smiling away. "Oh yes, ma'am, I can help you with that. He should be checking in from his afternoon round in just a minute or so." His obvious delight in being able to satisfy the request was heartwarming, if a little over the top.

"Would you like to wait in here with me?" He began to unlatch the door to let us in.

"No, thank you, sir, that won't be necessary," Bailey said, gesturing to the turna-round behind the guardhouse. "We're going to pull around behind here. If you could just wave and point him out when he gets in, that would be terrific."

"You got it, Detective. Not a problem.

Will do," Norman said, bobbing his head again and smiling broadly.

Bailey positioned the car behind the guardhouse, and we settled in to wait.

"'You got it, Detective,'" I teased. "Show him your gun—it'll make his whole month."

Bailey shot me a look that said she didn't appreciate my humor. Her loss.

We sat and watched the traffic as it passed in and out of the massive, electronically controlled iron gates. A brand-new Hummer sailed out, driven by an acned boy with pierced ears and a supergelled Mohawk. He was talking into his iPhone, moving his head to the heavy bass line of a gangsta-rap song that boomed out through an impressive set of speakers. The Hummer was followed by a brand-new BMW convertible being driven by a young girl with long, jet-black hair that flew out behind her. She wore a leather-and-bead bracelet that shone in the sun as she carried on a heated conversation on her jewel-encrusted cell phone. I wondered whether, after watching these idle children of the rich drive by him every day, Duane Pickelman had seen one too many and snapped.

A cyclist dressed in bright-yellow spandex with black stripes and matching yellow-and-black helmet pedaled up the incline and turned onto the drive leading to the gates. He waved toward the guardhouse, and Norman waved back gaily as he pressed the button to let the cyclist in. The man drove in circles, waiting for the gates to swing open. I looked closer, then tapped Bailey on the arm. "Check out the bumblebee on the bike," I said with a grin. "Isn't that our boy Densmore?"

Bailey turned to look. She nodded and chuckled. "The getup serves the purpose, but it does look stupid," she remarked. "Gotta admit, though," she said, watching him. "He's in great shape."

He was, but still. Yellow and black? Spandex? The gates finished their stately swing, and Frank Densmore rode up the hill, ending the show.

As he headed out of sight, a perfectly groomed, manicured, and Botoxed woman of deliberately indeterminate age pulled through the gates in a convertible Porsche. She too was on her cell—what did these people have going on that they couldn't even drive to and from their homes without talking on the telephone? The woman stopped at the curb just inside the gates to finish her call, talking and gesticulating broadly.

Just then, Normie waved a hand outside through the Dutch door and pointed to a pickup truck with a light bar on the roof and signs on both sides that said PALISADES SECURITY—24-HOUR PATROL. The truck drove out through the gates and parked next to the guardhouse. Bailey was out of the car and at the door of the pickup before he got a foot out.

I watched as she badged the guard, then stepped back to let him get out of the truck while she blocked the door to discourage any fancy evasive moves. I got out and moved into position in the backseat of Bailey's car.

Pickelman was about five feet ten, lean, and rangy. His white uniform shirt and black pants hung loosely off his frame. He pushed a greasy hank of dirty-blond hair out of his eyes and peered at Bailey nervously as she pointed to her car. I saw him hesitate briefly, then nod reluctantly and accompany Bailey to the vehicle. She showed him to the front passenger seat and stood behind him as he opened the door and got in. She then returned to the driver's seat. I sat behind our passenger, my hand on the gun in my purse in case he got "creative."

Bailey introduced me. "This is Rachel Knight, the prosecutor on the case."

Not wanting to either shake his hand or let go of my gun, I just nodded.

Pickelman looked over his shoulder and nodded back at me briefly, then turned to Bailey. "I didn't see nothing that night."

"You were on duty, though, right?" she asked.

"Yeah. So? Lotta guys were on duty. Whyn't you ax them?" A hint of belligerence creeped into his voice.

"'Ask.' It's 'ask.' Not 'ax,'" I said, annoyed. Seriously, it's a three-letter word. What's so hard?

Pickelman looked startled but obediently replied, "Ask."

"Because we're asking you, Duane. Can I call you Duane?" I paused half a beat. "So, Duane, did anything unusual happen during your rounds that night?"

"Nuh-uh . . . ," he said, groping for an answer.

The reaction told me he knew he'd

missed his checkpoints. What he didn't know was whether we'd found out about that.

"That wasn't a word, Duane. Did anything unusual happen that night?" I tried again.

"Not . . . not that I remember right now. I mean, it's been a while." He stumbled over this line, which for him was probably quite a speech.

"But it was a big night—little girls don't usually get raped in this hood, from what I hear. So try thinking back. You see anyone on the street near Susan's house? Any unfamiliar cars?" I asked, hoping he'd take the bait.

Duane Pickelman frowned, making the "thinking" face that probably never even fooled his kindergarten teacher. Then he shifted to his "oh yeah" face.

"Yeah, yeah, I think I might've seen a white Camaro. I know I seen one around that time, and I remember thinking it was kinda, you know, outta place."

I could tell he was proud of this effort.

"What time was that? Roughly?" I asked.

Duane screwed up his face even harder, looking like a Cabbage Patch doll but not as cute. "Prob'ly late, like toward midnight. I'm not sure . . ."

"You remember where you saw it?"

"Uh . . . nuh . . . I'm not sure," he said, glancing sideways at Bailey.

"But it was here in the community, right?"

"Oh yeah. Yeah, it was here, all right," he said, looking relieved.

"Interesting how you remember seeing that, Duane," I said. "Because, according to the records, you missed all your checkpoints after eleven o'clock that night."

Duane blanched so quickly I thought he might faint. His mouth opened and closed silently, then he finally used some good judgment and clamped it shut.

"Want to explain why you missed those checkpoints, Duane? Now's your chance."

"I . . . uh . . . I don't know. I don't remember missing 'em . . ." Duane's verbal engine ran down again.

"How about I make it easy on you?" I said. "Why don't you come downtown with us and give us a saliva and blood sample so we can exclude you? Because, frankly, if you're not involved and you were just goofing off on the job, it's no skin off my butt. I won't tell a soul. That way we can rule you out, and no one will ever know you played hooky."

Duane Pickelman's face settled into a grim expression that told me he'd shut down. He shook his head slowly. "Nuh-uh, not doing it. No."

"See, that makes me think you did the rape, Duane. You didn't do the rape, did you?"

"I din't do no rape, no, ma'am. But I'm not taking any tests," he said, his face set stubbornly, like a toddler determined not to do naptime.

I couldn't have scripted it better. I hadn't expected him to agree, and I couldn't force anyone to give a DNA sample without a court order. I didn't know if we could get one either. It was tough to get a judge to sign off on an order to take DNA samples without consent if the donor wasn't in custody. That pesky Fourth Amendment. But maybe, with Duane's refusal in pocket, in addition to the fact that he couldn't explain why he'd missed his checkpoints, a judge might give us the order.

"Okay, no problem. Then listen up, Duane: better stick around in case we need to talk to you again. Because if we come back and find you've beat feet out of here, it's going to make you look very guilty, and I know you wouldn't want to look guilty. Right? Duane?"

Duane continued to peer straight ahead, but I saw his eyes stray to the corners as he gave me a sidelong glance, his nostrils pinched and flaring as two bright-red circles flamed on his cheeks. "I got no reason to run. You can't prove nothing."

I nodded and gave him a cool smile, then pointed to the door. "That's the spirit. Thanks for your time. Have a nice day."

Duane didn't wait for me to change my mind. He opened the door and vaulted out, then headed into the guardhouse. I wondered what he'd say to Normie.

I grabbed a spare napkin out of Bailey's glove compartment and wiped off the seat before getting in, then Bailey drove out.

"Maybe it's time for you to break down and get a 'carry,'" she said with a pointed glance at my purse, where my .357 nestled peacefully. "Put your rebel youth behind you," she said dryly.

"This is the thanks I get for being your loyal backup? You make me get a permit?"

"You shoot somebody, I've got to do

double the paperwork." Bailey gave me a warning look.

Paperwork, the scourge of all cops. I had to admit, it would be embarrassing if Bailey had to write me up for illegal weapon possession. And the possibility had grown considerably since I'd become someone's favorite target. Besides, now that I could count on support from both Bailey and Graden, there was no way I'd get turned down.

"Fine. Set it up. I'll get the friggin' permit," I said, grouchy with the knowledge that this would mean paperwork for me.

"You know, a normal person would be glad to do it," Bailey said. Realizing that meant nothing to me, she shifted gears. "Think Pickelman's our guy?"

"Maybe. Or maybe he knows who is. Or maybe he's guilty of something else."

"Glad you could narrow it down," Bailey replied.

"Always here for ya."

33

We were about two blocks from the Biltmore when my cell phone hummed in my purse. I fished it out absently. "Yep."

"Rachel?"

I recognized Graden's voice.

"It is."

"I called because I'm in the neighborhood, wanted to say hey . . ."

His purposely neutral tone made my ears perk up. Beyond that, neither of us ever said hey, and there was nothing special about him being in the neighborhood, since we both worked in the area. I deduced he was letting me know he wasn't in a safe place to talk. Likely because the FBI clones Ted and Fred were standing at his shoulder.

"Can you meet me at the bar?" he asked quietly.

I would've liked to have had a few minutes to pull myself together. My hair was still a mess, and I was dying to wash the county jail off me. But I knew why he'd called, and I didn't want to put this off just to spruce up. I'd have to suck it up and let him see the real me.

"See you in five," I replied, and hung up.

I snapped my phone shut and gathered my briefcase and purse. If I ran, I could make it to my room in time to spray on some cologne and run a comb through my hair. It wasn't much, but it was better than nothing. I was calculating how long it would take to run for the elevator and get up to my room when Bailey broke in.

She must have heard it was Graden on the phone, because as she pulled to the curb, she turned and gave me the once-over. "I'd get to a mirror if I were you."

I jumped out of the car, saying, "I'll call you later."

I ran for the door as Bailey peeled out.

Some big meeting had just concluded, and a group of office workers crowded the entrance. I mentally groaned with frustration as I slowly wove my way through them. I trotted across the lobby and hurriedly pushed the elevator button, facing its brass doors to shield myself from the public eye. Unfortunately the polished doors gave me a full-on view of my reflection. My mascara had run into circles under my eyes, my hair hung in limp, scraggly clumps, and I'd managed to smudge the collar of my blouse with . . . who knows what. It couldn't have been food—my hollow stomach told me that much. The sign above the elevator told me it had just stopped on the second floor. And then, of course, the inevitable happened.

"Rachel, hey," Graden said as he came up beside me and touched my arm.

I fought down the wild urge to run and made myself turn to him and smile coolly. "Hey."

He looked at me, and a smile tugged at his lips. "You've had quite a day."

"What makes you say that?" When in doubt, brazen it out.

He chuckled. "I'm betting you wanted to clean up before I got here."

Busted, I felt no need to state the obvious. I sighed in defeat.

"Go ahead," he said. "I'll order the drinks."

I made my way up to my room, repaired what I could quickly, and slid into the booth across from him just ten minutes later. Two icy martinis sat invitingly in the middle of the table. I saw that Graden's was still untouched.

He nodded toward the drinks. "Nice timing. They just got here. I knew you cleaned up well, but I didn't know you did it that fast," he said with an appreciative glance at my combed hair and change of blouse.

Before he could ask about my day and force me into a lie I didn't have prepared, I quickly changed the subject. "You've still got the Feds breathing down your neck?"

"Oh yeah. They want to get the credit for solving this one, so they're here to stay until the case gets cleared."

"You still working on it with them, or have they shut you out?"

"They're not ready to dump me just yet.

If they get rid of me and then get stuck, they'll look bad. So we're doing a little dance where they try to hoard all the toys and squeeze me for ideas," Graden said, shaking his head.

"Does that mean you can't . . . ?"

Graden cracked the smallest of smiles. "No, it means you should be impressed at how I overcame these obstacles to slay your dragon."

I felt something tickle my right knee under the table and looked down to see that it was a small manila envelope. He'd managed to get the photograph of Kit Chalmers that had been found on Jake. I took it and gingerly slid it into my purse.

"Don't worry, it's already been processed for prints and all," Graden assured me.

I looked at him with gratitude. "I am impressed. I can't thank you enough, Graden. I know this was risky."

"It was. But it was worth it. I can't say what the Feds are doing, but I can say this much: the more I see the way they're pursuing this, the more I think it's a good thing that you're looking into it yourself."

I took in this sobering information. Whatever hope I'd had that the FBI would look beyond the obvious and possibly find an innocent explanation for Jake's presence in that motel room evaporated in that moment. It was all on me now. Me and Bailey.

"I'll do whatever I can, Rachel. But you've got to be careful. You get caught, and you'll be lucky if all you lose is your job."

Disbarment, possible arrest for obstruction . . . those were the least of my worries, after having my car savaged and getting shot at and kidnapped. But I decided this probably wasn't the best time to tell him that. Instead, I proposed a toast.

"To my new career in ostrich farming."

We clinked glasses carefully and sipped our martinis. I filled Graden in on the fact that we'd been able to eliminate Luis Revelo as the rapist—though of course I didn't tell him about our visit to Bauchet Street. And I told him about our contact with Duane Pickelman, who was starting to look good for the rape.

"You've got tabs on him, right?" Graden asked when I'd finished telling him about Duane's refusal to come in for DNA tests.

"As much as we can. Bailey's getting the court order as we speak."

Graden nodded, though he didn't look

all that hopeful. He wasn't wrong—getting a judge to authorize forcible testing on someone who hadn't been arrested yet was no easy thing. But I didn't want to make that arrest until I was damn sure I had the right guy. The defense always loves to tell the jury about all the people we arrested and had to release before we finally landed on his client. It doesn't look great, to put it mildly.

From there, we segued into judges we did and didn't like, which of course took us to Toni and J.D. and how much we admired them, singly and as a couple.

"He was a great guy on the force too," Graden remarked. "I wish I knew what his problem was."

"What do you mean?"

"With Toni. I know he's really into her, but he never manages to pull the trigger." Graden shook his head, confused.

"I figured it was a commitment-phobia thing on both sides."

"Uh, I think maybe on just one side."

I looked at Graden quizzically.

"I think she's commitment-phobic. He's afraid to get turned down."

"Seriously? Are you sure about that?"

Graden shrugged. "In my experience, women tend to think men are commitment-challenged when the truth is, we're a lot more willing to settle down than most women are."

This conversation had taken an unexpectedly serious — and uncomfortable — turn. My own uneasiness with the topic forced me to consider the possibility that he was right. I had to admit that the moment any man wanted me to say I wouldn't see anyone else, I felt the walls closing in. That moment had led to the death of more than one relationship. At least it had until Daniel. I caught myself midrumination and realized that Graden was waiting for a reaction.

"They do say that single women are a lot happier than single men," I joked, tossing back my drink.

He acknowledged my deft evasion with a small smile. "Another one?"

I looked into my glass. "This one does seem to be empty."

We moved on to lighter topics, including my intention to get a gun permit, and we chatted and laughed companionably as customers came and went. Graden walked me to the elevator.

"By the way, I'll approve your permit," he said.

"Thanks for the vote of confidence."

"I *am* confident . . . that you'll carry anyway," Graden replied, chuckling.

I laughed my acknowledgment, and he joined me. I didn't feel a pressing need to tell him I'd been carrying all along.

The elevator dinged its arrival, and when the door opened, I put out my hand to hold it there.

"Thank you," I said on a more serious note. "For everything."

He looked into my eyes for a moment. "Any time," he replied softly.

Back in the room, unsure whether I was buzzed from that look or the two martinis, I watched some television then showered and fell into bed early. The possibility of a serious relationship with Graden floated luminously in the distance. Whether it would materialize—whether I even wanted it to—was unclear. Too tired to ponder the question further, I closed my eyes and was asleep within minutes.

34

When I awoke the next morning, I uncharacteristically popped straight up, jangling with a sense of urgency. There was something I had to do right away. What was it? I got out of bed, went into the bathroom, and splashed cold water on my face.

Then I remembered. I quickly threw on some jeans and a sweater, grabbed my laptop and purse, and ran out to the elevator. I got off at the second floor and went straight to the corporate office of the hotel.

"Zoey, do you mind if I use your scanner for a quick minute?" I said.

Zoey was not exactly who you'd expect to see in the corporate office of a huge hotelier. She'd been born in the '60s, so hippies were an artifact by the time she was old enough to become one. Undaunted, Zoey wore colored granny glasses and dressed in wide, colorful skirts, sandals, and beads. Incense always seemed to circle the air around her long hair. Zoey never walked; she flowed like a babbling brook—everything about her was mellow. Yet she managed to run the office like a Swiss clock. It was an act of legerdemain: she moved at warp speed while appearing to stand still.

Zoey looked over the top of her granny glasses. "Sure, man, help yourself. Want me to show you?"

"No, that's cool. I know how."

I went over to the scanner and prepared all the settings, then slipped the photograph of Kit onto the platen, closed the cover, and hooked up my computer. Within seconds, I'd captured the image, stuck the photograph back into my purse, and disconnected.

Zoey was on the telephone, so I mouthed my thanks. She waved, and I headed back to my room. I quickly opened my laptop; drafted an e-mail to Clive, my vigilante buddy; and attached Kit's picture.

I was about to tuck the photo back into the zippered pocket inside my purse when I stopped to study it again. Kit didn't appear to be posing—in fact, the shot seemed to have caught him in an unguarded moment. In spite of all the cool-guy tatts and piercings, Kit had the hollow-eyed look of a lost child. I felt my heart twist at the sight. I'd seen that look on the faces of too many kids in juvenile court. The ones who'd been brought into the world by accident and left to grow like weeds. The closest they ever got to finding a parental figure who cared enough to lay down some rules was the judge and their probation officer. I turned my attention back to the picture and studied the background area behind Kit, looking for clues as to where it had been taken. There wasn't much to go on. No tables, no chairs, no furniture. But I did notice that there was a vertical black line in the background. I held the photo closer. What was that? Was it on the wall behind Kit, or just some artifact caused by a flaw in the camera? I couldn't tell. I made a mental note to check it out with a magnifying glass and went to shower.

I'd just finished toweling off when my phone rang.

"Dress casual," Bailey said, the sounds of traffic behind her telling me she was in the car.

I put my jeans back on and topped them off with a long-sleeved T-shirt and heavy cable-knit black sweater. I did a quick, per- functory job on my makeup and hair, then checked my e-mail. Clive had written to say that he'd gotten the photograph and that he'd let me know what he found out. Feeling efficient and for once loving our computer age, I closed my laptop, stuffed it into the carrying case, grabbed my purse, and had one foot out the door when I realized I'd for- gotten my nemesis. Even though I'd be with Bailey, if we were going casual, that meant we'd be outside. I tromped back into the room, dragged the bulletproof vest out of the closet, and grumpily took off my heavy sweater. After I'd strapped myself into the vest and gotten redressed, I stomped out, feeling like a child who'd been forced to wear saddle shoes instead of sneakers.

"I can't believe I have to wear this thing

the whole damn day," I said when I got into Bailey's car.

She just looked at me. "Deal, Knight."

I tried to cross my arms in front of me indignantly, but the vest made the reach too wide and they slid apart. Out of the corner of my eye, I saw Bailey smirk.

We turned onto Fairfax and headed south. As we crossed Beverly Boulevard, the famed hangout known as the Oki-Dog came into view. It was only 10:30, too early for the outdoor tables to have filled up, so we'd have the place to ourselves for a little while. As Bailey parked in a public lot across the street, I marveled at the popularity of this dumpy little hut. With its barred windows and fading paper signs announcing the various forms of its artery cloggers du jour, it couldn't by any stretch be called inviting. But for some reason it attracted a wide array of devoted customers. And if baby gangster Hector Amaya had been telling the truth, one of them had set him up for the burglary in Susan's neighborhood. Once we figured out who that guy was, we could work on why he'd done it. It might not be related to the rape, but if it was, we'd be a big step ahead.

Since there was literally no one there, Bailey and I decided to stop into Canter's and grab a quick nosh. The deli had had its ups and downs in popularity, but it still managed to serve up some great-tasting food. I threw caution to the wind and ordered a bagel and lox with cream cheese and capers, and Bailey got whitefish on a kaiser roll.

"We get the results back on Revelo yet?" I asked her.

She shook her head. "Soon, but we know they're gonna exclude him."

I nodded. "I told Graden we'd pretty much eliminated him. I'm going to really love telling Densmore he was wrong."

Bailey sprouted a satisfied smile. "Sweet." She paused and asked, "What'd you tell Graden about how we managed to get Revelo tested?"

"Same way we're going to tell Densmore—and Vanderhorn. By keeping it vague. Just said we'd caught up with him and he'd agreed to give samples."

Bailey nodded approvingly.

By the time we got back to the Oki-Dog, it had started to fill up. Bailey and I found seats strategically located at the periphery of the action, where we could scan the crowd and look for our target, the Aryan Brotherhood guy. Although neither of us was hungry, the smell of fried food drove us to distraction. I got a large Diet Coke to keep myself occupied and sipped it slowly to avoid needing a bathroom run. After three hours, two refills, and a bursting bladder, and with no sighting of our man, I turned to Bailey.

"I could talk to some uniforms who work the area. Ask them to keep an eye out," she suggested.

We both knew the odds were very long that the unis would find him. They had their own work to do, but I didn't have any better ideas. I reached down to get my purse when I noticed someone who looked familiar. He was a tall, slender black kid with an Afro, and he was standing with a group of teens to the left of the door. I looked at Bailey and nodded toward him, and she glanced over, then nodded back. We stood quietly, walked around the back of the hut, and came up behind him.

"Hey, Dante," I said practically into his ear. "What's up?"

35

The kid literally jumped at the sound of my voice. Just in case he thought he had a shot at running, Bailey stepped around in front of him. "Hey, Dante," she said. Then she turned to the others. "Would you guys mind if we borrowed him for a sec?"

Dante, who wanted to make it clear to his associates that he wasn't a snitch, said, "This about Kit again?"

"It is. We just want to let you know what we think so far, get your opinion," I replied, giving him a face-saving exit.

He had no choice, but he wisely nodded

to make it look like he did and accompanied us back to our table.

As we sat down, I noticed that he looked mighty skinny. It could've been drugs, but it didn't feel that way. "Dante, you want some lunch? I'm buying."

He looked at me for a second, but only one, and said, "Yeah, sure. I'll have two Oki-Dogs, a cheeseburger, and some fries."

"Drink?"

"Uh, Dr Pepper's great, thanks."

I talked to him while Bailey went to get the food. "You heard anything on the street about Kit? Maybe what he was into just before he died?"

"Nah," Dante said, rubbing his hands on his jeans and looking impatiently toward the hut.

"Where's your home, Dante? Where do your folks live?" I knew that was a safe question because, wherever that was, this kid obviously didn't live there.

"Dad"—he shrugged—"don't know. Never knew. Mom lives up in Jordan Downs with my grandma."

Mom lived in the heart of the ghetto in Watts, a very tough, very poor neighborhood. I looked at his neat but threadbare jeans, multiply washed shirt, and clean but worn-down sneakers. He'd been taking care of himself on very little money for a very long time. If I thought about this too long my heart would break right in front of him. I looked around at the Oki-Dog customers. It was the usual motley crew: Emos with their black-painted fingernails and hair and white faces, and some preppy types who'd wandered over from the Rossmore mansions to mingle with the rougher crowd—looking "cool" in their Lacoste T-shirts and neatly pressed khakis.

Bailey came back, her arms laden with food, a Dr Pepper sticking out of her pocket. It looked as if she'd doubled Dante's order, but then I realized that was how big the portions were. No wonder the place was such a hit with the kids—big servings, low prices, and, judging by the smell, tasty food. Dante tucked into his feast, and we sat back to let him eat in peace. When he was done, he politely wiped his mouth with a napkin. "Thank you, guys. Really," he said.

"It was our pleasure, Dante," I said. "Mind if I just ask some general questions about Kit?"

Dante looked at me, his expression perplexed. "I don't mind, but I thought they said that DA guy, Jake, did it. So isn't that it? I mean, what're we gonna talk about?"

It was a fair question, and it deserved an honest answer. "I think it might not have been Jake who did it."

Dante considered this for a moment. "For real? Don't get me wrong, if I was you, I wouldn't want my homie to get accused of nuthin' that nasty either, but sometimes you got to face facts, you know?"

The wisdom of the gods, from the mouth of a sixteen-year-old. I nodded. "I do. And if it turns out I'm wrong and Jake did it, then that'll be that. But if I'm right, then the guy who did it is still out there." I paused to let that sink in. "And I'm guessing you wouldn't mind helping me get him. Am I right?"

Dante looked away, and I saw him swallow hard. Kit's death had hit him where it hurts—in his own vulnerability. "If you're right, I want you to fry his ass," he said quietly.

I nodded. "Kit was hooking, wasn't he?"

Dante took a deep breath, and I saw him mentally turn the corner. He looked down at the table and nodded.

"He have any regulars?" I asked.

Dante shook his head. "Not that he ever told me about."

"You know any of his johns?"

He shook his head again.

"He ever pose for porn?"

Dante shrugged. "We all did whatever we could. Posing was the easiest money."

"Can you remember who he posed for?"

"I never knew. Me and him, we'd, like, hang sometimes. You know, similar circumstances and all, but we weren't that close. 'Sides, I barely remember who I posed for. It's not the kind of thing you want to think about a lot, and I never did it as a regular thing for anyone, so . . ."

I nodded. In his place, I wouldn't have wanted to give it all that much thought myself. "Would you recognize someone you'd posed for if I found his picture or gave you a description?"

Dante shrugged again. "Maybe. Hard to say until you do."

I didn't have anyone yet, but I hoped that Clive would come up with some leads. In the meantime, I had an idea.

"I may have some pictures or descriptions for you pretty soon, but I need to ask one favor. Can I take your picture?"

He looked at me, wary. "What for?"

"It might help me track down who was taking pictures of Kit. This will not come down on you in any way, so don't worry, Dante."

He frowned, tilted his head to look down his nose at me, and thought for a moment. Eventually he said a reluctant "Okay." I pulled out my cell phone and took his picture. Then, just to be sure, I scrolled through my contacts and hit the send button. Dante's phone rang.

I smiled at him. "Just checking."

He looked away, then turned back, his expression serious. "I don't have nothing against gay, you know? Everybody gets to be . . . whatever. But I want you to know, I'm not gay, I just need the money."

"I get it, Dante," I said quietly, meaning it. "What about Kit? You think he was gay?"

Dante paused. "He hung out with Eddie a lot, but that don't mean nothing. So I guess my answer is, I don't know." He tilted his head. "Why?"

"Might help with motive and possible suspects," I replied. "You thought it mattered to me personally?"

Dante nodded.

I shook my head. "Couldn't care less."

36

"If the unis don't find our guy, we're going to have to go back ourselves," Bailey remarked as she drove on Fairfax, heading for the freeway that would take us back downtown.

I nodded. We passed Fairfax High School. Looking at the drab exterior, you'd never guess that it'd spawned geniuses such as James Ellroy and Larry Gelbart . . . and Slash.

"Hello? Earth to Knight," Bailey said, interrupting my effort to imagine what it would be like to be in the same classroom with guys like that.

"What? I'm here."

"I want to remind you that the more we float around out in the world, whoever's been after us—" Bailey stopped midsentence to swerve around a car that was crawling at a snail's pace. "We're giving them a plenty big target."

True. A plan was forming in my mind, but I needed another minute to make sure I liked it. In the meantime, I asked, "Did the cops find any ammo at our shooting scene?"

"Report said two bullets, no casings."

"So probably a revolver," I remarked. "Caliber?"

"Firearms Unit said it looked like a thirty-eight. Six left."

Six lands and grooves with a left-hand twist. That would narrow down the make of the gun that'd been used. "That a Colt?"

"Think so."

"What's going on with the court order for Pickelman's precious bodily fluids?" I asked.

"No dice so far." Bailey sighed. "Be easy if we just arrested his ass, but that's . . ." Bailey trailed off.

I finished the sentence in my head: a risky move if he wasn't the right guy. I

pondered the two most immediate problems on our plate. We drove in silence as I
mulled over a way to handle them both.
"I'm thinking about planting a story that
we've got the rapist in custody—no description. That way Pickelman won't be inclined to run while we try to get the court
order. And if that's who's been dogging us,
it might calm him down, get him off our
backs. Only problem with that is—"

"It might make him feel safe enough to
do it again."

I nodded.

We both fell silent, searching for other
solutions. We flew down the surprisingly
open freeway, and the skyscrapers of downtown came into view in the distance. It was
nearly 5:00, and the sun was getting lower
in the sky. I watched as twilight spread
through the air around me.

"Thing is, since we're pretty sure it's not
Luis, the rapist could go after another victim anyway," Bailey remarked.

I couldn't argue with that. "You said
we're getting Luis's DNA results soon?"

"Could be by the end of the day if our
tech is one of the guys who does Satur-
days—but for sure by Monday."

I sighed. "Okay, I'll get hold of my contact at the *Times*. Story should come out online by morning, in print the next day. And I'll have to call Frank Densmore and let him know what we're doing."

I didn't relish the thought of reporting to Herr Densmore. On the other hand, it might be kind of fun if I had information that would slap him down.

"Bailey, on the off chance we might get lucky for a change, would you mind checking with the crime lab now? It's sort of the end of the day."

Bailey smiled, understanding. She handed me her cell phone and dictated the number of the tech who was doing the test.

I dialed the number. Sure enough, a high Asian voice answered, "Lab—Fukai here."

"Hang on a sec. It's Bailey Keller." I handed the phone to Bailey.

"You got the results on Revelo's DNA test?" she asked.

I waited while she listened without comment for a solid, excruciatingly slow minute and a half. I kept looking over at her for a sign, but she was squinting at the road. Her expression told me nothing. Finally she snapped the phone shut and handed it to me. "Well?" I said impatiently.

She glanced at me out of the corner of her eye. "Revelo's a no-match."

"Yes!" I said, punching the air. It would feel good to tell that self-righteous egotist that he'd been wrong about Luis. But first I'd tell the one who most needed to hear this.

I fished out my phone, found the number, and pressed the button. "Susan? Hi, it's Rachel Knight. Do you have a sec?" I gave her the news.

Susan's response was what made the long nights and weekends of this job worth every second.

After a brief pause, I heard her blow out her breath. Then she gave an uncharacteristic yelp, her tone triumphant. "I knew it! I just knew it!" she said excitedly. "I tried to tell him, but he wouldn't listen. And now . . . wait, you're sure, right?"

Him. Meaning Densmore. "Yep, there's no doubt about it," I assured her. "It's safe to celebrate. You were right all along, Susan, and I'm so glad to be able to tell you that."

This would give her back some sense of

control over her life, not to mention a restored faith in her own judgment. That's important for anyone, but it's especially critical for a rape victim.

Hearing the newfound jubilation in her voice was like watching the sun come out from behind a dark cloud.

"Are you going to tell my father now?" she asked.

"As soon as we hang up," I promised.

"Oh, okay," Susan said quickly, now in a hurry to speed me on my way. "Then you should go. Thank you again! And thank Bailey, okay? Oh, and tell Luis I said hey."

Eager to get to that call myself, I told her we'd be in touch and ended the conversation. "And now," I told Bailey, pumped by my talk with Susan, "for an encore, I get to play Slap the Asshole."

In the end, like so many of life's highly anticipated moments, it was less fun than I'd hoped. When I told Densmore the DNA tests had excluded Luis Revelo, he'd harrumphed and immediately asked whether we'd moved on the security guard. Not even a breath between the answer I'd given and his next order for action. I closed the phone and tossed it into my purse with a little more vigor than I'd intended, drawing a knowing smile from Bailey.

"Didn't you have people shaking the trees for suspect neighbors and workers?" I asked.

"Yeah."

"Anyone fall out?"

"A pool guy, a gardener, and one kid whose family used to live in the hood until hard times hit. Apparently he and Susan got into it during lunch after he cheated on a friend of hers."

"And?"

"The pool guy wears a leg brace from ankle to thigh—he couldn't have climbed a ladder if his life depended on it. The gardener had a solid alibi; the kid, we're still working on, but I don't like him for it."

"You don't 'like him for it,'" I said dryly, mimicking the cop lingo.

Bailey glared at me sideways. "Nope. And he didn't even give us an alibi. Said he was sleeping, of all things."

If we couldn't get a court order for a DNA sample on Pickelman, we sure as hell couldn't get one for a kid who hadn't even bothered to come up with a phony-sounding alibi.

"Well, at least we can go back to the Oki-Dog tomorrow," I pointed out. "That hamburger smelled fantastic." I started planning the workouts I'd have to do to make up for tomorrow's lunch.

But, as they say, "Man plans and God laughs."

37

My phone rang at 6:30 the following morning. I grabbed the receiver and looked at the number on the screen so I could see who I'd be cursing. It was Bailey.

"Pickelman didn't show up for his shift last night."

"And they're just telling you now?"

"Director didn't know till he got in. We need to get out there and get his info so we can track him down." She hung up.

I groaned and pushed myself out of bed. A fast shower later, with no time for makeup, I pulled on jeans, a white thermal shirt, my trusty bulletproof vest—I didn't mind wearing it for a change, because the early-morning air was frosty — and a heavy coat. Bailey was idling in the driveway right in front of the door. She gestured to the cardboard cup of coffee in the holder on the passenger side and said, "Get human." I nodded and pried off the cover to let the steam out, then blew on it and took the first scalding sip. Five decreasingly scorching sips later, we were rolling down the freeway along with the rest of Los Angeles.

"He never checked in at all last night?" I asked.

"And he hasn't checked in to say why either."

Normie, the DOS (director of security), was apologetic and eager to supply us with all known phone numbers and addresses for Duane Pickelman. Bailey called for backup to meet us at his last listed address.

It was in Koreatown. A banged-up two-story apartment building with outdoor hallways that overlooked the street. An old couch was lovingly placed next to the Dumpster at the end of the parking lot. As we drove up, a flock of crows that had been feasting on something in a fast-food wrapper in the driveway flew off. I tried not to consider it an omen. Backup arrived as we parked in front of the door to apartment A—our destination. The door sported a bumper sticker for a local radio station and a couple of flower decals. I thought Duane's decorating style lacked focus.

Four attractively burly, uniformed officers spoke briefly to Bailey, then two of them ran around to the back of the building while the other two brandished their lethal-weapon flashlights and pounded on the door. Bailey and I held our guns down at our sides at the ready, just in case, and stood back.

"Mr. Pickelman, police! You need to open up!"

After a few seconds passed with no answer, they pounded again. I stepped in closer to listen and heard the sounds of running footsteps and lowered voices. Bailey gave the nod, and one of the officers pounded again. "Police!"

When this produced no response, one officer stepped to the side with his gun drawn, and the one who'd knocked threw his shoulder heavily into the doorjamb, then leaned back and gave the door an impressively solid kick. It flew open, and the sounds of girls squealing came pouring out.

Bailey and I looked at each other. This was not what we'd been expecting. The officer who'd kicked open the door pulled out his weapon and signaled his partner. I stood back as they covered each other and entered the apartment. Seconds later, two teenage-looking girls in T-shirts and capri-length, teddy-bear-covered pajama bottoms slowly emerged. They were crumpled in on themselves, their hands raised and heads bowed as if to ward off anticipated blows. The two backup officers moved to clear the apartment and make sure no one was lurking in the back with a bad idea. The first team, which had kicked the door in, took charge of the girls, leading them by their elbows.

When the girls passed by, I could see that one of them was probably closer to twenty, while the other looked to be around sixteen. Both were ashen-faced. As they stepped out into the cold morning air, the younger of the two began to weep uncontrollably.

"You think you can handle it from here?"

one of the officers asked, his tone a mixture of sarcasm and amusement.

"Yeah, probably so," Bailey said. "The other team's going to finish clearing the place?"

"Being done as we speak. They'll stay. Me and my partner have to head out."

"Not a problem. Thanks, Red."

"Hey, Red?" I said as he turned to go. "Linebacker?"

"Go, Saints." He smiled, made a gesture like the tip of a hat, and got into the patrol car with his partner.

I turned back to the girls, who were shivering in their thin jammies. The second team came out and gave us a thumbs-up. With the apartment now available, I turned to the shivering girls.

"Wanna take this inside?" I asked.

We all settled around a cheap imitation-wood coffee table. The girls sat on a battered sofa that looked worse than the one next to the Dumpster. Bailey and I settled on folding chairs across from them.

"Names?" Bailey asked as she took out her small notepad and pen.

"Amy Pickelman," said the younger-looking one. The family resemblance was obvious, now that I knew. She was pale, thin, and rangy, though shorter than Duane, and her hair hung in the same limp dirty-blond strands.

"Deandra Scorper," said the twenty-or-so-year-old. She was a little on the chunky side, but she was pretty, with blue eyes and wavy brownish hair.

I studied them for a moment, then turned to Amy. "Let's see your ID, Amy."

She looked stricken. "I, uh, don't know what I did with it."

I waited for her to fess up on her own. She didn't, so I did it for her. "You're a runaway," I said mildly.

After a brief silence, Deandra, who I'd predicted had some starch to her, said, "Oh, give it up, Amy. It's beyond obvious." Deandra turned to me. "We were just letting her stay for a little while until her mom could come get her. They live in Phoenix."

Amy favored Deandra with a look that would have petrified wood. "I'm so sick of that stinking place!" she exclaimed. "And my stepfather won't let me do *anything!* I'm not going back!"

I turned to the quasi-adult of the duo. "When did you last see Duane?"

"Yesterday, just before I left for work."

"Where do you work?" I asked for no particular reason other than it seemed the logical thing to say.

"T.G.I. Friday's. I'm a waitress. He called after I got home. Said he had some important job to do, that he'd be right back and not to worry." She stopped and looked at us. "I'm guessing that was bullshit."

"We saw him a couple of days ago and told him not to leave town," I replied, then let her draw her own conclusion.

"Well, fuck that. How'm I supposed to pay the rent all by myself? Especially with her to support?" she said, jerking her head toward Amy.

"He call you on your cell?" I asked.

"Yeah," Deandra said as she pulled her purse out from under the coffee table and handed over her phone.

I scrolled through the calls for last night. "You remember what time you got home?"

"Ten thirty. He called around eleven."

I scrolled down to the last call of the night and, sure enough, there it was. I highlighted the number and hit send. Duane's voice came on, telling me to leave a message. I cut off the call and handed the phone to Bailey so she could write down the number.

"You have any idea where he might be?"

"I'd tell you if I knew."

I believed her. Bailey and I looked at each other. There wasn't anything more to get here. She summoned over the patrol officers who'd stayed behind.

"This one"—Bailey gestured to Amy—"is going with you. She's a runaway and she's going to give you her mom's name and phone number." Bailey stopped and looked straight at Amy.

Amy appeared for a moment as though she wanted to defy the order, but it took all of five seconds for her to wilt under Bailey's gaze and give the officer the information in a small voice.

"Thanks, Deandra," I said as Bailey and I stood to go. I handed her my card. "Call me if you hear anything."

"No worries, ma'am. I will."

The determined note in her voice told me she meant it.

As Bailey and I left, I heard one of the patrol officers on the phone talking to Amy's mother. From what I could hear, if Amy thought she had it bad before, she was really going to hate her life now.

38

On our ride back downtown, the effects of the early wake-up call began to show. It felt like lead weights were attached to my eyelids. My head kept dropping forward onto my chest, and I wanted a nap so bad I could taste it. But I felt guilty about leaving Bailey to navigate while I slept, so I kept myself awake by focusing on our next step.

"You got a friend who can track the cell sites for Pickelman's phone?" I asked, my voice thick with exhaustion.

"I'll start making the calls when we get back to your place," she said, stifling a yawn.

I was a habitual night owl, so getting up early was always a problem for me. But Bailey was an early riser by nature. She was yawning for a different reason. "Tough working a day job when you're dating a bartender," I remarked just to see what she'd say.

Bailey glanced at me quickly, then focused on the road, a small smile playing on her lips. "It's worth it."

Apparently the Bailey-and-Drew connection was still going strong. I was happy for them. And impressed.

We got off the freeway and pulled into the hotel driveway. We made a beeline for my place and called room service, loading up on coffee, fruit, and baked delights. Bailey started working the phone while I doctored my coffee with no-calorie sweetener and 2 percent milk. I drank about half the cup and tried to ignore the siren song of the chocolate muffin Bailey had cruelly ordered and placed on the table between us. There's nothing like sleep deprivation to make my dietary discipline go down the drain.

"Okay," she said as she snapped her phone shut, "the wheels are in motion. Let's hope this techno stuff works fast. If he dumps that phone, we're toast."

Bailey broke off a chunk of the chocolate muffin and chewed. I watched her like a dog at the butcher's. "Here, have some," she said, and tauntingly held out the other half.

"I hate you," I said, and grabbed my disgustingly healthy apple.

Bailey the Sadist put her feet up on the coffee table, leaned back, and took deliberately long, loving bites of her muffin.

Her phone rang, and she peered at the number, then looked at me quizzically. "It's Dispatch," she said, then opened the phone.

I was equally confused. Dispatchers don't call detectives; they call patrol officers.

"Keller here," she said, then listened for a moment. Suddenly she dropped her feet to the ground and sat up. "Give me that address again?" She took out her notepad and pen and wrote something, then thanked the dispatcher and hung up.

"What do we always say?" she asked me.

"Why don't you stop screwing with me and tell me what the hell's going on?"

"No. We say, 'I'd rather be lucky than good.'"

That was true.

"And?" I asked.

"We've got Pickelman."

We flew out the door as Bailey called for backup for the second time that day. Once we'd navigated back onto the freeway, Bailey explained.

"After I heard this morning that he'd split, I let the patrol sergeant and Dispatch know I was looking for him. Apparently someone just called nine one one and asked whether there was a reward out for Pickelman—"

"Why would anyone think that?" I interjected. I'd called in my chit with the *L.A. Times* and gotten a story planted about already having the rape suspect in custody, so I didn't think the online news story had inspired the 911 call.

"I'm guessing Pickelman told whoever he was staying with that he was trying to ditch the cops. That person probably doesn't even know about any rape case. But maybe once he heard Pickelman was wanted, that person decided to turn in our little buddy and make some dough. So he calls and asks about a reward, and the operator, being smarter than this nimrod, keeps him on the phone long enough to get his location. Then she tells him his reward is that he won't get busted for harboring a felon and for obstruction of justice if he gives up Pickelman's location immediately and makes sure Duane stays there—"

"That dispatcher deserves a reward. How much farther?"

"We're here," Bailey replied as she pulled off the freeway in Boyle Heights.

I crossed my fingers and tried not to count on finding Pickelman, just to avoid a jinx. But it was definitely a good omen that he was so close.

Backup had already arrived, parked out on the street in front of the building I assumed was our destination. It was a one-story ranch-style apartment building in the shape of a horseshoe—a big pink horseshoe that had faded and withered in the fifty years since it had been painted that unfortunate color. The front doors of the apartments all faced the U-shaped area, which was filled with weeds, random food wrappers, and bottles.

Bailey signaled for the uniforms to follow

quietly, and we ran up to the door marked
with the number 9 in the middle of the
horseshoe. One of the unis knocked, which
prompted a loud yell from somewhere inside the apartment.

Without waiting for an answer, two of the
unis reared back and threw themselves
against the door. It gave way as if it were
made of kindling, and they practically fell
inside. They drew their guns and ran in,
with Bailey and me close behind them. We
hurried through a nearly empty living room
and down a narrow hallway that forced us
to move single file, following the sounds of
angry grunts and male voices. When we
reached the back bedroom, I saw Pickelman standing on an unmade twin bed,
struggling to climb out the window. A couple
of skinny young men—one white, with a
patchy, uneven beard; the other looking
like a Native American, with long black
hair—had their hands on Pickelman's legs
and the seat of his pants and were trying
to pull him back inside.

The white kid called to us, "Help, goddamn it!"

I could swear I heard one of the unis
chuckle as they moved forward in tandem

and easily lifted Pickelman off the window-sill. He squirmed and kicked and managed to knock heads with one of them in the process. That did it—the unis got serious and dumped him facedown on the ground, folded his hands behind his back, and cuffed him. I allowed myself a sweet moment of elation.

"He's a pig, man. He got sick all over the place, acted like he was insane. Get him out of here. He's a friggin' menace!" the white kid yelled hoarsely. "I only let him stay because I thought you guys wanted him and there'd be a reward or something."

I briefly wondered what the "or something" was that he had in mind. Then I looked down at Pickelman. He seemed a lot worse for the wear. And not just from having been bounced around a little. He had the pale, sickly, awful look that takes some time to achieve.

I crouched down and turned his face toward me. "What's wrong with you, Duane? You look like shit."

Duane was breathing hard, and he tried to turn his face away. But since he was being held down by a uni and he was in handcuffs, it was a futile effort.

"Come on, Pickelman. You're already screwed. We've got your ass for resisting arrest, which means we're going to get your DNA, so you're toast. You may as well tell me why you look so bad."

At this, Duane huffed and squeaked out, "I didn't do no rape! I ran 'cuz I didn't want to lose my job! If I gave you my DNA you'd find out I been doin' crank. I had to take off so I could detox and give you a clean test!"

Bailey and I took this in. Pickelman was a crystal-meth addict. I'd had a feeling this bust was too good to be true. My heart sank as I admitted that Duane's tale of woe unfortunately had the ring of truth, and it was convincingly backed by his pale, sweaty face.

"Take him in," Bailey told the unis. "He's probably still under the influence, so book him on that, and make sure to get him swabbed. I'll get the swabs to the lab."

But we already knew the tests would show he was a no-match.

We got into the car, and Bailey drove us back downtown. I looked out the window at the passing cars, too tired and depressed to think. What I wanted was Susan's rapist behind bars, a suspect for Jake's and Kit's murder, and a shower.

For now I'd have to settle for one of the three.

39

For the next three days, we hit the Oki-Dog. Sitting as far away and unobtrusively as possible, we scanned the motley gathering for the Aryan Brotherhood guy Hector had described, and made plans for how we'd squeeze him like a lemon when we found him. So far the only thing I'd squeezed was my gut as my jeans got tighter by the day. If we didn't catch this guy soon, I'd have to buy a whole new wardrobe.

It was late morning on our fourth day, and there wasn't a cloud in the sky. Bailey and I were wearing big sunglasses that hid our eyes.

"Here's your 'carry,'" Bailey said. She passed me the laminated card, and I slipped it into my pocket. For the first time ever, I was legally carrying a gun. It didn't feel any different.

"I do like our working hypothesis that this AB guy's got some connection to the rape, since it looks like he set up the Sylmar Sevens to take the fall on the burglary in Susan's neighborhood," I said in a low voice.

Bailey nodded without looking at me.

"But even if we grab him," I continued, "that doesn't mean he'll give us anything. And I don't have any connects in the AB who'll help loosen him up for me. Luis was a fluke. You got any skinhead buddies in your back pocket?"

Bailey looked at me. "Sure, me and Mazza used to shoot pool. I'll just give him a jingle."

Mazza, a big gun in one of the larger skinhead clans, had been on twenty-four-hour lockdown in the heaviest maximum-security prison in the state for the past several years. This led me to believe Bailey's offer was insincere.

My cell phone buzzed in my sweatshirt

pocket, and I unfolded it and quietly answered, "Yep."

"Are you in a library?" Graden asked.

"No, Bailey and I are on a stakeout . . . sort of. What's up?"

I was momentarily distracted by a low-flying seagull that was swooping in for the kill on a half-eaten Oki-Dog someone had left on the lid of the Dumpster.

"The Feds cleared out for the day. Some big drug bust down near the border. I was thinking you might want to come over and see what we found in the motel."

Suddenly I was a ball of energy. "What time?"

"I'm guessing that means yes," Graden replied, amused. "I'll call you when it looks like it's about to get quiet enough."

"Sounds perfect," I said, and we hung up.

As I closed my phone, Bailey cocked an eyebrow, having overheard. "It's good to know the king, huh?"

I nodded. Out of the corner of my eye, I noticed that a group of skinny young boys and girls with shaggy hair, tight jeans, and small T-shirts had gathered at a table close to the sidewalk. One of the boys stepped back and put his foot on the chair to tie his green-and-purple Converse sneaker, and I glimpsed an older man in dark glasses sitting in the middle of the group.

A black mustache drooped over his mouth, which sagged down at the corners, and his hair—too black to be natural—was gathered into a ponytail. He was tough-looking in a way that went beyond his black long-sleeved henley and leather vest. He seemed guarded, yet he exuded an aura of dominance that showed in the way the teens moved around him.

I watched as he leaned over to the girl on his right and held out a crumpled pack of cigarettes. The girl took one, and as the man drew closer to light it, a creepy feeling washed over me. I slowly took out my cell phone, scrunched down in my seat, and snapped his picture. I tried for a second shot, but a bushy-haired boy had moved into the gap and blocked my view. I sat and watched the group for a few more seconds, then turned to Bailey and saw that she too had spotted them, although her face was pointed off to the left.

"You got him?" she asked softly.

"Think so," I said as I held my phone

under the table to look at the image. Other than the mustache, he fit Hector Amaya's description. "Think it's him?"

"Could be," Bailey replied. "Can't see his neck, though."

"Want to push in closer?" I asked, thinking that if we could see the tattoo, we could bust him. I knew that busting him now would mean we'd have to get Hector Amaya to come out front with his story. But that was a problem I'd just have to deal with later.

"Better wait. I don't want to cause a scene with all those kids around him."

I nodded. Then it occurred to me that we could skin this cat another way. I quickly hit my speed dial.

"'Lo?" Luis croaked.

Not even noon yet—way too early for the shot-caller of the Sylmar Sevens to be verbal. I didn't even want to think about what had kept him out all night. "Luis, wake up. This is urgent. Does Hector have a cell phone? I've got a picture he has to look at for me, like, five minutes ago. Can you handle this?"

Inmates weren't supposed to have cell phones, but an impressive number managed to get them anyway.

Luis yawned loudly, then said, "Send me the picture. I'll take care of it."

"I mean it. I'm in a hurry, Luis."

"Okay, okay, jus' send it to me, will ya?"

"It's coming now," I said, then sent him the photo.

"Heads up," Bailey said quietly, beginning to stand.

I looked over and saw that our target had stood up to talk to a young blond girl behind him, letting us see that he was just under six feet tall, medium weight. I figured Bailey and I could take him — especially if he didn't have a gun. I didn't have an ID from Hector yet, but I had a hunch and I was willing to bet on it. I stood up, and Bailey and I started to move slowly through the tables toward him, trying to act casual. For the second time since I'd been forced into it, I was glad to be wearing my vest. I put my hand into my coat pocket and wrapped it around my .357, just in case.

We were less than ten feet away when one of the boys at the table said something to our target and jerked his head in our direction. The man looked over his shoulder, and for a brief moment he and I locked eyes. Then the group suddenly closed around him. Sensing the need for urgency, Bailey and I started to push through the tables, abandoning any effort at stealth. By the time we got to his group, he was gone. I quickly scanned the area. Off to my right, I spotted him moving fast through the parking lot, toward the gas station next door.

Bailey and I gave chase, running full-out, legs and arms pumping. As I ran, the vest compressed my chest, making it hard to breathe. I wanted to call for backup, but there was no time. He headed for the gas station and disappeared into the mechanics bay. Still running, I pointed the area out to Bailey. If we didn't take cover, we'd be perfect bull's-eyes. She nodded and gestured for us to get in position at either end of the station.

I ran to the far end and stopped just outside the wall of the bay, gun held in both hands in front of me, pointed at the ground. Still gulping air from the sudden manic sprint, I tried to quiet my breathing. Across the way, I saw that Bailey stood near the wall between the office and the mechanics bay, her gun down at her side. I heard men's voices, but none sounded out of breath or amped up. Puzzled, I hazarded a look inside. Two men in coveralls were bent over the engine of an old Mercedes—no ponytail, no vest. Bailey and I exchanged a look across the garage.

I glanced around the station. A woman was pumping gas into a new red Corolla, and a man in a white T-shirt and motorcycle helmet was screwing the gas cap on his tank. I looked back inside the mechanics bay. A car was up on the lift, and I noticed something dangling from the window. I badged the mechanics and barked, "Police." Not exactly true, but this was no time for technicalities. "Bring that car down."

The shorter and balder of the two stared at my gun for a moment, then quickly punched the button. When the car got within two feet of the ground, I saw what it was: a leather vest. At that moment, the roar of engines being gunned hard turned me toward the pumps—just in time to see the motorcycle speed out. I ran and nearly bumped into a young guy with big black hoops set into his earlobes who'd come out of the office right behind me. He frantically yelled out, "Hey!" at the receding motorcycle.

I ran to the sidewalk to see if I could get

an idea of which way he'd headed, and Bailey joined me one second later. I pocketed my gun as we watched the motorcycle recede into the distance, heading south on Fairfax.

"That guy stole my bike!" he yelled.

I handed him my cell phone. "Call the cops."

He looked from me to Bailey, perplexed, then took it and said, "Thanks."

I nodded and turned to Bailey, who was staring down the street. "Shit," she said, echoing the mildest of my thoughts.

I leaned back against the gas pump, and Bailey continued to stare off in the direction the motorcycle had gone, her hands on her hips, her expression grim. The hoop-eared guy returned my phone, then walked off, shaking his head. I dropped it back into my pocket.

"He ran the minute he saw us."

Bailey nodded.

"He recognized at least one of us," I said.

She nodded again. "Seems so."

"Unless the sight of women always makes him run—"

"Or he made us as cops."

I glanced at Bailey. "Not likely."

She looked me up and down. "True."

"I'm willing to bet he's the one who did my car, and the one who fired the shots at us."

Bailey thought for a moment. "Makes sense."

"And you know what else?" I asked.

"No. What else?" she said flatly.

"This means our play worked," I replied. "When he saw the *Times* story about us having a suspect in custody, he figured it was safe to crawl out of his hole."

Bailey nodded.

"That's something," I said.

Bailey nodded again.

"You know, the way you go on and on is a problem sometimes," I said.

Just then, my cell phone buzzed in my pocket. I pulled it out and looked at the number.

"Yeah, Luis?" I said.

"Hector says tha's the guy."

40

He was "the guy" all right. In more ways than one, based on what I'd seen at the Oki-Dog. I didn't know when or even if the cops would catch up with him for stealing the bike. Vehicle theft was not a high-priority crime. And I couldn't tell the cops how I knew the AB guy had set up the burglary in the Palisades, because that information had come courtesy of my clandestine and highly illegal visit with baby gangbanger Hector. The good news for Hector was now we wouldn't need him to go public with his story—we could bust our AB guy for auto theft. Assuming we could find him.

"Can you try to find out who this guy is without getting noticed?" I asked Bailey.

She nodded. "Soon as I drop you off."

But I was impatient. Now that we were closing in, I didn't want to just wait; I wanted to do something. So when Bailey dropped me back at the Biltmore, I immediately sat down to e-mail Clive the photo of our AB guy. If I was right, and the guy was involved in Susan's rape somehow, he might show up in a database somewhere. Clive had ways of getting into such child-molester databases, and he worked fast.

When I logged on, I was surprised to find that I had a message from Clive waiting for me in my in-box. "Per your request, I've attached photos that look like the kind that were taken of your victim. Let me know if there's anything else I can do."

I sent the AB guy's photo to Clive with a request to find out if the suspect showed up anywhere. Then I opened the attachment from Clive's e-mail. There were seven photos of young boys, all around the same age as Kit. As I looked closely, I saw that they all had the same background as Kit's photo—the lighting, the dimensions of the seemingly unfurnished room, and something else: a black vertical line. I started to focus in on that detail, then got a sudden jolt when one of the faces sprang out at me: it was Dante.

I felt the adrenaline rush I always got when the pieces of a puzzle started to fit. If Dante saw this picture, it might trigger the memory of who took it and where. I called him, nervously pacing as I willed him to pick up. Instead I got his voice mail. Frustrated, I left a message telling him to call me immediately. Then I returned to the photos to study the background detail again. I went from photo to photo. There it was, in every single one. I pulled up Kit's photo, just to make sure—I was right; it was there too.

I took out my magnifying glass to get a closer look and pored over every millimeter of the line in the background of each photograph. One by one, over and over. But there wasn't enough detail to tell what it was—the photographs were surprisingly grainy and unprofessional-looking.

Whatever it was, it had to have been part of the room, not just a random shadow or developing artifact. This was proof positive that all of the photos had been taken in the same place. With a little luck, Dante could tell me where that was.

I wished I'd kept the original photo of Kit, but I hadn't wanted to risk getting Graden in trouble, so I'd sent it back to him through Bailey. As I paced, my cell phone—now off vibrator mode—played the refrain from "Love Street" by the Doors. I'd downloaded the tune in a fit of boredom during one of our stakeouts at the Oki-Dog, though I had to admit it was a little on the nose.

It was Dante. Eager for answers, I got right to the point.

"I found a photo of you on the Net. I'm going to send it to you right now. I need you to tell me what you remember about it," I said.

Dante blew out a long breath, and there was silence on the line for a few beats. Finally he said, "Send it."

I told Dante he'd have the photo in five seconds, then hung up and sent it. My phone rang twenty seconds later.

"That photo of me, I don't remember it at all. And it's kinda weird-looking, not like the usual stuff we do," Dante said, his voice puzzled.

I'd hoped for more, though I wasn't surprised. He'd warned me before that he washed out memories of his photo shoots. But the fact that the photograph was out of the norm was an important little nugget. It didn't do much for me now, but it might at some point. I told him I'd stay in touch, and we hung up. I remembered an earlier text message from T'Chia, Kit's girlfriend. She'd decided to come clean, and told me Kit had bragged to her not long before he died about being into some big-money deal. She'd figured it had to do with dope, which she didn't want to hear about, so she hadn't asked for any details.

It wasn't such a big revelation. With Kit's nude photo in Jake's pocket, blackmail had been in the center ring right from the start. The question was, who was Kit blackmailing?

I started to pace again and stepped out onto the balcony. The sun was nearly gone, but remnants of the light lingered like a shimmering cloak trailing behind a departing king. The sky above the horizon had begun its infusion of purples and indigos that would seep down into the glow and envelop the last rays of sunlight.

All in all, it hadn't been such a bad day, productivity-wise. We'd lost the AB guy at the gas station, and I couldn't yet say whether he was the rapist, but I had to be right that he was the one who'd vandalized my car and taken shots at Bailey and me. And now that he'd seen us go after him, he had to know we were on to him. This was as safe as I was going to get until we locked him up.

My cell phone played "Love Street" again. I enjoyed the song for a moment, then answered.

"I never realized how packed this place is," Graden said without preamble.

"What place?"

"The evidence room. Next time some defense attorney whines about all the shit we forgot to do, I'll show him around this joint," he remarked dryly. "Anyway, you still in the mood to check out what we've got?"

I'd barely hung up before I was out the door and on the street, headed toward the Police Administration Building. I moved briskly, wondering if it would be pushing my luck to ask Graden to check out the photo of the AB guy and see what he could find.

His door was open, and he was standing

at the conference table to the right of his desk. Strewn across the table were bags with evidence tags. I knocked on the door frame, and he looked up and motioned for me to come in.

"It's a lovely evening for sifting through evidence of a homicide, don't you think?" he said with a grin.

"Is there ever a bad time?" I asked, smiling.

"It'll be a bad time if anyone sees you in here, so close the door."

I did as he said and walked over to the table.

"They basically cut out the entire carpet and pulled off every piece of lint, flint, and loose change they could find. And, of course, every possible surface was examined for DNA, then dusted for prints," Graden said, scanning the table.

"And?" I asked.

"No dice on the prints or DNA—"

"Damn," I said, disappointed.

Graden nodded, agreeing. "We door-knocked the motel for witnesses."

"I'll bet that was fun," I said dryly.

"The junkie down the hall from the room thinks he saw a guy walking out of the motel right after the shots were fired, but he can't remember size or weight, just said the 'dude wasn't big and wasn't small.' He didn't see his hair, so we don't even have the hairstyle or color. And he didn't see what room the guy walked out of, so this mystery man may not even be related to the case," Graden said, shaking his head.

"So I guess you're about ready to make an arrest," I replied.

"Yeah, we're on the brink," he said, shaking his head again. He gestured to several plastic baggies in a box at the corner of the table. "I've gone through it all. That's what they found on the carpet."

I looked through them one by one. Loose change, a lighter, some cigarette butts, burnt matches, a single cheap earring. Nothing exciting. "I'm not seeing much here," I said, sighing.

"I know," Graden agreed. He opened his drawer and took out a bag of what looked like M&M's and offered it to me. "Consolation prize? And what's probably going to be your dinner."

I looked at the bag. "It seems different somehow," I said as I dumped some candy into my hand.

"It's their latest development. Not on the shelves yet."

I looked at Graden. "It's a free sample, right? They give you this kind of stuff because of your video game."

"Guilty," he admitted.

"This is shameless swag," I said, amused.

"Which doesn't bother me because I am shameless." Graden grinned. "But it's pretty good, no?"

I nodded, thinking that it wasn't, actually. It was supposed to be coconut-flavored, but it tasted kind of soapy. I handed the candy back to him, then turned to the table and sifted through a few more evidence bags. "What's this?" I held up a plastic baggie with a sparkly round . . . something.

"I'm thinking it probably fell off a hooker outfit," he replied.

That fit. "And what about those?" I asked, pointing to the cigarette butts. "No DNA?"

"Not much, and what we did get didn't match either Jake or Kit or anyone in the database."

I sighed, feeling defeated. "What about the bathroom? Find anything in there?"

"Nothing you want to hear about," Graden said. "But I do have something for you."

I gave him a sidelong glance. "Careful. Remember, I've got a permit now."

"If you shoot, you won't get to hear this," he said, returning my mock warning look. "One of the senior ballistics experts is a buddy of mine from a big gangland murder a couple of years ago. You might've heard of it. Some bangers went out for retaliation and shot up the wrong apartment. Wound up killing a little boy who was asleep in his bouncer."

I remembered. It was a heartrending case that even the shooters were ashamed of. "From what I remember, your expert clinched the case for first-degree murder, didn't he?"

Graden nodded. "The defense couldn't touch him. He's top-of-the-line. I slipped him the autopsy and crime scene reports on Jake and Kit, and asked him to tell me what he thought of the FBI's murder-suicide theory."

"And?" I asked, afraid to breathe.

"He said the angle of entry and the wound track in Jake's head are off. No way Jake's death was a suicide."

I let out the breath I'd been holding in a big whoosh as relief washed through me.

"And if Jake was shot by someone else, it's much less likely that Jake killed Kit. Which means it's much less likely he was being blackmailed by Kit." I paused to consider the significance of what Graden had just told me. "Your man would testify to that?"

Graden nodded. "He's solid on this one."

I sat down heavily, yet I'd never felt lighter. "Thank you." I looked at him gratefully. "Seriously."

"No, I should be the one to thank you. If you hadn't pushed for a deeper look, I might not have gotten into it. And who knows what the Feds would've done? So thank you for saving us all from making a big mistake," Graden said.

"As much as I hate to say it, Kit could still have been blackmailing Jake. It might just mean that there's a third party involved in the mess," I said.

"We can't rule that out. But nixing the murder-suicide theory isn't a bad start."

That much was certainly true.

"I think I'm ready for some more of that weird candy now," I said.

Graden poured some into my palm, took a little for himself, and closed the M&M's

in his hand. He held that hand out to me, and we bumped candy-filled fists.

"To a pretty good day," he said.

"To that." I popped the candy into my mouth and thought it didn't taste so bad after all.

41

Graden dropped me back at the Biltmore. Hoping I was on a good-news roll, I hurried to my room, eager to get to my computer and see if I'd heard from Clive Zorn. I logged on. Nothing. I could feel our suspect slip farther out of reach by the minute. Impatient, I looked at my watch. It was a little after 9:00, not too late to call Bailey.

"Got anything on our AB guy?" I asked.

"Not yet," she replied.

I was silent as I considered our next move. "The jerk may not show up in the database, and I don't like losing all this time. Why don't we push his picture around and see if anyone recognizes him? Hit all of Densmore's health centers? If we're right about his involvement in the rape, I want to figure out how he wound up targeting Susan."

"I'll pick you up first thing in the morning," Bailey said. "Seven thirty a.m. sharp. Be on time."

I hung up and took a hot shower to calm my nerves. That didn't work, so I opened a bottle of pinot noir. That worked a little better. I took an insomnia-curing murder-mystery novel to bed with my glass of wine. Before I knew it, I'd dropped off to sleep.

The next morning, I woke up feeling claustrophobic. I panicked for a second, then realized the book was spread open on my face. I tossed it onto the bed and went to take another long, steamy shower. After a quick blow-dry and makeup job, I dressed comfortably in wool slacks and a turtleneck. It was going to be a long day in the field.

"You've got the addresses of all Densmore's clinics — excuse me, I mean 'health centers'?" I asked Bailey as I buckled myself into the passenger seat. I handed her one of the coffees I'd purchased in the café downstairs.

"No."

"Oh good. Then we're just going to drive around and hope one happens to appear?" I asked. Morning is not my specialty. Bailey knows this and loves to take advantage of my weakened condition.

"Don't be ridiculous, Knight. No one would do that," she deadpanned.

See?

Refusing to be baited any further, I folded my arms and waited for the answer as we crawled through morning rush-hour traffic toward the freeway entrance.

"We're going to the main office in Beverly Hills. The administrator's going to be there, and she'll give us the list."

"I don't suppose you could've told me that to begin with," I said. The answer was obvious, so Bailey didn't bother. We drove on in silence.

The Beverly Hills Children's Health Center was located on a leafy drive unimaginatively called Elm Street, in the area known as the "flats." The homes were charming and extremely well tended, but they weren't the palatial manses to the north that the city was famous for.

When we entered the one-story building, there were only a few children waiting. Two of them were sitting on their mommies' laps, and one was lying on the floor, coloring a Little Mermaid book. None of them looked particularly sick to me, but kids are pretty tough.

Bailey and I walked over to the small reception area, and a youngish woman with a blond ponytail and pink lips looked up. "Can I help you?" she asked.

Bailey pulled out her badge. "We're here to see the office administrator, Evelyn Durrell."

The girl's eyes widened momentarily when she saw the badge. "I'll just go tell her you're here," she said. She got up and quickly disappeared into the clinic. Badges can be helpful.

Seconds later, the ponytailed girl emerged. In her wake was a woman of medium build, about Bailey's height, with short brown hair and glasses pushed on top of her head, sporting a nubby cardigan and slacks. She came out to the reception desk and motioned us in as she buzzed the door. When we entered, she held out her hand.

"Evelyn Durrell."

Her tone was curt, her movements direct, economical, and graceless.

"Bailey Keller," Bailey said as they shook hands.

"Rachel Knight," I said. We shook briefly. Her grip was firm, her hand cold. On closer inspection, I saw that the hair pushed behind her ears was gray at the roots. Her makeup was spare but tasteful: it emphasized hazel eyes—her best feature—and minimized thin, pinched-looking lips. In short, she looked like the office administrator she was—and one who'd probably begun her career as a nurse.

Evelyn got right down to business.

"You wanted a list of Dr. Densmore's clinics, correct?" she asked.

Bailey and I nodded. Evelyn lowered her glasses and held out a piece of paper, then pointed to the first entry with a pencil.

"He's got six, including this one: the Palisades, Brentwood, Sherman Oaks, Calabasas, and Hollywood—but he hasn't been to the Hollywood clinic in quite a while." She handed us the list. "What else can I do for you?"

"You can tell us where Dr. Densmore will be today," Bailey said.

"I believe he'll be in the Palisades center." Evelyn looked at us over her glasses. "Is that it?"

"Just one more thing," Bailey said. "Have you seen this man around any of the clinics?"

She held out the picture of the AB guy. Evelyn took it and studied it a moment, then handed it back.

"No, I can't say that I have," she said slowly. "Why? You think he's the one who raped Susan?" she asked, her tone alarmed.

"We don't know yet. This is just one of several avenues we're checking into," I replied.

"Mind if I ask your receptionist?" Bailey said.

"Go right ahead," Evelyn answered. "But . . . you're not going to show that picture to the patients' parents, are you?"

"No, that won't be necessary," Bailey reassured her.

I thanked Evelyn for her help while Bailey went over to the receptionist. When I joined them, the girl's eyes got even wider. She shook her head. "I've never seen him before," she said.

Or anyone like him, I was sure. We said

good-bye and drove to the Brentwood health center, where we met with similar results.

"Be easy to head out to the Palisades from here," Bailey said.

"It would," I agreed.

She turned onto Sunset, taking the scenic route, and I watched as we rolled past pretty people, nice cars, and palm trees.

We found the Palisades health center. It was just where Evelyn said it would be. And we found Densmore there—just where she'd said he would be. That Evelyn was one organized administrator.

Bailey showed the AB guy's photograph around, but no one recognized him. Densmore was in a meeting and wouldn't be out for another couple of hours, so we said we'd be back later and headed for his gated community instead. Now that we had a photograph, maybe one of the guards would remember seeing him.

Luckily cop-groupie Norman Chernow was on duty.

"What can I do for you, Detective?" he said cheerily, smiling and nodding at Bailey.

What was I, chopped liver? I had a badge

too. Maybe I should've shown it to him. Maybe I should've shown him my gun too.

"Have you seen this guy around here?" Bailey said. She handed him the photograph.

Norman held it close to his face and squinted. "No, doesn't look familiar to me. Want me to ask the other guards?"

"That's okay, Norm. I'll do it," Bailey said diplomatically.

It was as important to watch the guards' reactions as it was to hear what they had to say. If someone flinched, then claimed to know nothing, we'd need to dig further. We parked and went into the guardhouse to query the other two guards. Unfortunately they didn't so much as bat an eyelash when they said they hadn't seen him. *Damn.*

"Mind if we go on up and ask around the neighborhood?" Bailey said.

"Sure, absolutely, Detective," Norman said. He leaned in toward Bailey conspiratorially. "Tell you the truth, these guys aren't like us," he said, tilting his head toward the guardhouse. "They don't work too hard, if you know what I mean."

Norman hadn't left much to decipher in that statement. Bailey assured him she did know what he meant, and Norman opened the gates. We drove through and headed up the hill.

"Now what, Detective?" I asked sarcastically. "We going to door-knock everyone in the hood?"

"Do I hear a note of jealousy?" Bailey asked with a superior smirk.

"No," I lied. "But when he sees that my badge is bigger than yours, he'll say, 'Detective who?'" I replied smugly.

We pulled up to the Densmores' house. "Seriously, we can't knock on every door," I said as we got out of the car. "What's your plan?"

"Let's hit Mom and Susan. They should both be home by now," Bailey said. "By the time we're done with them, I'll have a plan."

42

Bailey rang the bell at the Densmore manse, and this time Janet herself answered the door. *Must be the maid's day off.* We exchanged the requisite pleasantries, and Janet ushered us in.

We told her why we were there and showed her the photograph. She took it and frowned. "I've never seen this man, and I'm sure I'd remember if I had." She handed the photograph back to Bailey, her expression puzzled. "What on earth could he be doing in this neighborhood?" she asked. Then she heard her own words and looked down. If we were showing her his picture, it was pretty obvious what he might've been doing in this neighborhood. "Let me call Susan." Janet pulled a cell phone out of the pocket of her khaki pants and punched in a number.

Seeing her make the call, I thought maybe Susan wasn't home after all. Then I reminded myself that in a house this big, you couldn't just yell and expect anyone to hear you.

Seconds later, Susan appeared in faded and torn jeans and a gray T-shirt with a zippered pocket on the chest. I estimated that worn-down-looking ensemble cost more than three hundred dollars. But Susan looked like a million bucks. Though I'd heard the elation in her voice when I'd told her Luis was in the clear, seeing her now gave me visible proof of just how much that news had meant to her. I felt fairly certain that the relaxed demeanor and easy smile I saw today wasn't just a return to the "old" Susan; it was the emergence of a new, more confident Susan. One who'd proven not only that she was right but that Daddy could be wrong. Maybe something good had come of this tragedy after all.

"Hey, Susan," I said. "How're you doing?"

"Okay," she said in a tone more buoyant than I'd ever heard before.

I asked her about school and we chatted for a moment, then I got to the point.

"We're working on another lead. Would you mind looking at a photograph and telling us whether you've ever seen this man before?"

Susan paused at first, but then she lifted her chin. "I don't mind," she said. Her brave expression made me feel proud and sad at the same time.

Bailey handed the photograph to her, and I watched her take a deep breath before looking at it. She peered down, then blinked twice as her brow furrowed. "I don't recognize him at all," she said. She looked at the photograph again, then shook her head and handed it back to Bailey. "I've never seen that guy."

Bailey and I glanced briefly at each other. No dissembling here — they really didn't know the guy. I couldn't say I was surprised.

We said we'd let them know what developed and headed back to the car.

"Now what?" I asked Bailey.

She shrugged. "We look around, I guess."

"That's it? That's your plan?"

"You got a better one?"

I thought for a moment and looked up and down the street. Bailey stood on the driver's side of the car, key in hand. I spoke to her over the hood.

"If our boy was in this neighborhood, doesn't it stand to reason that someone who's out on the street a lot would've been the most likely to see him?" I asked.

"Yeah. But that doesn't mean squat to the two geniuses we found in the guard-house," she said acidly.

"They're just two guys who roam all over the hood. I say we look near the Densmores' house and see who's floating around."

"And just hope to get lucky?" Bailey said derisively.

"You got a better idea?"

She shook her head.

We moved down the street and found three gardeners who deciphered enough of my broken Spanish to understand that they should tell us if they recognized the man in the photograph. They shook their heads. No luck. Two nannies strolling their babies together. "No, no. Don't see him here." Three more nannies walking dogs.

The nannies were happy for the chance to take a break, the dogs less so. But again, nothing.

Then I spotted a lithe young woman in spandex pants and a matching midriff-baring spandex top. She was running backward in front of a stringy older man, whom she was exhorting to "keep up the pace" and "pump those arms." She had a perfect tan and the kind of body bikinis were made for. I wanted to stick my foot out and trip her. I looked at Bailey, who nodded at me, and we headed in her direction. The woman's sun visor and glasses blocked a view of her face and eyes, so I couldn't tell if she saw us approach. But if she did, it didn't faze her. She kept barking orders as though she and the old man were the only two people on earth.

"Excuse me, ma'am," Bailey said, using her cop voice. That got the woman's attention. She paused and looked at us, an annoyed expression on her face.

Then Bailey pulled out her badge. "LAPD. We're investigating a crime. Could we have a few moments of your time?"

The woman's expression changed from annoyed to perplexed, but she stopped and the older man looked at us gratefully. He leaned forward, hands on thighs, and took the chance to catch his breath.

"Can you tell us whether you've seen this person in the neighborhood?" Bailey handed the photograph to the man first.

He looked at it while he continued to wheeze. His mouth turned down, and he shook his head. "Nope." He handed the photograph back to Bailey. "This about that little girl who got raped?"

Bailey ignored him and gave the picture to the trainer.

She took it and lifted her sunglasses to get a closer look. She frowned at first, then nodded. "Yeah, he looks familiar. I've seen him around, though I don't know who he was visiting. I remember thinking he looked . . . wrong, you know?"

We sure did. Bailey took the trainer's information. Her name was Miley Barone, and she was also a life coach. Of course she was.

"How many times did you see him?" I asked.

"Not a whole bunch. Three? Maybe four?" Miley guessed. "He mighta been here more than that, though, and I just didn't see. I'm up here a lot, but I work all over the neighborhood."

"Do you remember when you last saw him here?" I asked.

"Maybe two or three weeks ago. I think I was working with Sookie Tuckman."

Two or three weeks ago. Likely just before the rape.

"Where does Ms. Tuckman live?" I asked.

"On Briar Court, about two blocks from here." She pointed in the direction of the address.

Bailey and I exchanged looks. That was just one block away from where the Densmores lived.

Bailey got Miley to list the names of her clients in the neighborhood and promised not to let them know that Miley had been the source. The trainer didn't seem to realize that the older man might be her bigger problem, but I decided not to point this out. We thanked Miley and her client for their time and left. As Miley barked out, "Let's go!" the man looked back at us wistfully, then slowly cranked himself up to a slow trot, his expression grim.

We waited until we were in the car to high-five.

"Let's see, whose idea was it to walk the hood?" I crowed, rubbing it in.

"Mine," Bailey replied. She drove out through the gates, and I looked over at her.

"I swear, I will push you down," I threatened.

"Try it, Knight. We'll see what happens." Bailey grinned. She had at least three inches and some considerable muscle on me.

"But I will have the element of surprise on my side, grasshopper."

We laughed, and within a few minutes we were back at the Palisades Health Center for Children. This time, Densmore was waiting for us. Impatiently.

The receptionist buzzed us in, and a nurse escorted us back to an office at the end of the examination rooms. Densmore was standing next to the desk. Through the window behind him, the late-afternoon light was beginning to fade.

"I've got another meeting to get to, and based on your track record, this is going to be yet another dead end. So make it fast," Densmore said irritably.

"I don't know if your office administrator, Evelyn Durrell, told you, but—," I began.

Densmore cut me off abruptly. "In case you haven't noticed, I've been in meetings all day. No one's had a chance to tell me anything. What is it?"

"We have reason to believe that this man may be involved in the assault. We'd like to know if you recognize him," I said. Bailey held out the photograph of the AB guy.

Densmore took it and looked at it. His jaw twitched, then he shook his head. "No. Are you saying he's the rapist? Or that he's some kind of accomplice?" Densmore's voice was tense, angry. But I couldn't blame him. I'd sound pretty pissed off too if I thought I was looking at the picture of the man who'd raped my daughter.

Bailey took back the photograph.

"We don't know yet," I replied. "Once we get him identified, we can find out whether his DNA is in the database."

Frank Densmore nodded curtly, then looked at his watch and cleared his throat. "Call me when you know something. I'm late for my next meeting." He picked up his jacket and keys and herded us toward the door, but I stopped with my hand on the knob.

"Dr. Densmore, we're concerned as to

why this man may have targeted Susan—,"
I said.

"How the hell would I know that?" he
interjected angrily. "Isn't that what you're
supposed to figure out?"

"We're not magicians, Doctor," I pointed
out, my voice steely. "You've told us that
you have no known enemies, and you
couldn't remember having had any problems with patients' families. We can only
work with what we have."

"Then you'll just have to work a little
harder, won't you?" Densmore sniped.

The only response that sprang to mind
would've landed me in deep shit with Vanderhorn, so I opened the door and we all
filed out.

"So much for that," Bailey said as we
buckled our seat belts.

"I suppose after two strikeouts it'd be
too much to hope that old Frankie might
show us a little love," I said.

"That guy wouldn't have shown us any
love if we'd made an arrest on day one,"
Bailey groused.

She was right, of course. But the mention of the two strikeouts had given me an
idea.

"We still have Pickelman in custody?" I asked.

"Most likely," Bailey replied. "Want to go see him?"

"Yeah. Can you get us in now? It'd be on the way home." Pickelman had been booked into the county jail downtown.

"Done," Bailey said as she pulled out her cell phone.

"Make sure he's not lawyered up," I reminded her.

Bailey nodded. While she tracked down Pickelman, I got to wondering whether I'd see the same guard who'd been on duty when I met with baby gangbanger Hector Amaya. It seemed unlikely she'd be able to recognize me now that I wasn't in drag, but still. It was not a pleasant thing to wonder.

43

We made relatively good time, considering it was 5:15, the height of rush hour. We entered the jail and I tried to hide my face behind Bailey's shoulder as we approached the sheriff's deputy seated behind the bulletproof glass. I sneaked a look but couldn't see well enough to make out who it was, so I listened for the voice as the guard spoke into the microphone to the people ahead of us in line—the sound was too muffled. I knew that logically I had next to nothing to fear, but there was that off chance. . . . I could feel my scalp start to sweat.

The gate buzzed, and the people ahead

of us moved inside. Bailey strode over to the guard, and I feigned interest in something on the floor as I followed.

"ID, please," the guard said.

It sounded like a man. Encouraged, I lifted my head just enough to look inside. My heart gave a heavy thump. It wasn't a man. It was she. The same guard who'd been on duty when I'd come in with Luis Revelo. Jeez, what kind of crappy luck was that? Different time of day, but nevertheless there she was. Didn't she ever take vacations? But it was too late to bug out now. I moved forward and dropped in my ID. This time, I decided to brazen it out, and I deliberately looked straight at her, daring her to recognize me.

The guard scanned my ID. "You with her?" she asked, gesturing toward Bailey, who'd just stepped through the gate.

"Yeah," I said.

The guard buzzed me in, looking bored.

I enjoyed the irony of feeling relief at walking *into* a jail and followed Bailey, who'd found an officer to take us to an attorney room.

Bailey chatted amiably with the officer, who never asked to search a thing on us.

When we got to the room, he opened the door. "Here you go. He'll be out in a sec. You need anything, just holler."

In other words, nothing like my last visit. And he wasn't kidding—it really was "a sec."

The county-issued orange wasn't a good color for Duane Pickelman, but he looked a hell of a lot better than he had the last time we'd seen him.

"Hey, Duane. How's County treating you?" I asked.

"Sucks," he answered.

"I heard you cut a deal. Got six months and a drug-rehab program," Bailey said.

"Yeah," Duane replied glumly.

That Pickelman was quite the word-smith.

"We've got some questions for you, Duane. But before we get to it, I've got to read you your rights. You know the drill," Bailey said. She went through the routine, then asked if he wanted to waive his rights and talk to us.

"Depends," Duane said cagily. "What's in it for me if I talk?"

"Get you a better rehab program, maybe let you do work furlough," I said.

Duane nodded sagely. "What you wanna ax me?"

"'Ask,' Duane. The word is *'ask,'*" I said, annoyed. I thought we'd already been over this.

"Ask." Duane again complied.

"Tell us if you recognize this guy," I said. Bailey held the photo up for him to see.

Duane's eyes became saucers, and his jaw dropped. "Is that—?" he asked, his voice squeaking with fear as he put it together. "I d-din't know, you g-gotta believe m-me!"

I nodded, guessing what had happened. "He paid you off to let him into the neighborhood, right?"

Pickelman was gulping air, but he managed to nod.

"But you didn't know why he wanted in?" I continued.

"N-no. N-never." He stared at the floor, shaking his head as he put two and two together—without even using his fingers. "I n-never woulda done it if I knew he was gonna hurt that little girl." Duane looked up at us. "Please, you gotta believe me!" he said anxiously.

I did, actually. He was a pathetic addict,

and what few brains he'd been born with had been fried, but he didn't strike me as cold enough to knowingly facilitate the rape of a fifteen-year-old girl. But I needed to nail down more details.

"So, the night of the rape, did he pay you off to miss your checkpoints?"

Duane shook his head. "No. He never said nuthin' about missing my checkpoints." He sighed and paused a moment before continuing. "He gave me some real good glass." It made sense. The man didn't need to tell Duane to screw up his job. He just gave the security guard a nice load of crystal meth and let nature take its course. Duane looked down at his hands. I could swear he actually seemed ashamed.

"I got really revved. I mean, I was flying." Duane paused, carried away by the memory of his high, his shame already forgotten. He looked positively misty.

"You know his name, Duane?" I asked, holding my breath.

He thought for a moment. "Uh, Carl . . . something."

"Think harder, Duane. We need a last name," I said tensely.

He thought again. The visible strain of the effort was painful to watch.

Finally Duane shook his head. "You know, I don't think I ever knew," he said.

I looked at Bailey, and she nodded. That was all we'd get out of Pickelman.

We stood, and Bailey signaled for the officer to come fetch him.

"Thanks, Duane," I said.

"You gonna hook me up with somethin'? Work furlough, maybe?" he suggested.

"We'll do what we can," Bailey said.

The officer came and took Pickelman, and Bailey and I got out of there.

"So close," I said. I got into the passenger seat and slumped down. We'd learned some, but it wasn't enough.

"Don't worry," Bailey said, seeing my agitation. "I'll find the guy. We know he didn't get those AB tatts hanging out in church. It's just a matter of time before I get a name."

Eventually she pulled into the driveway of the Biltmore. "You want to come in for a drink? Or dinner?" I asked. It was after 7:00 p.m., and the rumbling in my stomach reminded me we hadn't stopped to eat all day.

"Thanks, but I've got to go back to the office to check up on some other cases."

I nodded. "Call me the minute you hear anything," I said. Bailey saluted, and I got out and headed for the elevator.

Back in the room, I dropped my coat and purse and perused the room-service menu. The seared ahi tuna and grilled zucchini looked good. I opened a cool bottle of pinot grigio to complement the experience and enjoyed a glass until the food arrived. One long shower later, I was in bed, too tired to even pretend to read a book. I snapped off the nightstand light and dropped into a deep sleep.

44

I woke up to the ringing of my room phone at 8:00 a.m. The phone continued to ring jarringly. I picked up the receiver, thinking it had to be Bailey. Only my closest friends called me on that phone, and only when they wanted to wake me up. I was right.

"Got good news and bad news," Bailey said.

"Good news."

"Got a name for our boy: Carl Stayner. He has a bust for burglary in Florida."

"Perfect! Did Fukai run his DNA against the rape kit?" I asked, excited.

"And that's the bad news," Bailey said, sighing. "Stayner's not there."

"What do you mean, 'not there'? How could he not be in the database?" I asked, exasperated. How did this asshole keep slipping through our fingers?

"No clue," Bailey said, sounding every bit as irritated as I felt.

"Okay, give me all you got on him. I'll find out," I said.

She gave me all of Stayner's identifying numbers, and I called the district attorney's office in Miami-Dade County, where he'd been convicted. After getting passed around a few times, I managed to get the deputy district attorney who'd handled the case, a man named Fred Goins. I introduced myself and explained the situation, then asked if he'd mind looking at my photo to see if it was the same guy.

"Sure, hang on while I boot up here. And while I'm at it, I'll send you my photo of the miscreant."

He pronounced "miscreant" with three long, slow syllables.

Within seconds, we were both looking at the photos.

"Yep. We got the same guy, all right," Fred remarked as he slurped his drink.

I agreed. The photo Fred sent showed a man who was slightly heavier, his hair a little shorter, but there was no doubt he was our guy.

"So what happened, Fred? Why isn't he in the database?"

Fred exhaled loudly and said with disgust, "You can thank Judge LetEmGo for that one. True name Lettingail, but you get the picture."

I did.

"Stayner's attorney argued that since his client was only a thief and hadn't been charged with a crime of violence, he shouldn't have to get entered in the database. Judge LetEmGo agreed, said there was no reason to make him endure the ignominy of a buccal swab."

Like "miscreant," the word "ignominy" rolled off his tongue with an unusual mixture of languorous cynicism.

"You've got to be kidding me," I said.

"Welcome to my world," Fred replied. "I threw myself a kegger when I got transferred out of his court."

"I'll bet. Congratulations on getting out of there, and thanks for your help, Fred. You're a gem."

"Go get 'em, Rachel. I'm sorry I couldn't be more help to ya."

I was too. We hung up, and I pondered what to do next. I figured I should probably start by getting dressed. The day had dawned cloudy, cool, and a little breezy. I wasn't sure whether I'd be outside or inside, and I didn't want to wear that damn bulletproof beast if I didn't have to.

I considered what my next step should be. I didn't have DNA, but I did have photos of Stayner, and we hadn't finished hitting Densmore's clinics yet. That meant I'd definitely be outside. I started to burrow through my drawers for comfortable walking-around clothes. I opened my phone to dial Bailey's number when it rang in my hand. Making a mental note to switch it to vibrate when I left for the day, I pressed the button. "Knight."

"News flash," Bailey said, uncharacteristically excited.

"Listening."

"We've got Stayner."

I gripped the phone as though it might fly away. "Where? How?"

"I'll tell you when I pick you up. Be downstairs in ten."

"Make it three," I said, but I was talking to dead air. Bailey had hung up.

45

I'd been waiting a full five minutes when Bailey roared into the driveway and jerked to a stop in front of me. I jumped in and yanked on my seat belt as she zoomed around the circle, barely stopping to check for oncoming traffic, then pulled out onto Figueroa and floored it onto 101, heading north.

Bailey was in the zone, weaving between cars, flying down the road the way only cops and immortal teenagers dared. It seemed unwise—perhaps suicidal—to distract her with questions, so I hunkered down in silence and consoled myself that I'd have the answers soon enough.

When we passed through the San Fernando Valley and got off at Las Virgenes, I started to ask where we were headed, but when Bailey turned left, I realized it could only be Malibu Canyon. The narrow road climbed up through the untamed Santa Monica Mountains with hairpin turns, and Bailey was still doing at least sixty-five miles per hour. I held my breath and the dashboard as she careened through the curves. Since I was now fully focused on surviving this ride, I didn't even *want* to ask questions. We flew up the mountain in silence.

We passed through the tunnel at the top of the canyon and had begun our descent down the other side of the mountain pass into Malibu when I saw the flashing lights of police cars, fire engines, and an ambulance. Bailey badged our way through the police perimeter and pulled over on the right shoulder. We got out, walked across the road, and went to the edge of the shoulder, where everyone had congregated.

I looked down into the ravine. There, nearly one hundred feet below, among the rocks and shrubs, was an old black Escalade, its grille smashed into the trunk of a thick, squat tree. The entire front end of the car had accordioned on impact, and at least one of the branches had broken through the windshield. The driver's door had been pried off by the Jaws of Life, and a gurney was set up next to the opening. As I watched, two paramedics lifted out a body that had a long, thin branch protruding from its neck.

"It won't be too hard to get a DNA sample out of him now," I remarked to Bailey.

"Questioning him is going to be kind of tough, though," she replied.

We headed down the ravine to see what we could see.

On the way, we passed the paramedics, who were huffing and puffing as they carried the gurney up the hill. I didn't envy them their task, but then again, I never did.

I took in the grisly sight of the branch that jutted from Carl Stayner's neck. "Possible DUI?" I asked the paramedic. Stayner wouldn't be the first or even the hundredth who'd gotten drunk, miscalculated a curve, and wound up airborne in this canyon.

"Don't think so. At least, I don't smell any booze," he replied.

I nodded and ran to catch up with Bailey, who was closing in on the wreckage.

A group of detectives who'd been huddled around the car made way for her deferentially. It was Bailey's case; they were just there to look on and help. When I reached the opening where the driver's door had been, I could see that there was surprisingly little blood, likely courtesy of the branch that had stopped his heart and all bodily functions before his wounds could bleed out.

Bailey was snapping on latex gloves. "Got any extras?" I asked.

She patted her pockets as she looked into the car. "Nope. But I can't move anything until the crime scene tech gets here anyway."

I nodded and peered in over Bailey's shoulder.

"See that?" I said, pointing to what looked like an old-fashioned motel key on the passenger floorboard.

Bailey leaned in closer and read off the name. "Surf Motel," she said.

The Surf Motel. I knew the place. The unoriginal name was its best feature. It was a ramshackle series of ten connected units that hugged the bluff on Pacific Coast Highway and afforded a commanding view of the Pacific Ocean. It had seen the days that would qualify as its better ones about forty years ago. Now it was an eyesore that inexplicably occupied prime real estate in one of the priciest neighborhoods in the country. I'd wondered whether it was still in operation. I had my answer.

We resumed our examination of the car. The backseats had been unhooked and latched to the sides to create a large cargo space. I peered in for a closer look and saw a few cans of Red Bull and other smaller items, but the tinted windows were too dark to let me see what they were.

I was craning my neck when a photographer and three crime scene techs wearing elbow-length gloves and hairnets approached.

"Uh, if you wouldn't mind stepping back, ma'am," said a young Hispanic woman whose net sagged under the weight of an impressive head of black hair.

I did mind but stepped back anyway and continued to watch from a few feet away as Bailey negotiated with the oldest of the group, a paunchy red-faced man with a tiny nose and squinty blue eyes, about proceeding to the Surf Motel with us.

The two younger techs stood back and waited as the photographer took pictures of the outside of the car from all angles. I followed him around. When we got to the rear passenger-side bumper, I leaned in and said, "Do you see that?" I was pointing to what looked like a dent in its center.

The photographer, a thirtysomething with freckles, firecracker bangs that shot straight out from his scalp, and horn-rimmed glasses that made his brown eyes look huge, seemed annoyed at first. Then he took a closer look and said, "Yeah," and snapped several shots of the bumper.

"'Course, we don't know when it got there," he said. "Damage looks kinda old to me."

"You can't have too many pictures, though, right?" I smiled winningly.

He shook his head, sighed, and snapped more photos. I could tell he was really enjoying my company.

Bailey had finished with the older crime scene tech, and I told her what I'd seen. She went around to look at the bumper. "That's old. Probably unrelated." She turned to the photographer. "On the other hand, a few extra pictures never hurt."

I enjoyed a brief moment of triumph.

"I miss Dorian," I remarked.

Bailey nodded. "But Ben's okay," she said, indicating the older man with the paunch. "He gets a little tired, but he's careful and he doesn't miss much."

The subject of our discussion had just opened the rear hatch of the Escalade. I moved closer to get a better look. It was cleaner than I'd expected: a few McDonald's hamburger wrappers, a can of Red Bull, a half-smoked pack of Camel cigarettes, a lighter, a pack of Quench Gum, and a box of condoms.

I turned to Bailey. "Condoms."

The rape kit had revealed lubricant of the sort commonly found on condoms.

She nodded. "So far, so good."

The photographer moved into position and began snapping pictures of the inside of the vehicle.

"Want to take a look up on top, see where he went flying?" I asked.

We climbed the hill, which was no easy thing. Between the steepness and the loose rocks and dirt, there was no traction. We moved slowly, grabbing on to bushes for leverage.

The cops had cordoned off a wide section where the tire tracks showed the car had gone off the road and over the cliff.

"Anything to talk about?" Bailey said to one of the crime scene techs.

"Some interesting marks in the dirt over there," he said, pointing to a spot just off the road.

"Interesting how? Brake marks?" she asked.

"No. Like weird little holes, just a couple of 'em," the tech said. Then he shrugged. "It might not be anything either. Dirt's real loose up here, doesn't give a good impression."

Bailey and I looked at the spot. I didn't know what to make of the small indentations. I glanced at Bailey, who shook her head. "Yeah," I agreed. "Let's hit the Surf."

I didn't see anything else to do here, and I was dying to get into Stayner's motel room.

She nodded and turned to the crime scene tech. "Get Ben up here," she said.

46

The clouds that'd been hanging over downtown L.A. were nowhere in sight out here, and the descent down the Malibu side of the mountain offered a spectacularly clear and sparkling view of the Pacific Ocean. For a few moments, I lost myself in the glorious panorama but got dragged back to earth when the Surf Motel, in all its dilapidated glory, came into view.

All ten units in the low-slung building had windows that faced the ocean, and doors that faced the Pacific Coast Highway. Convenient parking was provided on the unpaved stretch of dirt that separated the motel from the road. I noticed that an old VW Bug was parked in front of the door at the far end, and a Harley-Davidson chopper was parked to the right of the car. I did and didn't want to meet the owners of those vehicles.

Bailey and the cruiser behind us stopped in front of a sign that said OFFICE, and we all got out and walked up to the weathered door. Salt air is hard on paint, but it didn't look like anyone had put in even a nominal effort to fight the damage. The original wood of the door showed through in big patches, and what little paint still clung to it was in the process of peeling. Bailey tried the knob. The door was open.

The office was really just a tiny vestibule that'd been added on to the end of the single row of rooms. If the motel had been downtown, it would've been the kind of place that rented rooms by the hour—a lot like the one where Kit and Jake had been found. This seemed to be my new theme. We walked up to the small desk, and Bailey tapped the old-fashioned bell. Instead of a ring, it gave off a dull buzz. A shirtless, barefoot guy in his twenties, with board shorts and wild hair, came out

yawning and scratching his stomach. He
too gave off a dull buzz.

Bailey pulled out her badge. "We're investigating a rape, and we have reason to
believe that the suspect was staying here."

The young man looked singularly unim-
pressed with either Bailey or the uniforms
behind her. "Aren't you guys supposed to
get, like, a warrant or somethin'? I mean,
like, what if the dude sues us?"

"We just scooped what was left of him
off the side of the canyon," Bailey said. "I
don't think he'll be suing anyone."

He nodded to himself, then squinted at
Bailey again. "What room?" he asked.

"Got one rented to someone named
Carl Stayner?"

He opened a soggy-looking book with
lined pages and ran a dirty nail down the
entries. "Nope."

That figured. "Drove a black Escalade,"
I said.

"Looked like this," Bailey added, holding
out Stayner's mug shot.

He ran a hand through the mop on his
head as he peered at the photo. "Oh yeah,
number ten," he said. The young man pulled
out his master key. "'Kay, but don't, like,

mess it up too bad. I'll catch hell with the owner."

Bailey took the key, promised nothing of the kind, and moved down the concrete walkway that led to number ten.

The number hung crookedly on the door, rusted and dirty, held by one screw. I would've been disappointed if it hadn't. I appreciate consistency. Pulled-back dirty, torn curtains offered a glimpse into a room that was disgustingly filthy. I figured he hadn't been there long enough to give it the full treatment. Bailey opened the door, and the smell of sweat, pot, and dirty clothes rolled out in oily waves to greet us.

She stepped aside to let the photographer in first. He put on bootees to cover his shoes and moved slowly, snapping away from all angles to capture the scene before anything was moved. Then he got everything on video. When he finished and moved on to the bathroom, we put on bootees and gloves and followed.

A sagging, unmade bed, its worn, ugly gray chenille spread pushed to one side, was littered with clothes, an empty pizza box, and stray cigarettes. I didn't see a corresponding pack anywhere, so I couldn't tell the brand. I called out to the photographer. "You get those cigarettes on the bed?"

The camera clicks coming from the bathroom stopped. I heard an audible sigh. "Yeah, I got 'em," the photographer answered in a bored, tired voice.

I looked around the room. The window at the far wall offered the possibility of an ocean view out to Catalina Island, but the grime that had been allowed to accumulate over the years showed only a dim suggestion of that vista.

I looked back toward the door and saw a bulging canvas suitcase near the closet.

"Looks like Stayner was on his way out," I said to Bailey.

She nodded and motioned me over to the nightstand. I noticed an odd bulge in the carpet next to the wall between the nightstand and the bed.

Bailey and I exchanged a look.

She called the photographer over and pointed to the area. "Get this."

I noticed he didn't dare look annoyed at Bailey. He moved in and snapped several pictures.

"Ben, we need you over here," she ordered.

Ben quickly examined the spot, then got his kit, changed gloves, and knelt on the filth-encrusted carpet. I watched as he felt around for a loose edge, and for the second time that day I was glad I'd put myself through law school.

The carpet came up easily, and I leaned in to look. The lump was a gun and a stash of money. One immediate thought came to mind.

"Can you tell the make on that gun?" I asked.

Ben inserted a pencil through the trigger guard and lifted it for a closer look. Getting prints off a gun was always a long shot, but it'd be foolish to ruin any chance by being careless. "Colt, probably thirty-eight caliber," he replied.

I looked at Bailey. "An alarming coincidence?"

"After you bag and log the gun, Ben, give it to me," she said.

It was likely the same make and caliber of the weapon fired at us the day we'd visited the school. I wanted it to be *the* gun, but Colt .38s aren't exactly rare. And even if it was the right gun, that didn't mean Stayner was the one who'd fired it.

It could have been someone in league with Stayner.

Bailey turned her attention to the suitcase. She said to Ben, "Let's check that out first. You can go over the rest of the floor later. I'm betting that's all we're going to find under the carpet."

Again, the photographer went first, then Ben began to go through the bag, piece by piece. I watched, getting increasingly grossed out and bored by looking at this jerk's Skivvies, when Ben opened the zippered pocket on the back of the suitcase. And pulled out a man's blond wig.

47

Bailey and I exchanged a long look.

"Dorian hasn't matched those blond synthetic hairs in Susan's headboard to any of her dolls yet, has she?" I asked.

"Nope."

"I bet she'll find a match now," I remarked.

"Yep," Bailey replied.

"I get from this that the wig is significant?" Ben asked.

"Yes," we both said in unison.

Ben nodded. We watched as he carefully bagged the wig and filled out an evidence tag for it.

I called Dorian and told her we had a wig for her to look at.

"Well, make sure you get it bagged right. Knowing you two, you're probably playing Frisbee with it," she growled.

"Frisbee? With a wig? That would be silly, Dorian. It wouldn't fly right." I paused for her reaction. Dead air. "We've got it bagged, no worries," I said.

Dorian hung up without comment. I turned to Bailey.

"Assuming he wasn't hiding that wig for the rapist—"

She picked up my train of thought. "Which is unlikely—"

"And assuming we get a match on the wig—"

"Which is likely—"

"We may now deduce that Stayner's our rapist."

"Yep," Bailey agreed.

"I'll make the calls." I dialed her buddy Fukai at the crime lab and asked him to get a sample as soon as possible from the morgue and compare Stayner's DNA to the rape kit, then got the number of the Firearms Unit.

I gave the Firearms supervisor the

heads-up that we were sending a gun in for testing on the unsolved shooting near Marsden High School. Since Bailey never reported that we were the targets, I saw no reason to mention that detail now.

I noticed that the photographer had left, and Ben had moved to the bathroom. "Where are the print techs?" I asked.

"On their way," Bailey replied.

I nodded and fell silent, thinking about what we had now.

We were rolling in evidence on the rape, but we still had a bunch of unanswered questions. Not to mention a suspiciously timed dead body.

"We still don't know why this guy targeted Susan," I said. I looked around the room for a moment. "And I don't like the way he turns up dead just when we start showing his picture around."

"Yeah, smells to me too," Bailey agreed.

The more I thought about it, the less I liked it. "So let's assume that Stayner's accident was no accident—"

"That leaves a pretty open field of suspects," she said. "I'd imagine lots of people had a motive to kill that scumbag."

"Number one being revenge for Susan's

rape—which makes Mommy and/or Daddy look good for it . . ."

Bailey nodded. "Except how would they get to him?" she asked. "We have no known connection between Stayner and them."

"I know." I sighed.

"And it could be revenge for raping some other kid," Bailey said. "Odds are Susan wasn't his first."

I nodded. "Or it could've been a falling-out with some other scumbag."

As I paced, another possibility occurred to me. I started to voice it, but the small room had made my pacing circles a little too tight for comfort. I was beginning to make myself sick. "Let's get out of here," I said.

We walked toward the Pacific Coast Highway, and I took a few cleansing breaths. The ocean air felt good. I resumed pacing and tried not to get distracted by the sparkling ocean view.

"If this is about revenge for molesting or raping someone else, we're toast," Bailey said grimly. "Without a known victim, we've got nowhere to go."

"Right," I said. "But if our killer's a pissed-off partner-in-crime, we should get a hit on any fingerprints they find in the car," I said. "They're printing the car, right?"

"Every inch and everything in it," she replied.

Another theory occurred to me. I stopped pacing and turned to Bailey. "What about a certain gang shot-caller? For example, someone Stayner set up to take the fall for Susan's rape?"

Bailey looked back at me. "Luis Revelo," she said, nodding. "That could work."

I pulled out my cell phone and scrolled to find his number, then hit send.

"Get him to meet us now," Bailey said.

I nodded, and we moved toward the car.

"Senorita Knight," Luis said. "Whassup?"

"I need you to meet me on the West Side," I replied.

"What for?"

"I'll tell you when I see you."

"'Kay," Luis agreed. "When?"

"Now," I said.

There was a beat of silence before he answered. "Sounds good," he said slowly, his voice unusually warm. "But I'm kinda busy at the moment. How 'bout a little later? Say, tonight?"

I paused, puzzled by his tone. "No. Now.

Meet me at Du-par's," I said. I gave him the address. The old-school diner-style restaurant in West Hollywood was midway between Luis's stomping ground and Malibu.

"We havin' lunch?" he asked.

"Sure," I replied. I didn't want to tip him off about the true reason for this meeting.

"Cool," Luis replied and hung up.

"We're on," I told Bailey.

We got in the car, and she steered it back over the canyon, heading for the freeway.

"I could go for a tasty chicken potpie," Bailey said with a sadistic smile.

I gave her a frosty look. "Why not complete the torture and order the pancakes?" I asked acidly. Du-par's was famous for their heavenly pancakes.

"Good idea," she said. "Pancakes would be way better."

I spent the rest of the ride thinking of a suitable revenge.

48

Bailey was halfway through a stack of decadent butter-and-syrup-laden pancakes by the time Luis slid into the booth across from us. He shot a narrow-eyed look at Bailey, then at me.

"I thought this was just gonna be you an' me," Luis said.

"Why?" I asked.

"'Cuz when you called, you said, 'Meet *me*,'" he replied.

The reason for the warm phone attitude finally dawned on me. "Luis, you did not seriously expect to hook up with a DA," I said, trying to keep a straight face.

Luis gave me a sly smile. "Why not?" he asked. "Not the first time I gone slummin'."

This was not the attitude of someone who'd just committed—or ordered—a murder.

"You mind telling us where you were last night?" I asked. I watched him closely, gauging his reaction.

Luis looked at Bailey, then looked back at me quizzically. "At my *tia's*," he finally replied. "It was my niece's *quinceañera*."

There wasn't even a whiff of anxiety or nervousness in his attitude. Concerned, maybe, and curious, certainly—but not nervous.

"From when to when?" Bailey asked.

Her tone told me she'd noticed Luis's demeanor too.

He shrugged. "Like, from six o'clock on. I helped them set up."

"And you were there until when?" I asked.

"Until dawn, man. It's a fiesta," Luis said, annoyed. "I got at least a dozen homies an' prally fifty of *mi familia* gonna—*going* to—tell you I was there all night."

I could see he was feeling dissed for being challenged this way. And I also had no doubt that, true or not, he'd have a ten-page list of alibi witnesses who would not just "prally" but would certainly say he was with them. So the alibi was less significant to me than his attitude, which was way too cavalier for a recent murderer. Luis might be good, but he wasn't *that* good.

"You gonna tell me what the deal is?" he asked.

I couldn't see any reason not to at this point, so I told him.

Luis sat back and looked at us with a disbelieving smile. "You gotta be kidding me," he snorted. "No, ain't no friggin' way." He shook his head firmly. "Tha' don' make no sense at all."

Luis was so incredulous at the notion that he'd killed Stayner, he'd abandoned any attempt at grammar. But I knew what he was getting at. In gangland, payback requires that a message be sent, and that message cannot be delivered by setting up an accidental death. I'd still ask to have his and his homies' prints checked against whatever they lifted from Stayner's Escalade. But, all things considered, I was ready to let Luis go for now.

"Don' get me wrong. I wouldn' a' minded

nailing that *pendejo,*" Luis said, his tone steely. "But after Hector fingered him for you guys, I knew you'd be sniffin' around him. I'd be a fucking idiot to do anything right now."

Right now. It wasn't exactly a comforting way to exclude Luis, but after all he was a shot-caller, not the Easter Bunny. I glanced at Bailey, who'd resumed eating her pancakes. I knew what that meant.

"Okay, Luis," I said. "You're good to go for now."

He started to slide out of the booth, but then I remembered I had a message to deliver.

"Susan asked me to tell you 'hey,'" I said. "I think she hopes you're still going to go for your GED."

"How's she doin'? I been meanin' to call," Luis said.

"She's doing better every day," I replied. "And I'm sure she'd be glad to hear from you."

Luis paused, nodding to himself. "Yeah, I kinda fell off my game with everythin' — *everything* — that's been happenin'," he said seriously. "I got to get back to the books."

Luis slid to the edge of the booth, then

stopped and leaned toward me with a slow smile. "You ever want to check out the finer things in life, you just call. *M'entiende?*"

I raised an eyebrow. "Why don't you empty your pockets, and we'll see if you get to walk out of here?" I asked.

Luis stood up. "Jeez, I was jus' jokin'," he said indignantly. "You know what your prallem is? You got no sense of humor."

I had many "prallems" right now. A failed sense of humor was the least of them. Luis headed out. As I watched him go, I was reminded of another odd puzzle piece I couldn't fit into the picture. I picked up my heretofore unused fork and turned to Bailey. "We always figured the rapist had framed Luis Revelo to take the fall for the rape," I said. I took a forkful of the now-cold pancakes. They were still delicious.

"Right." Bailey nodded.

"But what we've never been able to figure out was how Stayner knew Susan was tutoring a guy who'd look good for it."

"No," she said with an exasperated sigh. "Somehow he had to get close enough to Densmore to know as much as he did. Any bright ideas?"

I lifted my fork again, and Bailey pushed

her plate toward me. I took one more mouthful of pancakes and savored the sweet, soft
morsels before I reluctantly put my fork
down and tried to come up with said bright
idea.

"We checked out everyone who worked
in or around the house," I thought out loud.
"But we didn't get to all of Densmore's
health centers yet."

Bailey nodded again.

"That's about as bright as it's going to
get right now," I said.

49

We managed to get to the Calabasas Children's Health Center, a Spanish-style, tile-roofed building with a lovely courtyard, in record time. It was a small operation, and the few who worked there were all present and accounted for. Not one of them recognized Stayner's picture. Not one of them gave me any reason to think he or she was lying about it.

We worked our way east, toward the health center on Ventura Boulevard in Sherman Oaks. This center was on the third floor of a large, dark-windowed office building. But the center was just as kid-friendly and freshly decorated as the others. The employees there didn't recognize Stayner either. We continued on a southeasterly route to our last stop: the Hollywood center.

When most people think of Hollywood, they picture stars set into sidewalks, the flashbulbs of paparazzi cameras . . . swimming pools, movie stars—to paraphrase an old sitcom. What they don't know is that Hollywood is also seedy, run-down apartments, flophouse motels, buckled sidewalks, and urine-soaked corners. Where the homeless, the runaways, and the drugged-out converge in disharmony. The Yucca Street clinic was in that Hollywood.

The small one-story building that housed the clinic had a parking lot marked STAFF ONLY at the rear. Bailey pulled into it and stopped. I checked out our surroundings. It was late afternoon, and a fair number of the residents in this neck of the woods were hanging out—at the curb, on the front steps of a small, dingy liquor store, and on the street corners.

We walked into the waiting room and looked around. Surprisingly, it was nearly empty. The only occupants were a too-skinny, tattooed blond girl leafing listlessly through an ancient copy of *People* magazine and, across the room from her, a young Hispanic man who was bent over a sloppily bandaged hand. There was no one behind the counter at the reception desk. To the right of the counter was a gate that led to a corridor and, I surmised, the examining rooms. Presumably the gate was meant for security.

"Hello?" Bailey called out.

"Just a minute!" replied a female voice. Precisely one minute later, a woman appeared in a nurse's uniform, with black, wiry, shoulder-length hair and glasses on a chain around her neck.

"You're the detectives?" she said, sounding surprised.

"Well, she is," I said. "I'm a DA. Rachel Knight."

"And I'm Bailey Keller."

"Sheila Houghton," the woman said. "Glad to meet you."

She briefly scanned the waiting room, then looked back at us. "It's just terrible what happened to Susan," she said quietly. "I hope you get that monster soon."

Bailey said we hoped so too and got right

down to business. She held out Stayner's photograph. "Ever see him around here?" she asked.

Sheila put down her clipboard, slid on her glasses, and took a look. "Yeah," she said, pulling her glasses off again. "He brought a lot of the teenagers in here. Usually runaways," she replied. "Carl . . . something, I think."

I nodded neutrally, careful not to show she'd hit a bull's-eye. "Was it mainly girls or boys?"

"Both. But more boys. Said he worked at one of the local runaway shelters," she said. Her brows knitted for a moment. "I can't remember which one, though."

It didn't matter. It was probably a lie anyway. I had a feeling I knew why Stayner was bringing kids to a clinic, and it wasn't because he was working for a shelter.

"When was the last time you saw him around here?" I asked.

"I don't know." Sheila thought for a moment. "Not long ago—maybe a few weeks?"

So probably sometime before the rape.

"Sheila, would you mind if I looked around a bit?" I asked. I was actually more interested in having a quick—and private—word with Bailey than in a view of the clinic. I've learned from hard experience that the less witnesses know about what we're thinking, the better. Witnesses like to talk—and usually to all the wrong people.

"Be my guest," she said. Then she turned to the waiting area. "Mr. Flores?" she called out. "Come on in. Let's take a look at that hand."

The doors to the examination rooms were open, and as I passed the first one, I looked inside. A young Hispanic woman with a sizable diaper bag on her shoulder was strapping a toddler into a stroller. She looked up and smiled at me briefly. I returned the smile, and then she wheeled the stroller out of the room. The area was clean, but it wasn't the spiffy state-of-the-art place that the other clinics were. It had an old-fashioned feeling to it: an aging scale in one corner, a height-measuring chart on the wall next to the table, and some beat-up-looking wooden toys in a bin near the door. Even the predictable child-friendly poster—Thomas the Tank Engine—was out-of-date.

Exam room two was empty. So was

exam room three. They were all in the same condition: clean but old, no-frills. Looking at the rooms, I could feel something tickle at the back of my brain, but I couldn't put my finger on what it was. I heard Sheila approach and saw that she was heading for exam room two with Mr. Flores, so I didn't have time to think about it. I quickly pulled Bailey into exam room three.

"My guess is Stayner was pimping the kids and bringing them here for checkups," I said.

"Yep," Bailey agreed. "And I'm thinking maybe one of those kids decided he didn't appreciate the job opportunity so much anymore."

I nodded. "But if it was a kid, there's less chance we've got his prints in the database."

Bailey sighed unhappily. "Exactly."

"Great," I replied. "Perfect."

We headed out and waved good-bye to Sheila, who was busy bandaging Mr. Flores's hand in exam room two.

Bailey edged the car out into the near-standstill traffic on Hollywood Boulevard.

"So we've got good news and bad news,"

I said. "Bad news: our list of suspects is now the size of a phone book. Good news: we can at least eliminate Luis and Nurse Sheila."

"Fantastic," Bailey said sarcastically. "We're almost there."

We rode on in silence. With nothing good to say, we found it was best to say nothing.

After a while, Bailey broke the stony silence. "Home?"

"May as well," I said glumly. "Feel like a drink?"

"Or ten."

It wasn't that either of us minded the fact that Stayner might've been murdered—he was no big loss to the human race. But his death deprived us of a lot of answers. The only person left who might be able to give us those answers was his killer. And, with each passing minute, that killer might be slipping farther away.

I watched the outline of the downtown skyscrapers draw near as office lights flecked the darkening night sky like fireflies.

50

Bailey and I hit the Biltmore bar in a grouchy mood. Neither of us was herself . . . or anyone better. Drew poured a round of martinis.

"How's it going, ladies?" he asked.

"Like shit," Bailey said, abruptly taking the olive out of her martini as though it had deliberately gotten in her way. She took a long pull from her drink.

Drew raised an eyebrow at me. "Bad day?"

I rolled my eyes, picked up my drink, and considered draining it. I restrained myself—barely—and took a healthy sip instead.

Bailey, looking distracted, tapped her fingers on the bar nervously.

"Anything I can do?" Drew asked.

"You just did it," she said tersely, nodding toward her drink. She took another sip and resumed tapping.

"Okay," Drew said, tilting his head toward the other end of the bar. "I'll just be down there."

"Wise move, Obi-Wan," I said.

"I'm a survivor," Drew said smoothly. He moved to the service end of the bar, where a waiter was trying to decipher the drink order he'd written on a small notepad.

When I turned back, Bailey was scrolling through her e-mail on her cell phone.

"Any word on the print run?" I asked.

"They promise results first thing Monday morning," she said, frowning.

"Coroner?" I asked.

She scrolled for a few more seconds. "Also sometime on Monday. Preliminary results only." She shoved her phone into her pocket and turned back to her drink.

"Look, it is possible that Stayner drove

off that cliff by himself, Bailey," I said. "Accidents do happen."

"Yeah, just like coincidences," she said acidly. "And we both know what you think of those."

This was true. I considered offering her a platitude about things looking better after a good night's sleep, but I had a feeling neither of us was going to get one. We drank our martinis in silence, as if they were medicine. Which I guess they were. After one more dose, we were both ready to call it a night.

"You're not going to drive home, are you?" I asked.

"I was," Bailey replied.

Drew, who'd been standing nearby, leaned toward her. "No. You wasn't," he said. "Either crash with her or wait for me."

"Crash with me," I said quickly. I knew that if Bailey waited for Drew in her current mood, nothing good would come of it.

"Fine," Bailey said, resigned. Drew patted her hand, and she gave him a tired smile.

"Call me tomorrow," he said.

Bailey nodded, and we headed up to

my room. I helped her make up the sofa bed, then went and took a long, hot shower. I didn't realize how tired I was until I got into bed. But the moment my head hit the pillow, my whole body sank in, and I was gone. That's what too many suspects and not enough evidence will do to you. That, and a few martinis.

Sunday passed without incident; Bailey found her way home before I even awoke. By the time I got up Monday morning, I'd recovered most of my sleep and then some. It was 7:30. I showered, brushed and combed, and went out to look at the day. The sky was blue and the sun was shining; the air was a friendly, medium temperature. I hoped this was a good omen. I went over to my closet to make my wardrobe choices. I didn't know what the day would hold—I just knew I didn't have to be in court. So I dressed casually in slacks and a sweater.

Did I still need to wear the vest? Whoever had killed Stayner—assuming we were right and it wasn't just an accident—was still out there. But that person didn't seem dumb enough to go after me. Take me out, and there would be a million

more in my place. I decided I was safe
enough with just my .22-caliber Beretta and
left the vest in the closet.

I felt good, if a little naked. And I could
move a heck of a lot faster. Within minutes, I was climbing the stairs to the back
doors of the courthouse building. I'd just
stepped inside when my cell phone rang.

"Where are you?" Bailey asked.

"Heading for the elevator."

"I'll be there in ten," she said, and
hung up.

Nine minutes later, she strode into my
office. I held up the cup of coffee I'd bought
for her at the snack bar.

"Thanks," she said, sitting down in front
of my desk.

"And?"

"Print run is mostly done," Bailey replied.
"Just about everything's got Stayner's
prints."

"Just about?"

She nodded. "One item did not. The
tech found a set of clear but unidentified
prints on it."

"Unidentified?" I repeated. "You mean it
didn't match anyone in the criminal database?"

"That's what I mean."

That ruled out Luis for good and probably eliminated some other scumbag crime partner of Stayner's.

"Where were the prints found?" I asked.

"On a pack of Quench Gum," Bailey replied.

I frowned, thinking it certainly wasn't what I was expecting to hear. But it was better than nothing. "It's a thread to pull," I said. "Since we got no hit on the criminal database, we'll have to assume for now that whoever put those prints on the gum isn't a criminal."

"For now," she agreed. "But if we eliminate the criminal element, the motive we're left with is—"

"Susan's rape," I finished. "And the only noncriminals we know who've got the motive to kill Stayner because of Susan's rape are Susan—"

"I'm going to go out on a limb and say we can rule out the little girl," Bailey interjected.

"A bold move, but all right," I said. "Which leaves Mommy and Daddy."

"But this one's tricky," Bailey said. "We need more than a hunch before we take a run at them. They'll go straight to my captain—"

"And Vanderhorn—"

"—in a heartbeat," Bailey finished.

I thought for a moment. "Aren't doctors' prints on file?"

Bailey tilted her head. "Not sure," she said. "But I can find out pretty quick."

She made calls while I waited nervously.

"You nailed it, Knight," she said appreciatively. "They're accessing Densmore's prints as we speak. We should have the answer within the hour."

"And Densmore will never have to know."

51

It was one hell of a tense hour. Bailey didn't want to leave the office because she thought she might wind up in a bad cell area and miss the call. I wanted to get out because I needed to move around, and my office doesn't have enough room for even minor pacing. But I felt I had to be there when Bailey got the call. So I sat, pinned to my seat, and waited.

An hour and twenty minutes later, Bailey's cell phone rang. She listened and said "uh-huh" a few times, then "Thanks," and hung up. She looked at me deadpan.

"Do not torture me," I warned.

Not one to be threatened, she waited another beat before speaking. "We've got Frank Densmore's prints on the gum."

"Boo-yeah!" I shouted.

Bailey laughed, and we high-fived.

"You know, it does fit, doesn't it?" I said. "Quench Gum didn't exactly seem like Stayner's style."

Bailey nodded. "As soon as you mentioned that Densmore's prints might be on file, I remembered that's what I chew when I'm bike-riding."

Right. Densmore was a cyclist. "You didn't say anything," I remarked.

Bailey shrugged. "I wanted to wait till we got the prints back," she said. "I didn't want us to get fired up just to crash down."

After our mood a couple of nights ago, I couldn't blame her. I thought for a moment about where we stood. "It's all good so far, but it's not enough to get a warrant," I said. "It'd be easy for Densmore to claim that Stayner picked up the gum at a clinic."

"Or even that Stayner found it outside Densmore's house," Bailey said, "now that we know Stayner was floating around the hood."

"But working on the theory that Densmore's our killer—"

"A fair bet."

"That means Densmore lied when he claimed he didn't know Stayner," I concluded.

Bailey nodded. "Or else he wouldn't have known how to find him."

"That means it was probably Densmore himself who gave Stayner access to his home, his family," I added.

We both mulled over that unsavory thought, then Bailey voiced the million-dollar question. "Why?"

I shook my head. "We don't even have enough to venture a good guess yet. But let's not jump the gun. First we need to nail down Stayner's murder. Then we can see where we stand."

"True." Bailey folded her arms and leaned back in her chair. "The fact that Stayner's prints aren't on the gum helps," she said.

"It does," I agreed. "But not enough." A person doesn't always leave detectable prints every time he touches something. So the absence of prints has some value, but it's limited.

"Also true," Bailey said. "So we need more on our guy."

"You shoot at the king, you better kill the king," I agreed.

We both sat for a moment, silent, thinking.

"What about the coroner? You hear from him yet?" I asked.

Bailey shook her head. "Couldn't hurt to goose him a little." She punched the numbers on her phone.

"If you can't get the coroner, I'll try Scott and see what he knows," I said.

Bailey nodded.

I stood and faced the window while Bailey made the call. The sky was so piercingly blue it looked unreal, and the bright sunshine made even the grass around city hall look inviting. At the far end of the grounds, a shirtless man furtively urinated against an imposing maple tree. The grass looked somewhat less inviting now.

Bailey waved to get my attention, and I gladly turned away from my window. She covered the phone, her expression ominous. "I'm on hold. The assistant thinks they found the cause of death," she said. "It's a heart attack."

I frowned. "Is the coroner going to get on the phone?"

"Waiting to find out," Bailey said. After a moment, she nodded to me, then spoke into the phone. "Yeah, hi, Dr. Loujian," she said, and paused. "Yes, Carl Stayner."

While Bailey listened, I considered the possibilities now that Densmore was a potential suspect. I pointed to the phone and whispered, "Ask him—"

She looked at me. "Could you hold on for just a sec, Doctor? The DA has a question." She handed the phone to me.

"Dr. Loujian, thank you for taking the time," I said. "Is this a final conclusion or a preliminary?"

"It's just preliminary at this point," he replied in his oddly high-pitched voice, which was even more incongruous when you saw him: he was a solid six feet five.

"Was his physical condition completely consistent with a heart attack?" I asked.

The doctor paused. "Well, let's say it wasn't inconsistent," he replied. "His heart wasn't good. Then again, it wasn't as bad as his liver. Now *that* was something to behold. It looked like it was ready to crawl out of his body on its own." He chuckled at the macabre joke. Not all coroners have that sick sense of humor, but enough do to justify the cliché.

I tried to give him a polite laugh, but it stuck in my throat. "If someone wanted to administer a drug that would make the cause of death look like a heart attack, what would that be?" I asked.

"A number of substances could do it," he replied. "It'll take me a while to screen for them all, though."

I thought for a moment. Stayner had been killed within hours after I'd shown the photo to Densmore. If Densmore had done it, the substance would have to be readily at hand. "I'm thinking of something a doctor could get ahold of relatively quickly."

"That should narrow it down," he said. "I'll have them redo the tox and see what shows up."

"That would be great," I said. "How long will it take?"

"As long as it takes," he replied.

A beat of silence passed as I tried to think of a polite way to tell him to get the lead out. Before inspiration could hit, the doctor spoke with a sigh. "I'll put in a rush, but I can't promise anything."

"Thank you, Doctor. I really appreciate it." Knowing I was pushing my luck but unable to resist, I added another request. "Would you mind faxing me your preliminary report?"

"Ms. Knight, you know that's not kosher."

"I won't let anyone else see it, I promise," I said. "You can trust me, Dr. Loujian," I said quickly. "Ask Scott. He'll tell you. We go back a long way."

I didn't think it would help to add that Scott could also vouch for me because no one had found out about his pilfering Jake's autopsy report at my request.

After a pause, the doctor spoke. "I'll do it," he said reluctantly. "But you've got to keep it to yourself. And when I write the final report, you'll have to destroy the preliminary."

"I promise," I said.

"Go stand by your fax machine, and don't let anyone see you," the doctor said. "I'll get back to you on the rest as soon as I can."

I told Bailey to come with me as I headed for the machine in Melia's office. As we walked, I told her what the coroner had said.

"Those tox screens can take some time," she remarked grimly.

"I know," I replied. When we entered the anteroom to Eric's office, I noticed with relief that Melia wasn't there. The last thing I needed was her nosing around and asking questions. "But this is pretty specific stuff he's looking for, so that should speed things up."

Within seconds, the fax machine lit up and started spitting out pages of the preliminary autopsy report. I took the sheets as they came out, and we went back to my office, where I plopped down in my giant judge's chair and prepared to read.

"Feel like a snack?" Bailey asked.

At the mention of food, my stomach came to life with an answering rumble, reminding me that I'd skipped breakfast. The clock on the Times Building said it was 10:00 a.m. already.

"I'm starving," I replied. I started to reach for my purse, but Bailey stopped me.

"This one's on me," she said.

I looked at her, suspicious. "No bagels and no muffins. I can't take the stress right now."

She threw me a mock wounded look

and moved toward the door. "You cut me, Knight," she said.

"Seriously," I said. "I'm hungry and I have a gun. Do not fuck with me, Keller."

Bailey raised an eyebrow and walked out.

I grabbed a handful of mini-pretzels from my bottom drawer to stave off the hunger pangs and picked up the autopsy report.

Stayner and Densmore. The Hollywood clinic a connection between them. I turned the triangle over and over in my mind as I scanned the description of Stayner's external condition: "A well-nourished adult male . . . weighing 189 pounds . . . measured at 70 inches." I stopped. *Measured at.* Something skittered through the back of my brain. I tried to make the phantom thought take shape, but it eluded me. I let out an exasperated sigh and slapped my desk in frustration.

At that moment, Bailey walked in and dropped a bag of celery and carrots and an apple on my desk. "What's your damage, Knight?" she asked.

"Something in the autopsy report . . . reminded me of . . . ," I said. I paused as the wisp of a thought floated closer. Then slipped away . . . again. I shook my head. It was maddening.

Bailey picked up the report and read out loud: "'Weighing one hundred eighty-nine pounds . . . measured at—'"

"Measured at," I repeated. I held up my hand to stop Bailey from reading any further.

I quickly grabbed my printout of Kit's photograph from the zippered pocket in my purse. Where was my magnifying glass? I eagerly rummaged through my desk drawers, slamming them closed one by one.

"Knight?"

I shook my head, looking around my desk, and was about to move to the file cabinet near the door when I spotted the magnifying glass on the table near the window. I jumped up, snatched it, and slammed back into my chair. I held the magnifier over the picture and peered closely at the vertical black line in the background. Now that I knew what it was, it seemed so obvious.

"What?" Bailey asked.

"Look at this," I said.

I held the magnifying glass out to her. She took it and studied the picture.

"That black line in the background?" Bailey asked.

"It's a height-measuring line," I said. "We saw one in every exam room in the Hollywood clinic."

52

"So the pictures Clive found on the Net were all taken in that clinic," Bailey said almost to herself as she looked down at the printout again.

"Which explains why none of the kids looked posed," I said.

"Yeah, none of 'em looked particularly sexy," she agreed. "Then again, kiddie pictures often don't." Bailey put down the magnifying glass and sat back.

I nodded. The innocent look was usually a big part of the allure. I moved off the nauseating thought as a more stunning revelation suddenly hit me. The force of it held me transfixed in my seat. I stared out the window as I mentally played out the implications of what we'd just learned.

"What?" Bailey asked.

I paused. My conclusion was incredible but inescapable. "If we're right about all this, it means that Susan's rape and Jake's case are connected."

Bailey stared at me for a moment, blinking rapidly as the realization struck her.

I spoke slowly, thinking as I put the pieces together. "Kit is photographed in Densmore's clinic. The photo is found on Jake. Densmore killed Stayner—and probably because Stayner raped Susan."

"I'll be dipped in shit," she said softly, her tone incredulous. "You're right."

There's no such thing as a case without surprises, but they're generally little minnow-size twists that only involve side issues. What we had here was a game-changing sperm whale.

"But how and why did Densmore hook up with a cretin like Stayner?" I asked.

"No clue," Bailey said. "But whatever we were thinking about the cases before, all bets are off now."

I nodded. At this point, anything was possible.

"So this means Densmore's a pornographer?" she asked, her voice heavy with disbelief.

"I'm having a hard time with that one too," I admitted. I shook my head. "It makes no sense that this multimillionaire power broker would do something like this. Even if he was bent that way himself—"

"Which, frankly, I don't get from him," Bailey said. "Not that I'm a fan."

"No, I agree," I said. "On both counts. But we can't rule him out."

She nodded. "And even if Densmore isn't the one doing the porn, it's got to be someone with easy access to the rooms."

"The only thing I can say for sure about that is I'm not liking Nurse Sheila for it," I said.

"Yeah, I'd guess that someone who says 'Be my guest' when cops ask to look around isn't someone who knows they've got something to hide," Bailey agreed.

I sighed and leaned back in my chair. The more answers we found, the more questions popped up. Bailey posed another one.

"I've been picturing the clinic in my mind," she said. "I don't remember seeing any place for a camera in the exam rooms. Do you?"

I thought for a moment, then shook my head.

"We could head out there, take a look," Bailey suggested.

"May as well. But we should come up with a cover story for Nurse Sheila," I said. "We don't want her telling anyone what we're doing there."

Even if Sheila wasn't involved, we couldn't risk the possibility that she might inadvertently tip Densmore off by telling him what we were up to. There was also the minor detail that I'd been specifically ordered not to get within ten miles of Jake's case. Twice.

"Shouldn't be too hard," Bailey replied. She stood up and moved to the door. "We'll figure it out on the way."

"One more thing," I said. "We're going to have to keep the connection between the rape and the murders to ourselves for now."

"No shit," she agreed with a small chuckle. If we told the powers that be about the link right now, they'd throw us off the Densmore case and hammer us for tromping on forbidden territory. But if they found out after we delivered both cases all nicely wrapped up with a bow, it'd be tough to justify any disciplinary action. All things considered, I decided to follow my motto: Better to ask forgiveness than permission.

"Of course, even if you did tell anyone—," I began.

"They'd never believe it anyway," Bailey finished for me.

We shared a rueful smile.

I picked up my coat, stuffed Stayner's autopsy report into my purse, and put the printout of Kit's photo back into the zippered pocket. We walked out and headed down the hallway.

"We could tell Sheila we wanted to score some Ecstasy," I suggested.

"Nah," Bailey replied. "It's a sappy drug. Make it crystal meth."

"Never figured you for the tweaker type," I said.

"I'm a control freak," Bailey said. "It's a control-freak drug."

"Interesting. I never thought of it that way."

We'd almost reached the main door when I heard Melia call out, "Rachel!"

I spun around to see her waving at me from the door of Eric's anteroom. Annoyed, I turned back. When I got close enough to avoid having to yell, I stopped. "Yes?"

"You've got a call," she said. "A doctor. I think his name is . . . uh . . . Luanne?"

Loujian. The coroner. *That was fast.* "Thanks, Melia," I said. Bailey and I rushed back to my office. I called out to Melia over my shoulder. "Tell him I'm coming."

I was breathless as I picked up the phone. "Dr. Loujian?"

"I suppose I owe you one, Ms. Knight," he said. "I went back to the body and found an injection site in the upper-right buttocks area. I decided to run some additional tests, and I suspect the killer may have used suc-cinylcholine, or Anectine—a smart move because its half-life is about two minutes, then it's gone. But I can still test for the me-tabolites."

"What's Anectine?"

"It's used to relax the respiratory mus-cles in order to insert a breathing tube for anesthesia. Basically it paralyzes the respiratory muscles, which makes an overdose look like a heart attack," Dr. Loujian explained.

"Is this something a doctor might have on hand?"

"Easily," he replied. "Though I wouldn't think he'd administer it without having an anesthesiologist present. Of course, that wouldn't be such a big concern if he was using it to kill people," the doctor said, chuckling at his own joke.

Actually it was kind of funny, so I chuckled with him for a moment. I promised to destroy the preliminary report, thanked him profusely, and hung up.

I brought Bailey up to speed, and she immediately pulled out her cell phone.

"Who're you calling?"

"I'm sending units out to Densmore's clinics to find out whether they stocked Anectine and, if so, whether there's any missing," she replied.

"Perfect."

While Bailey made the calls, I turned to my computer and started preparing search warrants for Densmore's house and clinics. Most of the personnel in the health centers would probably give us consent. But since

I figured the pornography was an inside job, there had to be at least one person who'd refuse permission to search if he could.

Bailey got off the phone and turned to me. "They'll be calling in with results as they get them. Assuming everyone at the clinics cooperates."

I told her I was working on the warrants. "But if we want to make sure the judge approves an arrest warrant for Densmore, we should lay out a scenario for how he could've done the murder," I said. "The judge isn't going to want to go out on a limb any more than we did."

"Right," Bailey agreed. "I've been thinking about that. My guess is that Densmore got Stayner to meet him somewhere—"

"I'd bet the Hollywood clinic," I said. "He'd need a private place he could control so he could knock Stayner out and inject him without being seen. And that clinic is the one point of intersection for them."

"Sounds right," Bailey said. "Then he loaded his bike and Stayner's body into Stayner's Escalade and drove up to the top of Malibu Canyon."

"And that Quench Gum fell out of his bike bag."

Bailey nodded. "Densmore took out the bike, put Stayner into the driver's seat, and sent the car off the cliff. Then Densmore rode his bike down the canyon."

"All the way to the Palisades? That's a pretty long ride," I remarked.

"Not for him," Bailey explained. "Don't forget, it's downhill all the way to the Pacific Coast Highway, and then it's level ground on PCH. For a rider like him, it's very doable. But even if he got tired, there's a bus on PCH that'd take him almost all the way home."

"Better add the bike to the search warrant," I said as I turned back to my computer. "And we'll need to check the records at the guard gate to see if they show him coming in late that night."

"I don't think there'll be a record," Bailey said. "The gate picks up the signal from the transponders that the residents have on their cars. His bike wouldn't have one."

"That's true," I replied. "Maybe one of the guards will remember letting him in." I thought about that for a moment. "On second thought, no. If I were him, I wouldn't chance that. I'd stash the bike nearby and climb the fence somewhere I wouldn't be spotted."

Bailey nodded again. "Then he could ride it back the next day without attracting attention. We'll have the search team check the perimeter of the hood for a point of entry."

Her cell phone rang.

"The troops checking in?" I asked.

"Hope so," she replied. "Keller." She listened for a few moments, then ended the call. "Brentwood, Palisades, and Calabasas do have Anectine," she said.

"And?"

"It's all present and accounted for."

I exhaled and sat back. "I'll keep working on the warrants," I said. "But I don't want to go to the judge with them until we've heard back from all the clinics."

Bailey nodded. After another ten minutes, her cell rang again. This was nerve-racking. I stopped and watched as she took the call.

After a few moments, she signed off and put her phone in her pocket. "Sherman Oaks and Beverly Hills—ditto," she said. "Nothing missing."

Worried now, and wondering whether we'd need to find out where Densmore had hospital privileges, I tried to refocus on the warrants. Bailey tapped her fingers nervously on the arm of the chair.

Five minutes passed. I couldn't keep myself from looking at the clock on my computer. I wanted to tell Bailey to stop that goddamn tapping.

Ten minutes—still nothing.

Finally, at 1:35 p.m., I finished the warrants and hit print. Just as the pages began to roll out, Bailey's cell rang again. I turned to her, and we exchanged a look.

"Keller." She listened for a few moments. "Okay, stay there for now," she said, then hung up.

"It figures," Bailey said flatly.

"What? What?" I said, aggravated and impatient.

"Hollywood clinic. They ordered two vials. Their records show neither of them were ever used," she said. After a brief pause, she continued, "But one of the vials is gone."

I sagged with relief. We had our missing Anectine.

Indignant, I remarked, "You punked me."

"Just a little," Bailey admitted with a grin. "It's a great tension-breaker, don't you think?"

"No." I turned back to my computer and added this latest information to the warrants, then hit print again. I handed the papers to Bailey. "You got a judge in mind for these?"

She smiled mischievously. "I thought I'd hit up Judge J. D. Morgan," she said. She looked at her watch. "He should just be getting back from lunch."

"Sheer genius, Keller," I said with an appreciative laugh. J.D. wasn't just a friend, he was a judge who was uniquely unafraid of political fallout. The perfect person to handle what was sure to be a hot potato of a case.

Bailey stood and moved to the door quickly. "Once I get these signed, we should get out to Densmore's house right away. If he's inclined to talk, we should be there to listen."

"I'm packing up right now," I said.

53

Soon after, Bailey and I were in her car, heading for the Palisades. The moment J.D. had signed the warrants, Bailey had sent out units to locate Densmore. They'd tracked him to his house and were parked just out of sight at the front and back gates to the community, waiting for Bailey.

As she drove through the tunnel to the freeway, I pictured the police converging on the mansion, and poor Susan and Janet feeling besieged. The elation of a few moments ago drained away. I couldn't imagine how they were going to deal with all this. On the one hand, it was somewhat noble that Densmore had killed his daughter's rapist. But on the other hand, the connection between Densmore and Stayner was bound to be bad news of one kind or another. I had been excited to question Densmore; now my curiosity was mixed with dread.

We got to the house quickly, but not before our backup arrived. Bailey got out and told them to follow her lead. No one thought guns would be needed here, but you never knew.

Bailey knocked, and when the maid opened the door and saw the phalanx of officers behind her, she stood frozen in shock.

"We're looking for Dr. Densmore," Bailey said.

"*Sí, sí,*" the maid replied. "*Allá,*" she said, nodding to her left. Then she turned and ran back into the house.

Bailey stepped through the open door, her gun held pointed down at her side.

Janet came into the foyer. "Yes? Can I help you?" she asked. When she saw that Bailey was holding a gun, her eyes flew open in fright and she turned as white as a sheet.

"I'm sorry, Mrs. Densmore. We're here for your husband. Is he here?" Bailey said.

"Frank?" Janet looked as if she were going to faint. "He's in the den." She pointed to her left.

Bailey motioned for two of the officers to join her, and they headed off to serve the arrest warrant on Dr. Densmore. I hung back to talk to Janet.

"What's going on?" she asked, her voice shaky.

"I'm so sorry, Janet. Your husband's being arrested," I said, "for murder."

Janet started to sway, and I quickly caught her by the arm. Somehow she recovered enough to let me guide her to the sofa in the living room.

After I got her settled, I offered her a glass of water. When she shook her head, I sat down next to her. I wanted to give her the solace of knowing that the person Densmore had killed was Susan's rapist, but we didn't have that confirmed yet.

"Can you tell me if you saw Frank last night?" I asked.

Janet started to speak, then her eyes darted to the foyer, where officers had begun to gather. Janet put her hand to her throat, and her mouth fell slightly open. Finally she spoke in a faint voice. "I — I don't think I should be talking to you."

Probably not, now that I thought about it. I wouldn't have wanted to talk to me either. At least at this point there was no reason to force the issue.

"Is Susan here?" I asked. I didn't want her to see her father taken out in handcuffs.

"No. She went to a friend's house," Janet replied, her voice barely a whisper.

"Do you have someone you can stay with tonight?" I asked.

She didn't answer. She stared out the window at the rolling gardens in her backyard, her features slack.

"Do you want me to call someone for you?" I asked.

Janet slowly shook her head. "I'll do it," she said, her voice thin.

I nodded. She probably wouldn't want me to do anything else for her — ever.

I joined Bailey and the officers in the den. Frank Densmore had been proned out and thoroughly searched. One of the officers helped him up off the floor and placed him on the leather couch. He was pretty mussed up.

"Dr. Densmore, I'm going to read you your rights—," Bailey began.

"Don't bother. I'm not talking to any of you," Densmore said, his tone steely. "Give me my phone. I want to call my lawyer."

The officer standing to his right went over to the desk, picked up the phone, and asked Densmore for the number. Densmore told him and the officer dialed, then held the phone to Densmore's ear. Oddly, even with his hands cuffed behind his back, he managed to look imperious.

I sighed, but it figured that he'd invoke. He had nothing to gain by talking to us, and he was smart enough to know it.

There wasn't anything for us to do here at the moment. Bailey tilted her head toward the door. I nodded, and we headed out.

"Want to check out the garage before we split?" I asked.

"Absolutely."

The garage was huge and spotless. Of course.

"That his bike?" I asked, pointing to the yellow-and-black racing bike hanging from the ceiling.

"Looks like it," Bailey replied. "It's in the

warrant. I should remind them to be careful bagging it so we can save dirt samples."

"I'm guessing those puncture marks in the dirt on the shoulder of the road were probably from his bike shoes," I said.

"Right," Bailey said. She punched numbers on her cell phone, then talked to someone about bagging the bike.

"They know to look for the shoes?" I asked.

She added that reminder too and ended the call.

"The clinic?" I asked.

"The clinic," Bailey agreed.

We headed for her car—and the opposite end of the world.

54

There was only one police unit at the clinic when we got there. Of course, as far as they knew, they were just babysitting a shelf in a medical-supply closet. They had no idea the clinic might be connected to Jake's murder.

We walked into the health center and found Sheila doing paperwork at the reception desk. She greeted us warmly, but I could see she was curious about what the Anectine search was all about. I planned to tell her . . . later.

"How often did Dr. Densmore come around here?" I asked.

Sheila pursed her lips, holding back words she couldn't afford to say. "Almost never. I think it's been a year since I last saw him here," she said, her voice tinged with disapproval. "Your officer is back there waiting for you."

"Yeah, I know," Bailey replied. "Thanks for your help, Sheila."

"Not a problem," she answered. She went back to her paperwork, and we sauntered down the hall slowly. I whispered to Bailey out of the side of my mouth, "You going to get rid of your guy?"

She nodded. "Go ahead and start. I'll catch up."

After a quick glance behind me to make sure Sheila wasn't looking, I walked into exam room three, closed the door, and faced the wall with the measuring line that had been in all the photos. I tried to place myself where the camera would have been positioned. When I'd hit the spot, I turned and looked behind me. Nothing. There had to be a camera somewhere near. Unless they'd already taken it down? But the only person who had reason to know that the clinic had become a focus of suspicion was Nurse Sheila. I never liked to rule anyone out based on appearances, but I felt safe doing it this time. Nothing about her said she was involved in this.

I looked more closely. The camera had to have been somewhere on the wall opposite the measuring line. I scanned the wall. It had a sink and a compact air ionizer, with cabinets above and below. The cabinets were either too low or too high to have the angle I'd seen in the photographs. I opened them and looked inside anyway. Nothing but cleaning supplies below, and paper gowns above.

I thumped on the wall above the sink, feeling for a hollow panel. Nothing. The air ionizer was plugged in next to the sink. I unplugged it and hefted it in my hand. Nothing unusual. I shook it for a second but didn't hear any odd noise. Then I noticed that the grille could be lifted up. And there it was. The camera. So innocuous, it hid in plain sight. I marveled at the technology even as I felt sickened at the way it had been employed. It would take some techno-savvy to pull video and stills off this for the purpose of sale, but not a whole heck of a lot. The computer age has opened so many doors.

I plugged the ionizer back in and was trying to figure out who might've set this up when Bailey walked in. I pointed to the air ionizer and held a finger to my lips, warning her not to say anything. Bailey looked at it, then back at me, and raised a questioning eyebrow. I motioned for her to follow and led her out to exam room two. I checked the walls, this time aware of what I was looking for. Sure enough, on the wall opposite the measuring line, just above the sink: another ionizer. Wordlessly, I pointed it out to Bailey, who nodded. We did the same thing in room one. There, I unplugged the object and opened the front grille. Bailey examined the camera.

I spoke softly to avoid being overheard. "Stayner had to be part of this operation, but I doubt he could've set these up," I said, gesturing to the ionizers.

"No," Bailey agreed. "But I'll bet Densmore's bust is already on the news—"

"So whoever did this has got to be getting ready to cut and run," I said, completing her thought.

Bailey nodded. "I say we stake out the place and see who shows up."

I paused. It might not be the best plan,

but it was the only one we had at the moment.

She looked at me. "Well?" she prompted.

"I'm in."

55

It was close to 7:00 p.m., and the clinic was empty. Sheila was walking toward exam room one, key in hand, ready to start locking the place down for the night.

"Sheila, I'm going to need you to leave things as is for now so we can get the medical-supply closet photographed and printed," Bailey said.

It was partly true. We did need to get pictures and prints, which was why Bailey had posted the officer there earlier. We just weren't going to do it tonight. Right now, the pressing need was to find out who'd installed the hidden cameras. Photographs could be taken anytime, and as for the prints, while it would be nice to find Densmore's digits near the bottle of Anectine, they wouldn't exactly be a smoking gun, since he had lawful access to the medical-supply closet. Then again, given his infrequent visits, it would be something.

"Not a problem," Sheila replied in her typical way.

"It'd help if we could stay here and wait for the techs," Bailey said. "That okay?"

Sheila paused a moment to think. "It's fine, Detective," she replied. "But let me show you where the doors are. If you don't lock up, the place will be gutted by midnight."

She showed us the back door. The reception area was actually deeper than I'd realized. At the far end of the room was a back door that led into the staff parking lot behind the building. The nurse demonstrated which key went to that lock, then led us down the hallway, past the examining rooms. At the end of the hall was a small office. A door at its side also gave access to the parking lot.

"Two back doors?" I asked. It seemed odd.

"Yeah," Sheila said. "This building used to be a house. If you look, you can tell where rooms were added on to make it into a clinic. I think the door in the office was actually the original back entrance." She picked up her purse and jacket. "Anything else I can do for you?"

"Can we get all your numbers?" I asked. "Just in case we have to reach you for any other questions."

Sheila furnished us with her cell and home phone numbers, then gave the keys to Bailey. "We open at seven a.m.," she warned.

"I'll be here," Bailey promised.

We watched Sheila leave the staff parking lot, then mapped out our strategy. Out of necessity, it was a simple one.

"We'd better monitor both the front and back doors," I said.

"Agreed. But I'm guessing our buddy is going to come in through the back door. So I'll take the back; you take the front."

"We've only got one car," I pointed out.

She nodded. "And it can't be all alone out there in the staff parking lot. It'll be like posting a neon sign. So you take it out front," she said, handing me her keys.

"Then where are you going to be?" I asked.

We turned to look out through the office window. The parking lot offered no cover. I scanned the area around it. An alley ran along the left side. Farther to the left, across the alley, was a small gas station. A low cinder-block wall divided them, but it wouldn't get in the way if Bailey had to move fast. And there were enough cars, people, and activity at the station to let her blend in.

I turned to Bailey and saw that she too had zeroed in on the gas station. "It isn't perfect," I said.

She nodded. "But it'll have to do."

"You got a jacket or coat in your car?" I asked. The night was getting chilly, and our suspect might not show up for hours—if at all. It was going to get pretty uncomfortable if Bailey had to stand out there for very long.

"Don't need it," she replied. "I'm sure they've got lots of bad coffee at that gas station. That'll keep me warm."

"That's like drinking acid rain, Keller. You'll blow our cover if you glow in the dark," I said with a tight grin.

Bailey's answering smile was just as strained.

"We'll blow our cover right now if we don't get these office lights off and get out of here," she said. "I'm going to get into position." She stopped and scanned the gas station, then she continued, her tone urgent, serious. "You stay here and watch so you can see where I'm going to be. I'll have my cell phone on vibrate. We should check in with each other every ten minutes or so, but I'll call you. You don't call me. I'm the one exposed, and you won't be able to see if someone's too close to me. Got it?"

"Got it." I nodded toward the door. "Go."

Bailey opened it a fraction and looked around to make sure the coast was clear, then sprinted across the parking lot. She stepped over the cinder-block wall and into the gas station. There were a few cars parked outside the now-closed service bay. Bailey slipped between two of them and stood facing me. I waved from the office to show her I had her position. She lifted her cell phone. One second later, I heard mine ring. I quickly shifted it to vibrate and answered.

"I've got you. I'm on my way out."

"Remember to lock the office door and check to make sure the other one's locked before you go," Bailey replied, then hung up.

I did as she said with the office door, then turned out the lights as I went through the clinic. By the time I finished locking reception, the only light was in the waiting area. My spine tingled with apprehension. I stopped and listened for a sound. Had I heard something? I looked around, seeing nothing but darkness. The stillness of the office suddenly unnerved me, and I quickly moved to the front entrance. I forced myself to turn off the light in the waiting room before opening the front door, so I could slip out as unobtrusively as possible. Then I closed the door softly behind me. With shaking hands, I turned the upper dead bolt and the lock in the doorknob and ran around to the staff parking lot as fast as I could without drawing attention to myself.

I stopped at the back corner of the clinic and looked around. The lot was dark, but life went on in the houses surrounding the clinic, and in the gas station where Bailey was positioned. Somewhat reassured by the sight of others nearby, I took one last glance to make sure no one was coming, then trotted over to Bailey's car. I pressed the remote to unlock the door, jumped in, and pulled out of the lot. I drove slowly toward Yucca, scanning for an empty spot on the street. I found one in front of a tiny house that had been boarded up and graffitied, just west of North Cherokee Avenue. I backed into the space and turned off the engine. I was parked near the clinic, with a clear view of the front door ahead of me.

I sank down to stay out of view and hoped no one would decide Bailey's car needed breaking into tonight. Moments later, my cell phone vibrated. I checked to make sure it was Bailey.

"Where are you?" she asked.

I told her.

"Good." She clicked off.

On the street, young teenage boys were starting to gather into groups of two and three. Some leaned against street signs; others against fences and the walls of houses. All were whip-thin, with long hair, almost androgynous. It wasn't hard to imagine Kit among them. Or Dante. These thoughts were distractingly sad. I promised myself I'd find a way to help Dante climb out of this cesspool, and made myself look away.

Bailey called twice more, checking in. The third time, she told me she was going in for a cup of coffee. If it'd been me, I'd have been on my fifth cup and I'd still have been a frozen block of ice by now. "I'll get out and cover you," I said.

"Stay put. I don't like you being seen getting in and out of that car. I'll be fast," she said.

I made a face at the phone and ended the call. Waiting was not my strong suit. Neither was sitting still.

"I got an e-mail from SID," Bailey said during her fourth call. "Stayner's DNA matched Susan's nightgown."

"Nice," I replied. I was surprised by how anticlimactic this news was—we'd been so sure about Stayner that it hadn't occurred to me to worry he might not be the rapist. But now that it was official, someone could tell Janet and Susan and let them salvage something out of the wreckage of their lives.

Bailey hung up, and I continued to watch the street.

Time passed. We checked in regularly. More time passed. Still nothing.

"I've got to get out and move around or I'll lose it," I said on our ninth call.

"Remind me never to bring you on a real stakeout," Bailey groused. "Fine, cover me. I'll take a bathroom break."

"Take your time," I replied.

I scanned the area to see if anyone was watching. There didn't seem to be. I slipped out and closed the driver's door as quietly as possible, locked it with the key to avoid the "beep" of the remote, and moved down the alley along the side of the clinic, toward the staff parking lot at the rear. There were a few bushes on the alley side of the building. I found a spot at the corner nearest to the parking lot and got between the bushes and the wall. The lot was still empty.

I was just about to head back toward the car when something flashed to my right. It looked like a light was on in the office. If so, someone had gone in through the front door after I'd left the car—of course, the minute Bailey'd gone. It figured. Scared but too curious to stop and think, I moved around to the front of the clinic and tested the doorknob. It turned in my hand. I pushed through, slowly and quietly, my heart thudding like a bass drum.

I closed the door partway behind me but didn't click it shut, afraid the sound would alert the suspect. I stood very still and listened. There seemed to be movement in the first examination room, the one nearest to the reception desk. I felt in my pocket for my .22, pulled it out, and flipped off the safety. I moved toward the reception area. I'd have to climb over the security gate. I swung a leg up onto the counter and pulled myself over, then stepped down on the other side, one foot at a time. The sound of footsteps emerging from the first examination room made me duck down, but they soon receded in the direction of the second room. By the time I ventured to look out, the hallway was empty.

I duckwalked into the hall, intending to corner whoever it was inside the second examination room. I held my breath and moved slowly, gun in both hands in front of me, pointed at the ground. I could feel my temple pulsing. I swallowed nervously as I moved toward the doorway. At that same moment, the intruder stepped out. I barely had a second to register that it was a woman when she swung her monstrous purse at my head. I ducked just in time, but as I raised my hands up for cover, the purse struck my right forearm. Whatever was in that bag was mighty heavy. By the time I straightened up, the woman was running down the hall toward the office.

I gave chase, blood pounding in my ears. She sprinted around the corner and turned into the office. I followed, but just as I reached the end of the hall, she slammed the door. I threw my body against it once, twice, and it flew open—just as she ran out the back door. Feet pounding on the asphalt, I chased her through the parking lot. We were running toward Yucca Street and probably toward her car. I ran full-out, trying to gain ground. As we hit the sidewalk, I knew there were only seconds left. In a combination of desperation and sheer stupidity, I jumped, trying to tackle her. And missed. I barely got hold of her ankles, and my gun went flying. She went down, but I'd fallen right behind her.

She got a foot free and landed a boot on my face, then turned over and started kicking me, hard and fast, in the chest and head. I tried to hang on to the one ankle and roll to my side to get my head out of range, but she managed to lean forward and pummel me with her fists, on the back, head, shoulders. . . . I felt myself starting to go under. My grip on her ankle loosened. I felt her begin to stand up. In desperation, I threw my whole body into her legs, taking her down again. I heard a *whump* and a dull thud as she fell over. Still dazed, I straddled her back and saw that her head had hit the pavement—hard. Blood trickled from her forehead. I looked around for my gun, knowing I couldn't hold her down for long. I spotted it a few feet behind me on the right. I leaned back and tried to reach for it, but just as I managed to get my fingers around the barrel, she got her hands under her and abruptly shoved me backward. As I fell, I finally got ahold of my gun and slammed the grip hard into the side of her head. She slumped just long enough for me to get an arm around her neck. Putting her in a choke hold, I shoved the muzzle into the back of her head and yelled, "Don't move!"

She finally lay still. Bleeding, bruised, my breath ragged, I thought, *Now what?*

At just that moment, I heard the most welcome sound imaginable.

"I can take it from here, Knight. You can stand down," Bailey said. "Or finish falling down. Whatever's good for you."

Relief rushed through me, and the adrenaline drained abruptly. My stomach lurched, and I crawled over to the bushes, where I retched until there was nothing left.

When I'd finished, I sat on the ground, my back propped against the wall of the clinic. I looked at the woman, whose hands were now cuffed behind her back. It was Evelyn Durrell. Office administrator. And, apparently, pornographer.

56

Bailey insisted I go to the hospital, although I knew there was nothing really wrong with me. The doctors had taken X-rays and poked and prodded me until I threatened a lawsuit, but in the end they found nothing had been broken or mangled. I was released that same night.

I took a long, hot shower; had a big, tall glass of Patrón Silver on the rocks; and fell into bed. In my dreams, the chase replayed with alarming detail—right down to the pain I felt every time I tried to turn over.

I woke up the next day feeling like a bulldog's chew toy. The slightest move made every muscle in my body scream. Needless to say I called in sick. But apparently word of my exploits had spread fast. Not long after I'd called in, I got a big bouquet of roses from Eric and the deputies in Special Trials, with a card that said I was pretty cool. Actually it said: "For Rachel, who goes beyond the call of duty—and the pale of sanity." Sweet. Graden had shown he knew who he was dealing with: he sent me a bottle of Russian Standard Platinum vodka. He also sent a sweet note: "Do that again, and I'll revoke your permit."

I noticed I'd gotten nothing from Vanderhorn. I guessed that might have something to do with the fact that I'd tagged one of his major campaign contributors for murder—what a spoilsport.

Toni's trial was over, so she was free to fuss over me. She did such a thorough job of it, I finally had to tell her to go watch television in the other room and let me get some work done. I had calls to make and research to do. Bailey was hard at work too, and we compared notes throughout the day, including an interesting nugget on Stayner that Bailey'd dug up.

The following morning, I hobbled down

to the hotel lobby and tried not to lean against the wall while I waited for Bailey. There was no part of my body that didn't hurt to be touched.

She pulled up in front of the Biltmore. I gingerly got into the car, trying not to wince.

"You look good," Bailey said.

"Thank you," I replied with as much dignity as my bruises and scratches would allow.

They were keeping Evelyn Durrell at the Hollywood Station jail. It was smaller and safer than some of the others, and the detectives there were good friends of Bailey's. Evelyn had told the officers who'd taken her in that she wanted to talk. But our forty-eight hours ended today. That meant I had one chance to see what I could get out of her.

When Bailey and I walked into the small interview room, Evelyn Durrell was already there, cuffed to the table. I was gratified to see that she looked bruised too. I glanced up to make sure the red light of the video camera was on. Then Bailey read Evelyn her rights, and she waived them.

"Since we found the ionizers and cameras in your purse"—hence the heavy bag—"we've got you dead to rights on the pornography charges," I began. "I can't even tell you how many counts you'll be facing, but it'll add up to a lot of years." Evelyn already knew she was in deep shit, but I wanted her to realize just how deep. "So if you think you've got information to bargain with, it better be good."

She lifted her chin, looking me in the eyes. "I know I do."

She sounded pretty confident. We'd see if she had reason to be.

I decided to start with the most obvious point. "Stayner rounded up the kids for you, right?" I asked.

"Yeah," she replied.

"So who first came up with the idea to use the clinic for child pornography?" I asked.

"Carl. He'd bring kids to the clinic a lot. We'd talk. He never told me what he was up to, but it didn't take long to figure out he was probably pimping them. After a while he brought up the pornography idea. Said those kids were selling it anyway, so what difference did it make?"

Even if that was true, Evelyn had been a willing accomplice. Pretty cold for someone who works with kids.

"And Densmore, was he in on it?" I asked.

"Up to his neck," she answered, her voice tinged with anger. "Matter of fact, that's how Carl knew where he lived. Densmore had him over to talk about putting cameras into the high-end clinics too."

I shook my head. "I don't buy it," I said. "Densmore's rich enough without this slime money. Why would he risk everything by getting in bed with you and Stayner?"

"Because he's one of 'em," Evelyn said. "He likes boys." She looked at me. "Didn't know that, did you?" she asked, a slight tinge of triumph in her voice.

As a DA in Los Angeles, few things had the ability to surprise me—this wasn't one of them. Still, I had to push back.

"Why would I believe that?"

"Because I can prove it," she replied smugly. "I've got him on videotape making it with one of those little hustlers in the Hollywood clinic."

I took a deep breath. "When?" I asked.

"A few years back," she said. "But, trust

me, he's still at it. He likes 'em older. Eighteen, twenty."

I paused a beat, considering what she'd said.

"You got Densmore on videotape with a hustler," I said.

"You bet," she said smugly.

I wanted to smack her. Really hard . . .

"That means you already had a camera in place, Evelyn. Your operation was already up and running."

That smug smile dropped away suddenly.

"I'll tell you what happened," I said. "You got lucky. You didn't mean to, but you caught Densmore on tape. Perfect blackmail material. A guy like him, big-shot businessman, he couldn't afford to have people know he's hooking up with street trade. A big break for you, because after that, you didn't have to worry if he found out." I leaned back in my chair. "By the way, we've got a warrant for your house. We find that tape, I'll have the pleasure of adding an extortion count to that impressive list of charges."

I don't know whether it was the mention of an extortion count or the mention of a search warrant—or maybe it was everything falling in on her at once—but for the first time she seemed rattled. What had she expected? On the other hand, she wasn't exactly your typical career criminal.

Evelyn said nothing, which worried me. I kept talking, hoping to provoke her.

"So I don't buy your story that Densmore invited Stayner to his house," I said. "Tell you what I think. I think Stayner showed up uninvited to pressure Densmore into putting cameras into his high-end health centers."

It was a shot in the dark, but judging by Evelyn's grim expression, I'd hit close to the mark. Still, she remained mute. This was not good. I pulled out the file I'd brought and opened it. I took a moment to review the notes I'd made the day before.

"I don't think you're really the criminal type. Or at least you weren't." I looked up from the file and studied her face a moment. "You've been with Densmore from the beginning, when he opened the Hollywood clinic. That was his first one, wasn't it?"

Evelyn nodded warily.

"Right. No pricey 'health centers' back then," I said. I deliberately looked down again to consult my notes. "And you were a single mom, struggling to support your teenage daughter, Katie. So you were grateful when Densmore said you could hire her to help with the filing at the clinic, weren't you?" I asked.

At the mention of her daughter, Evelyn's face suddenly froze. The story of Katie had come to us courtesy of Nurse Sheila, who'd started with Densmore at the Hollywood clinic at the same time as Evelyn. Sheila had proven to be a great source of information—once we knew the right questions to ask.

I noted Evelyn's reaction and shot a brief glance at Bailey, who was leaning against the far wall. She nodded and moved in closer. When Evelyn looked up at her, Bailey began to speak.

"But after Katie started working there, she got sick. Hep C. She fell for one of the young street boys, didn't she?" Bailey asked.

Shaken, Evelyn nodded, her expression bitter.

"And he gave her a potentially fatal disease," Bailey said, her tone sympathetic.

Evelyn nodded again.

"By the time you realized how sick she was, she'd probably had the disease for over a year. Densmore helped you out with the new interferon, but it made Katie horribly sick. And she was probably miserable, maybe even suicidal. So you bought into those so-called cutting-edge drugs that promised a miracle cure. But they were expensive—"

"And none of them worked!" Evelyn spit out angrily.

Bailey nodded in acknowledgment. "Katie's still very ill," she said. "From what I've heard, there's a strong likelihood she'll die of liver cancer. And it's all because you had to work in that place." She paused for effect. "No Hollywood clinic, no hep C. Right?"

Evelyn was stone-faced, but I could see the anger boiling just below the surface. I glanced at Bailey, who nodded. I leaned in and took over.

"And meanwhile Densmore's beautiful little daughter, Susan, never had to work a day in her life, let alone in a place like that," I said. "Bottom line, you needed money and Stayner offered you a way to make it, quick and easy. And it didn't hurt that you got to screw over Densmore in the process."

Evelyn sat up now, her cheeks flushed

with anger. "You watch your kid suffer like that, you'll do anything. Besides, Carl wasn't wrong. It wasn't like we were pulling any of those kids off their teeter-totters."

I wasn't a mother. Who could say what I would've done? Evelyn went on, her tongue loosened by anguish and fury.

"It would've been fine, but Carl got greedy and started pressuring Densmore to put cameras in the other health centers. I told him to let it be, but would he listen? Of course not," Evelyn fumed. Then she stopped, her face fell, and she grew quiet. A note of true remorse crept into her voice. "And then the sick asshole had to go and rape Densmore's daughter."

I could tell this was the turning point. I let a beat of silence punctuate her last words, then took the plunge.

"Where were you the night Kit was killed?" I asked.

Evelyn's eyes darted to Bailey, then back to me. She licked her lips, and I could tell her mouth had gone dry. If she dummied up now, we were toast. The air was thick with tension. I tried to make myself breathe normally as I waited and silently willed her to speak.

"That was Stayner," she replied.

I let her words hang in the air and deliberately said nothing. I've found that sometimes silence is the best interrogator. After a moment, she continued.

"Kit found his own photo online and managed to figure out where it had been taken. He tried to use it to blackmail Stayner." Evelyn shook her head at the folly of it. "I had no idea he was going to kill the kid."

Bailey glanced at me, and I sat back. She turned to Evelyn. "A dead man is an awfully convenient fall guy," Bailey said. "If you want me to help you out, you're going to have to give me something that proves it was Stayner."

Evelyn thought about it for a minute, then stared straight ahead as she spoke.

"I can tell you why that DA guy wound up dead."

I felt a little sick, not sure I wanted to hear what she was about to tell us. But, after all this time, I knew I had to find out. I only hoped that, good or bad, it would be the truth. Bailey nodded to prompt her, and she continued.

"Kit bragged that he was friends with a DA. Said that the guy helped him all the time and that he was going to be waiting outside the motel. I'm sure he figured that would scare Carl into giving him the money and getting out of there." Evelyn paused, then continued. "Carl didn't buy it. Thought the kid was just bullshitting. But Carl was wrong. The DA really was waiting outside. And even so it wouldn't have mattered, except Carl showed up late. So by the time he shot Kit, the DA had gotten worried and came in to find out what was going on. Once that DA came knocking on the door, Carl was stuck. Besides, he didn't know what Kit had told the guy." Evelyn paused and sighed. "No way Carl could just let him leave." She sat back and exhaled.

"So Stayner let the DA into the room and shot him, then set it up to look like a murder-suicide," Bailey said.

Evelyn nodded. "You check that DA's cell phone. I'm betting you'll see there's a call from Kit sometime that day setting the pickup spot."

I struggled to hide my emotions. My relief was mixed with profound sorrow. Jake would be cleared, but it was gut-wrenching to think that his act of kindness had led to his murder. And Evelyn's story didn't fully explain the nature of Jake's involvement with Kit. Much as I hated the thought, I resigned myself to the possibility that I might never find out. With an effort, I put aside my feelings and pressed on.

"But if Stayner didn't know Jake was coming, then how did our man just happen to have a photo of Kit to plant on Jake?" I asked, my tone deliberately skeptical.

"I told Carl to have Kit bring it with him. I wanted to have a look at it to see what tipped Kit off to the fact that we'd taken it at the clinic. If Kit could figure it out, so could someone else. I didn't want any more blackmailers out there."

Other than you, I thought. Not surprisingly, the irony was lost on Evelyn. But I had what I needed. Now it was time for the endgame.

"I'll buy that," I said with a shrug. "But it doesn't prove Stayner killed them. Where were you that evening?"

Evelyn made a show of thinking about the answer. "I believe I was at work. Matter of fact, I was at the Hollywood clinic."

"Till what time?" I asked.

"I was the last to leave that night, and I

seem to remember locking up around seven thirty," she replied.

It was a decent alibi. The murders were committed at 5:30. And it was a smart answer, because nobody punched time clocks at that clinic. So if Evelyn was alone, there was no one who could contradict her story. There was just one problem.

"Stayner's cell phone records put him in Santa Monica. Sixteen miles from the motel." I paused to watch Evelyn's reaction. She obligingly gave me one.

"Doesn't mean the phone was on him. He could've loaned it to somebody," she said.

"But he didn't," I replied. "We've got an intersection photo that shows him driving north on California Ave. At five thirty p.m. There is no way he could've been there if he'd just killed Kit and Jake. At that time of day, it would've taken him over an hour to get from downtown to Santa Monica."

Evelyn blanched so suddenly I thought she would faint. She stared at the table with sightless eyes as the shock of what I'd said sank in.

"And there is also no way you'd know

this much about the murders if you hadn't done them yourself," I concluded.

Bailey wrapped it up. "Evelyn Durrell, you're under arrest for the murders of Jake Pahlmeyer and Kit Chalmers."

And on that note, Bailey and I walked out.

EPILOGUE

I filed two counts of murder against Evelyn. We were still totting up the child-pornography charges. If the jury did the right thing, she'd get life without parole. As for Densmore, Bailey and I agreed there was no way he'd known anything about Jake's and Kit's murders or their possible link to his clinic. Much as he loved his daughter, he wouldn't have pushed her case that hard if he'd known it would lead to proof that his clinic was being used to produce child pornography. As for Stayner's murder, Densmore likely figured he'd never get caught—and he very nearly didn't.

I filed a few counts of child pornography and one count of first-degree murder with special circumstances against him, but it wouldn't surprise me if the jury dumped the pornography counts and convicted him only of second-degree murder, or even manslaughter. Juries don't mind vigilante parents, even when they're egotistical control freaks. But even if the jury did cut him a break, Densmore would get to live with the knowledge that his "associations" were responsible for his daughter's rape.

The memory of Densmore's arraignment was a painful one. The court had been crowded that morning, and the press had predictably shown up. I wanted to get it over with and get out of the limelight as soon as possible, but by the time the judge finally called my case, the reporters outnumbered the lawyers. I read the charges, and Densmore's lawyer, a slick New York–looking guy I didn't recognize, entered his not-guilty plea. We set a date for the preliminary hearing. The whole thing was over in minutes. I took my time packing up so I wouldn't have to face the reporters. When I thought it was safe, I picked up my file and turned to go. There, in the audience, were Janet and Susan. They were talking—or rather listening—to Densmore's lawyer.

I'd walked down the aisle toward them, unsure of what to say. My heart ached for the pain they'd suffered and would continue to endure. When I drew near, they looked up and saw me. I stopped.

"Susan, Janet. I'm so sorry," I said.

I wanted to tell them I'd never thought things would turn out this way, that I'd have changed it all if I could, that I'd had no choice but to do my job. But I could see there was no point. Susan had leaned away and deliberately looked down. Janet gave me a cool glare, then turned back to the lawyer. I left the courtroom.

All Susan could see was that I'd destroyed her father. And she probably couldn't stop thinking that it had all happened because she told her mother and father that she'd been raped. So she was blaming me, herself—everyone but Densmore. Maybe someday she'd be strong enough to blame the right person.

But one good and unexpected thing had come out of the arraignment. The next day, after it had aired on all the news channels, Olive Horner, Kit's foster mother, called.

"Got somethin' you're gonna want to hear," she'd begun.

"Do you want me to come out and see you?" I offered, curious.

"Nah," she replied.

I heard the muted sounds of a television in the background but no baby cries. I guessed the little one had been adopted after all.

Olive continued. "I got this fifteen-year-old, Adam, just came to me recently. One day he sees the picture of Kit I keep in my wallet. Says he knew Kit. Did time with him in the hall." Olive paused, and I heard a muffled voice that sounded like Janzy's come from somewhere in the room. Olive said, "Just a minute, okay?"

The phone banged as it landed on a hard surface, and I waited, somewhat impatiently. Where was this going?

A few minutes later, Olive returned. "Sorry."

"It's okay. So Adam knew Kit," I prompted.

"Yeah," she replied. "Then, yesterday, me and Adam were watching you in court and the news showed Jake's picture."

Jake. I sat down, the phone pressed tightly against my ear, and braced myself.

Olive continued as I rubbed my suddenly painfully throbbing temples. "Adam knew Jake. Said a bunch of the kids in the hall knew him. Jake would talk to 'em about how school was important, 'bout stayin' out of trouble, respectin' themselves. He'd bring 'em clothes, books. Even got some of 'em tutors so they could get their GED."

"So Jake was—," I began, my voice shaky.

"A kinda guardian angel, from what I hear," Olive said. "Knew he was your friend. Figured you'd like to hear that."

"Olive, I can't tell you what this means to me," I said, trying to rein in my emotions.

I literally couldn't tell her. Olive didn't really know of the suspicions that had been raised about Jake and Kit.

Relief mixed with painful remorse for ever having doubted Jake moved me to tears, and I let them roll down my cheeks unchecked. With an effort, I steadied my voice enough to ask, "Do you think Adam would mind talking to someone else about Jake?"

"Don't see why not," Olive replied.

I immediately placed a call to Jennifer, who'd broken down completely when I told her the story. When she recovered, I suggested that she might like to hear the tale in person, and she'd readily agreed. I arranged for her to meet Adam for lunch—my treat.

Now, weeks later, I was finally feeling like I'd recovered from my bout with Evelyn. And the obvious bumps and bruises had receded enough to let me put away the heavy concealer.

Graden had suggested that since I'd managed to close my case *and* his, maybe I could let him buy me dinner. I decided I could. Then we thought we'd make it a party. So tonight all of us were gathering at the Rooftop Bar above the Standard Hotel for a big celebration dinner.

Graden was going to pick up Toni, Bailey, and me at the Biltmore at 7:30. J.D. and Drew would meet us at the bar. It was only 6:30, so I had time to kill. I called Toni and Bailey and asked if they felt like coming by early to have a drink before Graden got there. They both said yes before I finished the sentence.

By quarter to seven, Bailey called me from the downstairs bar.

Bailey, Toni, and my martini were ready and waiting when I arrived.

"I figure you've earned that, after that textbook takedown of Evelyn Durrell," Bailey said with a smirk.

I sipped my martini and tried to ignore her.

"What do you call that move anyway?" she teased.

Toni laughed hard. Too hard. "What were you trying to do? Make her surrender out of pity?" she asked.

I shot her a look, then turned to Bailey.

"You're already going to be feasting on this for months. If I answer that question, I'll only be feeding the beast. No, *gracias*."

"It was a flying tackle, wasn't it?" Bailey grinned.

I sipped my martini and ignored her.

"At least you didn't nail a parking meter," she said.

I ignored her some more.

Instead I turned to Toni, resplendent in her long sparkling scarf and an armful of glittering bracelets.

"Putting it on for His Honor," I said. "Go, Toni."

"I couldn't stand it anymore," she said. "I just had to break out and enjoy myself tonight after wearing all those dull, disgusting suits for the past several weeks."

Nothing Toni wore was ever dull or disgusting, but it was pointless to argue.

"I meant to tell you," Bailey said to me. "I've got a bodywork guy who said he could give you a deal on your car. I promised to send him some pictures so we could get an estimate. What time is it?"

I looked at my cell phone. "Seven o'clock. We've got time if you want to do it now."

"Yeah, let's go confront the carnage."

"Let me just suck this up real fast. I think I'm going to need the anesthesia before I see that mess again." I took a long sip of my drink.

"Okay if I meet you all out front?" Toni asked, gesturing to her four-inch-heeled strappy sandals. "I don't really need to do any more walking than necessary in these."

"Meet us in five, Scarlett," Bailey said.

We took the elevator down to the parking lot. But when I got to my space, it was empty. I turned, disoriented, and looked around the cavernous lot.

"What the hell?" I said, perplexed.

"When was the last time you checked on your car?"

"Not since it happened," I admitted. "Maybe I've got the wrong spot," I suggested.

But after we'd combed the entire floor, I admitted defeat.

Demoralized, frustrated, and furious, I stomped out of the garage.

"Your insurance will cover it, Knight," Bailey said. "Besides, it looked like hell."

"But I had stuff in it. CDs, pictures. Damn it!" I said. "Where the hell is Rafi?"

I continued stomping all the way up the ramp, Bailey beside me. When we got to the valet stand, Toni joined us. "You won't friggin' believe this," I told her. "Someone jacked my car!" Toni was about to reply when we got distracted by the thumping bass of a loud stereo coming from somewhere up the street.

A midnight-blue car, blasting rap music, was slowly bumping and bouncing its way down Grand Avenue toward the hotel

driveway. A hand came out of the passenger window and waved, followed by
the grinning face of Luis Revelo. The car
came to a stop in front of me.

"*Hola,* Ms. Prosecutor," Luis said.

"Luis? What're you doing here?" I was
still pissed off but also surprised and pleased
to see him.

"What's it look like I'm doin', man? I'm
returnin' your ride."

I frowned, then looked at the car again.
My car! Only—not.

"You're kidding."

"I'm mos' definitely not kiddin' you." Luis
got out of the car and motioned for the
driver to step out. "Get in, man. You got
everythin' in here. Not like before. I hooked
you up with sound—"

"I heard." I laughed.

Bailey and Toni were smiling. "Go on,
get in."

"You guys knew," I said.

They nodded. "From what Luis told me,
you're gonna love it," Bailey said.

Luis held the door as I walked around
to the driver's side, then closed it gallantly.
I started to thank him, but he'd already
sprinted across the street. He had business

to attend to. The less I knew about *that,* the better.

I gestured for Toni and Bailey to get in and handed my cell phone to Bailey. "Call Graden," I said. "Tell him I'm driving tonight."

ACKNOWLEDGMENTS

This book would never have happened without the advice, support, and fortitude of Cathy LePard—a brilliant writer, a beautiful person, and my personal savior. My love, gratitude, and appreciation are boundless. You are a god/goddess-send.

Hard work takes you only so far; at some point you also need a little luck. I had the enormous fortune to find the best agent in the world: Dan Conaway, whose genius took the book to the next level, and whose charm, wit, and warmth made the process not only educational but a lot of damn fun. And here's to Stephen Barr, the marvelous, indefatigable assistant who was always a joy. What a team! I couldn't love you more.

To executive editor par excellence Judy Clain and publisher Michael Pietsch: my boundless and eternal thanks from the bottom of my heart for believing in this book—I'm so honored and thrilled to be with you, it almost leaves me speechless. And as if that weren't enough, working with you has been an unmitigated pleasure. You are the gold standard, truly. Special thanks to fantastic, hardworking editorial assistant Nathan Rostron, who kept the wheels turning smoothly. And kudos to senior copyeditor Karen Landry—what a great job! Thank you!

And my thanks to Marillyn Holmes, whose sharp eyes miss nothing.

My profound thanks to all of the wonderful folks at Mulholland Books—your smarts, creativity, and sheer resourcefulness are a wonder. I have had so much fun working with you! What a great and rare gift you are!

I want to specially thank my dear friend Lynn Reed Baragona for making the connections that set it all in motion—somehow, Lynn, you're always there at the critical moment. The magic of friendship never ceases to amaze me. You're simply terrific.

My great thanks also go out to Katharine Weber. Your advice, help, and insight were key to getting this book out into the world, and I've so enjoyed our time together. Thank you!

To Hynndie Wali, dear friend, who listened generously, suggested wisely, and in general put up with my ruminations beyond the call of duty. I can't promise it won't happen again, but I can promise that the drinks are on me! Thank you, girlfriend, for always being there in so many ways.

Marcia Clark is a former Los Angeles deputy district attorney who was the lead prosecutor on the O. J. Simpson murder case. She cowrote a bestselling nonfiction book about the trial, *Without a Doubt,* and is a frequent media commentator and columnist on legal issues. She lives in Los Angeles.